PENGUIN BOOKS

NOBODY'S FOOL

'A tense, suspenseful and action-packed thriller . . .
it'll have you staying up late into the night to
find out what happens next'
Independent

'Harlan Coben never disappoints'
Stephen King

'Coben is a phenomenon – the most reliable of American
thriller-writers, the least likely to disappoint'
The Times

'Harlan Coben never ever lets you down'
Lee Child

'Harlan Coben: simply one of the all-time greats'
Gillian Flynn

'Unbelievably brilliant'
Richard Osman

'Harlan Coben is the modern master of the hook and twist'
Dan Brown

'One of the world's finest thriller writers'
Peter James

'We can always rely on Harlan Coben
to have us enthralled'
Sunday Express

THE MYRON BOLITAR SERIES

Deal Breaker
Drop Shot
Fade Away
Back Spin
One False Move
The Final Detail
Darkest Fear
Promise Me
Long Lost
Live Wire
Home
Think Twice

THE DETECTIVE KIERCE SERIES
Fool Me Once
Nobody's Fool

THE MICKEY BOLITAR SERIES
Shelter
Seconds Away
Found

THE WILDE NOVELS
The Boy from the Woods
The Match

Harlan Coben

NOBODY'S FOOL

PENGUIN BOOKS

PENGUIN BOOKS

UK | USA | Canada | Ireland | Australia
India | New Zealand | South Africa

Penguin Books is part of the Penguin Random House group of companies
whose addresses can be found at global.penguinrandomhouse.com

Penguin Random House UK,
One Embassy Gardens, 8 Viaduct Gardens, London SW11 7BW

penguin.co.uk

Penguin
Random House
UK

First published in the US by Grand Central Publishing 2025
First published in the UK by Century 2025
Published in Penguin Books 2025
003

Set in 10.82/15.45pt Fairfield LT Std
Typeset by Six Red Marbles UK, Thetford, Norfolk

Printed and bound in Great Britain by Clays Ltd, Elcograf S.p.A.

The authorised representative in the EEA is Penguin Random House Ireland,
Morrison Chambers, 32 Nassau Street, Dublin D02 YH68

A CIP catalogue record for this book is available from the British Library

ISBN: 978–1–804–94343–4

To the other members of the "Core Four"

Nicola Shindler
Richard Fee
Danny Brocklehurst

Great partners, better friends

Prologue

Did it all go wrong the moment I saw you?

I was a mere twenty-one years old, just a baby now that I look back on it, freshly graduated from Bowdoin College and gamely beginning the backpack-through-Europe ritual so common amongst my ilk. It was midnight. The nightclub's music pounded and pulsed. I was nursing my first bottle of Victoria Málaga, the cheapest cerveza they served (hey, I was on a budget) at a nightclub on the Costa del Sol of Spain. I fully expected this to be a typical club night for me—lots of hope, fear of missing out, quiet disappointment (read: striking out)—when I spotted you on the dance floor.

The DJ was blasting "Can't Get You out of My Head" by Kylie Minogue, which, man oh man, would end up being the most on-the-nose tune imaginable. Still. Today. A quarter of a century later. You met my eye, held it even, but I didn't really believe that you were looking at me. Not just because you were out of my league. You were, of course. Out of my league, that is. No, the reason I didn't think you were looking at me was because I was surrounded by the Bowdoin lacrosse bros—Mikey, Holden, Sky, Shack, and, of course, team captain Quinn—all of whom were rugged and handsome and oozed good health like those pictures you'd see of young Kennedys playing football in Hyannis Port. I figured you were looking at one of them—maybe Captain Quinn, with his hair that was "wavy" to the tenth power and a physique that could only be produced by the optimal blend of weights, wax, and steroids.

As if to prove the point, I did a performative, nearly cartoonish look to my left, then to my right. When I risked turning my gaze back in your direction, you somehow resisted doing an eye roll and instead, in a show of mercy, gave me a small, knowing nod. You again met my eye or maybe you were like one of those old oil paintings I saw two days ago in the Prado where the eyes seemed to follow you no matter where you stood. I wish I could say that everyone else in the Discoteca Palmeras faded away except for the two of us, like in some cheesy movie where the music's volume would drop and then they'd zoom in to close-ups of you and me, but that didn't happen.

The dance floor was crammed with young partygoers. Someone bumped into you. Then someone else. Other undulating bodies swarmed between us.

You vanished from view—as if the crowd had swallowed you whole.

I stood up. The Lax Bros at my table didn't notice. I was more of a mascot than a friend, comic relief, the weird little guy who drew the ultra-popular Captain Quinn as a roommate freshman year. Most of the bros thought I was Indian, often calling me Apu and mimicking some kind of South Asian accent, which was annoying because I was born and raised in Fair Lawn, New Jersey, and sounded like it. The Lax Bros hadn't been my first choice of European travel mates, but my best friends Charles and Omar had both already started jobs, one at Bank of America in Manhattan, the other doing genetic research at Mass General. I'd been accepted to Columbia's medical school and would start in the fall—though in truth, it was pretty cool, flattering even, to be traveling with the Lax Bros, even if it was at Quinn's urging.

I swam more than walked onto the dance floor, fighting through the sweat-drenched bodies like they were incoming waves. The DJ switched songs to "Murder on the Dancefloor" by Sophie Ellis-Bextor, which again in hindsight seems perhaps apropos or maybe ironic, but I've been confused about the actual meaning of the word *ironic* ever since Alanis Morissette sang that song and even now, a quarter century after that night, I don't want to get it wrong.

It took me a full minute of shoving through flesh before I found you in the center of the dance floor. You had your eyes closed, both hands in the air, and you moved slowly, languidly, silkily, and I still don't know what the name of that dance move was, but I was mesmerized. Raising your arms over your head made your top ride up so that your tan midriff was visible. For a moment I just stood there and stared. You looked so lost, so at peace that I almost just let you be.

Imagine if I had.

But alas, my courage was uncharacteristically up. Nursing that one beer emboldened me enough to step forward and tap you on the shoulder.

You startled and opened your eyes.

"Wanna dance?" I asked.

Look at me, just going for it. I don't think in my life I had ever been that forward. A beautiful woman dancing alone, and I had the simple gall to approach.

You made a face and shouted: "What?"

Yes, it was that loud on the dance floor. I leaned in closer. "Do you want to dance?" I yelled, trying to get my mouth close to your ear but angling off a little so I didn't puncture your ear drum.

You made a different face and shouted: "I'm already dancing."

This would have been the part where I—and to be fair, most guys—would normally slink away. Why didn't I? Why did I see something in your eyes that told me to give it one more shot?

"I mean with me," I shouted.

The right side of your mouth curled up in a small smile that I can still feel in my veins. "Yeah, I got that. I was joking."

"Good one," I said, which I don't know if you took as truth or sarcasm, but for the record, it was sarcasm.

We started to dance. You are a total natural. Relaxed,

sensual, magnetic. You have that ability to completely let go, to somehow look both spontaneous and choreographed. I do my best dance move, which basically involves moving too consciously side to side, aiming not so much to look like a good dancer as to pass, to blend in and go unnoticed—to not look like a total fool. My dance moves were an attempt to not embarrass myself, which of course makes me look extra self-conscious—or maybe that's me being self-conscious.

You didn't seem to mind.

"What's your name?" I asked.

"Anna. Yours?"

"Kierce." Then for some reason, I added, "Sami Kierce." God, how dumb I sounded. Like I thought I was James Bond.

You gestured toward the Lax Bros with your chin. "You don't look like you belong with them."

"You mean because I'm not tall and handsome?"

That small smile again. "I like your face, Sami Kierce."

"Thank you, Anna."

"It has character."

"Is that a euphemism for 'homely'?"

"I'm dancing with you, not them."

"To be fair, they didn't ask you."

"True," you said. Then that smile again. "But I'm also not leaving here tonight with them."

My eyes must have bulged, because you laughed a beautiful laugh and took my hand and we kept dancing and I started to relax and let go too and yes, two hours later, I left the nightclub with you while the Lax Bros pumped their fists and hooted and hollered and chanted "Kierce, Kierce, Kierce" in drunken unison.

We held hands. We walked the Fuengirola beach. You kissed me in the moonlight, and I can still smell the salt of the Mediterranean. You took me back to your place in a modest high-rise; I asked if you had roommates. You didn't reply. I asked how long you'd been in Fuengirola. You didn't reply.

I had never had a one-night stand. Or picked up a girl at a nightclub. Or, more aptly, had a girl pick me up. I wasn't a virgin. I'd dated Sharyn Rosenberg during our junior year at Bowdoin and we did it plenty of times, but still I was nervous. I tried to channel Captain Quinn. That dude had confidence to burn. Our freshmen year, Quinn would always score and come home super late or early the next morning. When I asked Quinn once why he never brought a girl back to our room, he said, "I don't want any part of her staying on me, you know what I'm saying?" and then he would hit the shower for a full half hour.

Captain Quinn had—probably still has—serious intimacy issues.

That first night, you and I cuddled on a couch and made out for a while and then you fell asleep or maybe you passed out, I still don't know. We had all our clothes on. I thought about leaving, but that seemed wrong, maybe rude, so I closed my eyes and tried to make myself comfortable and pretended to fall asleep too.

When you woke up in the morning, you smiled at me and said, "I'm happy you're still here."

"Me too," I replied.

Then you took my hand and led me to the shower and let's leave it at that.

Two days later, the Lax Bros left for Sevilla. I met them at the train station in Málaga to say goodbye. Captain Quinn put his giant hands on my smaller shoulders and looked way down at me and said, "If you finish tapping dat in the next three days, meet us in Sevilla. Day four and five, we will be in Barcelona. Day six we cross the border into Southern France."

Quinn kept going on like this before I reminded him that I was the one who booked our itinerary and knew where they would be and when. He gave me a quick yet ferocious hug. The other Lax Bros gave me fist pounds. I waited and watched them board the train.

Here's an odd sidenote, Anna: I never saw any of the Lax Bros again.

Holden called me once because I was a cop at the time—I'm not anymore—and his son had gotten arrested in a bar fight. But I never saw Holden. Or Mikey. Or Sky. Or Shack. Or even Captain Quinn.

I never saw any of them.

But I will always wonder what my life would have been like if I had just stuck to the itinerary and gone with them to Sevilla.

I wonder what your life might have been like too.

Maybe it would have changed everything for you too. I don't know.

I'm stalling, Anna.

We weren't in love, I don't think. It was a vacation fling. It's not like my heart was ever broken by you. I wish. That I could have gotten over. I've had my heart broken before and since. A few years later, I would even suffer a far more devastating loss than this, but at least with Nicole there was closure.

You need closure, Anna.

But with you . . .

Still stalling.

It was our fifth day together. We agreed I should give up my bed at the hostel and move in with you. My heart soared. We spent our nights in various dance clubs. We drank. We took lots of drugs, I guess. I don't know what. I wasn't much of a party guy, but if you wanted to party, then I was game. Why not? Live a little, right? You had a "source"—a slightly older Dutch guy dubbed Buzz, who had purple spiked hair and a nose ring and a lot of rope bracelets. You always handled the buys. That's how you wanted it. You and Buzz would meet up on that corner behind the El Puerto Hotel. I remember you two whispering, and sometimes it seemed to grow animated. I figured you were negotiating before you slipped Buzz cash and he slipped you whatever.

What did I know? I was young and clueless.

Then we would party. We would go back to your place, usually around three in the morning. We made love. We passed out more than fell asleep. We woke up at noon at the earliest. We rolled out of bed and onto the beach.

Rinse, repeat.

I don't remember that last night well.

Isn't that odd? I know we'd gone back to the nightclub where we first met, the Discoteca Palmeras, but I can't remember leaving or walking up that hill to your high-rise—why did you stay at an apartment in Fuengirola anyway? why weren't you staying at a hotel or a hostel like everyone else our age? why didn't you have any roommates or friends or seem to know anybody other than this Buzz guy? why didn't I push to know more?—but what I do remember is the hot Spanish sun waking me up the next day.

I was in your bed. I remember groaning when the sunlight hit my face, realizing that if the rays were hitting from this angle it had to be at least noon and we had yet again forgotten to close the shade.

I made a face and blinked and lifted my hand to block my eyes.

Except my hand felt wet. Coated in something wet and sticky.

And there was something in my hand.

I slowly lifted it in front of my face.

A knife.

I was holding a knife.

It was wet with blood.

I turned toward your side of the bed.

That was when I screamed.

There are scientists who believe that no sound ever dies, that it grows softer, fades, decays to the point where we can't detect it with our ears anymore, but that it's there, somehow, and if we could ever be silent or still enough, we would be able to hear that sound for all eternity.

That was how this scream felt.

And sometimes, even now, in the quiet of the night, I can still hear the echo of that scream.

1

TWENTY-TWO YEARS LATER

I stand behind the tree and snap photos of license plates with a long-lens camera. The lot is full, so I go in order from the most expensive car—I can't believe there's a Bentley parked by this toilet—and move on down the list.

I don't know how long I have before my subject—a wealthy man named Peyton Booth—comes out. Five minutes, maybe ten. But here's why I take the photos. I send them to my shadow partner at the DMV. Said partner will then look up all the license plates and get the corresponding emails. She'll email the pics and threaten exposure if they don't transfer money into this untraceable Cash App account. Only $500. No reason to be greedy. If they don't respond—and ninety percent don't—it goes nowhere, but we make enough to make it worthwhile.

Yeah, times are tough.

I'm positioned across the park and dressed like what we used to call a vagrant or hobo or homeless. I forget the proper euphemism they use nowadays, so I ask Debbie.

"'Unhoused,'" Debbie tells me.

"Really?"

"'Unsheltered' too. They both suck."

"Which do you prefer?"

"Goddess."

Debbie the Goddess says she's twenty-three, but she looks younger. She spends a lot of her days standing in front of various, uh, "gentlemen's clubs"—talk about a euphemism—with tears in her eyes and yells "Daddy, why?" at every guy that walks in or out. She started doing it for kicks—she loves the way some guys turn white and freeze—but now a few of the regulars say hi and maybe throw her a twenty.

"I do it as an exercise in capitalism and ethics," she tells me.

"How's that?"

"The capitalism part is obvious."

Debbie has good teeth. That's rarely the case out here. Her hair is washed. She's sleeveless and her arms are clean.

"You make money," I say. Then: "And the ethics?"

Her lower lip quivers. "Sometimes a guy hears me and runs off. Like I knocked some sense into him. Like I reminded him who he should be. And maybe, just maybe, if some girl had yelled that at my daddy, if some girl like me did something, anything, to stop my daddy from going into a place like that . . . "

Her voice fades away. She looks down and blinks her eyes and keeps the lip quivering.

I study her face for a second and then I say, "Boo friggin' hoo."

The blinking and quivering stop as if her face is a shaken Etch A Sketch. "What?"

"You think I'm buying the Daddy Issues cliché?" I shake my head. "I expect better from you."

Debbie laughs and punches my arm. "Damn, Kierce, you must have been an awesome cop."

I shrug. I was. I don't know how Debbie ended up on the streets. I don't ask and she doesn't volunteer, and that seems to suit us both.

I check my watch.

"Showtime?" Debbie asks.

"Has to be."

"You remember the code?"

I do. If she yells "Daddy, why?" that means wrong guy. If she yells "But Daddy, I'm carrying your child," that means my man Peyton just exited. Debbie came up with the code. I'm giving her fifty dollars for the job, but if I land what White Shoe needs, I'll up that to a hundred.

Debbie heads down the path to a spot where she can see the club door. I can't see it from my perch. Debbie saw Peyton Booth's pic on my phone, so she knows what he looks like. You probably guessed this, but Peyton is getting divorced. My job here is simple.

Catch him cheating.

This is what I've been reduced to since getting chucked off the force for messing up big-time. Worse, even though I'm working for a high-end, whitest-of-white-shoe Manhattan law firm, I am not getting paid. This is a barter arrangement. I'm being sued by the family of a high school kid named PJ Dawson. According to the lawsuit, I perilously pursued PJ onto the rooftop of a three-story building. Because of my negligence, young PJ slipped and fell off the roof, plummeting those three stories and sustaining critical injuries. The White Shoe law firm (actual name is Whit Shaw but everyone calls them White Shoe) is representing me in exchange for my working jobs like this off the books.

America is grand.

Peyton is head of a major conservatively based conglomerate and reportedly, because we are all hypocrites, a big-time playah with da ladies. According to his wife's statement to her attorney, her soon-to-be ex has a weakness for "bottled blonde skanks with giant fake cans." The wife had been convinced that Peyton was messing around with his neighbor, but I checked it out thoroughly and yes, the neighbor matches this description, but no, he isn't messing around with her.

Peyton made sure to leave his Lexus in a remote corner of the lot, far from prying eyes. That's why I'm set up on this hill, in the one spot where I can position my camera and record any action that might take place. If I set up closer, I would be spotted. If I set up farther away, I would get nada. The only way to make this work is to be here and to know when my man Peyton leaves.

The parking lot is also cleverly set up so that it shares its spaces with an old-school convenience store called Get Some and a florist called—get this—Rose to the Occasion, thus giving the clientele who are visiting the "gentlemen's club" proper cover. Point is, if I capture Peyton leaving here or parked here, it won't be a big deal in court. But if I can capture him with a dancer (again with the euphemisms— don't we all miss the days when you could just say what you mean?), that would be huge.

"Daddy, why . . . ?" Debbie calls out.

I have the camera on a tripod. I check the aim. Yep, right through the windshield of the car. I'm still looking down the barrel of the lens when I hear a voice behind me.

"Where's Debbie?"

A quick glance tells me it's an unhoused (or unsheltered) guy.

"She's working," I say.

"My name is Raymond."

"Hey, Raymond."

"Debbie usually brings me a sandwich."

"Give her a few, okay, Raymond?"

"She knows I hate mayo."

"Got it."

"Debbie tell you how jet planes stay in the air?"

"No."

"Want me to?"

"Do I have a choice, Raymond?"

"Witches," he says.

"Witches," I repeat.

"Flying witches, to be more precise. Three of them per plane. One holds the right wing, one holds the left wing, the third witch, she's in the back, holding up the tail."

"I've been on planes," I say. "Even sat by the wing a few times. I've never seen a witch."

I don't know why I say this, but I sometimes speak and act without considering all the consequences. That might explain why I've gone from catching murderers and hardened criminals to quasi-Peeping-Tom-ing near Rose to the Occasion.

Raymond frowns. "They're invisible, fool."

"Invisible flying witches?"

"Of course," he said, as though disgusted with my stupidity. "What, you think gigantic metal tubes can just stay up in the air by themselves? I mean, come on. You just believe everything the government tells you?"

"Fair point, Raymond."

"Your average Airbus weighs at least 150,000 pounds. Did you know that?"

"No."

"And we're supposed to believe something that heavy can stay up in the air all the way across an ocean?"

"Uh-huh."

"Take the blinders off, man. The Man has been gaslighting you. Ever hear of gravity? The physics don't work."

"Ergo, the witches," I say.

"Right. Witches, man. And it's all one big joke on mankind."

I can't help myself. "What do you mean, Raymond?"

He scowls. "Ain't it obvious?"

"Not to me."

"One day," Raymond says, rubbing his hands together and licking his lips, "when we rubes are least expecting it, all the witches, all at the same time, they're all going to let go."

"Of the planes?"

He nods in satisfaction. "That's right. All the witches will just let go of the planes at the same time. Cackling. Like witches do, you know. Cackling and watching the planes, all of them, plummet back to earth."

He looks at me.

"Dark," I say.

"Mark my words. Get right with the Lord now before that day."

Down on the street below, I hear Debbie shout, "But Daddy, I'm carrying your child."

Bingo.

"Can we talk about this later, Raymond?"

"Tell Debbie I'm waiting on that sandwich. And no mayo."

"I'll do that."

I look through the camera lens and see Peyton in full business suit. My heart sinks when I see he's alone. He gets in the driver's side. I wait, hoping someone will join him. No one does. He starts up his car.

But he doesn't back out.

I smile now as I watch through the lens. My man Peyton is waiting for someone. I know it.

Still looking through the lens, I hear Debbie shout "Daddy,

why?" as a mustached guy in a business suit makes his way into the lot.

My phone rings. It's Arthur, my young attorney-handler at White Shoe law firm. "Are you on him?"

"I am."

"Good. We sign the papers first thing tomorrow."

"I know."

"If we don't get evidence he cheated, she can't break the prenup."

"I know."

"Will you have something or not?"

Someone opens the passenger door of Peyton's car and slips in. Peyton turns.

They start making out big-time.

But it's not a chesty bottled blonde he is making out with.

It's the mustached man in a business suit.

2

That night—a few minutes before it all went wrong yet again—I was teaching a night class at the vaguely yet fancifully named "Academy Night Adult School" on the Lower East Side. The school still advertises in those free magazines-cum-pamphlets you see on the streets and interior subway cards above the seats on the F and M lines. The pamphlet advertising my course calls me a "world renowned ex-police detective" alongside a headshot of me so unflattering the DMV is jealous.

My class runs from eight to ten p.m., and it's pay-as-you-go. We charge sixteen bucks a class. Cash. I split that fifty-fifty with Chilton, "headmaster" of the Academy Night Adult School, which is why we make sure the amount is an even number. Chilton is also the sole custodian of the building, so I don't know how legit the whole enterprise is. I don't care much either.

We are situated in the shadows of the Baruch Houses,

high-rises near the Williamsburg Bridge on Rivington Street, a street you may or may not find on a map. The building is more ruins than edifice, opened in 1901 as a public bathhouse, the first in the city. Upon hearing this, some people feel this locale will be exotic or glamorous. It's not. Public baths were built for hygiene, not leisure.

I looked it up once. Back in the day, there was one bathtub for every seventy-nine families on the Lower East Side. You can almost gag on the stench of that statistic, can't you? There are few signs of what this place used to be, though my classroom is cavernous concrete and has pretty good acoustics and sometimes I can see, if not smell, the ghosts from the past.

But I'm prone to that.

My class is on criminology. I decided to call it—get this—No Shit, Sherlock. Right, yeah, fair, but admit it's catchy. At the start of every class, I write a different quote from Sherlock Holmes (from Sir Arthur Conan Doyle, for you literalists) on the roll-in whiteboard. We then discuss it. And we go from there. I started six weeks ago with two students. Tonight, I count twenty-three, twenty-one of whom paid for the class, and two—Debbie and Raymond—who are here gratis on a Sami Kierce scholarship. Debbie is enthralled and wide-eyed. Raymond clips his toenails the entire class, studying each nail before cutting them with the precision of my grandmother's lunch group dividing a check.

The class makeup is eclectic. In the front of the room are three women in their seventies who call themselves the Pink

Panthers. They are amateur detectives who love to watch true-crime shows or find a story in the paper and investigate it. I've seen some of what the Pink Panthers can do, and it's pretty impressive. Weirdly enough, as though de-aging, there are three matching young women in the back, twenty-five-ish I'd guess, attractive, who, I'm told, are minor-league Instagram influencers who just started a true-crime podcast called *Three Dead Hots*. There are several wannabe true-crime podcasters in the room, I suspect. There are also true-crime fanatics. A guy named Hex, who always wears gray sweatpants with matching hoodie, wants to solve his aunt's murder from 1982. There is also Golfer Gary, who always wears an ironed golf polo with a logo from some ritzy club. I would say he's a poser, down here in the Lower East Side with us, but I'm a trained detective, and something about his demeanor reeks of old money. I don't know his deal, but I'm curious. Everyone is a story, but this class feels like a bit more than that.

We are a little more than halfway through class when someone slinks in through the side door.

My spidey senses tingle. Or maybe that's hindsight.

I only see the form in my peripheral vision. I don't take a close look. People wander in here all the time. Last class, a man with a dirty-gray beard so bushy that it looked like he was midway through eating a sheep shuffled in. He cupped his hands around his mouth and screamed, "Himmler likes tuna steaks!" and then left.

This part of the class is show-n-tell. Leisure Suit Lenny is up. I don't know what to make of him. He sits a little too close to the influencers, but there is something harmless about him too. He puts a box on a decrepit concrete slab we use as a table and starts taking out gizmos.

"These are tracking devices," Lenny tells the class.

You've probably heard the "Yep, that's me, you may be wondering how I ended up here" record-scratch movie cliché on some meme. That summer with Anna knocked me off the rails. When I came home, nothing felt right. I hid in my room a lot. I didn't want to go to medical school anymore. My parents understood the best they could, but they were also sure it would pass. Defer a year, they urged me. So I did. Defer another year. I did. But I still couldn't go back. I spent my life wanting to be a physician. I tossed it away. This crushed my parents.

"I always carry at least three tracking devices with me," Lenny continues.

Instagram Influencer One says, "Seriously? Three?"

"Always. See this one here?" Lenny lifts what looks like, well, a black rectangular tracker in the air. "This is an Alert1A4. Do you remember those 'Help, I've fallen and I can't get up,' commercials?"

Lots of nods. Raymond presses down on the nail clipper. The cut nail flies.

Golfer Gary grabs his cheek: "Ow, what the . . . ? That almost went in my eye!"

Raymond raises his hand and then points to himself. "My bad, that's totally on me."

Lenny remains steadfast in his presentation. "This is a more advanced tracker because it can do more. I can mute it from this end"—he demonstrates—"and leave the speaker on so this can be both a listening device *and* a tracker. Problem is, the battery life isn't great." He looks around the room. "That's true for all of these, by the way. The GPS's battery drains too fast. Now this one—" He pulls out a device shaped like a thick coin. "This can last for up to six months—but you have to be within twenty yards to pick it up."

Instagram Influencer Two raises her hand, chews her gum, and says, "This is kind of stalker-y."

One (also chewing gum): "Definitely."

Three (also chewing gum): "Perv-level stuff."

Two: "Like, there's other ways to meet people."

One: "Do you carry zip ties too?"

"No!" Lenny's face turns red. "I don't use these for anything like that!"

One: "Then, like, what do you use it for?"

"In case there's a crime in progress. Like this one." He lifts a small GPS tracker high in the air with both hands like it's Simba in the beginning of *The Lion King*. "This one has a strong magnet. I can stick it on a car."

Two: "Aaaaaand you've definitely done that before, right?"

One: "Like, more than once."

Three: "Like, to meet a girl."

One: "I had a guy do that to me once."

Two: "Get out."

Three: "For realz?"

One: "Like, he slapped a GPS on my car so he could set up a time for us to"—finger quotes—"'bump' into each other."

Two: "Ew."

One: "You mean like a pervy meet-cute?"

Three: "Exactly."

Two: "Did it work?"

Three shrugs. "Kinda, yeah. But he drove a Porsche."

One: "What do you drive, Lenny?"

Lenny throws up his hands. "I don't do any of that."

One: "Feels pervy to me."

Two: "Creepy AF. Unless, well, what car do you drive, Lenny?"

Lenny whines, "Mr. Kierce?"

"Okay," I say, and I move next to him, picking up the first GPS and casually tossing it in the air. "I think we should . . ."

And that is when I see Anna.

I stop, blink. I almost do one of those headshakes to clear out the cobwebs.

I know this is impossible, and so for a few moments, I don't really react. I try to let the moment pass.

This would not be the first time I've seen dead people.

Last year, I went through a stage where I would hallucinate and even have full conversations with my "other" murdered lover, Nicole.

Yes, murdered.

I guess I'm not safe to date, ladies.

Tasteless joke.

But when I had visions of Nicole, she hadn't aged. I saw her as she was back then, the way she'd looked on the day she was murdered—the same heartachingly beautiful twenty-six-year-old that I'd known as my fiancée.

I've also imagined seeing Anna before. You know how it is. I'd be in a crowded park or maybe a jam-packed Manhattan bar and I would see a woman with long auburn hair and for a moment I would be certain it was Anna, but then I would blink or tap her shoulder and I would see her face and reality returned.

I do that now. I blink. I blink again. Now I go through with it and give my head a tiny shake to clear it. But even as I do, I know this isn't the same. In the past, the "Anna visions," which is way too strong a term for it, was always the Anna I knew, age twenty-one (or however old she really was) Anna. She'd have the long auburn hair and nebulous eyes, which is weird. I don't remember Anna's eye color—maybe because her eyes were shut the last time I saw her—but now, among the malodorous ghosts of the former bathhouse, I see the hazel in this woman's and yes, now I remember.

Anna had hazel eyes.

Someone—I think it's Golfer Gary—says, "Kierce? You okay?"

But this woman doesn't have long auburn hair. It's short and blond. Anna never wore eyeglasses when I knew her. This woman has stylish round wire frames. Anna was twenty-one-ish years old. This woman is in her midforties.

It can't be her.

The Maybe Anna startles back now. She had been leaning against the wall but moves fast, hurrying out of the room.

"Kierce?"

"Continue your show-and-tell, Lenny. I'll be right back."

————

I sprint after her.

All heads turn. The students, of course, know something is up. They're in a criminology class and so are both inherently and situationally nosey. They're hyperaware. I hear the squeak of chairs as if readying to join me.

"Stay," I command.

They listen, though grudgingly.

I exit the room. I hear footsteps echoing below me. Everything in here echoes. I start toward them. As I do, some degree of sanity returns. I remind myself again that I've hallucinated before. I mentioned that before, with my murdered fiancée, Nicole. I had entire conversations with Nicole. At one point, Hallucination Nicole even talked me down from a bridge from which I planned to jump. She had sagely advised and then convinced me—a hallucination, mind you—to go home to my pregnant fiancée (now my wife), Molly.

Before you think me completely insane, I eventually learned these hallucinations were not my fault. They were a side effect of a terrible drug, one that nearly killed me, blended with whatever weird chemical makeup courses through my body and, not to dismiss my own role in this, a past that had involved excess drinking.

But once I stopped taking the drug, the hallucinations stopped.

Still, wasn't a hallucination the best explanation?

It can't be Anna.

It makes no sense.

And yet, in another way, it might explain everything.

It is funny how fast your perception changes. I'm already accepting that what I've believed for the past quarter century was wrong.

Only one way to find out.

Everything echoes in here so I can clearly hear her heading down the stairs. I follow, taking the steps two or even three at a time. I can see her. She has hit the ground level.

"Stop," I say.

I don't yell. No need to yell with all the echo in this place. But more than that, I don't want to scare her. I simply want her to stop running.

"Please," I add. "I just want to talk."

Perhaps she saw the crazy look in my eye and just figured that I was a threat. Perhaps, like Tuna Himmler, she had just wandered in, seeking a little shelter from the outdoors, a safe place to sit and reflect and let down her guard.

But she didn't look poor or down on her luck or any of that. I spotted what looked like a thick gold bracelet on her wrist. Her camel coat reeked of cashmere and big bucks.

She is almost at the main door.

I move faster now, caution to the wind and all that. I see Maybe Anna reaching for the knob that will lead her outside into the Lower East Side night. No time to delay. Her hand lands on the knob and turns it. I leap toward her and grab her by the forearm.

She screams. Loudly. Like I stabbed her.

"Anna," I say.

"Let go of me!"

I don't. I hold on and stare at her face. She turns away from me, tries to pull away. I hold on tighter. She finally turns and looks up at me. Our eyes meet.

And there is no doubt anymore.

"Anna," I say again.

"Let me go."

"Do you remember me?"

"You're hurting my arm."

Then I hear a familiar deep voice: "Kierce?"

It's Chilton. He's in his tight white custodial suit, the sleeves rolled up his bloated arms like tourniquets. Chilton is Jamaican, a big man with a heavy Rasta accent, shaved head, hoop earring. He wants to be called Black Mr. Clean. No one calls him that, but to be fair, he isn't far off.

Anna doesn't hesitate. She uses the distraction to pull her arm free of my grip. I reach for her again, grabbing the camel—yep, cashmere—coat and making my move because in my peripheral vision I can see Chilton bearing down on me. Time is short. I don't want to let her out of my sight, but I know that forcing her to stay would be the wrong move. Every mistake I've made in my life—and there have been plenty—has derived from moments when I've acted impulsively.

Chilton gets to me and puts a hand on my shoulder. His hand is the approximate size and weight of a manhole cover. He gives my shoulder an eagle-talon squeeze, and I almost drop to my knees.

Anna runs outside.

I couldn't move even if I wanted to. Which I don't. I don't need to follow her.

I got what I want.

Chilton lets up the pressure. I stand to my full height, which is probably a foot shorter than his. He stares down at me, hands on his hips now.

"What the hell, Kierce?"

I am nothing if not fast with the lies. "She didn't pay for the class."

"Say what now?"

"The woman came in, she took the class, and when I asked her to pay—"

"And you chased her?" Clinton asked, shock in his voice.

"Yes."

"A white woman?"

"Don't be racist, Chilton."

"You think this is funny?"

I lift my hand, palm down, and rock it back and forth in a gesture indicating "maybe a little."

"You don't chase after a white woman," he says. "Not in this city. What did I say to you on the very first day you came to work for me?"

"'If you don't make me money, you're dead to me.'"

"And after that?"

"Not to chase white women?"

Chilton shakes his head. "Not to cause trouble."

"Oh," I say, "right."

"I gave you this job as a favor."

"I know, Chilton."

It wasn't so much a favor as a quid pro quo. My old cop partner, Marty, tore up three parking tickets in exchange for Chilton giving me this gig.

"Don't make me regret my generosity," Chilton says.

"Sorry, you're right. I overreacted." Then I point up. "I have over twenty paying students upstairs."

That gets Chilton's attention. "Seriously? That many?" He shoos me toward the stairs. "Go, go."

He doesn't have to tell me twice, even though he just did.

"Maybe next week, we move the price up to eighteen dollars," Chilton suggests. "See if we lose anyone. Then the next class, twenty."

"Subtle," I say as I hurry back up the stairs. The class is totally silent when I get there. They all stare at me.

"Lenny," I say, "can I see you in the hallway for a second?"

The class "ooo"s like this is third grade and I'm sending Lenny to the principal's office. Lenny actually looks nervous, so I add, "You're not in any trouble."

When we are clear of the door, I unlock my mobile phone with my face and hand it to him. "I need a favor."

Lenny looks down at my phone. "What?"

"Download the GPS app," I tell him.

When I grabbed Maybe Anna's coat at the door, I dropped one of Lenny's trackers into the pocket.

"What's that?"

"I need the app," I say.

"Why?"

"I'm on my way to a meet-cute."

3

Maybe Anna is already on the FDR Drive.

That means she is either a world-class sprinter or she drove here. That surprises me. No one drives here. You take the F or M train. There is no nearby parking. Very few taxis pass this way. She could have called an Uber, I guess, but judging by where she is now, the Uber would have arrived in seconds, something again that doesn't happen often in this part of the Lower East Side.

But maybe.

I, of course, don't have my car. Garages are too expensive, so I mostly leave the decrepit 2002 Ford Taurus I bought off a sports agent ten years ago in my friend Craig's driveway in Queens. He charges me fifty bucks a month. You may say, "Some friend," but if you live around here, you know this is a bargain among bargains. I debate grabbing a taxi and telling the driver vaguely where to go as I watch the tracker, but that

32

would be both suspicious and costly. Lenny's GPS tracker is in her pocket. It's working. I can afford a little patience.

I take the M line north into Queens and walk three blocks to Craig's house. The lights are off. No one home. Craig keeps a car key in his kitchen. I have mine on me at all times. I get in the car, back out onto the road, and check the tracker app. Maybe Anna is stuck in traffic around 125th Street, not far from where the FDR Drive becomes the Harlem River Drive. I don't know why they change the name of the road there. It's the same road. It just confuses everyone, even locals, but heavy traffic on the FDR/Harlem River is the norm not the exception. The road's main feature is a lot of nighttime closures for construction. I switch over to a navigation app to figure out how to get to her. Crossing at the RFK Bridge would be the best way to get close if she stays in Manhattan, but odds are, her car will keep heading farther north. With this much traffic, if Maybe Anna wanted to stay in Manhattan, she would have pulled off the FDR and taken local roads.

Still. I have zero idea where she is going, so I have to keep a steady eye on my smartphone screen. As I do, the phone rings. My wife Molly's beautiful face lights up over my tracker app.

I hesitate, consider ignoring the call, but no, that won't do. I hit the answer button, slide my thumb to bring the tracker map back up, and try to keep my voice neutral. "Hey," I say.

"Hey, handsome. How was class?"

"Good," I say.

I've kept a lot of secrets in my life. You do that when you

drink too much. That's not exactly a news flash. I've had a past of telling lies too often in relationships, and Molly's had a past of being on the receiving end of them. When we got married last year, I promised her that was over for both of us, that no matter how bad or how big, there would be no lies or secrets between us. I have kept that promise, though I never told her about Anna or that summer in Spain. That might be a lie of omission, I don't know. The only person in the world I've told the full story to about that night is my father. His response was short: "Get the next plane home."

He and I haven't talked about it since. Not once.

"Are you on your way home?" Molly asks.

"Not yet," I say. "I have to follow up on something."

"Oh?"

I hear something I don't like in her voice. I want to comfort her, but I am not going to lie. I am going to keep my promise.

"It will be impossible to explain on the phone," I tell her.

"I see."

"But it's okay. I'll tell you everything when I get home."

I check the tracker. Maybe Anna is on the Cross Bronx Expressway heading east.

"How's Henry?" I ask her.

Henry is our infant son. He is about to turn one. When Henry was born, my entire world shrank down into a six-pound, fifteen-ounce mass. Your world is one thing before you have a child. It is another after. I don't mean this to advocate for or denigrate the act of having a child. Do your thing. But the reality is, want it to or not, a child changes absolutely everything down to a molecular level. No one is immune.

"He's up and wired for sound," Molly replies. Henry is not a great sleeper. Then she asks in a tone I still don't like: "Do you know what time you'll be home?"

"Not really," I say.

"So this is something big, right?"

I am not sure how to reply to that. "It's a lot, yeah. But it's okay."

"You're being a tad cryptic," Molly says.

"I don't mean to be. I can try to explain now—"

"But you'd rather do it in person."

"Yes," I say. "Very much."

"Okay. I love you, Sami."

"I love you more," I say because I do.

Molly disconnects first. I make up time on the Major Deegan and before I know it, we are both on Interstate 95 heading toward Connecticut. I check my gas gauge and am happy to see I still have half a tank. Craig often uses my car, which isn't part of the deal, but he knows I don't care and he's usually good about putting gas back into the tank. Craig works administration for the Bronx Zoo. He lost his wife, Cassie, a boisterous explosion of a human, to ovarian cancer two years ago and now when Craig smiles, it never reaches his eyes.

I keep my eyes glued on the road. The tracker veers off at Exit 3. I do the same. I try to think it through, try to figure out how it could be Anna and why she came to my class, but then I remember the Sherlock Holmes quote on that old blackboard:

It is a capital mistake to theorize before one has data. Insensibly one begins to twist facts to suit theories, instead of theories to suit facts.

In short, keep your mind open. Don't theorize so fast. Wait until you know more.

Yeah, that's not going to happen.

I flash back to that cop in Fuengirola, Carlos Osorio, his youthful yet world-weary face indicating he didn't believe one word I said when I was telling the truth. Or part of the truth anyway. Not the whole truth. Who would tell a police officer the whole truth in that situation? Who would mention, for example, waking up with the murder weapon in your hand? But I was a dumb kid—I'm sure Osorio could sense I wasn't coming completely clean. I remember the way he folded his arms and waited patiently until I was wise enough to shut up and then he launched the pointed questions: "How much did you drink? . . . How much did you smoke? . . . How much did you snort? . . . Should I give you a drug test right now?"

I follow the tracker down a high-rent main street that Molly would call "cutesy," with upscale restaurants and well-coiffed boutiques that seem more hobby than business. My old clunker of a car fits into these wealthy environs like a cigarette in a health club. I crank down the window so I can smell the money. I curve off to the left and onto streets lined with ever-growing mansions—the farther you move from the main street, the larger and more remote the estates.

A mile passes. Then two. I can still see the occasional home, but only via twinkling lights through thick hedges. There are gates at driveways and elaborate iron fencing. It is hard to believe that this exists in the same world as the Lower East Side, which again is neither an indictment nor an acquittal of one over the other. I'm clearly not a rich man, and while I get the primitive draw of the ginormous mansion—the simple human need for "more"—who really needs or wants that much space? How many rooms can you be in at one time? There is an idiom my father used as a warning about greed: You can't ride two horses with one behind.

I think that fits here.

The tracker hasn't moved, according to the app, in seven minutes.

Is she home? Don't know. But if I'm reading this tracker correctly, she is not on a street. I use my fingers to zoom in. From the tracker's viewpoint, it appears as though Anna is 1.8 miles away from where I'm now driving, in a remote spot at least two or three hundred yards from the nearest road.

Odd.

A satellite view option would be handy, but the tracker doesn't have one. I pull my car onto the shoulder of the road and click the three dots on the top right-hand corner of the app. The drop-down menu offers up the target's precise latitude-longitude coordinates. I copy and paste them into Google Earth and wait as the globe spins around.

When it stops, I say to myself in a low voice, "Oh boy."

The spot where Anna—just for ease, I'm going to call her Anna instead of Maybe Anna for now—the spot where the tracker claims Anna has now stopped for the past nine minutes is blurred out on the satellite image.

Blurred out?

That's fairly unusual. The government can request that satellite maps blur sensitive locations like military bases or certain bureaucratic buildings. I doubt this is either, because the rent out here is too high for such riffraff. But it's a possibility. Google Earth will sometimes blur out a location if there is a compelling reason for privacy or sensitivity in a private home. They do not do it often. And it usually costs.

In short, someone with some power or money wants to keep this location—the location Anna seems to be at—a secret.

Now what?

I should go home, of course. Take a breath. Talk to Molly. Do some research. I have Anna's location now. At least, I think I do. For all I know this is just a pit stop. Or she's visiting a friend who lives here. Or she's spending a few hours or just one night. She could, in fact, move on in an hour or tomorrow or anytime.

I check the battery icon in the upper left-hand corner. The tracker only has eleven percent left. What's that give me in terms of tracking? Another hour tops?

Then Anna could disappear again.

Can't risk that, can I?

The streets are still, the only real illumination coming from my headlights. I don't think I've seen another car in the past three or four miles. I head down the wooded road closest to where the tracker tells me Anna is. There is a driveway through the break in the trees. I slow and see that the driveway is blocked by a wrought iron grill gate. The gate is tall with spikes on top. There is a hut next to the gate. The light is on in the hut, and I can see the silhouette of what I assume is a security guard.

Hefty protection for a private home.

If this is indeed a private home.

I quickly look for a sign or house number or anything like that—I don't want to linger—but there's nothing. I debate driving up to the gate, but then what? It's after ten p.m. I can't pretend I'm delivering a package—and saying "I'm here to see Anna," well, I just don't think that's going to play.

Impulse Me still wants to make that play. Impulse Me wants to drive right up to the security guard and say, "I'm here to see Anna. Tell her it's Sami Kierce and we met in the Costa del Sol of Spain twenty-two years ago." Impulse Me often makes mistakes. Impulse Me was the one who ran out of that bedroom and left Anna behind. Impulse Me was the one who went to the Fuengirola police station and reported a murder to Osorio. Impulse Me chased PJ onto that roof and made him fall. Impulse Me let Maya Stern go unaccompanied to Farnwood, Judith Burkett's enormous estate, a mistake which led to my fall from quasi grace.

Maybe Impulse Me should stay out of this—but either way, I'm not just going home.

I drive slowly down the heavily wooded street and pull off where I see a little opening. My car is still visible from the road, but only if you're looking hard for it. I turn off the engine and make sure the interior lights are off. I don't think anyone will see, but then again I don't plan on being here long enough for the police to call a tow truck. I grab a piece of paper and pen from the glove compartment and scribble a note: "Car Broke Down, Back Soon." I debate adding that I'm a police officer, but that is both beside the point and no longer true.

I get out of the car. The night is crisp, the tang of autumn in the air. The stars are bright out here in a way you never get in the city. I'm holding the app like a compass. The tracker I put in Anna's pocket is two-tenths of a mile from where I now stand, but the entire trek is through the woods.

No reason to dawdle.

I start into the trees. I debate turning on my phone flashlight, but out of an abundance of caution, I'd rather leave it off for now. It is hard to see more than a few feet in front of my face. I walk Frankenstein style, arms lifted and parallel to the ground, hands stretched out so I don't walk into a tree face-first.

Once I'm inside the woods, the trees thin a bit, making my trek faster. I don't know what kind of security they have out here. The manned gate was impressive, but that didn't mean you could guard an entire estate that way. It may have been for show. They could have trip wire in the woods, I guess, or motion detectors, but that's unlikely. There are many deer and squirrels and assorted suburban wildlife out here. There would be too many false alarms.

I keep moving. I'm not quiet about it, hearing twigs and leaves beneath my feet, but what else can I do? When I am within a tenth of a mile of the tracker, I start seeing lights filtering through the trees. I move closer and, as though on cue, a huge estate begins to rise on the horizon. I stop and look at the tracker. According to the help section on the app, the tracker is accurate to within ten meters. Assuming that's correct, Anna and/or her coat is inside the estate.

The tracker battery is down to eight percent. I am at the clearing now. I stay on the edge, half in the woods, half on the start of a large expanse of lawn. The house itself is a jaw-dropper—an enormous Colonial-style stone castle that looks like something out of *The Great Gatsby*. The landscape lights illuminate sprawling symmetrical gardens with matching topiary on either side. There is a pool and a glass-house cabana. Two cars are parked near the door—a Porsche and a Mercedes, both black.

No other movement. No guards patrolling the grounds.

As I watch, debating what to do, a light goes on in an upstairs bedroom on the left. I duck down, even though I'm still a good one hundred yards away from the house. I get my breathing back under control and look toward the window.

Anna walks by it.

I check my watch. Almost eleven p.m. I quickly run through my next possible moves. Should I just knock on the door or ring the bell or whatever? Just be direct? That seems weird and I don't know how security, assuming there is some, might react. Still, it's a possibility. I could also maybe, I don't know, grab some pebbles and toss them at her window. That feels a little too "movie," if you will—and the most logical outcome from such a move would be her screaming for help.

But do I care if she does?

I want to get to her. I want an explanation.

It is then, as I stand there and consider my options, mere seconds after I saw Anna at the window, that I hear dogs.

I should point out that I love dogs. When Henry is a little older, Molly and I want to get a friendly little Havanese for our family.

This doesn't sound like a friendly little Havanese.

This sounds like—and now looks to be—several snarling Doberman pinschers. They are hurtling full speed right down the center of the symmetrical gardens.

Toward me.

My heart leaps into my throat. No need for Impulse Me to tell me what to do. I snap-turn to run back through the woods, knowing I have no chance of outrunning the dogs. Zero. I jump two steps back into the woods and I can tell by the barking the dogs are mere seconds away. I take one more step and then one of the Dobermans leaps up and he knocks me down.

I scream as I crash to the ground.

I don't know if I should try to fight my way out of this, but I distantly recall my police training on dog attacks. If you're already down on the ground, stop moving. Curl in a ball and cover your neck and head with your arms. I do that now, go into a protective shell, my phone still in my hand.

The dogs are on me now, surrounding me. The barking has stopped. They are low-growling, staring at me with black eyes and bared teeth. They look ready to pounce. I stay very still and wait. It is, to put it mildly, terrifying.

Then a man shouts, "Down!"

The growling stops immediately. The dogs' teeth vanish. Their tails wag as they back away. I risk a look and see the silhouette of two men standing near me. One of them is pointing a gun in my direction.

I blink up at them and say, "I'm sorry for the intrusion. I was just taking a walk and got lost."

"Were you now?" one of the men, the smaller one, replies, his voice thick with sarcasm. "Get up."

I manage to lift myself up and move back onto the edge of the grounds. Yep, two men. The bigger one, the one with the gun, has a moon-shaped head, complete with old-zit craters.

"Nice place," I say.

"Who are you?"

"I'm a cop."

"Can we see your badge?"

"Ex-cop actually."

"An ex-cop hiking in the dark on private property," Smaller Guy says. "Is that what you're telling us?"

I try a smile. "Well, I have had a bit to drink," I say, hoping that explains it. His face tells me that it doesn't explain a damn thing. Gun Guy looks at Smaller Guy and nods. Smaller Guy takes out his phone.

"Spell your name," Smaller Guy says to me. I do. Gun Guy keeps the gun on me while Smaller Guy types into what I assume is his phone's search engine. While he does, Gun Guy strolls over to me and, without the slightest warning, punches me deep in the stomach with his free hand. The air whooshes out of me. I drop yet again to my knees, trying to gather a breath.

Gun Guy grabs me by the hair. "Can't leave us alone, can you?"

I try to gather a breath. Gun Guy looks back at Smaller Guy. Smaller Guy says, "Sami Kierce, ex-NYPD detective, fired for endangering civilians and incompetence."

Gun Guy still has his hand in my hair. "Who hired you, Sami?"

I shake my head, the breath finally returning. "No one," I manage.

"One way or the other," Gun Guy says, "you're going to tell us why you're here."

I decide to go with something close to the truth. "I'm an old friend of Anna's."

I check their faces for a response, but the lighting makes it difficult to see expressions. I am still on my knees. He still grips my hair.

"I could just shoot you," Gun Guy says. "What do you think, Tee?"

"Hmm." Smaller Guy Tee is reading off his phone, his face

aglow from the screen. "Whoa, check this out. This is the guy who messed up the Burkett case." He looks up at me. "Do you know we're friends with the Burketts?"

I say nothing.

He looks back down at his phone. "Kierce here was fired for violating police protocol. Multiple times, it says here, including the Burkett case. Being sued up the wazoo for putting a civilian in the hospital. Lots of his arrests are now being challenged, including—get this—the murder of his own fiancée. Described as erratic and dangerous." Smaller Guy Tee looks up from the phone and grins. "Yeah, we could definitely kill him and claim self-defense. I mean, he's erratic, dangerous—and trespassing."

"Right," Gun Guy says. "Exactly. Oh, and guess what? I have another gun on me. Untraceable."

Smaller Guy Tee is warming up to this. "So we just say he pulled it on us. Our word against the word of a dead man."

"Yes. And once we shoot him—once he's dead—we can put the gun in his hand. Fire it even, so he has powder residue."

Smaller Guy Tee nods. "No one will question it."

"No one," Gun Guy agrees. "We make it look like we had no choice."

They both smile at me, clearly warming to this plan.

"So"—Gun Guy aims the gun at me—"what do you say to all that, Sami Kierce?"

Now it's my turn to smile. I have a good smile. You should know this about me. It's far and away my best physical feature. Molly said she fell for me when I smiled. But that's not the smile I'm displaying now. This smile of mine is far more maniacal. This smile is just south of sane. It makes both men, even the one holding a gun on me, step back.

"Say it louder," I say.

Gun Guy looks confused. "What?"

I shake his hand off my hair. Then I lift my other hand into view. My phone is still in it, only now they can see a face on the screen. While they talked, I managed to hit my FaceTime.

"Come on, Tee," I say as I rise to my feet, the maniacal smile still plastered on my face. "Or should I call you 'the Tee-ster'? I'm not sure my friends at the NYPD heard you clearly. Say how you're going to kill me louder."

4

Smaller Guy Tee and Gun Guy escort me back to my car. I try to get them to talk, but they clam up. I ask about the woman in the upstairs window, no longer using Anna's name. They still don't talk. After they let me out of their SUV, Smaller Guy Tee rolls down the window and says, "You stay away from her."

Then they drive off.

Craig is still on my phone's FaceTime, and no, he was never a cop. There was no time to scroll around for Marty's number or anyone's number really. I just hit the redial and since the last person I called was Craig to tell him I was picking up my car, I got lucky he picked up.

"What was that all about?" Craig asks me.

"What did you hear?"

"Not a word. It was all garbled."

"What did you see?"

"Same. It was too dark."

I thank him for staying on the line and tell him I'll call him later. I get in my car and start down the road before they have a chance to change their mind and come back. I dropped a pin when I was near the edge of the grounds. When I hit a red light back on Main Street, I text the pin's location to Marty with a brief message:

Need to know who lives here ASAP.

I check the car clock, but then I remember that it doesn't work. I check my phone's clock instead. It's late. Marty is a health nut who is in bed every night at ten p.m. and wakes up precisely at six. He's annoyingly regimented, which is to say he's anal, and I know a stronger word for anal, but I love him too much to call him that. At the time of my firing, Marty was my junior partner, foisted on a reticent me by a boss who sarcastically insisted Marty would benefit from the wisdom of an older, more experienced officer.

He didn't.

I debate calling Molly to let her know I'm on my way, but it's late and a call may wake up Henry and I just don't know what to say to her right now. I settle for a text. I take the car back to Craig's driveway. He is waiting there for me.

"You okay?" Craig asks.

"Fine."

"Do you want to talk about it?"

Yes, I think, *but not with you*. "I'm fine, Craig. Thanks, man."

"Want a brandy before you head home?"

"Not tonight," I say.

I head to the subway station. My app says the train is one minute away, so I hurry down the stairs. By the time I'm home it's nearly one in the morning. The house is silent. Molly left one of those plug-in nightlights on for me. I tiptoe down into the nursery and peek in on Henry. My son—man, just those two words: *my son*—sleeps peacefully. I watch him for a minute, maybe two. My chest grows tight. My eyes water. If you're a parent, you know the feeling, that heady mix of wonder and fear.

Molly is asleep in the dark in our tiny bedroom. I get ready for bed with as much stealth as I can muster and slip under the covers. I immediately feel the heat from her body. I like that. I scoot closer to her because I sleep better when part of me is touching her skin. Molly stirs. She wiggles into the spoon, and I melt into her.

All the dumb things I've done in my life, all the mistakes and oversteps, and yet I ended up with this spectacular woman as my wife. I am never not awed by this.

Molly is my warmth and my center and yes, she makes me talk in clichés and greeting-card jingoism and country-song lyrics. But that is the thing with my wife. She makes my life better, yes, but she makes every room she enters better. Her love is effortless. It is just who she is. The fact that she chose me is what I want to be the defining moment of my life. It is also a rationale, an excuse, a get-out-of-jail-free card—how can I possibly be bad when this woman chose me to be her life partner?

I expect sleep tonight to elude me. It does not. I conk out

immediately and sleep like the dead. When my phone rings at seven in the morning, I startle awake. The spot in the bed next to me is empty.

My phone was put on quasi-silent—that setting where the phone will only make noise when people on a certain list call. I have six people on this list, including Molly, my dad, my brother, Marty—and this morning's caller, Arthur from the White Shoe law firm. Hardly a surprise.

"What do you want first," Arthur says without preamble, "the news more important to me or the news more important to you?"

"You choose."

"Let's make it about me to start, shall we?"

I'm pretty sure I know what he's going to say. "Go ahead."

"At eleven this morning, Peyton Booth—and more importantly, our client his lovely albeit vengeful wife Courtney—will be ensconced in our fanciest conference room on the forty-seventh floor for their divorce negotiations. You know this."

Yep, no surprise. "I do."

"And yesterday you took photographs that will untangle the Booth prenup."

"I did."

"So why don't I have them?"

I switch hands holding the phone. "You will."

"Why the holdup?"

"I'm developing them."

"Developing them?" Arthur repeats. "What is this, 1987? Are you going to bring us video on a Betamax?"

"Betamax," I say. "That's funny."

"No, not really."

"Most people might have gone with DVD or VCR. But Betamax is far funnier."

"Kierce."

"No worries, Arthur. I'll bring them today. I promise."

"I don't like this."

"Yeah, I didn't think you would," I say, and then try to move this along. "So what's the news more important to me?"

"You're not going to like it."

I also don't like the way his tone has suddenly shifted. Molly appears in the doorway. She smiles at me and lifts a cup of coffee in my direction as if to ask whether I want one. I assume this is a rhetorical question because I always want one.

"What is it, Arthur?"

"Do you remember how upset you were when Judith and Caroline Burkett were released on bail?"

The sickening power of money. "Yes," I say.

"This is worse."

"Just tell me, Arthur."

"I just got word. They're releasing Grayson this morning."

My heart sinks. Molly spots the expression on my face. Grayson is Tad Grayson, the man who has—or, I guess, *had*—been serving a life sentence for murdering a police officer named Nicole Brett.

At the time of her murder, Nicole Brett and I had been engaged.

"He's . . . " I can barely say it. "He's going to be free?"

"Yep, the judge ordered his release last night."

I see the concern on Molly's face. She's heard enough to figure out what Arthur is telling me. We knew this was a possibility, and I had tried to brace myself for it. After my dismissal for cause from the NYPD, attorneys and activists started poring through my old cases, searching for or making up "misdeeds" to claim I was being, to quote that article, "erratic and dangerous," not to mention, I guess, corrupt. So far, three people who had been serving time—*guilty* people, no matter what the court now says—had already been released. Worse, an advocate group called the Equitable Liberty Initiative (ELI, like the name, for short) had started poking into the seemingly solid Tad Grayson conviction, especially when it was discovered that I had participated in the investigation and conviction of my own fiancée's murderer. Attorneys working pro bono for ELI claimed any evidence recovered by the police, even if it hadn't been collected by me personally, should be deemed fruit from the poisonous tree and thrown out.

I swallow. "So when does Grayson get released?"

"At eight."

"Wait." I can't believe what I'm hearing. "Eight this morning?"

"Yep."

I check the clock on the nightstand. It's almost seven. I swing my legs out of bed.

"Don't go, Kierce," Arthur says to me.

"Okay."

"You're lying, aren't you?"

"Maybe a little," I say before disconnecting.

Molly moves toward me. "Are you okay?"

I am sitting on the edge of the bed. I nod.

"You're going to watch him walk out of prison?"

"I have to."

"What good will it do to see that?"

"None at all," I say.

Molly sits next to me. She takes my hand. For a moment or two, we don't move. Then Molly asks, "Does this have something to do with where you were last night?"

"No," I say. "Nothing."

She stares out, stays silent.

"I know this sounds crazy," I continue, "but last night involves something that happened to me when I went to Europe after I graduated college."

She makes a face. "You went to Europe after Bowdoin?"

"It wasn't for long."

"Like a backpacking kind of thing?"

"Yes. I went with a few friends. But something happened. It has nothing to do with us, I promise, and I want to tell you all about it."

"But not right now."

"I want to be there at eight. I need to see his face."

"Go get dressed," Molly says. "I can wait."

5

Tad Grayson steps through the prison gates.

The sky is gray. The building is gray. The street pavement is gray. I don't want to say the mood is gray, but that's what we are left with, aren't we? I count three news vans and about ten members of the press standing outside the prison gate. His release is a story but not a huge one. It might have been a few years ago, but nothing is a huge story anymore. We read about something awful, we get pissed off, a new outrage comes along, we move on. The cycles of news, like the cycles of life, are getting faster and tighter with time until eventually we reach oblivion. But now I'm getting deep.

I watch from behind a tree. I don't want to be spotted, but I won't care much if I am. Tad Grayson looks awful, I'm happy to say. I hadn't seen him since they led him out in handcuffs after the guilty verdict, so maybe that's part of it—the sudden skipping of twenty years and so he's aging to me all at once—but I think it's more. I've aged. We've all aged. But Tad is barely recognizable. Only a few wispy strands remain from his thick mane of jet-blue Superman hair. Those strands are plastered down into a classic combover. His cheeks are sunken. His skin tone is—here it comes again—gray. His walk is an old-man shuffle, though he's only forty-eight.

He spent more than two decades in prison for murdering a police officer. That might make you a hero among your prison peers, but I am sure the gatekeepers made sure the time passed slowly and with difficulty. My hate is still fresh, raw, but I would be lying if I didn't say it felt tempered a bit because Tad Grayson looks so broken.

A woman in a business suit—his lead lawyer, I suppose—spreads her arms and Tad steps into them. She hugs him. He rests his face into her shoulder. He may be crying, I can't say for sure. The woman pats his back and whispers something. With his face still hidden, I can see him nod.

A voice from behind me says, "I figured you'd be here."

I turn and look up. It's Marty, my partner when they threw me off the force. Marty's young and naïve and tall. He's far too good-looking to be likable—Molly says that he looks like an "underwear model, only more handsome"—and yet he is also adorably dorky with the annoying enthusiasm of a born-again puppy. You can't help but love Marty, even when you want to kick his shins.

"Deducing that I might show up for the release of the man who murdered my fiancée," I say. "Boy, I'm proud to be your mentor."

"You're being sarcastic, aren't you? I can never tell."

"No," I say, "you can't."

"Kierce?"

"What, Marty?"

"You use sarcasm as a coping mechanism to obfuscate your true emotions."

I look up at him and say nothing. A few seconds pass.

"I got a vocabulary-building app on my phone," Marty says in way of explanation. "*Obfuscate* was Tuesday's word."

"Glad you could find a real-world use for it," I say. Then: "Why are you here?"

"One, to make sure you don't do something stupid. Like, I don't know, showing up here."

"So 'one' is answered. What's two?"

The media has set up a podium with their various logoed microphones. The woman in the business suit heads toward it. She is flanked by two what look like male colleagues.

"You sent me a pin last night," Marty says. "For a location. You wanted to know who lived there."

"Today," the woman at the microphone begins, "a terrible injustice has been corrected."

The woman introduces herself as Kelly Neumeier and then says more stuff around righting wrong and fighting injustices and how the police's incompetence means the real killer is still out there, but there's no need to repeat it. I get the need for groups like the Innocence Project and ELI. I get that I had corrupt colleagues and that the blue line protects them and all that, though I found most of the evidentiary abuse comes from being lazy and wanting to cut corners rather than trying to subvert justice. Also arrogance—you know who did it and you just need a little extra juice to prove it, so why not play God a bit?

Yes, I know it's wrong.

But I also know that Tad Grayson killed Nicole, that the bust was righteous, that the conviction was untarnished except for nonrelated grievances involving me. Their case in a nutshell was this: I, Sami Kierce, violated rules once or twice, ergo every other case I was involved in should be thrown out.

Just so we are clear: I never violated rules for personal gain or profit or even to expedite a conviction.

I wonder what Neumeier and her boy-band background lawyers really think. Do they honestly believe Tad Grayson is innocent—or is this about a higher cause to them? They looked at the evidence. Sure, they were able to use my downfall to get him loose. But they know he did it.

The question is, what can I do about it now?

"Mr. Grayson has gone through an incredible ordeal and injustice. But he still would like to make a brief statement."

Kelly Neumeier steps aside for Tad. The streets seem to go quiet. Marty moves closer to me, as though worried that I might make a run at him. I won't. I feel disoriented and not at all like Impulse Me. I don't think I could move if I wanted to. A weird, horrible thought enters my head. It is so awful and self-centered I am afraid to say it here, but I can't help it: If Tad Grayson hadn't murdered Nicole, my son, Henry, would have never been born. This isn't a profound thought.

It is not a thought that gives comfort or changes anything. In fact, when I think about it, it's ridiculously trite.

Goodbye, Impulse Me. Welcome, Trite Me.

Tad clears his throat. His eyes are on the ground. He blinks and again he looks old and broken. "There are some people I need to thank," he says, as though this is an Oscar speech. He names people. The lawyers all nod and give a tight-lipped smile when their names are mentioned. When he finishes with the thank-yous, he stops, lowers his head again, raises it again, does the whole summoning-up-the-strength thing again. Now I can see the rehearsed quality to it. I don't think the media does though.

"Since the day I was arrested," he begins, "I have claimed my innocence. I was offered a lighter sentence if I confessed. But I didn't."

This is a lie, but never mind.

"I was offered more privileges inside if I confessed. But never, not once in the past twenty years, have I wavered. I will say this again. I didn't kill Nicole Brett. I know most of you don't believe me. I do admit that I became obsessed. I do admit that I did things that I'm not proud of. Those awful texts? I sent them. But I didn't kill her."

The "awful texts" came in incremental threats, the final one stating "I'm going to put a bullet in your brain," which is exactly what happened. Nicole didn't tell me about the texts. Tad Grayson was a mistake, she said. An obsessive ex and harmless. She had it handled. When I noticed him hanging around, when I wanted to sneak up on him and send him a message—yes, beat the living shit out of him—Nicole admonished me for my sexism. Did I think she couldn't handle herself? Did I think she needed a man to protect her?

So we stopped talking about him.

A reporter shouts out, "Do you blame the police for this? The prosecutors?"

Guess what Tad does? He lowers his head, raises it. The dude is half marionette. I wonder how he will handle this question. Finally he says, "I've thought about that a lot." He manages a wry smile. "You get a lot of time alone to think when you're in a cell for twenty-three hours a day. I have looked at it from every conceivable angle. I have gone through the gamut of my emotions—and the emotions of others. There were times of great anguish and of great resolve."

I get up on my toes to whisper in Marty's ear. He bends down to meet me halfway. "Does this sound completely rehearsed?" I ask him.

"He had to be expecting the question, to be fair. And like he said, he's had plenty of time to think about the answer."

I frown.

"In the end, I don't know for sure, and I'm confident that my attorneys will tell me that their actions were malicious, but I think the authorities honestly believed that I was the killer. I've been told that is too generous a response."

I almost stick my finger in my throat to indicate that what this lying scuzzball is saying makes me want to hurl.

"And this certainly doesn't excuse their actions. But at the end of the day, I didn't kill Nicole. That means whoever did may still be out there."

Another reporter shouts out, "Are you going to swear to find the killer?"

Another adds: "Like OJ?"

That leads to some snickers. I like that. Tad, I can see, does not. He opens his mouth as though he's going to reply, but then Neumeier puts her hand on his back and steps forward and says no more questions. She leads him to a car. He slides into the backseat. She slides into the backseat. They pull away.

And that's it.

I'm just standing there with Marty.

The news crews grab their microphones. I don't move. I just stand there. Marty gives me the space. I watch as the news vans drive away.

Then I say to Marty, "You were saying about my dropped pin."

"Yes."

"What about it?"

"You were in Connecticut."

I turn and again look up at him. "I can't tell you what pride I take in the fact that I trained you."

"You also use humor as a defense mechanism."

"I wish I still carried a firearm."

"More humor."

"I know I was in Connecticut, Marty. Of course I know. I thought this was clear from my text, but just in case: I dropped that pin at someone's residence. I want to know whose."

"You also realize, I assume, that you were in a very high-end district when you dropped that pin."

"I do."

"On private property."

"Yep."

"I checked several satellite maps. The aerial footage over that area is blurred on all of them."

"I know," I say.

"You also dropped the pin late at night."

"Marty?"

"Yes?"

"Why do you keep telling me things I already know?"

"What the hell were you doing there, Kierce?"

I don't answer. There is no one left by the prison gate. I still stare at the spot where Tad Grayson had been standing. He was free. The man who had murdered Nicole was free. I bet his lawyers take him out for dinner. Probably a fancy steakhouse. Celebrating the man who blew away Nicole's beautiful face.

Marty isn't good with silence. I know that. He is a babbler. It takes a few more moments and then he lets loose a sigh. "The property is owned by an LLC."

"Any name attached?" I ask.

"Not yet."

I am not surprised by this. Someone is working hard to keep that property secret. Why? And why would Anna, a woman I thought was murdered in my presence over twenty years ago—perhaps by my own hand—be staying there?

"I tried a few other ways to look up the owners, but I didn't get anywhere. Yet. You know how it is. You sent me that location late last night. Most places are just opening now. I'll make some calls."

"Thank you," I say.

Then he asks the same question Molly did: "Does this have something to do with . . . ?" He gestures toward the prison gate.

"No," I say.

But then I tilt my head.

"What?" he asks.

I met Anna in Spain more than twenty years ago. Five years later, I was engaged to Nicole and she was murdered by Tad Grayson. I never put the two together. Why would I? They had nothing to do with one another. The only connection was, well, me. And I certainly see no connection between Anna—should I keep calling her Anna or should I move back to Maybe Anna, I don't know anymore, let me stick with Anna—showing up at my class yesterday and the release today of Tad Grayson. None. Except for one thing.

The timing is curious.

Coincidences happen more often than we know. I've done a lot of studying on this. Fatalism, Jung-Pauli theory on synchronicity, probability, chance, apophenia—but I mostly go with something closer to a chaos theory. Coincidences happen. But coincidences assume a randomness, that there is no connection, not even a casual one, between two events.

But again there is a connection. The connection is yours truly.

So though I can't see—the real definition of *coincidence* states that it is a remarkable occurrence of events or circumstances without *apparent* causal connection—could somehow the reappearances of both Anna and Tad Grayson in my life be connected? Or am I the one now guilty of narcissism or metaphysical solipsism or, more simply put, egocentrism— that is, the world revolves around me?

My head is starting to hurt.

My phone buzzes. It's a text from Arthur:

WHERE ARE THE PHOTOS??!!

I check my watch—an old Casio I found abandoned on a bus bench. I had taken the visitors' bus out here from Jay Street and the MetroTech Center in Brooklyn, but the bus back was still forty-five minutes away from leaving.

"I assume you drove here?" I ask Marty.

"Yes."

"Can you give me a lift back to midtown?"

6

Marty tries to get me to talk, but I don't give him much. He hates silence and fills it with self-help jargon and discussions about his new workout regimens. Right now, he is singing the praises—yes, the upcoming pun is intentional—of something called Cycle Karaoke, which is exactly what you think it is.

"Guess what my favorite cool-down song is," he says.

"'If I Die Young'?"

"No!" he says with that puppy-like enthusiasm. "'Save a Prayer' by Duran Duran."

He glances at me to see my reaction. When we first met, "Come Undone" by Duran Duran came on my car radio. He had never heard of the song. He had never heard of Duran Duran.

We are on Park Avenue now.

"Okay," I say. "You can drop me off on the corner over there."

The White Shoe law firm is on Park Avenue and Forty-Seventh Street, near the MetLife Building and across the street from the Lock-Horne Building. I jump out fifteen minutes before the Peyton Booth divorce mediation.

I am nothing if not ready.

Like almost everyone in New York City, I wear a backpack. In it, I have caps from various delivery services—Prime, UPS, DHL, FedEx. I have caps from Con Ed, Verizon, Sprint, Spectrum. I can't carry uniforms for all these companies, obviously, but I can (and do) carry a neon-green reflective vest with the word SECURITY printed on the back. It does the trick. I also have various fake identification/credentials I can slip into a clear plastic name badge. You'd be shocked at how easy it is to move about with these, but in this case, I don't need much.

I've already donned the FedEx cap and the reflective vest. I hold the envelope in my hand and wait on the corner. I hope that I'm not too late, but Arthur is blowing up my phone like a stalker. Up ahead I see a black SUV pull up to the front of the building. Peyton Booth steps out with a confident air. He sports a fake tan, a light gray business suit sans tie, and a crisply ironed shirt so white I almost reach for sunglasses. I don't know what brand of shoes he's wearing and I'm too far away to know for sure, but I can tell they even smell expensive.

I hurry toward him, envelope in hand. Two other suited men, both with ties, step out of the car with him. His attorneys, I deduce. That may make this all the more delicate for Peyton, but that's all up to him.

"Courier delivery for Peyton Booth," I say.

As I hand him the envelope, one of the two lawyers, a big guy, steps in my way and puffs out his chest. I know this kind of poser. I'm small and South Asian. Easy pickings, he thinks. But I also always mentally prepare. I focus on—need be—how my knee will slam into his balls.

Takes away the size advantage.

"Is this a subpoena?" Puffy Chest asks me.

I point to my FedEx cap. "Does this say subpoena delivery service?"

"Oh, I've seen servers pretend to be a lot of things."

"That sounds unethical," I tell him with top-notch fake earnestness. "But no, I'm not a server. I was told to give this to Mr. Peyton Booth and that it was very private."

Puffy Chest doesn't like it, but I scoot around him before he can ask more questions. I jam the envelope into Peyton Booth's chest, try and fail to make eye contact, and hurry away. When I'm around the corner on Forty-Eighth Street, I take off the cap and vest. Then I wait and watch. Peyton Booth and his attorneys enter the building. I give them a little bit of a lead before following. I want them to get up to White Shoe before me—but not *too* long before me.

When they get their passes and head down the corridor, I make my move. I show my real ID to the woman at the same security desk on the Forty-Eighth Street side of the building and get a pass to the tenth floor.

Arthur is waiting for me when the elevator opens.

"What the hell, Kierce? Our client is already in the conference room."

Arthur is not what you expect. He's a tall, lanky glass of water, only twenty-four, and already a partner here. How did he make partner so young? He's a genius. He graduated law school at sixteen. He wears his hair long. He favors suits with vests, a pocket watch, and dangling feather earrings.

Behind him I see Peyton Booth's two attorneys. No Peyton. That's good.

"The mediation," Arthur continues, "starts in five minutes. I need—"

"Here."

I hand him the other envelope I had in my backpack. The one I gave Peyton Booth was unsealed so he could open it fast. This envelope is the opposite—sealed with envelope moistener and one of those long strings you have to keep unwrapping.

Arthur frowns and starts on the string. "Are you serious?"

"Gotta hit the head," I say and rush down the corridor toward the bathroom. I have been in this bathroom maybe five other times in my life. I have never seen anyone else use it. I'm hoping my luck will hold, but if not, I can wait.

Peyton Booth is there. And only Peyton Booth. My luck, if you call this that, holds.

"Who are you?" he asks.

I lock the door behind me. If someone needs a toilet, they can always find another one.

"That doesn't matter," I say.

His face goes as white as that crisply ironed shirt. "So this is, what, a shakedown?"

The only shaking I see is his hands. He has the envelope. The photos of him with that other man, the ones I took near Rose to the Occasion, are back in the envelope as though even he doesn't want to see them again.

"I was hired by your wife's attorney to see whether you were abiding by the infidelity clause of the prenup you and your wife signed." I point at the envelope in his hand. "This is the evidence that you were not."

"So how much?"

"Pardon?"

"To keep this quiet. How much?"

I'm genuinely curious now. "How much are you offering?"

He raises his chin, the businessman again, back in control. It's a business deal now, a corrupt one, and that puts him back on terra firma. "Give me a number."

Yep, master negotiator. Or so he thinks. Negotiation 101: Never be the first to give a number. Let your opposition make the first move. You can learn this from reading pretty much any book on negotiating or watching repeats of *Pawn Stars*. Rick and Corey always ask, "How much do you want for it?" as they launch into making any deal.

"How much do you want for it?" I try.

"You go first."

"Ah never mind," I say. "I can't think of a price, so let's just move on."

I start for the door.

"One hundred grand," he says.

Whoa. That's the opening bid. I could probably get a lot more. That would change everything, wouldn't it? Get me out of debt. A better apartment for Molly and Henry. Maybe some babysitting help so Molly can go back to work. I'm tempted to counter at a million, but I've let myself get distracted with this long enough.

"Here's what's going to happen, Peyton," I say to him. "You're about to head into a meeting. You are going to agree that your prenup is null and void and then you and your soon-to-be ex will negotiate what one hopes will be an equitable deal for you both."

He waits for me to say more. Another negotiating tactic. I don't bite.

"And then?"

"That's it. I was hired to see if you broke the infidelity clause of your contract. You did. Mission accomplished."

"And what becomes of these . . . ?" He can't say it so he just raises the envelope in the air. He keeps his eyes on me as though he's afraid to make eye contact with what's inside. Just to clarify, I gave him my three clearest photos of him with the man. I also left him a note to meet me here and not to say anything to anyone. To make sure, I wrote on the envelope, "Look at these right away but don't let anyone else see." Seems he abided by that.

"I destroy them," I say.

"Just like that?"

"Just like that."

"How do I know you won't keep a copy?"

"You don't. Come to think of it, I had planned on deleting everything, but you're kind of scaring me now, Peyton. So I'll keep a set with my will. Just in case something happens to me."

"Suppose something happens to you and it's not because of me."

"Too bad now," I say. "You should have thought of that before you made that veiled threat."

"I don't understand any of this."

"We don't really have time for this," I say. "If we aren't back soon, someone is going to think you have a case of constipation that would take down a mule. Simply put, I'm okay with exposing that you committed infidelity per your prenup. That's my job. That's what you signed on for when you drew up the deal with your wife. What I'm *not* okay with is unnecessarily outing you. I'll do it if I have to—to prove that you broke your prenup. It gets morally hazy if we swim into that space and I'd rather stay on dry land. Does that make it clear?"

"That photo is blackmail," he says. "You're not the good guy here."

I think about that. "Yeah, I kinda am." I turn and unlock the door. "Either way, I'll see you out there."

———

The Booth divorce mediation does not take long.

It takes place in a conference room with a big glass wall,

so I'm able to watch from down the corridor. I can't hear, of course, but I find it odd how many conference rooms have glass walls which both intrude on privacy and cause unnecessary distraction. There are six people in the conference room. Husband Peyton and wife Courtney sit across from one another, their lawyers on both flanks. The body language tells me everything. Peyton caves quickly. This surprises his wife. I can see a stunned Courtney Booth turn to Arthur, seemingly unhappy in victory. The lawyers all shake hands. Husband and wife avoid eye contact.

Team Peyton exits first and briskly. Arthur follows. He beams and gives me a thumbs-up. Courtney Booth is right behind him. She looks perturbed.

"Thank you," Arthur says to me.

I nod. I'm ready to move on, but Courtney Booth has other ideas.

"What the hell was that?" she snaps.

"A win," Arthur replies. "Your husband just agreed to rip up your prenup."

"Right, sure. Out of the goodness of his heart?"

"This is a divorce action," Arthur says. "No one does anything out of the goodness of their heart."

"I don't like it," she says.

"This was a good meeting, Courtney. A really, really good meeting."

She turns to and on me. "You're the one who took the photos?"

"Yes."

"Was he screwing Britney Griffin?"

I don't say anything.

She glances back at Arthur. "Didn't we hire a private investigator to take photos?"

"We hired him to break the prenup. Mission accomplished."

"So that whore Britney gets off scot-free? Oh no. I want that bitch outed. She was my neighbor for God's sake. My friend. And then she—"

Here I make a mistake. I say, "It wasn't Britney Griffin."

That surprises her. "It wasn't?"

In for a penny . . . "No."

"So who was it?"

"I don't know a name."

She steps up closer to me. Courtney Booth is very attractive and far taller than I—statuesque, modelesque, and I confess she smells great. "Why haven't I seen the photos?"

I look toward Arthur.

Arthur says, "It doesn't matter, Courtney."

"Don't tell me what matters, Arthur. You work for me, correct?"

"Yes."

Courtney is still glaring at me. "I want to see the photos. All of them."

"There are a lot," I say. "It's a big file."

"I don't care."

I nod. "Fine," I say. "I can email them to you."

"You do that."

With one last glare she must have learned at soap-opera-acting school, Courtney spins and struts away. Arthur moves next to me. We wait until she's in the elevator.

Arthur asks, "Did you watch Tad Grayson get released?"

"I did."

Neither one of us says anything for a moment.

"The head lawyer ELI assigned to overturn his conviction," Arthur says. "She works here. Her name is Kelly Neumeier."

I flash back to the lawyer who spoke at the prison. "I know."

"She worked the case pro bono."

"I know."

"Kelly is good, Kierce. Ethical. Principled. I like her."

I don't care, but I don't say that. I don't blame the lawyer. I don't blame the system. I blame mostly me, but I don't bother with that right now. "His conviction wasn't overturned," I say.

"Right," Arthur says. "It was vacated."

"So the DA could retry him."

"They could," Arthur says with great care. "But . . . "

I know. He knows. They won't. There isn't enough evidence anymore. It would be impossible to reconvict, and the DA's office doesn't really have the stomach to try. It would be embarrassing and an unpleasant reminder for all. I get all that. No one really cares anymore.

Arthur reads my mind. "It can't be you, Kierce. Anything you find, any evidence you dig up, will be dismissed."

I nod. "I better go."

"Aren't you forgetting something?"

I wait.

"Courtney Booth's email address," Arthur says. "Do you want it?"

"No."

"You're not sending her the photos?"

"I'm not sending her the photos."

"She won't be pleased."

"I gather that."

"She probably has a legal right to them."

"You're the one with the law degree."

"Work product on her case. She could sue you."

I shrug and start toward the elevator. "What's one more?"

7

I pick up Debbie on the way out to Connecticut. She wants a day out of the city, and I figure that maybe I could use her. We follow my late-night pin drop back to the lush estate of Maybe Anna. I don't have much of a plan here. I consider trying to make some kind of approach as a delivery man, but that won't work here. Whatever packages get delivered here are left at the gate, I'm sure. I debate casing the place from down the street, parking and waiting for a car to come out and then following it, but my guess is, the local authorities notice old beater cars held together by duct tape idling on these fair streets. Debbie might help with that. It's one thing when a guy is in a car by himself. It's a little less conspicuous with a couple.

Debbie has her window down and sticks her nose out of it like a golden retriever. "Can you believe all this green?" she asks in wonder.

"Is there no green where you're from?"

"Not green like this," she says. "It's like even the trees smell like money."

I get what she means.

"Can we go for a hike, Kierce?"

"This is all private land."

"For real?"

"Yep."

"There must be some walking trails nearby though, right?"

"I guess," I say.

"You like hiking?" she asks.

"No."

"Why not?"

"Because it's boring," I say. "It's hot. It's dusty or muddy. And then it's all 'Oh, look honey, there's a tree! Oh, and there's another tree! And another! Oh, I wonder what's around that bend . . . Oh wow, looks like a tree!' I get thirsty and hungry and, I mean, if you want to take a long walk in the city, yes, sure, I'm with you. You see people's faces. You can window-shop. You can gaze upon architectural wonders or meander through a bookstore or head up to that flea market on Columbus Avenue. That's stimulation. That's interesting."

Debbie smiles and sits back in her seat. "I like you, Kierce."

"I like you too."

"I still want to try hiking someday," she says. "Get some fresh air."

"Fresh air is overrated. Your lungs are strong from a lifetime of street fights."

She laughs at that. "So what's our plan?"

I shrug. "I'm open to ideas if you have any."

We circle the streets and hope something comes to mind. Nothing does right away, but I've learned that there is something to literally and figuratively spinning your wheels. Patience is a virtue and all that. Wait enough and sometimes something happens.

Or this is what I tell myself to excuse the fact that I'm a shit planner.

We drive around like this for about twenty minutes when I see a car, a Mercedes-Benz CLE convertible with its top down, pull out of the driveway down the road from Maybe Anna's. There are four young women in the car. They wear sunglasses and wide smiles and give off major "not a care in the world" vibes.

"Speaking of smelling like money," Debbie says.

"How old do you think they are?" I ask.

"Like, I don't know—high school seniors, college maybe? Why, you interested?"

I make a face at her and swing the wheel so that I'm following the Mercedes.

"You got a plan?" she asks.

"I do."

"Care to share it?"

"They live across the street from our target house."

"So?"

"So they probably know who lives there."

"You think they'll tell you?"

We follow the car to the outskirts of town. The Mercedes

pulls up to some fancy converted barn, the kind of place you'd find an overpriced pottery store or one of those upscale wine-n-paint party joints. Molly went to one of those wine-n-paint parties last year. She brought back a painting of what might be a nature scene and gave it to me. It couldn't be uglier and I think Molly knows that, which is why I hung it in our bedroom and I'll be damned if I ever take it down.

A valet takes the convertible and the four—can I call them girls? teens? women?—head inside. I look for a sign telling me where I am. There is none. Debbie is on her smartphone trying to look the place up.

"It's called the Ivy," she says.

"What is it, a restaurant?"

She shakes her head. "A rejuvenation center."

"Does that mean spa?"

Debbie shrugs. I pull my Ford Taurus up to the valet. The valet crinkles his nose and looks at my car as though it just plopped out of a dog's backside. We get out and I toss him the keys.

"Don't scratch it," I say.

The valet looks at the exterior. "Might make it look better," he replies.

"Good one," I say. "If I had cash, I would tip."

"I take Venmo and Zelle."

"Let's chat later, shall we?"

Debbie and I enter a sea of white. The barn has high ceilings and big picture windows. Plush white leather chaise lounge chairs line all four walls, with what looks like a round cocktail bar in the middle. The clientele wear white terrycloth robes and lay on the chaises.

They have IVs in their arms.

Debbie leans toward me and says sotto voce, "You know what this reminds me of?"

"What?" I ask.

"My mother getting chemo."

I say nothing for a moment. This is the first time Debbie has ever revealed anything even slightly personal.

"Except this is way more ritzy." She thinks about it. "Do you say 'more ritzy' or 'ritzier'?"

"'Ritzier,' I think." Then I add, "I'm sorry about your mom." I'm thinking about asking how her mom is or if she's dead or alive or still going through chemo or in remission, but Debbie shakes me off like a baseball pitcher who doesn't like what the catcher is signaling.

"Do you think that's what this is?" Debbie asks. "Like rich-people chemo?"

"No," I say.

"Me neither. Everyone at chemo had brittle yellow skin. These rich people glow like rich people."

A receptionist with a constant blink, as though midseizure, steps in front of us. "May I help you?"

"My dad wants to buy me a treatment," Debbie says. "It's my birthday."

"Oh wow, how wonderful."

I smile at her. The proud father. In my peripheral vision I see the four girls from the convertible come out in white bathrobes. They are led to four chaises on the right wall. They sit-lie, and four women dressed in pink scrubs like pediatric nurses put IVs into their left arms. They sip what might be piña coladas from cocktail glasses with small umbrellas.

"Ivy," I say softly. "Like IV."

"Yes, that's our service," the receptionist says. Her voice turns a tad condescending. "Our IV therapies start at eight hundred dollars."

"American dollars?" I ask.

"I have a brochure."

She opens it. There are treatments called Super Immunity and Beauty Boost and Elite Energy. There is something called a Myers Cocktail and HydroBlast and VeinVitalizer and HornyHelper. I look at Debbie and then toward the Convertible Girls. Debbie understands my meaning.

"Can we talk about the options over here," Debbie says, trying to look embarrassed, "like away from my dad?"

"Oh of course."

They move away, leaving me be. The girls are all lying back as though tanning on a beach. Now or never.

I stick out here like a snowman in a sauna. Still, the initial looks I'm getting from the four girls are more curious than accusatory. They are in a peppery, animated conversation punctuated with an indiscernible blend of young exclamations including "I know, right"s and "sus"es and "it's giving"s and "sending me"s and "mid"s and "simp"s. They barely look up until I am standing over them. I don't say anything. I wait. The conversation fades away like the end of a song more than it stops. Then a few "what the f" giggles start up as I just stand there and give them my warmest smile.

The girl who was driving is the first to speak. "Uh, can we help you?"

"My name is Sami Kierce," I say. I hold up my phone with the photo I took of the gate blocking Maybe Anna's driveway. "Could you tell me who lives here?"

Sometimes you try subtle. Sometimes you just dive right in.

The girls all share a glance, but the convertible's driver keeps her eyes on mine.

"Are you a cop, Sami Kierce?" she asks.

"Used to be."

"Why aren't you one anymore?"

"Got thrown off the force."

Again the other girls turn their heads and mutter. They are almost background noise now. It's just the driver and me.

"Why do you want to know who lives there?" she asks.

"More than twenty years ago, when I was probably around your age, I fell hard for a girl when I was backpacking through southern Spain."

"Like a summer romance?" one of the girls says.

"Exactly like that," I reply.

The other two girls say "aww." The driver keeps her eyes on me.

I continue: "Anyway, like I said, I fell for a girl in Spain. Up until last night, I thought she was dead."

"What happened last night?" Driver Girl asks.

"She showed up at a class I was teaching in the city. Then

she bolted out when I spotted her. I followed her back here, but she disappeared behind that gate. I tried to get in, but her security guys threw me out."

"Oh that's sweet," another girl—the other three all seem to be one mass to me now—says. They all stare up at me with classic doe-in-the-headlights expressions. They are engaged, paying attention, wanting to know more.

That's the thing about truth—it has its own unmistakable odor. You can smell truth. Authenticity can disarm the opposition.

"Wait," Driver Girl says, "how do you not know the name of your old girlfriend?"

"She said it was Anna."

"But you don't believe that?"

I shrug.

"Are you sure it's the same girl?"

"I guess I can't be. It's been over twenty years. She's changed a lot."

"But?"

"I'm pretty sure it's her. But if I'm wrong, there's only one way to find out."

"This is so weird," one of the girls says.

"Kind of stalkerish too."

"Maybe she was, I don't know, ghosting him?"

"Then why come to his class?"

"Oh right, right."

"Hold up," Driver Girl adds. She has these intense blue eyes that bore holes. "You said you thought she was dead."

"Yes," I reply. "Worse, I thought maybe I was responsible for her death. I've lived with that guilt and worry for twenty-two years. As for stalking and ghosting or whatever, I have no interest in her in that way. It was a long time ago. I'm happily married. We just had a baby."

I show them a photo on my phone of the three of us. Molly had set her phone up with the timer and then she used some app that created a cheesy rainbow background like we used to get at Sears department stores as kids.

The girls in unison, almost as though they'd practiced it, say, "Awwww."

"So cute!"

"Adorbs!"

They take my phone from me and pinch-zoom the photo to get closer in.

"Is that your wife?"

"Yes," I say. "Molly."

"She's so pretty."

"She is," I agree.

"Does she know you're here?"

"Yes. We don't keep secrets. I just need answers. Molly—that's my wife's name—she gets it."

They all share looks, not sure what to say next.

"Please," I say. "I just need answers. I don't mean anyone any harm."

The girl on the far right says, "But you don't want to go there."

"They aren't nice people," another adds.

"My mom said it's an old mobster's place," Girl Three says, "and they shoot anyone who tries to get to him."

"No," Far Right Girl says, "it's some rich Russian guy who wears a lot of chains."

Driving Girl signs and sits up. "Excuse me, Gardenia?"

One of the women in pink scrubs comes out from behind the circular IV bar. Driver Girl motions toward the IV in her arm. Gardenia attaches it to a metal IV stand with five wheels on the bottom and two hooks at the top. Driver Girl rises and gestures for me to follow her.

"As you can see," she tells me, glancing back at her friends, "the family that lives there works hard on maintaining their privacy."

"So they aren't rich Russians or mobsters?"

"No." She looks down, chews on her lower lip. "But they have good reason to want their privacy."

"That being?"

"The family has suffered a lot of tragedy. The woman you saw. Your girlfriend from Spain."

"What about her?"

"How old is she?"

"Around my age."

Her face pales. "Still."

"Still what?"

"She could have just been someone who worked at the estate. Like a housekeeper or groundskeeper or something."

"I don't think so," I say.

"Why not?"

"I tried to sneak to the house through the woods. Before security caught me, I saw Anna in an upstairs bedroom window. I mean, maybe she was just dusting or whatever, but it was late at night."

"Still," she says again. "It doesn't mean it was her."

"Wasn't who?"

"I mean, no one is even sure she lives there." Her words are coming fast now. Driver Girl had been so poised, so mature up to this point. "But that's what my parents told me. I've never seen her. I don't think anyone has."

"Slow down a second," I say. "Take a deep breath."

"No," she replies. "If I slow down—if I think about it too long—I won't tell you. I'll back out. The family that lives there."

"What about them?"

"Their last name is Belmond."

It feels as though the air has been suddenly sucked out of the room. Her eyes stay on mine.

I almost take a step back. "Belmond," I repeat. "As in?"

She nods. "Victoria Belmond. The girl you call Anna? She may very well be Victoria Belmond."

8

I don't even know what to say.

"What?" Debbie says when we are back outside. "What happened?"

I don't reply. We pick up my car from the valet. My head spins as I put it in drive. When we are down the block, I pull over and take out my phone.

"Kierce?"

I bring up the WhatsApp group called No Shit, Sherlock. I have the contact info for twenty-eight students. I pare it down to what I consider my top ten students—the Pink Panthers, Golfer Gary, Leisure Suit Lenny, Debbie, a couple of others. I call this new group No Shit Elite.

With a slightly shaky hand, I type a message:

> Special Secret Class Tonight at 9 PM.
> Group Project: We are going to try to solve one
> of the most famous cold cases of the twenty-first

century: The kidnapping of Victoria Belmond.
All students are expected to research the case
and be prepared to present facts, evidence, and
theories.

When I hit send, I hear a ding. That's Debbie's phone. She reads the message on her phone.

"What the hell, Kierce?"

I am wondering how to reply to that when my phone rings. It's Arthur from White Shoe. I put a finger to my lips to signal that Debbie should stay quiet. She nods that she understands. I hit the answer button.

"What's up?" I ask.

"I need you to come to the office."

"You sound tense, Arthur."

"When can you be here?"

"Look, if Courtney Booth is upset about me not sending the photos—"

"It's not that—"

"—I can send her a bunch that don't show what I don't want to show."

"It's not about the Booth divorce, Kierce."

"So what's going on then?"

"Kelly Neumeier is here."

The lawyer who sprung Tad Grayson.

"So?"

"So she asked me to make this call. She's here with Tad Grayson."

"Here as in . . . ?"

"Our office. Tad Grayson wants to meet with you."

———

Tad Grayson sits in the same chair that Peyton Booth had occupied just a few hours ago. Divorcés. Cop killers. This room handles it all, I guess. Tad's hands—the hands that killed my fiancée—are folded on the long conference table. His eyes are down and on them. Kelly Neumeier smooths her gray pencil skirt and paces behind him.

I stand outside the windowed door with Arthur. They haven't seen us yet.

"I'll go in with you," Arthur says.

"Why?"

"You should have counsel."

"Why would I need counsel?" I ask.

"Out of an overabundance of caution."

"You're worried I'm going to do something stupid."

"Definitely. But mostly"—Arthur gives a loose, young man's shrug—"I don't want you going in there alone. I want someone in there on your side, you know what I mean?"

I nod that I do and I'm grateful. We are both trying to make light of something that is anything but light. My heart is pounding hard in my chest. I want to slow it down. I reach for the door, trying to be all casual about it, but I haven't been in the same room with this monster since I testified against him in court. I didn't go to hear the verdict. I didn't go for the sentencing. This man murdered my fiancée. I felt rage, of course. I wanted to tear him apart in so many ways. But back then I also felt something else when I was near Tad Grayson: Fear. Indistinct, blurry fear. I don't know if that emanated from his obvious psychosis or the personal circumstance—or more, what I felt capable of doing to him. I haven't felt that way since I left the courtroom, but now, as I open the door and Tad Grayson looks up at me, that fear is back.

It is Kelly Neumeier who speaks first. "Thank you for agreeing to see us, Mr. Kierce."

I say nothing. Arthur towers over me like an overgrown weed. He stays right by my side. He even leans a little against me to show he is there for me. It comforts me, which is something of a surprise. Neumeier starts toward me, hand extended for me to shake.

"Let's not," I say.

She stops, looks at her extended hand, pulls it back. "Why don't we sit?"

"No," I say.

I look toward Tad Grayson. He finally raises his eyes. When our eyes meet, I feel the fear awaken in my chest and start slithering, making it hard to breathe. Tad's eyes aren't black— they are a prison-dull gray that had once been blue—but they feel black. The temperature in the room drops. I struggle not to blink, to maintain the eye contact, but I can feel something inside of me start to quake and give way.

There is snap in my tone. "What do you want, Tad?"

"I didn't kill her."

"Yeah, I heard your press conference. You did things you aren't proud of. You sent awful texts, including the one that said you were going to put a bullet in her brain. But you didn't kill her. Anything else you want to tell me?"

"My conviction," Tad said slowly, "was set aside. Not overturned."

"But—let me guess—you want to clear your name," I say, my voice booming with sarcasm, "because gosh darn it, you didn't do it and the killer is still out there!"

Tad doesn't even blink. "Yes," he says. "And no."

I look up at Arthur as if to say, "Can you believe this crap?" Then I turn back to our adversaries. "Tad, whatever bullshit you're peddling, I'm not buying. Your lawyer here"—I motion toward Kelly Neumeier—"I don't think she buys it either. This wasn't about guilty or innocent for her. She knows you did it. It's about issues of procedure and what she sees as law enforcement abuses."

Kelly Neumeier doesn't like that. "Don't speak for me, Mr. Kierce."

"You're the one who dragged me down here."

"Exactly," she says. "Do you think I would do that if I didn't believe what Mr. Grayson had to say had merit?"

"Then I do apologize, Ms. Neumeier. Seems I was wrong about your motives. He's snowed you too."

"You're missing my point," Tad says.

"And what point is that, Tad?"

"The conviction was set aside, not overturned."

"Yeah, you said that already."

"That means," he says, "I can be retried."

"And for that reason," Neumeier adds, "I have advised my client not to say anything to you. It leaves him unnecessarily exposed. I advised him to keep a low profile or perhaps leave the area, at least temporarily. With the illegally obtained evidence now thrown out, he is scot-free. There is currently no path toward retrying him, much less obtaining a conviction, so if my client takes counsel's advice and just keeps his mouth shut, he will be in the clear. But despite all that, Mr. Grayson is ignoring what I've recommended and insists on talking to you."

Tad gives me the pleading eyes. "I didn't do it, Kierce, and yeah, I know you don't believe me. I'd like you to, I guess, but in a sense, I don't care either."

"Then what do you want from me?"

"I want you to help me find Nicole's killer."

"Don't say her name." I feel the rage now. "Don't you *ever* say her name."

"I'll answer any question," Grayson babbles on. "I'll take a lie detector test." He rises slowly and walks creakily toward me. Like an old old man. I like that. I like that he's weak and beaten. He keeps trudging forward. I make a fist. I want to hit him. I also want to step back, but then again I don't want to show fear. So I stay where I am. I hold my ground. I let Tad Grayson come right up to me, face-to-face, so close I can smell the decay coming off him.

"And here's the best part for you," Tad Grayson says to me. "If the new evidence we find points to me, well, then you can use that to retry me. You want her killer in prison? Cool. Let's find them. And if the killer ends up being me"—he spreads his hands—"then you'll know that too. A fresh bite at the apple, Kierce. This is your only chance of getting enough evidence to send me back to prison."

Everyone just stands there, all eyes on me.

"Ballistics matched your illegally purchased Walther PPK as the murder weapon," I say, because I'm stupid and can't help myself. "How do you explain that?"

"I don't know."

"You've had a long time to sit in a cell and think about it. No theories?"

"Just the obvious one: The killer stole the gun and framed me."

"The gun you bought under a pseudonym at a gun show in Pennsylvania?"

"Yes."

"Wearing a disguise. Trying hard to cover your tracks."

"Yes."

"Just one week before Nicole's murder—and the day after you sent the text about putting a bullet in her brain?"

"Yes."

"A gun—a Walther PPK, to be exact—that was dumped far away from your home and in a way that no one could trace it to you?"

For the first time, Tad Grayson smiles. "Oh, that's not true."

"What's not true?"

"You said 'no one could trace' the gun to me." His smile, his smile with tiny Tic-Tac teeth, grows. "And yet, somehow the police were able to do just that. Odd, don't you think?"

So we are there now. The two of us. Standing at the precipice.

"Somehow," Tad continues, "the police were able to find the gun and figure out that I was the owner of the gun, even though I, as you put it, wore a disguise and covered my tracks."

I had heard his explanation for all this already. His ridiculous story was that the timing was just a coincidence, that he'd planned on buying a weapon this way (illegally) for months because he was already a convicted felon and New Jersey's strict gun laws wouldn't let him assert what he saw as his constitutional right to bear arms. And yes, sending a life-threatening text to Nicole was admittedly wrong and appalling, but perhaps the idea to send it had been subconsciously planted in his brain because he was on his way to buy a gun. When he sent the threatening text, he was, in fact, gassing up his car for his trip across state lines to buy the Walther PPK. So that explains it somehow.

Yes, that was his ridiculous defense.

Needless to say, the jury didn't buy it.

"If we do nothing," Tad Grayson says to me, "we know the outcome: The killer stays out of prison. There is never justice for . . . for her. Or you. Or perhaps me. If we investigate, there are three possibilities: One, nothing changes. Two, you gather enough new evidence to convict someone. Or three, you find enough new evidence to convict me." He tries to meet my eye again, but I'm not in the mood. I step back. "Either way, I don't see the big risk to you."

"The risk," I say, "is that I'll have to be in the same room with you."

Neumeier doesn't like that. "Is that a threat?"

Arthur: "It most certainly wasn't. My client is understandably disgusted by the idea of being in the same room with the man who murdered his fiancée and was just released on a technicality."

"It wasn't a technicality," Neumeier counters. "The court found that most of the evidence against Mr. Grayson collected by the police, including former detective Kierce, was gathered in violation of a constitutional right."

"That was not what was proven," Arthur countered. "The case you presented was the flip side of guilt by association. Detective Kierce has been accused of police impropriety in a specific situation—therefore, you claimed, he is guilty of impropriety in every case he handled. The court's decision was unconscionable."

Kelly Neumeier is getting pissed. "Are you serious, Arthur? Need I remind you that you're still only a junior partner—"

I've had enough. I interrupt with a forceful: "Are we done here?"

No one knows how to respond.

"Tell you what," I say to them. Then I look directly at the scraps of a man that used to be Tad Grayson. "If you come up with some kind of evidence that points to someone other than you, I'll listen. Until then, fuck all the way off."

———

Arthur follows me to the elevator. He presses the down button and waits for me.

"Thanks for that," I say to him.

Arthur nods. Something crosses his face.

"What?" I ask.

"Don't bite my head off."

"Go on."

"I kinda believe him."

"Psychopaths are good liars," I tell him.

"Yeah, I know."

The elevator dings and opens.

"Kierce?"

"What?"

"You're a great cop. If Grayson is indeed the killer, you'll find that out, so I'm not sure I see the problem with"— Arthur makes quote marks with his fingers—"'helping' him investigate."

The elevator is empty. I'm thankful for that. I step in and let the door close on me without another word.

9

The first PowerPoint slide reads: **The Kidnapping of Victoria Belmond**.

The Pink Panthers, three women, start us off. We are in our public-bath classroom. The lights are out. Golfer Gary brought some kind of fancy projector in, and the three Pink Panthers are using it now against the grayish white of the concrete wall.

The head Pink Panther is an exceedingly tall, thin woman named Polly. She sports a Ticonderoga-yellow pantsuit. Match that up with her short-n-spiky gray hair colored pink, and the overall effect is that Polly looks something like a giant Number Two pencil. Pink Panther Polly could be Pencil Polly.

I'm big on thinking in terms of nicknames.

Polly has a good, clear speaking voice. My guess is, she has done a lot of presentations in the past. "Victoria Belmond, daughter of the Belmond fortune, was a seventeen-year-old high school senior when she vanished from a New Year's Eve party on December thirty-first, 1999. She and a bunch of high school friends rented out a space above McCabe's Pub in the East Village."

Lenny interrupts: "Hey, I threw up in that place once."

"Me too," Gary says. "Freshman year. Projectile vomit. Hit the jukebox."

"Guys," I say.

Polly is unfazed by the interruption. "The last time Victoria was seen was on a CCTV camera leaving the bar at 11:17 p.m."

One of the other Pink Panthers—I don't remember her name—clicks the mouse. We all have our eyes on the concrete wall as a blurry black-n-white still comes up. The angle, like seemingly all CCTV images, is from way above her head.

"Pretty bad quality," Golfer Gary says.

"The technology used was old," Polly says. "This image was taken from a VCR security tape. Some theorize it may not be her at all."

"Can't see the face," Lenny says.

"No," Polly says, "but that's what she was wearing. That's her hairstyle. That's the right height. Her friends identified her, so the police seem pretty certain that this is the last sighting of Victoria Belmond before she vanished."

Golfer Gary raises his hand as though waiting to be called on. I frown in his direction, and he puts his hand down. "This bothers me," Gary said.

"What bothers you?" I ask.

"Okay, first off, it's not just a New Year's Eve party—it's a New Millennium's Eve party."

"Right, so?"

"Do you remember what that night was like?"

The young influencers look at us blankly, as if we are discussing the Eisenhower presidency.

"I mean, it was such a big deal," Gary continues. "The end of the 1900s. The end of the 1000s, really. The start of not only a new century but a whole new millennium. Y2K and all that. Like Prince sang, we're gonna party like it's 1999. The buildup was huge. Everyone was ready for the party of a lifetime."

"So?" I say to get us back on track.

"So," Gary continues, "Victoria Belmond and her rich friends—most of them probably underage—rent out a space above a bar so they can party their brains out and watch the ball drop in a once-every-thousand-years event. And what does Victoria do?" Gary points to the projected image. "Forty-three minutes before the big countdown, she just leaves on her own. Doesn't anyone else find that weird?"

Murmurs of agreement.

"Good point," I say. I turn back to Polly and nod for her to continue.

"That's the last image we have of Victoria Belmond," she says. "No credible source remembers seeing her after this moment. Maybe she grabbed a taxi. Maybe she took a train or hitchhiked. Or maybe someone grabbed her right then and there. Nobody knows. Even now. Even today. There were no

ATM withdrawals, no credit card transactions, nothing. It's like Victoria Belmond was just swallowed whole."

The room falls into silence for a moment.

Lenny breaks it. "When was Victoria first reported missing?"

"That was part of the problem," Polly says. "No one realized she was missing at first. Her mother and father traveled that night to Chicago for a few days. Victoria has one brother—Thomas, age twenty-three at the time. He ended up at his girlfriend's. The staff had the night off. In short, no one checked in on Victoria, so no one even knows if she came home that night or what. Same with the next day. And the next. No one was around. When the staff came back, they figured Victoria was staying with one of her high school friends. Even when her parents came back from Chicago, they wondered where she was but, given her independent streak, nobody was overly worried. Her friends had rented a few ski homes in Cornwall to welcome in the new year. Her family figured she was at one of the other ones."

"So when were the police first contacted?"

"The night of January fifth. And even then, it wasn't all that urgent. The father, Archie Belmond, seemed somewhat concerned, but the mother, her name is Talia, thought Victoria was probably hiding from them on purpose. They'd had a fight before she left for the party."

"About?"

"College. Victoria had made Tufts University her early decision, mostly because her parents both went there and gave a ton of dough. Victoria wanted to travel instead, she said.

Maybe not go to college at all. Her mother threw a fit, according to what we know."

"Routine family argument," Gary says.

"Which was the problem. No one was really worried about her. If there were clues, they were vanishing day by day. The other thing that made it all seem okay is that the family received texts from Victoria's phone, purportedly from Victoria. The texts were vague." The slide changes, and Polly reads the texts out loud. "One says, 'Happy New Year.' Another says, 'I'm fine, I'll be back soon.' Another read, 'With C'—like the letter—'on a last sec trip, back in a week.'"

"Who's C?" Lenny asks.

"Yet another part of the problem," Polly replies. "No one knew for sure who C was. Victoria had two friends named Chloe, one Caroline, one Cora. It was Christmas break, and in these wealthy circles, I don't know, I guess it didn't ring any alarm bells."

"Or the parents were negligent," Gary adds.

"Right, could be," Polly says. "I'm trying not to be judgmental right now. I'm just giving the facts as we have them."

"And doing a good job," I add, giving her a thumbs-up.

"Thank you."

"Victoria didn't send those messages," Lenny says. "Her kidnapper did."

"That's now the most likely theory, yes. But the texts help add to the delay and confusion. In many ways, the kidnapping was the perfect crime. Everyone is distracted by the big celebration and the worry about Y2K. Her parents are away. Her brother is with his girlfriend. School is out, so no teacher would miss her. All in all, it took five days to report Victoria missing—and even then, for all the reasons we've gone over already, very few people took it seriously. But as the days turned to weeks, everyone grew more and more worried until—"

Polly nods. The other Pink Panther clicks the remote and a blank slide comes up.

"—there was nothing."

Polly pauses for effect, letting us stare at the blank screen. Then she starts speaking again. "No clues. No sighting. No witnesses. No leads. Not a trace of Victoria Belmond. Days turn to weeks. Then months. The legend grows. A true-crime documentary called *Vanishing Victoria* became a big hit. *48 Hours* did a two-hour special on the rich-girl Y2K vanishing. *20/20*. The ID network. Whenever something new aired, there'd be a lot of excitement and someone would claim that they saw Victoria in an airport or on a beach or something, but it never went anywhere. Time passes."

They click to a slide reading: **One Year**.

Click to the next slide: **Five Years**.

Click to the next slide: **Ten Years**.

The Pink Panthers have a flair for the dramatic, but the effect is pretty devastating. The room falls into respectful silence. Polly stands there and watches our reactions.

Golfer Gary shakes his head. "I have daughters," he says.

Lenny: "Can you imagine?"

Debbie: "That poor family."

"Everyone gave up hope," Polly says. "The pain became too much. The family withdrew from public life. At first they'd had a lot of support, but as time went by, people started making awful accusations."

"What kind of awful accusations?" Debbie asks.

"That the family was involved in what happened to Victoria."

"What?"

"The Belmond Corporation got entangled in some ugly business scandals. There were those who wondered out loud about that, claiming that Victoria wanted to blow the whistle."

"Blow the whistle on her family?"

"Yes," Polly says. "Suddenly rumors started to take root and spread. Her parents' trip to Chicago was last-minute. Maybe they took it so they'd have an alibi. Her brother, Thomas, had a bit of a checkered past—school suspension, dropped assault charges, too many DUIs. He also dropped her off in the city that night, so some wondered whether he had something to do with it. Victoria had a boyfriend whose father worked for the Belmonds. How come he didn't notice she was missing from the party? Victoria lived in this wealthy community and knew all their rich-people secrets, so maybe someone in town had to silence her. From what we can see, the police didn't take any of these too seriously. They were the stuff of tabloids."

"What other theories were out there?" Gary asks.

"The usual. I think after a few weeks, the police believed Victoria was dead. That she'd been murdered right away, and her body dumped in the river or buried in the woods. Or

NOBODY'S FOOL

maybe she was still being held by a kidnapper somewhere belowground. Stuff like that. Others believed that Victoria was behind it all. She had this fight with her mother, so she ran away."

I stand up. "That's a lot of theorizing," I say. "Does anyone remember our Sherlock quote on theorizing?"

Debbie raises her hand and without hesitation says, "'It is a capital mistake to theorize before one has data. Insensibly one begins to twist facts to suit theories, instead of theories to suit facts.'"

We all look at her, stunned by her memory.

"Very good, Debbie," I say. "So let's not fall into that trap. Let's get some more facts." I look at Polly. "What happened next?"

Polly nods again toward the other Pink Panther. I wish I could remember her name. The next slide comes up. It's a photograph of a diner straight out of a painting by Norman Rockwell by way of Edward Hopper. "This is the Nesbitt Station Diner located in Briggs, Maine. There's nothing much in Briggs other than a maximum-security penitentiary. On March eighteenth, 2011, eleven years and nearly four months after Victoria Belmond vanished from McCabe's Pub in Manhattan, someone claiming to be a waitress at the diner called the FBI and said that a woman sitting in the corner booth reminded her of the missing Victoria Belmond. The FBI didn't take it too seriously, but they did call the local police. Two cops happened to be eating there anyway, so they checked on the woman eating alone in the corner booth. They asked her

103

who she was and if they could see some ID. But the young woman either couldn't or wouldn't talk. Her head was shaved. They gently asked her to empty her pockets. She only had one thing in them . . . "

Polly swallows and nods. The slide changes.

"This."

It is a yellowing three-row library checkout card, the kind of thing they used when I was a little kid, though they were dated even then. You'd bring your book to the library desk. The librarian would stamp the due date in the column on the left. She'd remind you that it would be a dime for every day you brought it back after that. Then you'd write your name in the center column. When you brought the book back, the librarian would stamp the return date in the right column.

On the top of this card, the one on the slide, where it says Author, someone had typed:

Belmond, Victoria

Next line was the book title:

Captive

Under that, there are, as I mentioned before, three columns.

On the far left was the Date Due. Someone had stamped in:

Jan 31, 2000

Back in those days, you kept the book out for one month. This date, January 31, 2000, would be exactly one month after Victoria had vanished.

The middle area, where you put the Borrower's Name, someone had scrawled:

THE LIBRARIAN.

And then the final column, Date Returned:

March 18th, 2011

That day's date, more than eleven years after Victoria had vanished.

Under that, scrawled in script: *I know I owe a heavy late fine, but I really enjoyed the book. My apologies for being tardy.*

More silence. The room's temperature has dropped at least ten degrees.

Someone finally mutters, "My God."

Then Lenny says, "Man, that's pretty psycho stuff."

Polly continues, her voice properly somber now. "The police call in the parents. Victoria Belmond was seventeen when she left. If this is Victoria, she would be twenty-eight now. But the woman still won't speak. She's nearly catatonic. But when she sees her parents and brother, she starts sobbing uncontrollably. No one can console her. No one can get her to talk. When doctors run a full physical on her, they find signs of trauma and abuse, but they don't release anything specific.

She's fifteen pounds thinner, but that's not a huge surprise. At first, some officials are even suspicious of the woman."

"In what way?" Lenny asks.

"Like maybe the girl is a fake, a con artist. Rich family, missing girl suddenly home. To be fair, it's happened before."

"I remember a case like that in Texas," Gary says.

"Nicholas Barclay, right," Polly answers. "And that boy was only missing three years. Victoria had been gone for eleven years, and even her own family isn't sure it's her at first. The father has doubts, I guess. The mother doesn't."

"Why didn't they run a DNA test?"

"They did," Polly said. "That's why I said 'at first.' Back in those days DNA tests took a few days, so there are a few rocky days, but eventually the test confirms that the young woman found in the Nesbitt Station Diner is indeed Victoria Belmond."

Silence.

Gary turns to me. "I don't get something," he says.

"Go ahead," I reply.

"It'd been eleven years. Her head was shaved. She's thinner. Her own family barely recognizes her. And yet some random waitress spots her and calls it in?"

"That's a good point," Polly says. "Did anyone else catch that?"

"We did," one of the young influencers says, the first time they've said a word. "No waitress admitted making the call. We think it was probably the kidnapper."

"Except the record shows it was a woman's voice."

"So maybe the Librarian is a woman?"

"Or maybe a woman who works with the Librarian. Or the caller could have used a voice changer. Even back then the technology was good enough to make the deepest male bass sound like a little girl."

I try to get them back on track. "What happened next, Polly?"

"We don't really know much. Eventually Victoria Belmond was able to talk, but it's like the previous eleven years didn't exist. She has no idea where she'd been or who took her or anything about a kidnapping."

"Correction," Gary says. "She *claims* to have no idea."

"Maybe," Polly says. "All we know is that Victoria started being treated by the best psychiatrists money can buy. But we really don't know much more. The family asked for privacy, which makes sense, and they had the resources to make that happen."

"But Victoria Belmond was found, what, fourteen years ago," Gary says.

"Correct."

"So where has she been in all that time?"

"That's a mystery," Polly says. "Victoria has never spoken publicly or given interviews. According to the public record, the case remains unsolved. No one knows who kidnapped her. No one knows where she was for those eleven years. The family is superrich and has residences in several states and at least two out of the country. She could be holed up in any of them or none of them. No one knows."

"Almost twenty-five years since the crime initially took place," Golfer Gary says with a shake of his head. "This case isn't cold, Kierce. It's frozen in ice."

They all turn to me.

"Come on," I say, spreading my arms. "Don't you want a challenge?"

"A challenge, sure. But there hasn't been a new development in years."

I lean back in my chair. "Oh, I wouldn't say that."

10

After the students are given their work assignments and empty into the night, I stay behind and call Marty. He picks up and says, "Busy day here. I still only have an LLC for that Connecticut residence. Whoever owns that place is working hard to keep it quiet."

"I think it's the Belmond family," I say.

"As in—?"

"Yes."

"Oh," he says. "That would explain it."

"I also think Victoria Belmond lives there."

I can tell by his hesitancy that Marty isn't sure what to say to that one. "I see. Why do you believe that?"

I answer with a question. "Do you still have friends in the FBI?"

"I never had friends in the FBI," Marty says.

"But contacts?"

"I know a guy who may know a guy," Marty says.

"Can he get you the FBI file on Victoria Belmond?"

"As in the young woman who was kidnapped, what, thirty years ago?"

"Twenty-five," I correct. Then I add, "Yes."

I hear footsteps echoing outside of the classroom. Someone is coming up the steps.

"May I ask why you want the file?"

"Sure," I say. "There's a chance I could break the case."

"The kidnapping of Victoria Belmond?"

"Yes."

"You might be able to break it?"

"You sound skeptical," I say.

Sounds more like two, maybe three sets of footsteps.

"Maybe a tad," Marty says. "Do you care to elaborate on why you think you can solve one of the great mysteries of our time?"

The footsteps are closer, louder.

"I thought you said it was a busy day."

"Kierce."

"I'm not saying it's likely," I say, "and it's a really long story and I'll tell you about it later, but in the meantime can you look into the file?"

"No promises."

"I didn't ask for promises, did I?"

"No. No, you didn't."

The footsteps stop at my door. Leisure Suit Lenny leans in as I click off. Golfer Gary is with him.

"Got a second?" Lenny asks.

"Sure."

Lenny hitches up his pants. He does that a lot, I notice. I can't tell if the waist is too big or the bulge in his belly pushes the pants too low or why I'm wondering weird stuff like this. But it's distracting. He hitches them up and steps into the room. Gary follows him.

Gary starts it off. "We are here on behalf of the class."

Oh, this is going to be interesting. I lean back in my chair and throw up my feet. "Okay."

"We'd like to know," Gary continues, "why you are so interested in the Victoria Belmond case."

"Does it matter?"

"I guess not."

"It'll be a fun class exercise," I say, trying to keep my voice light. "Research. Investigation. Surveillance."

Gary folds his arms across the golf shirt with a logo that looks like a red basket on top of a stick. Golfers are weird. "But," he says, "there's more to it, right?"

I don't reply.

Now it's Lenny's turn. "The woman who crashed our class last night. The one you followed. I don't mean to pry, but that tracker goes to my phone too. You just asked us to run surveillance near Greenwich, Connecticut, in the exact same spot where the batteries on my GPS tracker died."

Man, I am getting sloppy.

"In conclusion," Gary says, sounding like a TV detective who has finally gathered all of the suspects in the drawing room for our denouement, "you saw a woman enter our class."

"A woman," Lenny adds, "who would be the approximate age of Victoria Belmond."

Back to Gary: "That woman ran off."

Lenny: "You followed her using a GPS tracker."

"Right to the spot where you now want us to surveil for a possible Victoria Belmond sighting."

They both stop and look at me. I nod in appreciation.

"I'm some teacher, right? I'm going to have to up the class fee."

Lenny hitches up his pants again. "So the woman who was here last night, the one who came to our class. You think there's a chance that—"

"—that she's Victoria Belmond?" I finish for them.

It is an interesting question. You'd think I would know for sure, right? There are photographs, of course, of Victoria Belmond online. Not as many as you would think. But enough. In most she is a teenager, which would be when I knew Anna. There are far fewer—almost none—since her return. The parents asked the press to leave their traumatized daughter alone and had the resources to make that a reality. But when I look at the photos of seventeen-year-old Victoria, I can't tell you for certain it's the Anna I met in Spain—but I think it is. If it's not, the resemblance is uncanny. The reason I can't say for absolute sure it's Anna is an odd one. I try to think back to what Anna looked like and when I do, I can describe her to you, I guess—but I can't actually *see* her anymore. Quick: Think about an old love, one from all those years ago, one you knew only a week. Really really picture them. Do you have the specifics? Like a photograph? Yeah, I didn't think so. Memory doesn't work that way. Memory doesn't take photographs. Memory is about trying to fill in the blanks, and while I see similarities, my memory won't let me make a definitive match.

So the mystery deepens.

I was also not the most perceptive of boys back then. Don't hate on me for this, but I don't remember Anna's eye color, for example. Anna's hair was different, a different color and longer than Victoria's, but that doesn't mean much. Plus Victoria wears glasses. Anna did not.

And yet, when I saw Anna/Victoria in the flesh in my classroom, I was sure it was Anna in a split second.

Crazy.

"So what we are saying," Gary continues, "is that Victoria Belmond showed up to your class last night."

"Could be."

"And when she saw you, she ran away."

I smile. I know where they are going with this, but I play along. "I startle people."

"True," Lenny says, "and we might buy that if it ended there."

"But?" I say.

"But, see, you chose to run after her," Lenny says.

"Chased her," Lenny clarifies.

"You didn't hesitate a second. A crazy look crossed your face and bam, it's like you were a world-class sprinter all of a sudden."

"And let's face it, Kierce. You don't like to run."

"Physical activity isn't my bag," I admit.

"Conclusion," Gary says with a flair for the dramatic. "This isn't just a class assignment. You, Professor Kierce, know—or knew—Victoria Belmond."

"Or at the very least," Lenny adds, "you have some personal connection to her or this case."

I look at Gary. Then at Lenny. I nod to show that I'm impressed.

"I will neither confirm nor deny your allegation," I say, mostly because I don't really know for sure what to tell them or even if the allegation is true. "But let's suppose I do. Then what?"

Gary takes a step forward. He grabs a chair, pulls it up near me, swivels it around and sits reverse pony. "This is a class of curious detective wannabees."

"Meaning?"

"Meaning we all googled you before we joined the class. We know your background. We know you were a decorated NYPD homicide detective, of course. And we know why you lost your job. We also know that another case where you had a personal connection has suffered a severe setback."

I try not to bristle at that. "I found her killer," I say a little too defensively.

"And now he's free," Lenny says.

So there we have it. The two men look at me and wait for my reply. I turn my hands palms up in a quasi shrug. "If you don't want to do this—"

"We didn't say that," Gary says quickly.

"But we think you should come clean."

"Because it may help us solve the case."

Gary rises, making a big production of putting the chair back where it was. "Either way we are still going to help you."

"Because we like you," Lenny adds. "And we think you're a good man."

"But we wanted you to know that we aren't patsies," Gary says. "We are going into this with eyes open."

They wait for me to say something. I settle for "Thank you."

That seems to be all they need.

———

Molly and I sit at our kitchen table finishing up breakfast.

Maybe it's thinking about the Belmond money or whatever, but this kitchen suddenly feels too small and dated. I want better for Molly and Henry. I want to have a job again with a steady paycheck. I don't want to see her worry, especially about money. Not ever. Old-fashioned thinking, and Molly would probably hit me for even considering it, but it should be my job to make sure she never has to worry about how we will pay our bills. I don't say this in a bitter way or any of that. A wise (rich) man once told me that the best part about having a lot of money is that you didn't worry about money. I feel that right now. I want that for us. For Molly.

"My coming home late last night has nothing to do with you and me," I say.

"I know."

"You do?"

"Yeah, silly. You love me. It's written all over that goofy face of yours."

I can't help but smile. "It is, isn't it?"

Forget what I said before. What man is wealthier than I?

"So what's wrong?" she asks.

I decide to just say it. "Do you remember the case of Victoria Belmond?"

Her face indicates that wasn't what she expected to hear. "The rich girl who was kidnapped?"

"Yes."

"You didn't kidnap her, did you?"

Gallows humor. I love this woman.

"Uh, no," I say. "But I may have dated her."

"Wow." Molly tilts her head. "When?"

"About two years after she was kidnapped."

She waits for the punch line. None comes. "You're serious?"

"Twenty-two years ago, I went to Europe with a bunch of guys from college after we graduated."

"You told me that earlier—"

"Right, I know."

"—but not before today. Not a word about a college trip with the boys. Which I thought was strange."

"Because I didn't stay with them very long," I say.

"Why not?"

"Early on, I met a girl named Anna. We hooked up in the Costa del Sol of Spain. I liked her, so I told the guys to go on without me and I stayed with her."

I stop.

"Sami?"

"And now, for the first time in all these years, I saw her again."

"Anna?"

"Yes."

"When?"

"Last night. She showed up to my class. But then she ran. I followed her, but . . . "

I shake my head. I can't speak.

Molly puts her hand on my arm. "This Anna," she says. "You think, what, that she might have been Victoria Belmond?"

When I finally manage to nod, Molly sits back, stunned. My nod turns into a headshake. Finally, I spout out, "Yes, no, maybe. I don't know. I'm still trying to put this together. It's a . . . it's a mess."

"It's okay. Shh, don't worry."

I shake my head again.

"You were young," Molly says. "Even if it was her, you'd have no way of knowing. How could you have possibly known?"

I don't know what to say.

Molly tries again. "In Spain, did this girl—this Anna—did she try to give you a signal?"

That confuses me. "A signal?"

"That she was kidnapped. That something was wrong or that she was there under duress."

I get it. Molly thinks I feel guilty because I hooked up with a kidnapped girl and didn't realize that she was in danger. I hadn't thought of that until right now, oddly enough, but maybe Molly has a point.

Was Anna in trouble that whole time? Did I miss the signs? My phone buzzes. It's a text from Pink Panther Polly.

> Car just left estate. We think it's her. Gary and I following.

My heart leaps and so do I. Molly watches me rise.

"Sami?"

"She's on the move."

"What? Who?" Then: "Victoria Belmond?"

I nod. "Or whoever she is."

"How do you know?"

"My students."

"What?"

I quickly explain that the Pink Panthers set up a schedule for my students to run surveillance near the estate in shifts. Ethically questionable, I guess, but certainly economical. I'm not a cop anymore, but we learn to make do.

"Can we finish this up later?" I ask. "In a few hours I may know if this is nothing but my imagination."

"Go," Molly says. "But one thing."

I look back at her.

"It's something I said before, Sami."

"I'm listening."

"This Anna or Victoria or whatever shows up in your life at the same time Tad Grayson is released from prison."

I shake my head. "I can't see a connection, Molly."

"Then you better look harder."

11

I'd just taken my first step down to the subway, hurrying to catch the next train which, according to my app, would leave in three minutes, when Polly called me back.

"They're on the highway," she says. "I think she's heading into the city."

"Are you sure she's in the car?"

"We think so, yeah. She's sitting in the back. A male is driving. Dark blue Cadillac Escalade. Connecticut plates. Gary and I are following. I'll drop a pin so you can track us."

I check my phone when I hear the proverbial and literal pin drop. Their car is heading west on 95 toward the George Washington Bridge. If she'd stayed in the Greenwich area, it would have made sense for me to drive up and try to confront her. But now that Maybe Victoria is this far on the move, it is better to stay still and see where she is going. I head into the simply named Hot Bagel Shop and order up a sesame bagel with a schmear—Molly taught me that word—of whitefish spread and cream cheese. I keep an eye on the pin drop. When the car takes the Hutchinson River Parkway, I figure the odds are Polly is correct about her heading into New York City.

Twenty minutes later, New York City is confirmed when the car pulls onto West Forty-Eighth Street heading toward Broadway. The traffic is, as expected, stop and go, mostly stop. I'm still standing at the counter at the bagel shop. A few minutes later, Polly says, "Photo incoming."

I check my WhatsApp. The little wheel spins, and the photo comes into focus.

A woman wearing a baseball cap and sunglasses is stepping out of a Cadillac Escalade. She's innocuously dressed in blue jeans, a gray sweatshirt, white sneakers.

It's Anna/Victoria.

"That's her, right?" Penny says.

"Yes."

"I'm following her on foot," Polly says. "We are in Times Square. Gary is going to continue following the Escalade."

"I'm on my way," I say and rush back to the subway. I look for any train heading toward the Times Square area. There are always plenty. I jump on the subway and check the app. There's spotty service down here so I'm not getting an update. When I arrive at Forty-Second Street/Broadway, I head up into the sunlight and the cacophony, and the app springs back to life.

The pin is four blocks away.

I call Polly. "What's she doing?"

"Just walking."

"How about the car?"

"Hold on, let me link in Gary." A few seconds pass. "Gary?"

"The driver parked the Escalade in a garage," Gary says. "He's walking toward you guys, I think."

"Do you have eyes on him?" I ask.

"Negative," Gary says. "I figured it would be smarter to double-park and wait by the garage. When they come back, I'll be back on them."

"Smart thinking," I say.

"Thanks, Teach."

"Kierce," Polly says, "how far away are you?"

"Three blocks and closing," I say.

I look at the screen as I move, which is no easy feat in Times Square. It's still fairly early in the morning, but the costumed beggars or whatever you call them are already out in force. As anyone who has visited Times Square in the past decade knows, it is flooded with costumed Batmans and Spider-Mans and Olafs and Minions and Elmos and Mickey Mouses (Mice?), hoping for tourists to take a photo with them in exchange for fees or tips. I always find this particularly weird. Mickey Mouse is about Disney, right? Not New York City. Why would you want a photograph with Mickey Mouse here? And these costumed cretins may seem harmless, but I know from my time on the force, they create a lot of crime. Some tourists snap photos not realizing that Mickey expects a tip for that and when you don't pay, it leads to intimidation and even violence. Some of those hidden by costumes get overly "handsy," if you catch my drift, and there is a fine line between quirky and creepy, or maybe the line isn't so fine, but too often, the whole experience lands in the creepy and flirts over toward the downright criminal.

I wish I'd brought earphones, but I hadn't, so I have to keep the phone next to my ear.

"Oh, one other thing," Gary says.

"What?"

"The driver."

"What about him?"

"Stiff gait. Too big a sports coat. Shifty eyes. I think he may be carrying."

"He probably doubles as her security," Polly says.

"We know Belmonds like their privacy," Gary adds.

"Hold up," Polly says.

"What is it?" I ask.

Polly says, "I'm on Forty-Second Street in front of the New Amsterdam Theater and . . . Gary, is the driver wearing a camelhair sports coat?"

I'm getting bumped by too many people, so I press against the window of a Red Lobster that feels like it's coated with drawn butter. I stick to it. Diners stare at me. I check the phone and see that I'm within a hundred yards of Anna. She's right here on Forty-Second Street. I hurry my pace.

And suddenly, there she is. I pull up.

Anna. Victoria. Whatever.

She's talking with Camelhair Coat Driver, though I know him by another dumb in-my-head nickname.

Gun Guy. He's Gun Guy from the other night at the estate.

My hands form fists. I owe that dude a sucker punch.

They finish talking under the marquee. There is a big crowd now flowing into the theater. Gun Guy opens one of the doors. Anna walks through a metal detector—a metal detector to see a Broadway musical—what a country—and enters. Gun Guy watches through the windowed door. Satisfied he moves away.

I say into the phone, "Polly?"

"I'll stay on him."

Gary asks, "Could you see anything, Polly?"

"She went inside and got her ticket scanned," Polly says. "I guess she's seeing the musical."

Gary: "Is it *Hamilton*?"

"No."

"*Wicked*?"

"No."

"Should I keep guessing, Polly, or do you want to tell me?"

"Guys," I say.

I'm not sure of the move here. I head toward the box office. A security guard has me go through the metal detector. I head over to the box office window. "Any seats available?" I ask.

The guy behind the window could only look more bored if he were unconscious. He sighs and says, "For when?"

"The current show?"

"Sold out."

"Standing room?"

He frowns. "What part of 'sold out' is confusing to you?"

"Boy, you're a turn-the-world-on-with-your-smile kind of guy," I say. "Thank you for just brightening my day."

He manages to hide the bleeding psychological wound made by my rapier wit. I head back outside and stand under the marquee. In the old days you might find some guy, usually in a shiny Mets jacket, scalping an extra ticket. No more. Even safe-scuzzy moments like whispering to a strange guy "Got a ticket?" have been ruined by apps and the internet.

So I wait for the show to end. Or should I say *we* wait.

Polly follows Gun Guy to the Yard House where he orders a burger, fries, and a beer. Gary stays in his double-parked car by the garage. I first go to one of those crap souvenir stores and buy a pair of AirPod knockoffs. I hook them up to my Bluetooth and test them with Polly and Gary. The treble is terrible, but I can hear them fine. I spend the next couple of hours waiting for the musical to end. I try to sneak in during the intermission, but I get rebuffed. I take a few moments to think about all this. By all accounts, Victoria Belmond is a recluse. She has done no interviews since her return from kidnapping. Every once in a while, a journalist will try to track her down, but by and large, journalists have moved on to easier prey. If this happened back in the seventies or eighties, like, say, Patricia Hearst, the story would still be worth pursuing. Sure, people might still have an interest in Victoria Belmond, but it isn't as though it would be an everyday thing. Stories no longer capture our collective attention that way. We don't all watch a kid being rescued from falling down a well anymore, and I don't know whether that's a good thing or bad.

Add into all this the obvious: Big money eases the way. The Belmond family has been willing to spend a great deal of capital to keep Victoria out of the spotlight. No one really knows whether she eventually remembered anything about her time in captivity or not. Is her mind still a blank—or did she process it all—or heck, has she been faking amnesia? I saw one rumor online that Victoria Belmond eventually remembered everything, and rather than have the kidnapper arrested, the wealthy Belmond family hired a mercenary group to handle the justice in their own brutal way.

I doubt that, but who knows?

Point is, it has been years, and no one is really paying much attention anymore, so trips like this into Manhattan are no longer a big security risk for her, I imagine. If anything, it is wiser to hide in plain sight. She lives her life, it seems, albeit quietly and uniquely, blending the clandestine domicile on the enormous Connecticut estate with seemingly the freedom to enjoy a Broadway show in the Big Apple.

I wonder what her life has been like. I wonder whether this is really my Anna from Spain or just a case of mistaken identity. I wonder about what really happened that awful morning in the Costa del Sol. Not to get too deep here, but part of me is still there, in that bed, waking up in the bright sunlight and screaming, screaming still, screaming so that even now, nearly a quarter century later, I still feel, more than hear, the echoes.

See what I mean about getting too deep?

After I flew home from Málaga Airport, once I listened to

my panicked father and hurried to the airport and boarded the first plane out to the United States, I found sleep elusive. I don't know about PTSD or something like that, but I kept dreaming I was waking up next to a faceless dead girl. I couldn't move on. I would check the Spanish news for updates, but there was nothing. It was then I started to drink. Just a little. Just to help me close my eyes. I had no ambition left, so I deferred medical school for a year. Then two years. Then the little drinking became a lot of drinking. I didn't go to med school. I forgot about all my plans, my lifelong goal of becoming a physician, all of that lost in a bottle with a dead girl I now know is very much alive.

A little more than two hours after the show began, Polly dings me. I hit answer and we are all on the same call. Polly says, "The driver paid his tab. He's on the move, walking back toward the theater."

That means I can't just hang out here anymore. Gun Guy will see and probably recognize me. I head toward the ticket scanner/security guard on the other side of the marquee, the one who hasn't already seen me try to enter before. "Can I ask you a favor?" I say.

"You can ask, I guess."

"I went to this play with my niece Pammy last Thursday."

Note: When you lie, add specifics. Names. Dates.

"Okay."

"Anyway, Pammy loved it and so I was hoping that I could just quickly run inside and buy her a souvenir sweatshirt."

"I think they sell them at that shop next door."

"They do," I say, "but they're pretty shoddy knockoffs. Also—and I know this is corny—but I want to get her the official sweatshirt from the theater itself. You know. As a real memento."

The guard has heard it all before, but he's also a human being. "You have to wait for the show to let out."

"Of course," I say. "I mean, I know it gets crowded so maybe the moment the show ends?"

It takes a little more haranguing, but the ticket scanner agrees. When the show lets out and the crowd begins to rise from their seats, he lets me in. I hurry over toward the souvenir vendor and feign studying the various items. The ticket scanner loses interest in me as the theatergoers stream out in a waterfall of flesh. There are side exits off the orchestra seats, I see now, and I worry Anna may depart that way. I swim upstream, against the tide of musical emigrants, so I can try to position myself to see all exits. I have my new "AirTods" in my ears, so I check in with my students.

"Polly?" I say.

"I'm here," she says.

"Where is the driver now?"

"He's pacing out front. Under the marquee."

Okay, good. That means Anna will most likely be exiting out the front. My eyes scan the crowd while I'm also trying to blend in. I don't want Anna to see me first and bolt again. That part still confuses me, by the way. Anna or Victoria or Whoever came to my class. Not the other way around. That couldn't be a coincidence. My class in the old public bathhouse down on the Lower East Side—that's not a place you happen by or casually stroll through.

She had come to see me. She had sought me out.

The crowd surged and then began to thin out. Still no sign of Anna. I wondered whether I had missed her. As I said before, there are plenty of exits. I can't keep my eyes on all of them. I move closer to the standing-room area and look down at the stage.

That's when I spot her.

She is still in her seat, facing the stage, her back to me. She seems to be still watching the show. Or something. I don't know what. The dark maroon curtain is closed now. I can't see her face, but I wonder what the deal is, why she remains in the seat. Does she not want to deal with the crowds? Was she emotionally overwhelmed by the musical? Does she just want to spend a few moments to soak in the grandeur of the ornate art nouveau interior? Does she want to prolong the time she has alone in this quiet theater before Gun Guy bustles her back to her prison-mansion?

I have no idea. But I see no reason to wait.

I start down the aisle toward her. Her seat is primo, center orchestra, eight or ten rows back. Three, four hundred dollars at minimum. There are a few stragglers, maybe twenty or thirty people left, but there is no one near Anna.

I whisper "Going on mute" into the AirTod microphone and hit the mute button.

Polly says, "Driver is checking his watch, starting to look impatient."

I keep moving until I reach her row. Anna's seat is third from the end. I slide in quickly and take the chair next to hers. When I land, she startles and looks at me.

"Anna," I say.

"Stay away from me."

She starts to rise. I gently but firmly put my hand on her forearm, trying to figure a way to keep her in place but not wanting to use force. This isn't easy and I realize I'm probably crossing a line here.

I try again. "Anna—"

"Why do you keep calling me that? That's not my name."

I meet her eyes now. In my mind, there is no doubt it's Anna from Fuengirola, but I also recognize the very human capability of deluding ourselves via our own wants and narratives. So I work to stay neutral.

"Would you prefer," I say, "that I call you Victoria?"

Her eyes flare and settle. I hit a nerve.

"How did you find me?" she whispers.

"I followed you from my class," I say. "Didn't your security guards tell you they threw me off your estate?"

Confusion crosses her face. "What are you talking about?"

"Your house in Connecticut. I tried cutting through the woods, but your driver came at me with a Doberman and a gun."

Anna shakes her head. "I don't know you," she insists, but

I hear doubt in her voice. She starts to rise again. When I tighten my grip, she glares at it and then at me. No choice. I have to let her go. She stands. I do the same. I follow her down the row of seats toward the opposite aisle.

"We met in Spain," I say.

"I've never been to Spain."

"Fuengirola, to be precise. On the Costa del Sol. We met there twenty-two years ago."

She continues to move, shaking her head almost as though she's trying to convince herself.

"You're mistaken."

"It was you," I say. "I thought you were dead."

She shakes her head harder.

"You went by the name Anna. We met on the dance floor of the Discoteca Palmeras. You had an apartment nearby."

I see her hesitate now.

"I checked the dates," I say. "It would have been about three years after you first"—I can't find the right word so I settle for—"disappeared."

In my earphones I hear Polly say, "Driver is talking to ticket taker. Looks like he's heading inside."

Shit.

Anna says to me, "I've never seen you before."

"Then why did you come to my class?"

"I can't stay," she says. "He'll be worried."

"Who?" But there's no point. I have a business card in my hand, which only has my name and phone number on it. "Take this."

"What? No."

"Call me," I say.

She shakes her head, but she also takes the card. Then she looks at me and says, "You're not lying? You really knew me?"

Before I can say yes, I hear Polly in my earphone: "The driver is inside now."

"Your driver," I say to her. "He's in the theater."

"Duck down!" she says in a panic. I do. I drop down to my knees and stay low as I hear that same Gun Guy voice call out, "Hey, are you okay?"

"I'm fine," Anna says quickly. "I just . . . I'm sorry. This theater is just so beautiful, you know."

"Uh-huh," he says. Then: "We better go."

Anna nods. Then, before she disappears up the aisle, she looks down at me and whispers, "Don't tell anyone you saw me. Please."

12

Polly calls off the surveillance on the estate in Connecticut. What would be the point? She grabs a downtown C train to her townhouse in the Village. Marty calls and tells me he has some info from the FBI on the Victoria Belmond kidnapping.

"For one thing," he says, "it's never been solved."

"You have the file?"

"A lot of it."

"Where is it?"

"My place."

He gives me the address. I tell him I'm on my way. Golfer Gary offers me a ride uptown, and I accept. Gary drives a high-end Range Rover.

We head north toward the park. I'm sitting in the front passenger seat next to him. I watch his profile. I'm guessing Gary is in his early fifties. He's got a classic dad-bod beer belly, skinny arms, hunched shoulders. When I was twelve years old, my father taught me a lesson I try to live with every day. We were walking through Washington Square Park on an early-summer Saturday. If you've been there, you know that the park is a microcosm of the entire globe jammed into fewer than ten acres. You will see every variety of human in just a few short minutes.

"Hopes and dreams," my father said with a wide smile, spreading his hands like he was preparing for a hug.

"What do you mean?" I asked.

He bent down so he could look me in the eye. "Good rule of thumb: Whenever you see a person—rich, poor, young, old, tall, short, whatever—remember one thing: That person has hopes and dreams."

My father didn't elaborate any further. I think that was intentional on his part because it is still something that provides endless curiosity. I still do it every time I look at someone. I think my father wanted to teach me about empathy. You pass a man on the street. Maybe he's angry and seems mean and he's lashing out. Or someone is ugly or stupid or whatever. Somewhere, my father wanted me to remember, underneath all that excess, there is a human being with hopes and dreams. It's a simple thought. Hopes and dreams. And maybe this person with the unremarkable exterior has had their hopes and dreams crushed along the way. Doesn't matter. Hopes and dreams never fully die. They remain somewhere, dormant perhaps, but never totally gone.

Honor that.

"Gary?"

"Hmm?"

"What's your deal?" I ask.

"Deal?"

Everyone has hopes and dreams, I thought, which also means that everyone has a backstory. Every human you meet is a novel different from every other.

"Where do you live?" I ask. "What do you do? What led you to take my class?"

"Do you always take a personal interest in your students?"

"Sure," I say. "Especially the ones driving me in a high-end Range Rover and wearing golf shirts from fancy golf courses."

He smiles, steering now with his wrists. "Do you play golf?"

"Never."

"So how do you know the logos on my shirts are from fancy courses?"

"Google."

He nods.

"I assume you play, Gary?"

His grip on the wheel tightens. "Used to."

"Not anymore?"

"Not anymore," he repeats.

"Look," I say, "if you don't want to say anything—"

"No, I get it," he says. "It's weird—me taking your class. I don't fit the profile, though judging by some of your other students, there isn't much of a profile for this class, is there?"

"It's an eclectic bunch," I agree.

"Can I ask you something?"

I spread my hands. "I'm an open book."

"Are you married?"

"I am."

"Kids?"

"A son. He's a year old."

"Nice," Gary says.

"Yeah."

"I googled you before I joined the class."

"Yeah," I say. "You mentioned that before."

"They say you were fired for breaking rules. You endangered a witness by chasing him onto a rooftop—"

"PJ Dawson."

"—and you also acted in an illegal manner that led to a death."

"There a question coming here, Gary?" I ask. "Never mind. Let me save you the trouble. Yes, it's true."

"Many believe you should have been prosecuted."

"They might be right," I say. "In the end, I cut a deal. Resign. Lose my entire pension. In exchange I don't get prosecuted."

"I'm sorry," he says.

"I messed up big-time," I say. And when I do, he adjusts himself in his seat, eyes fixed on the road. I decide to try a gentle push. "So what's your deal, Gary? Wife, kids, any of that?"

"Divorced," Gary says, and again I see something cross his face. "Two daughters. Ellie is nineteen. She's a freshman at Clemson. Tanya is a senior in high school."

"Do you see them a lot?"

Gary shrugs. "Not as often as I'd like. They live with their mother in Short Hills. You know it?"

Short Hills is a tony enclave in New Jersey. Big-money town. "I do."

"Wendy and I raised our girls there. They went to the Pingry School."

"Expensive," I say.

"I had my own hedge fund back then. We had a five-bedroom house on Dorset Lane. Wendy and I were married twenty-four years." He glances at me, then back on the road. "Does your wife love you?"

"Yes," I say.

"I don't think Wendy ever did. But maybe I'm being unfair. I destroyed her life. That's the truth of it. I thought we could get past it. But she couldn't. That's why I'm alone now. No job. Wendy is dating an old friend of mine. The girls are embarrassed to be seen with me. Well, Tanya is. Ellie is better about it."

"I'm sorry."

He smiles. "I messed up big-time."

"Want to tell me how?"

"You wouldn't believe me if I did."

"I'm a pretty good listener," I say. "Nonjudgmental too."

"You don't golf though."

I hold up my hands in mock surrender. "Don't hold that against me. And to be fair, it is a dumb sport that takes up too much real estate and time."

"Can't argue with that," he says. "Ever heard of Vine Ridge?"

I think about it. "It isn't completely unfamiliar."

"It's an exclusive golf club. It's also hosted several PGA tournaments including the US Open twelve years ago."

"Okay, yeah, I think I watched that on TV."

"Vine Ridge is up there with Augusta or Pine Valley or Merion or Winged Foot."

"Okay," I say again, though these words mean nothing to me.

"Wendy and I were both longtime members. In Wendy's case, third-generation members. Well, sort of. Women can't join. Her grandfather and father were members. So it's the same thing, really. Me, I was a really good amateur golfer. Was on the team at Amherst College. That's how Wendy and I met. So when we got married and joined as junior members, I was technically the member. Because only men can be members. You know what I'm saying?"

"I think so. A bit sexist."

"Very sexist," he says. "But Wendy didn't care. She loved Vine Ridge. She grew up there, really. From the time she was a little girl, she spent summers there with her parents and grandparents and uncles and aunts, and you get the idea."

"I do," I say.

"Wendy and I, we'd have dinner at the club three or four times a week. Always with friends. Tables of six or eight. Lots of laughs and drinks. Wendy played in the women's nine-hole group every Tuesday and tennis on Wednesdays. I was one of the best male players in the club. We knew everyone."

Gary takes a breath now, makes a very labored left turn, hand over hand.

"Three years ago, I was playing for the club championship against Richard Belthoff. This was the first time I had reached the finals. I lost two years in a row in the semis, once to Richard on a pretty controversial call. He hit his ball behind a tree and got a free drop because he claimed his ball was resting in a gopher hole. Can you believe that?"

I say, "No," even though I'm not fully following.

Gary shakes it off. "Anyway, we were friends, Richard and me, but we were also super competitive. I'll try to make this quick because it's hard to talk about and you probably aren't interested."

"Oh but I am."

Gary smiles and shakes his head. "We are playing for the club championship. We reach the eighteenth hole. That's the final hole. And we were tied. See, this was match play. You win, lose, or tie holes. I'd won four, he'd won four, and we tied the other nine. So it all came down to this final hole, a par three over the trees. It's a signature hole because you can't see the green from the tee.

"Anyway, here's what it came down to. I teed off first. I hit what I thought was a great shot. But the trees hadn't been trimmed because of a recent storm. So there was a branch still in the way. We heard my ball hit it solidly. I couldn't believe it. I remember Richard trying not to smile. My heart sank, but then, when I thought about it, I still had hope. The ball could have still bounced into play, maybe landed in the sand trap or something. So we hurry down there. Richard's ball had landed on the edge of the green, but it was still a hard two-putt. If I could find my ball and hit a decent chip, I'd be okay. Except I couldn't find it. We all figure that it hit off the stupid branch, the one that shouldn't have still been there, and bounced deep in the woods. If we didn't find the ball within five minutes, I'd get a penalty stroke and the match would for all purposes be over. Richard Belthoff would have won. Looking back on it . . . I mean, who cares? You get your name on a wooden plaque in the Men's Grill. Big deal. But, I don't know, I just wanted to win so badly. Who knows why. I was still fuming about how last year Richard had cheated with the gopher hole story. So I figured this would even out the score. It wouldn't make me the winner. If I got lucky, we'd still be tied after eighteen. Then we'd go to a sudden-death extra hole, and that would be fair, and I wouldn't lose because of some flukey branch."

"What did you do, Gary?"

"My golf ball is a Titleist Pro V with my initials GG written in red ink. I always do that. Write my initials in red. So you know it's my ball. And of course, all golfers carry an extra ball or two in our pocket. So you don't have to go back and hunt through your bag if you snap-hook one into the woods or lose one in the water."

"Okay."

"So when no one was looking, I took my extra ball out of my pocket and let it drop out of my hand behind the sand trap on the right."

I nod. "And then, what, you said you found it?"

He smiles. "Oh no, that would look suspicious. I walked

away, searched in the woods, pretending I'm a class act, being the gracious guy who suffered the bad luck of a bad bounce. Yep, that was me. The gracious guy. Everyone in the club liked me. So I moved away and hoped someone else would find my ball. And sure enough, Belthoff's caddy, Manny, suddenly yells out, 'Hey I found it.' I actually closed my eyes when Manny calls that out. I almost hoped that no one would see it. I could still go back and change everything. But once I dropped the ball there . . . "

"So what happened next?"

"I act all surprised and relieved. Then I grab my sixty-degree, take two practice swings, and chip the ball onto the green. Not to brag, but I hit the chip of a lifetime. The shot leaves me with only a three-footer for par. By now everyone in the club is coming down from the overlook deck to watch the last hole. They have drinks in their hands. Wendy is there. Her father. Her uncle. I'd say forty or fifty of our friends. And now it's Richard's turn. He lines up his putt. Manny helps him with the read. If he makes it, he wins, but I mean, come on, he's like thirty feet away. Chances are he will two-putt. That means I need to make my three-footer to force the playoff, a clean slate. We would then keep playing until a fair winner emerged. So Richard hits his long putt. It's a really good stroke. The ball is tracking right to the hole but—whew—it stops inches short of rolling in. Like only three inches. The spectators do that golf groan and then politely clap for him. Then all eyes turn to me. I'm getting ready. I need to make this three-footer putt. Richard walks over to his ball to tap in his three-incher—"

He stops. Tears rush to his eyes.

"Gary?"

He shakes me off.

"What happened?"

He blinks hard. He looks as though he's going to burst into sobs.

"It's okay," I say. "We can—"

"No," he says a little too loudly. "I've never told this story to anyone. I need to get through it."

I wait.

Gary swallows, his jowls shaking, and pushes out a hard breath. "So Richard goes to tap his three-incher into the hole," he says, starting up again. "And that's when he sees it."

"Sees what?" I say.

"There's a ball in the cup already."

He turns and looks at me. I feel my heart sink for him.

"My first ball," he says, though I guessed that already. "My original ball I hit off the tee. The one that hit the tree. It did indeed take a fluke bounce, I guess, but not into the woods. It rolled onto the green and into the cup. I'd hit a hole in one."

I say nothing.

"Richard slowly reaches down and picks the ball up. My initials are on it, clear as day. Everyone is silent. They all know now. I'd hit a hole in one—and outed myself as a cheater."

Gary grows silent now. I fear that I am going to say

something stupid or patronizing, something like "one momentary lapse" or "hey, we all have our moments" or "it's not really a big deal." But I get it. Even before he continues to explain: The cheating destroyed the life he knew. Gary became an immediate social pariah. We love building people up. We love tearing them down even more. No one wanted to play with him anymore. The dinner invitations dried up. The local online newspaper, the *Short Hills Patch*, got wind of the story and published it. Their friends fled. Gary suggested they move, start fresh. They had a place already on Old Marsh Golf Club in Florida. They could move down there permanently. But the members at Old Marsh had heard the story too. And Wendy loved this life. She didn't want to give it up. Yet there was no escape. So Wendy did what she could to survive: She divorced him, "cutting out the cancer so she could survive," Gary said. Now she'd taken up with one of Gary's friends—Richard Belthoff's cousin, ironically, who had recently become a widower. Then the leftover cancer spread. A lot of Gary's clients had been members of the club. They pulled their money out of his hedge fund.

In the end, Gary lost everything.

"I lost my membership, of course," Gary says. "I don't play anymore. But for some reason I still wear the clothes. A reminder maybe. Punishment. My own personal scarlet letter, albeit in bad golf fashion."

Again I just want to say, "You got caught up in the moment, you made one little mistake," and again I know not to insult him with something like that. Do you want the hard truth?

Life isn't about the big mistakes. It's about the little ones. Think about the line between in play and out of play at a soccer pitch or any game. The costliest mistakes are made right near that line, right when someone has laid down the line and you trudge back and forth across it and that line gets messy and now you see the ball go just over the line but maybe you can grab it in time, kick it back into play before anyone sees. Those are the mistakes that stay with you. Those, the small ones, the ones you didn't have to make— those are the ones that haunt you and change your life.

So I don't offer Gary words of comfort. He looks shattered. There are some shrinks I know who would say Gary did it on purpose. This country-club life was suffocating him and so he found the only way out was through an act of self-destruction. I doubt that was the case, but why not embrace it.

"Gary," I say.

"Yeah."

"I'm glad you're in my class."

He smiles. "Me too, man. Me too."

13

Marty lives in a three-story penthouse in the storied Beresford on Central Park West near the American Museum of Natural History. I googled the price on StreetEasy when Marty first moved in. Yes, it is none of my business, but this is the world in which we live. I don't make the rules. It was on the market for $19 million. It sold for "far less" than fair normal market value because the previous occupant had been a notorious hoarder and criminal, who hid a stolen Vermeer on the premises. So Marty got a "steal" and paid a mere $14 million.

No, Marty, who I doubt is more than thirty years old, didn't buy this place on his cop salary. He comes from money. Lots of it. His family lives in Houston and are what we used to call oil barons. He's fourth-generation oil rich.

We sit on the terrace overlooking Central Park. The Beresford is noted for its three corner octagonal towers atop its twenty-two floors (there isn't one on the northwest corner for some reason). Marty's apartment has one of them. It looms next to us.

"I want you to know," Marty says, "that we are going to put serious resources into reconvicting Tad Grayson."

I don't reply. I'm not saying the sentiment isn't authentic, but no one in the department will care enough. That's not a criticism. It's just the way of the world. If Nicole is going to get justice, it's going to be on me.

"But you're not here about that," Marty says.

"I am not."

"So let's get to it. The Victoria Belmond case. First off, it's three steps beyond bizarre."

Marty hands me a power shake of some kind. It's green. He loves power shakes and working out and eating right and he looks like it. It is hard to imagine a more perfect physical specimen than Marty. Tall, handsome, muscular, gorgeous, while I look more like something left in the bottom of a laundry hamper. We made, in that short time we were NYPD partners, quite a pair.

"I'm listening," I say.

"First off, the FBI case file is locked, sealed, classified, private, not in the system. Only the top guys can access it."

"Theories on why?" I ask.

"Not really, no."

"Why would the FBI seal a file in general?"

"Officially? It means the contents of the file are, and I quote, 'intelligence-driven and threat-focused,' meaning it relates to national security. They also make files private to protect sources or method or to safeguard evidence. In this case though, I think they are claiming privacy concerns. Files containing personal information about individuals are often restricted, if you have enough juice. But like I said, the Victoria Belmond case is weird—starting on the night she vanished."

"How so?" I ask.

"So you have these rich high school kids renting out a room above a bar on New Year's Eve. You know that part, right?"

"Right."

"For starters, no one reported Victoria Belmond missing because her parents were traveling, and everyone thought she was at a rental house with her friends."

"That part I know."

"Right, and we also both know how crucial the first forty-eight hours are in an abduction."

"We do."

"This was far worse—more like three or four times that amount. By the time law enforcement finally did take it seriously, none of the kids at this New Year's Eve party would even admit there had been a party that night. When the police finally got wind of it, the kids attending all lawyered up. Or should I say, their parents lawyered them up."

"Suspicious," I say.

"Yes and no. The kids were all underage and had fake IDs. They'd all just been accepted to elite colleges, which as you know, means more than anything to people in these communities."

I make a face. "So they lawyered up on their classmate being abducted because they were worried their college acceptances would be rescinded?"

Marty smiles. "What, you find that hard to believe?"

"Not really, no."

"That's what the rich do—they lawyer up. Better safe than sorry. College acceptance was probably enough, but maybe they worried their kids had done worse."

"Like?"

"I don't know. Got drunk that night, fought with her, whatever. Remember these are early days. Most people believed she'd either run away on her own or they'd find her dead somewhere. Either way, the legal advice they got was to shut up."

"And meanwhile," I say, "Victoria's trail grows colder and colder."

"Right. By the time the legalese was done—waivers, NDAs, all that—and the kids questioned, it led nowhere. No one remembered seeing Victoria leave the party. No one remembered any big incident involving her."

I think about that. "Victoria had a boyfriend, right?"

"Sort of, a Trevor Rennie. Wrong-side-of-the-tracks kind of kid, which in this case meant his parents only made a few hundred grand a year. The police looked at Trevor hard, but all evidence indicates they'd broken up a few weeks before the party."

"Was Trevor at the party?"

"He was, but think about it, Kierce. I mean, now. With hindsight." Marty lifts his hands. "How could it be the boyfriend?

Or for that matter, any of Victoria's high school friends? I mean, if she was found dead a few days later, sure, you'd really focus on this Trevor Rennie. But that's not what happened. Do you really think a high school kid could kidnap a classmate and lock her up for eleven years? Eleven years, Kierce."

Marty had a point. "I know," I say. "Makes no sense."

"And so we get to something else I think is weird."

"Go on."

"McCabe's Pub was willing to look the other way on the underage crowd, but they couldn't completely break rules that could put them out of business." -

"Meaning?"

"Meaning the person who signed the rental agreement had to be of age. No fake ID or any of that."

"So who signed the agreement?"

"Victoria Belmond's older brother, Thomas."

I consider that. "Interesting."

"Or meaningless," Marty says. "The FBI asked him about it. Thomas said yeah, his sister said they needed someone of age to sign it, so he figured why not. Supposedly Thomas and Victoria were close."

"Thomas Belmond has a record, right?"

"In his youth, he was in and out of trouble. DUIs. Some drug dealing. A few stints in rehab. He got arrested in a bar fight. There were rumors of him being aggressive with women, if you catch my drift, but this was before Me Too and so my guess is, a lot of it was swept away with money."

"What's Thomas Belmond's deal now?"

"He's married and working in the family business, but . . . hold on a second. Let me google." Marty leans toward his laptop and starts typing in and nods. "Yep. According to his bio, he's an executive vice president of the Belmond Corporation and lives in Greenwich, Connecticut, with his wife, Madeline, and two daughters, Vicki and Stacy."

Marty spins the laptop so I can see. There is a photo of Thomas wearing a blue blazer and green tie. I've seen him before. Thomas. Tee for short. The Tee-ster.

It's Smaller Guy Tee.

Marty watches my face. "You know him?"

"Yeah," I say. "He threatened to kill me."

———

Every other Thursday night for the past thirty-five years, the Kierces have had "family dinner" at a Chinese restaurant in West Orange, New Jersey, not far from where I grew up. When my father and mother emigrated to the United States, they lived in Newark, eventually settling into a two-family home in nearby Orange. They shared the house with the Weinbergs. Sam Weinberg, the patriarch, and Dad soon became best friends. The Weinbergs' extended family—Sam, Sam's parents, his sister, his brother, their kids—had Saturday night "family dinner" at the Golden China in the Essex Green Mall, usually somewhere between ten and fifteen of them. My dad admired the Weinbergs and liked the idea and thought it would be ideal for his own family.

We too started out at the Golden China, but they closed and then we tried Shun Lee in New York City, but that was too expensive and now we go to Moon Garden. We never had a lot of family like the Weinbergs. For years, it was just the four of us—my dad, my mom, my older sister. Tonight we are four again—me, Molly, Henry, and my dad.

Dad always orders and he always orders the same thing—dim sum, shrimp with lobster sauce, fried rice, spareribs. Sometimes he will order a wild-card dish, but that dish will never make the steady rotation. My mother died eight years ago from ovarian cancer, and my dad suddenly became a desirable widower. He doesn't shy away from that. He dates a lot, has become what we used to call a "playah," and while he has introduced us to five or six of his "lady friends," none has ever been invited to the family dinner.

"They're beautiful and smart and I enjoy their company," my dad told me once after he'd had a few too many Woodford Reserves. Then he tapped his chest with his index finger. "But only your mother could reach my heart."

My dad is the epitome of dapper. He wears vintage suits. He has a thin, perfectly symmetrical mustache; his steel-wool hair is loaded with product and slicked back. He always carries a pocket comb. He is the kind of man who looks like he's opening a door for a woman even when he isn't.

Henry gets super excited every time he sees his "Paw-paw"—his face lights up, his feet kick wildly, as if his whole body wants to express what he is unable to yet say in words. Molly adores my dad too, once telling me that my father "closed the sale" for her. We often hear that a woman becomes her mother, Molly explained to me once. When she met my dad, she hoped the same were true for a man. Sweet sentiment, but I have never been dapper in my entire life and take after my mother.

I try to not appear distracted as I mix the lobster sauce into the fried rice, but my father and my wife are the two humans who know me best. I'm not fooling anyone. Henry is in a high chair, his hand coated in rice, the insides of a dumpling leaking out of his tiny fist. Molly stands and reaches for him.

"I'm going to change him," she says.

"I can do it," I say.

"Let me. I need to pee anyway."

It's a weak-ass excuse, but I get it. She wants to leave me and Dad alone for a few minutes. I've wanted that all night too, and yet I've also been content with avoiding this discussion; my dad and I have been avoiding it for almost a quarter century.

Dad picks up on the opening. "So Nicole's killer is out."

Not the topic I have in mind, but: "Yes," I say.

"How are you handling it?"

"Fine."

"Not tempted to, I don't know, take matters into your own hands?"

"Tempted? Perhaps. Acting on it? A definite no."

Dad narrows his eyes. I think he believes me. "There's something else, isn't there?"

I look at him. I don't say anything. I just look at him. And he knows. "Oh damn." He leans back and pats the area beneath the bow in his tie. "Tell me."

I do. I quickly tell him about the class, about Anna showing up, about following her, about our confrontation at the Times Square theater, all of it. As I do, my mind keeps flashing back to that long-distance call from Spain, the panic in my father's normally smooth voice:

"Just go to the airport. Right now. Don't talk to anyone. Get on the next plane home. Or at least, to the USA. I don't care what city . . . "

My father taps his finger on the table as he listens. When I finish, he says, "I won't insult you by asking if you're sure it's the same girl."

I don't reply.

He keeps tapping. "You realize, of course, this is good news. It means you didn't . . . "

I feel something welling up inside me, but what he is saying is true. I had wondered about the truth and considered every possibility after stumbling away from that "dead" body, after realizing I didn't have my wallet or phone, after visiting the local police, that cop Carlos Osorio who didn't believe me at first, and then suddenly wanted to talk to me, though I never found out why because—

". . . Don't talk to anyone. Get on the next plane to the USA. I don't care what city—"

"But, Dad—"

"You are a brown kid in a foreign country."

"But maybe—"

152

"No one cares about the truth. You have to listen to me. You'll be blamed. Here's my credit card number. Get on the next plane."

I listened. I took the next flight out, which ended up going to Atlanta. By the time I arrived my father had already arranged for me to stay with my aunt in Tulsa for a little while. Just a month. Then two. Just to be on the safe side. We kept expecting Carlos Osorio to call my house in New Jersey, kept expecting law enforcement to knock on our door with some kind of extradition warrant for me to return to Spain.

But that never happened.

We never heard from Osorio. We never read about a body being found. And once I came back from Tulsa, my father and I never talked about it again.

Dad puts down his chopsticks. "So your Anna is really Victoria Belmond."

"Seems so."

"So what's your theory on all this?"

I thought again about Sherlock's axiom warning against theorizing too quickly. "I'm not sure."

"When we first came to this country," my father says, "the Patty Hearst kidnapping was a big story. Do you know about it?"

I nod. I had thought about that too.

"She was nineteen when radicals kidnapped her," Dad continues. "Soon she was making statements against her own family and holding up banks. At one point, two of her kidnappers were arrested for shoplifting. She jumped out of the getaway van and sprayed the store with machine gun rounds."

"I remember."

"When they found her, Hearst claimed—still claims—that she was brainwashed and coerced, even raped. But they still found her guilty. So no one fully knows the truth. Something like this might have happened to Anna . . . I mean, Victoria . . . or maybe not. She could have been forced into it. She took a lot of drugs. You told me that yourself. The dealer, the one who told you to run, he could have been the kidnapper. Or working with them. They could have kidnapped the girl and brought her to Spain and got her hooked on drugs."

I nod. I've thought about this possibility already, but I can't make myself buy it. Yes, we took drugs. Yes, a more potent chemical was probably sneaked into what we—or at least, I—took that last night. But Anna didn't have cravings or track marks or any of that. I'd have known if she was addicted or controlled by some kind of narcotic.

Wouldn't I?

Her best friend back then, her only friend, was our dealer, a man from the Netherlands everyone called Buzz. I had figured that Buzz was how Anna kept herself financially afloat, that she sold drugs for him or something. I didn't look too hard into this. I was on vacation. It was new. I was having fun. Was I supposed to have done more?

It had been Buzz who first heard my scream and burst into the room.

"Oh my God, what did you do . . . ?"

My dad put his hand on my forearm. "It's okay, Sami."

I can barely nod.

"If they find her body, we will both go to jail . . . "

"Have you told Molly?" Dad asks.

"Some of it."

"When?"

"Yesterday. I didn't want to lie about it."

Dad nods. "What did she say?"

"She mentioned Tad Grayson."

My father lowers his eyebrows. "Why?"

"She thinks it can't be a coincidence. Seeing Anna. Tad Grayson getting released."

Dad thinks hard, and as he does, I can see my own expression echoed in his face. "I don't see how."

"That's what I said."

"But that doesn't mean there isn't a connection," he says. "Maybe we can do some quick research on it."

"Research?"

"Where was Tad Grayson when you were in Spain? Has he ever been to Spain? Could his life have somehow intersected with Victoria Belmond's?"

I make a face. "And he, what, kidnapped Victoria years before we crossed paths and dragged her to Spain and then came home and started dating the woman I'd eventually propose to and then he killed her while he continued to imprison Victoria Belmond for, I don't know, another eight or nine years?"

My father leans back now. He has an old-fashioned. That's his drink. He slowly takes a sip. "I have another suggestion."

"What's that?"

"It's similar to what I told you back then."

"You told me to move on, to forget it."

Dad smiles. Like yours truly, he has a good smile. "Exactly."

I don't want to tell him what I'm thinking right now because it's pretty bad. I also hate when people blame their parents for their own problems. But the truth is, I took Dad's route back then. I tried to move on from Spain. I tried to forget. And how does a man do that? In my case—and I'm sure I'm not alone—you forget with the help of some sort of psycho-active substance. Again I'm not going to be so pat as to blame my father for my drinking. But is it okay to place some of the blame on whatever happened on that hot summer night on the Costa del Sol?

"We should all move to Florida," my dad says. "St. Petersburg. Let's be honest. There's nothing left for you here. You put the NYPD behind you. You put Tad Grayson behind you. Now that you know she's alive and well, you can even put Anna behind you too. We start anew. You remember my friend Akash? He opened a private security firm down there. He said he could use a guy with your experience. The salary starts at six figures."

We see Molly slowly move back toward the table. She's holding Henry, who gives me a big smile and stretches his arms toward me and does that "baby lean" from her grip. The cliché answer, the expected answer, is to tell my father no, that I'm not running away again, that I'm taking a stand, that this is my home, that I was born and raised here, all that. But that would be stubbornness on my part.

"Let me think about it," I say.

"Okay."

"And obviously talk to Molly."

"Obviously. But how about this? Until you decide, you just let the past be."

"It ruined me," I say without thinking, regretting the words as soon as they leave my mouth, even before I see my father flinch as though I slapped him.

"I don't mean that," I say quickly.

"It's okay."

"I just . . . You didn't raise me to walk away from a fight."

"Yes, I did," my father says, and then a wistful smile comes to his face. "But alas, your mother didn't."

14

It is later that night, two in the morning, when Molly says, "I left you alone with your dad on purpose."

Both of us are lying in the dark on our backs.

"I know."

"Did it help?"

"He thinks we should start again."

Silence.

"There's a corporate security job in Florida for me. Apparently, it pays well."

"How do you feel about that?"

"I'm married to a fabulous woman, and I have a son with her. This isn't just my decision."

"Kind of patronizing."

I smile in the dark. "I realized that the moment the words escaped my lips."

"I wasn't asking you to make a decision."

"I know."

"I wanted to know how you felt about it."

"Right," I say. "There are pros and cons."

"Want to go over them?"

"At two in the morning?"

"Neither one of us seems able to sleep," she says, turning to her side and putting a warm hand on my chest. "Pros: the weather."

"Neither of us likes the cold," I agree.

"The winters get long."

"Yet we've lived here our whole lives."

"Does that go in the con column against moving to Florida?" she asks.

"I think so."

"We are from here," she says. "We grew up here. We like it here."

"Even if we don't like the winters."

Molly continues: "More pros. The rent would be cheaper in Florida."

"Much cheaper."

"You'd have a job with good pay. I'd be able to find work."

"True and true."

"Henry could grow up with a real backyard."

I tilt my head. "Is that a pro?"

"The NYPD would no longer be an issue," she continues. "You'd be able to move away from your past."

Silence.

"Sami?"

"You can't move away from your past," I say.

"Sure, you can. There is something to be said for out of sight, out of mind. Yes, you're the same you—but the same you in a different environment is like adding a fresh catalyst to a compound. I know you have demons, Sami. We all do."

"Not you," I say. "You're perfect."

"Man, do I have you snowed. And I said 'move away' from your past, not 'run away' or 'escape' it. But here is the thing. I get you've dealt with demons. So have I. But whatever awful things we went through, it led to us, you and me, being here right now. It led to me having a baby and a life with the most marvelous of men. And you are marvelous, Sami. So the mistakes, the pain, even the deaths—maybe we learned something from all that."

Her hand is still on my chest. I put my hand over hers and we interlock fingers.

"Suppose," I say, "that part of what I learned—part of what makes me 'marvelous'—is that I can't let it go?"

She takes a second. "Touché."

"Do you want to go to Florida?" I ask.

"Hell no."

"Then case closed," I say.

I manage to fall asleep at five a.m.—and promptly at six, Henry wakes up with a cry. I whisper to my beloved that she should stay in bed, that I'll handle the wee one, and Molly replies with a gentle snore and closed eyes. I swing my feet onto the floor, grab my phone from the night table, and head to Henry. My son is a happy baby. Even his current cry is soothing rather than alarming or shrill, designed, it seems, to gently wake his parents, rather than agitate them into action. As soon as I bend down over his crib, Henry realizes his basic need is about to be met, and so the crying stops immediately. He smiles at me and coos and figuratively wraps me around his finger. I lift him high, change his diaper, carry him into the kitchen, place him in his high chair. I toss a few Cheerios onto his tray, and as I start to prepare his breakfast, I check my phone.

The first two texts are from Arthur and came in at 6:04 a.m. The first message reads:

> Don't kill the messenger.

I don't like this. I scroll down to the second message:

> At Tad Grayson's request, I am forwarding this message to you: 'Tell Kierce I want to show him the evidence. He should please come to my mom's place at 198B City Blvd in Staten Island. I'll be around all day. A call would be appreciated so I know he's coming.'

I hit reply, and type back to Arthur:

> Why do I have to go to him?? Let him come to me.

The dancing three dots tell me Arthur is typing a reply. Then it arrives:

> He's taken over hospice care for his mother. She
> won't be around much longer.

I don't care about Tad Grayson or his dying, lying mother. To express this, I find the violin emoji and type, "Tell him to pound sand—and play the world's smallest violin," but I don't hit send and end up deleting it in a rush of maturity. Then I start again:

> If he has evidence, why couldn't he tell me
> yesterday?
> I asked him that.
> What did he say?
> His reply: 'Only can see it at my house. Can't be in
> the office.'

Again I make a face. I look at Henry. Henry is frowning too, mimicking me. I look at him and say, "I know, right?"

That makes Henry laugh.

My phone pings. Arthur's text says: Are you going to go?

I type back to Arthur:

> Tell him I'll be there six PM on the dot.

This is a lie. No reason to let him prepare.

I move fast. I hope Molly is awake. She isn't. So I do it. Gently. Like Henry. She groans but gets it. I slip Henry onto her chest, shower, dress. Then I hop on the subway to the Staten Island ferry.

By eight a.m., I am on City Boulevard on Staten Island staring up at the house where the monster Tad Grayson had been raised. The house could politely be called *weathered*, but it looks more like it's shedding or even actively falling apart. The structure is oddly asymmetrical and looks as if it was drawn by a child in preschool. All the shades are pulled down except the upper right window, which has wood planks rather than glass. The neighborhood prides itself in small front yards so green they seem ready for a pro golf outing. Not the Graysons'. The weeds here are tall enough to go on the adult rides at Six Flags. I would say the concrete walk had a few cracks in it, but it would be more apropos to say the cracks had a few bits of concrete in them.

I step gingerly toward the door, trying to remember when I had my last tetanus shot. I look for a doorbell. No go. When I knock, careful not to scrape my knuckles or get a splinter, paint chips fly off. I wait. Nothing. I knock again and hear a voice I recognize as Tad Grayson's say, "Just a minute."

When he opens the door, I am again surprised, if not pleased, at how gaunt and awful Grayson looks. His breath is ragged as though he'd just finished a run. He wears rubber gloves and is holding a white plastic bag in his hand. I get a whiff of something that is both divinely human and makes me want to hurl.

"You wanted to show me something?" I ask.

"I thought you were coming at six p.m. on the dot."

I say nothing.

"I should have known from the 'on the dot,'" Tad Grayson says with a sigh. He steps back. "I'm in the middle of helping Mom get dressed. You'll have to give us a moment."

As if on cue, I hear an old woman croak: "Tad?"

"I'll be right there, Mom."

He gestures for me to enter. I debate the right move. I don't like the idea of entering this decrepit dwelling. I could wait outside, where the air will be far fresher, but I had learned from my years as a police detective that when a suspect invites you into their living quarters, unless you suspect serious danger, you accept. A person's home tells you about them. It is their setting, their choices, their mood. You never know what someone might leave out.

So I enter.

The small house's tiny foyer bleeds into the living room. The sofa is open to a queen-sized pull-out bed. I assume Tad slept here last night. The pull-out takes up all the space, so I just stand there—not that I'd want to go in and sit down on the threadbare furniture anyway. The television is an old-school box console with rabbit ears on the top. The bulbs in the room's lamps are yellow, so that everything looks jaundiced. There are faded photographs in fingerprint-smeared frames. I study them. Most feature a family of four—mom, dad, two boys. One photo was taken in the front yard of this house when the grass looked more like the neighbors', another in this very room with the same television. The father, I know, died years ago. I remember that Tad Grayson had a brother named Nathan. Nathan moved to Los Angeles sometime before the murder. I don't remember him coming back to support his brother after the arrest. That left the mother, Patricia. I recognized her from the trial, though she looks even younger here.

I hear running water and flushing toilets. Two voices— I assume Tad's and his mother's—are muffled. His sounds caring, comforting, calming. Hers sounds distressed, confused, scared. I don't like being here. It's dark and gloomy, and the entire place reeks of disinfectant and death. It is a smell, oddly enough, that reminds me of Henry's diapers and yet feels the direct opposite.

Life cycle via odors of human excrement.

I'm finding it hard to breathe.

The bedroom door off the back opens, and Tad Grayson shuffles out. His eyes are red now, I'm not sure from what. I also don't care.

"She's dying," he says to me.

I don't reply.

"I asked for temporary furlough, you know, a compassionate release. Just for a day or two. So I could say goodbye to her. You know what they told me?"

I don't reply.

"They said maybe I could get temporary furlough to attend her funeral." He shakes his head in bewilderment. "What a weird system, right? Funeral leave is compassion, but saying goodbye while the person is alive, while they can still hear and be comforted by it and maybe get some closure, that's a bridge too far."

He looks at me as though he expects me to agree.

"Nicole's mother died four years ago," I tell him. "Toward the end, she would call out her only daughter's name. It was the saddest sound I ever heard."

We just stand there for a moment.

"Where's your evidence you didn't do it?" I ask.

"Tell me, Kierce, how does a man prove a negative?"

"That's what you wanted to tell me?"

"No," he says. "I didn't want to tell you anything at all."

I step back. "I'm not following."

"My mother does," Tad Grayson says. "She's the reason I asked you here."

He turns back to her door and puts his hand on the knob. He looks back at me to make sure I'm ready. I really don't want to go in. I'm not good with these sorts of things. Who is? I don't like hanging with sick people. I'm a bit of a germophobe, and this place is crawling with too many varieties.

But I follow him into his mother's sick room.

I expect her to be hooked up to a million machines. She is not. She is sitting up in the made bed, the cover over her lower extremities. Her hair is thin and gray. I can see her scalp. Her skin is ashen. Her eyes seem too large, too bright, too blue, as they follow us. I try to match the woman I see now with the woman in the photographs, with the one I saw take the stand during her son's trial all those years ago. It's hard to make that match anyplace but those blue eyes that stare into mine, trying to pierce me, just as she did when she was on the stand.

I don't flinch.

"Tad?" his mother says.

"Yes, Mom."

"Did you offer our guest a drink?"

I handle that. "He didn't, I'm not a guest, and I don't want a drink."

Her eyes slide toward her son. "Wait outside please."

That seems to catch Tad off guard. "Mom?"

"Please, Tad," and while the voice is weak, I think he still hears steel from his childhood in it. "Wait outside."

Tad leaves, closing the door behind him. I don't move. The smells are all still here, fighting past some kind of lemon-scented spray which somehow makes them even worse. There is a chair pulled up next to the bed. I don't take it. I don't move. I just stay standing.

"Tad was here with me," she says, "the night Nicole was shot."

This is not news to me.

"Yeah, I was in the court when you testified, remember? You had nothing to corroborate your alibi. No one else who lived on your street saw Tad that night. The jury didn't buy it then. I don't buy it now."

"I'm dying."

"I know," I say. "That doesn't change anything. A mother's dying declaration to get her son off doesn't add weight to your testimony. Another witness saw your son right near the murder scene at the same time you claim he was here."

"Brian Ansell," she says.

"Yes."

She closes her eyes, takes a deep breath, and says, "I've thought about that for a long time."

"And?"

"Ansell lied on the stand. That's what I thought for a long time."

"And now?"

"Now I wonder," she says, her voice breaking. She struggles to sit up. I don't go to help her. "Did you ever think that maybe it was a setup?"

I say nothing.

"Tad went to Pennsylvania to buy a gun," she continues. "Maybe someone knew about that. Maybe someone followed him and stole the gun and dressed like him."

"Mrs. Grayson," I say. "I think I should leave now."

"She came here two days before she was murdered. Did you know that?"

I stop.

"Nicole, I mean. She came to visit me."

I try to slow my pulse. "Why?"

"Because Tad was acting out. Nicole didn't love him anymore. We both knew that. But she still cared about him. Nicole . . . she was that kind of person."

Part of me wants to slap her silent. The other part of me

wants to hear anyone who knew Nicole and could talk about her because, outrageous as it seems, the world has moved on from her.

Me, the love of her life, especially.

"Nicole and I were close," Mrs. Grayson says. "You know that, Sami."

I don't like her using my first name. It enrages me. But I need to keep myself steady. The man who murdered Nicole is right outside my door. Between his release and Victoria/Anna's return, my emotions are ricocheting all over the place. I'm not thinking straight. I know that.

"So," I say, trying to be analytical, "Nicole came to you because she was worried about the violent threats your son was subjecting her to—your son, who had just purchased a gun that was used to kill her. Do I have that right?"

No reply.

"I don't know how to break this to you, Mrs. Grayson, but this information hardly clears him."

"That's not all she said."

"Oh?"

"Nicole told me about a case."

"A case," I say, arching a skeptical eyebrow.

"Yes. She was investigating someone she thought might harm her."

"How convenient," I say. "Mrs. Grayson—"

"Patricia."

"Mrs. Grayson," I say, "Nicole was a cop. We looked into all her cases to see whether there was anyone who held a grudge who might have done it. We checked every lead in that direction. There was nothing."

"It wasn't a police case," Mrs. Grayson tells me.

I try not to roll my eyes. "You don't say."

"It was something personal. Something involving her own family."

"So she came to you to tell you that your son was threatening her—"

"She wasn't scared of Tad. She knew he was harmless."

"—and then say, 'By the way, I'm looking into a case that isn't a police case but it involves my family and I'm really scared about that too.' That just about do it?"

Her bright eyes flash dark now.

"And, just so I have this story completely straight," I continue, "you never told anyone about this visit, correct?"

"Correct," she says. "And you know why."

I spread my hands. "I really don't."

She coughs into a handkerchief. She turns and looks at the water next to the bed. I don't know if she's expecting me to help her get it or what. I don't move. "If I told the police that Nicole came to me about Tad's texts, the prosecutors would have twisted what I said to use against him. Like you just did. But listen to me. I won't last much longer. Tad was with me that night. I have never wavered from that. Not once. Someone . . . maybe someone Nicole was investigating and worried about . . . they're the ones you should be after. You need to find out what Nicole was working on."

I nod, more than ready to leave. "Is there anything else?"

Patricia Grayson is growing exhausted. Her head is back on the pillow. She is no longer looking at me, but the ceiling above her. "What if you're wrong?"

I don't reply.

"What if you put my son in that hellish prison for eighteen years and left him the husk of a man you see today because you wouldn't face the truth? And what if a small part of you now knows it, knows you did some grave injustice, but simply can't let yourself see because it would be too horrible for you to ever admit? How will you live with yourself, if it ends up Tad didn't do it?"

I say nothing.

"I'm a dying woman. This is my deathbed confession. My son was with me the night Nicole was murdered. He didn't do it."

15

I don't say a word to Tad Grayson. I just hustle out of there and catch the ferry back to Manhattan. The New York Harbor air feels good—I suck it in through the twenty-five-minute ferry ride. When we get off at South Street in Lower Manhattan, I walk north along the East River. I don't know how long. Hours for certain. I am in no rush. I have nowhere to be. Molly took Henry to some sort of Mommy and Me hour in the park. They won't be home yet. So I try to walk and shake off the feel and stench of the Graysons' house.

I replay what Tad Grayson's mom said to me. All of it. Repeatedly. She was lying to save her son, just as she had on the stand. I know that.

But there are parts of what she said that I must admit have the ring of truth.

For example, I know Nicole liked Patricia Grayson. Tad's mom had been kind to Nicole during her parents' contentious divorce. Nicole had spoken fondly of her on more than one occasion. She'd had it rough, Nicole had told me. The woman's crooked nose, the sunken cheeks—they had broken under an onslaught of fists from her husband, Tad Grayson's father. So I'm not surprised Nicole might have visited Patricia Grayson. I know Nicole took her to lunch sometimes. I know Nicole invited Patricia Grayson to our NYPD academy graduation.

Nicole never told me about the most threatening texts from Tad. I get why, of course. She feared I would do something. She could handle it herself.

So how would Nicole have handled it?

She might very well have tried to reach Tad through his mother. She might have gone to Patricia so they could figure a way to get Tad help before he went too far.

If she had, they had both obviously failed.

I don't know what to do with all this. Tad Grayson killed Nicole. The evidence proves it. But am I being stubborn? There was a serial killer caught recently who would set up innocents to take the fall, many serving life sentences when the real killer was caught. So is what Patricia Grayson is proposing that far-fetched? If I'm being objective—if I step back and try to look at the facts from a distance and coldly . . .

No, sorry, it doesn't change my mind.

"How will you live with yourself, if it ends up Tad didn't do it?"

Just fine, thank you. I followed the evidence. A jilted man sends the woman I love horrible, violent texts. He threatens to shoot her in the head. He buys a gun. That gun is used in the murder. Those are facts even Tad doesn't dispute. So even if he didn't pull the trigger . . .

Hold up. Am I actually entertaining this insane idea?

I am not. Patricia Grayson is lying to protect her son. But maybe I can use that. Maybe if I can prove that she is lying, maybe if I can get close to her and listen to her and see when she stumbles in her defense of her son and reveals a deeper truth . . .

Did I rush out too soon? Should I go back?

I am wondering this as I use my key to open the door of my (thankfully) rent-controlled apartment. I am surprised when I hear voices coming from my kitchen. One, of course, belongs to Molly. The other, I see as I come closer, is Victoria Belmond's. Victoria sits across the table from my wife. They are having tea. Molly takes tea seriously. She makes it fresh, buying the ingredients from a local farmer's market or growing specific herbs on our windowsill. She takes her time. She knows how to perfectly bruise the mint by rolling it between her fingers. She uses wooden spoons, not metal ones. She times how long she steeps, usually twelve minutes. She has a muddler to crush the leaves. We have infusers, strainers, airtight canisters, a variety of kettles.

Both women turn to me at the same time. I don't like myself for what I think first. You will judge me for it, but hey, warts and all, right? My first thought—and I'll defend myself by saying the thought was fleeting and instinctive and not considered—is that these two women are beautiful and that I've made love to both. There you go. Sorry not sorry.

Under any other circumstances, I would probably preen.

Molly speaks first, stating the obvious. "We have a visitor."

"I'm sorry," Victoria says. "I should have called, but if I did, I worry I'd lose my nerve."

"It's okay."

Molly says that, not me. She reaches a comforting hand across the table and puts it on Victoria's forearm. Victoria's hands are wrapped around the teacup as though she needs warmth. She looks up and gives my wife a grateful smile. Molly keeps her hand there another second or two, then rises.

"I'll leave you two to talk," Molly says.

"No, don't go," Victoria replies. "In fact, it may help if you stay."

Molly isn't sure how to reply to that. She looks at me. I'm not sure how I feel about it, but I nod that it's okay. She slowly sits back down.

We fall into silence. There is a chair in the corner of the room. I'm tempted to pull it up and sit with them, but right now I feel better standing. I don't know whether I should start or give Victoria space. A few seconds pass. Victoria uses both hands to bring the tea to her lips. We give her time and space. When she puts the cup back down, she turns to me.

"I don't know you," she says.

I say nothing. She didn't come all this way to tell me only that. So I wait.

"Or at least, I don't remember you. But there is something . . . I'm not sure of the term. It's not déjà vu. But there's something . . . familiar. There is something drawing me to you." She smiles awkwardly and shakes her head. "I'm not saying this right."

Molly puts her hand back on Victoria's forearm. "You're doing fine."

"I don't mean drawn to you in that way. I mean, and this will sound weird, like the opposite. Like I could offer you some kind of comfort. Does that make any sense to you?"

They both look at me and wait. I swallow, not sure what to say to that. I try to take it step by step. "You came to my class the other night."

"Yes."

"Could you tell me why?"

Victoria Belmond stares down at the teacup. "I saw your photo in the news. It was a story on how you'd been fired and how a killer was going to be freed because of your misconduct."

Molly leans back in her chair as something clicks for both of us. We'd tried to find the connection between Tad Grayson being released and "Anna" showing up in my life again. Now we had it.

"Anyway, once I saw your photo, I kept coming back to it. Like it was calling out somehow. I also kept thinking—and again, don't take it the wrong way—but I liked your face." She sees my expression. "What?"

"That's what you said back then," I tell her. "The first time we met."

"Really?"

"Yes."

"You said we met in a nightclub in Spain."

"In Fuengirola," I say. "A place called Discoteca Palmeras."

"And when we met, I said that I liked your face?"

"Yes. You said it had character."

Molly smiles. "I totally get that. It does, doesn't it?"

"There's a kindness, right?"

"Yes," Molly says. "Something you can trust."

Don't preen, I remind myself.

"Then I googled you," Victoria continues. "I read everything I could find. I saw you taught a night class. So I thought, I don't know, I would just come to the class and see you in person and maybe something would connect. I remember so little about . . . " She stops, closes her eyes, opens them, starts up again. "I wondered whether seeing you in person would shake something loose."

"And did it?" I ask.

"No. When you spotted me, I don't know, I just freaked out. I ran. I have a driver. My family doesn't like me going out alone. I ran to the car and told him to take me home. I can't imagine how you followed me."

I don't really see much reason to get into the GPS tracker right now.

"So," Molly says, "how can we help you?"

Victoria turns toward me. "Can you tell me everything you remember?"

"About Fuengirola?"

"Yes."

When I hesitate and glance toward Molly, my wife laughs and says, "It's okay, Sami. I know I wasn't your first."

"Yeah, but that doesn't mean I'd want to listen to you talk about an ex."

"That's because I'm more mature than you," Molly says. Then: "Do you plan on going into sexual details?"

"No."

Molly gestures with a sweeping hand for me to go ahead.

So as best I can, I recount the story about my trip with the Lax Bros, about meeting her at the Discoteca Palmeras, about her apartment in Fuengirola, about the lazy days on the beach, about the partying, about the only person who seemed involved in her life, Buzz the Dutch drug dealer. I watch her eyes for signs of recognition, but I don't see that. I see a woman engaged and a great listener. That takes me back. Anna had been a great listener. We had stayed up to all hours as she coaxed stories from me and admissions of flaws or inadequacies (no, not like that) and I had never been that vulnerable with a girl before. In my experience, women liked to hear their men admit to their flaws and vulnerability, but they never want you to appear weak. I don't know if that's a contradiction, but it is what it is.

"Tell me more about Buzz," she says.

I try to, but I don't really know much. I describe his looks and say that he spoke with a heavy Dutch accent.

"How old would you say he was?"

"Older than us. Thirty-five, forty maybe. Which felt old at the time."

I stop. I wait. We are getting to it now, and I'm still wondering how to handle it.

As though reading my mind, Victoria says, "So how did we end it?"

I'm still a cop. You don't give without getting. When you interrogate a suspect, you don't want to show your entire case. Of course. You want to hold something back—to entice the suspect to speak or perhaps to trap them in a lie. I think Victoria Belmond is on the up-and-up, but I don't know for sure yet.

I want her more relaxed for this part, and my still standing is starting to feel like a move that might make her defensive. I grab the chair in the corner and pull it up to the table, making sure it's closer to Molly than Victoria. I want to give Victoria space.

I try very hard not to sound like a cop. I smile as disarmingly as I can and try to show her the face that she'd said she likes. "Can I ask you a couple of questions first?"

She blinks, but says, "Of course."

"You are Victoria Belmond, correct?"

"Yes."

"What do you remember?"

"About you?"

"For starters."

"Nothing. Like I said. I'm sorry. I don't remember you or Spain or this Buzz or any of it. I don't want to sound deflated, but nothing you've said has stirred any memories for me."

"Which is what you came here for?"

"Yes."

"You hoped that maybe I could fill in some of the blanks about the time you went . . . missing."

"Yes. But there was something else. There still is."

"What's that?" I ask.

"It's what I said before. When I first saw your picture—and when I saw you teaching that class—I wanted you to know it was all okay."

I feel again the past pushing into my eyes, making me well up. Molly says, "Sami?" but I shake it off. I am moved and feel connected, and the truth is, seeing her, knowing she's alive and okay, has lifted a tremendous weight off me.

Victoria tilts her head. "Why do I feel that way?"

"I don't know," I say, but now both women look at me as though they can read the lie. I try to get back on track, try to channel my inner cop. "Could you tell me what you do remember? Not just about me."

Victoria lifts the cup back to her lips, though this time her hand has a quake. Molly notices that the cup is close to empty now. She stands and moves toward her kettle and starts preparing more.

"Do you know how they found me?" Victoria asks.

"In a diner in Maine," I say.

"I was in a fugue state, I guess. It's like I was living behind a shower stall or something. Like I could hear people talk to me, but the words were barely audible. I couldn't understand. And I felt like I was talking back, screaming even, but nobody could hear me. I didn't know anybody. I didn't know who I was. I couldn't really see their faces. I didn't even know my name at first. Nothing. When I saw my parents and my brother, that's when something started to crack through. But it was like everything I thought or felt was fragmented, like I was a shattered glass that couldn't be put back together, but there were shards that made me know I'd been a glass. I'm not doing a good job of explaining."

"You're doing fine," Molly says.

"You want to know what I remember about those eleven years," Victoria says, "so I'll tell you." She looks at me straight in the eye. "Nothing. No, worse than nothing. That's how I describe it. Nothing would be okay. I'd just be a blank. Like I went to bed when I was eighteen and going to a New Year's Eve party and woke up when I was nearly thirty. That would be nothing. But I do have flashes to memories. The dark. Blindfolded. I remember someone punching me repeatedly. When I got back, the doctors said at some point I'd suffered a broken nose and shattered cheekbone. I remember fear. Being scared all the time. I don't remember Spain, but I sometimes have visions of blinding sun. I worked with psychiatrists, of course. They were patient with me. We tried to put together what happened. But something in my brain wouldn't let me go there."

Molly again reaches her hand toward her. "I'm so sorry."

"It's okay now." Victoria forces up a smile. "This was all a long time ago."

Molly stands and pours her more tea. She glances at me to see whether I'd like one. I give a small head shake.

"Is there anything else?" I ask.

"Like?"

"Did the police ever find out who abducted you?"

"No."

"Did they get any serious leads?"

"No," she says.

"So whoever did this—"

"—is still out there? I don't know. They could be dead. That was one theory that was bounced around."

"What, that the kidnapper died?"

She meets my eye again. "That I killed him. That I killed him and escaped."

Molly sits back down. We sit in silence.

"Time passed," Victoria continues, her tone now pensive. "After a while, the police moved on. Everyone did."

"And you?"

"I've tried. But the accusations never stopped."

"What do you mean?" Molly asks. "What accusations?"

"There are other theories," Victoria says now, almost casually.

Molly takes that one. "About your kidnapping?"

"Yes. Many."

"Like what?"

"Like that I was never kidnapped," she answers, the small smile still toying with her lips. "That I was never in danger. That I made the whole thing up. That I ran away with a guy. Or that I ran away with a guy and then he turned on me. Or—for those who want to be kinder—that I had some sort of psychotic break and had amnesia the whole time. Why would someone kidnap a girl from a wealthy family and never ask for ransom? Or maybe they did. Maybe a kidnapper did ask my parents for money. Maybe they even gave it to them and never told the FBI. Or me."

"Do you believe any of that?" I ask.

She shrugs, but says, "No. My point is, the FBI doesn't know what to believe. One moment I was leaving a party. The next moment, poof, it's eleven years later and I'm in a diner."

We all take that in. We hear a small cooing noise coming from the other room. Henry is awake. Molly smiles and rises to get him.

When we are alone, Victoria/Anna puts her hand on mine. "I'm right, aren't I?"

I say nothing.

"When I saw your photo, something told me to find you and let you know it's okay. There's something to that, isn't there?"

"Yes."

"And are you? Okay, I mean. Or at least, better. Did seeing me help?"

I manage a nod. "Yes," I say. "It helped."

"I did something to you. In Spain."

"It doesn't matter anymore," I say.

She smiles at me, and it's the most genuine smile I've seen from her. "Then maybe that's enough," she says.

"Did it help you too?" I ask. "Seeing me again?"

She thinks about it a moment. "It did," she concludes. "I don't know how or why. But I feel more at peace." She lifts her phone, checks the time, swipes to a ride-share app. "I should go."

She stands up. I follow her to the door. Molly and Henry join us. Victoria spends a few moments cooing with Henry and hugging Molly goodbye. The Uber arrives.

"No one knows I came," Victoria says.

"What do you mean?" Molly asks. "Do they watch you?"

"They worry about me," she corrects. Then she turns to me. "I don't think we should see each other again, Sami."

She slips into the waiting car and waves to me. I wave back—and as I do, I realize something.

She's lying to me.

16

I sit on the kitchen floor with Henry and read our favorite book. It's a somewhat chewed cardboard edition of P. D. Eastman's classic *Are You My Mother?* My dad read it to me when I was a boy. It's the gripping story of a recently hatched baby bird who thinks his mother abandoned him and thus goes on a search (walking—he's too young to fly) to find her. He asks the titular question to a kitten, a hen, a dog, a car, and a boat, and he finally ends up on the scary tooth of a giant steam shovel. It's a creepy and kick-ass book. When you think about it, *Are You My Mother?* is our first experience with horror.

Molly finishes up in the shower and comes out in my bathrobe. We are about the same size, and I love when she uses my bathrobe or dress shirts or boxer shorts. It's a different kind of intimacy.

Molly says, "You okay?"

"Fine."

"That was . . . "

". . . bizarre," I finish for her.

"Yes. I feel sorry for her."

Henry reaches out and pulls down on the book. This is his signal he wants to hear more. We are on the page where the baby bird sits on the head of a large dog. I don't know what breed the dog is. I once googled it, but there was nothing out there. I have a dormant social media account, so I asked on that too. The most common answers were bloodhound or basset hound.

I can waste time with the best of them.

Molly sits with us. "Do you know what I found particularly strange?"

"Tell me."

"You spot an ex-girlfriend at your class. Someone you were only with a few days, maybe a week. You haven't made clear how long you were with her."

"Five days," I say.

"Five days," Molly repeats. "And now, more than twenty years later, you spot her in your class—and when she chooses to leave, you react by chasing her and trespassing on her property. I remember when you dated Jayme Ratner before we met. If you saw her in your class now and she took off, would you go through all that trouble?"

"No."

And then I tell her. I tell her about waking up with blood. I tell her about the bloody knife in my hand. I tell her how Buzz suddenly burst in and started shouting, *"Oh my God, what did you do . . . ? Get out! If they find her body, we will both go to jail. They'll think you killed her and I . . . just get out!"* I realized a long time ago, when I replayed what happened, that whatever compound Anna had gotten from Buzz was more potent, that I still wasn't thinking straight, that Buzz was able to get me to acquiesce because I was roofied or drugged. I complied. He dragged me out. I went downstairs and outside and ran and ran. I don't really remember much about that, just bumping into things and ending up on the beach and passing out, and by the time I was back awake, I didn't know what to do. I was confused and scared, and I just wanted to leave. I wanted to forget all this and chalk it up to a bad dream. It would be simple enough—just rejoin the Lax Bros and keep backpacking. . . .

But I couldn't do that.

Even as a stupid kid, I knew I couldn't just do that.

So I went to the local police station on the Avenida Condes de San Isidro. I met with a young detective named Carlos Osorio. But as soon as I started explaining to him that an American girl named Anna had been murdered, I could hear how bizarrely the words echoed in my own ears. Part of the problem was that it all did feel a bit like a bad dream. The drugs probably made that happen. Or maybe, I don't know, maybe it never really happened.

Except I knew that it did.

The other part of it was that, well, I was lying to Inspector Osorio, at least by omission. I'm a kid of Pakistani descent in a tourist destination jammed with white Europeans. I'm not dumb enough to say, "Oh, I woke up with a bloody knife in my hand," so even as I'm trying to convince Osorio that I'm telling the truth, I'm lying to him, and I think he knew that.

Eventually Osorio agreed to go with me to Anna's. But her apartment was in a complex of like-size buildings. I had trouble remembering which building was hers. When we finally found it—this was now a full day later—the place was empty and clean. Osorio gave me a look. I wanted to argue. I wanted to say that Buzz must have cleaned it up, like he said he would, but even then, I realized that Buzz would probably have that knife with my fingerprints on it and remember, this was twenty-two years ago—taking or possessing illegal drugs in a foreign country could lead to a hefty prison sentence no matter what.

So what could I do?

I didn't know.

I went back to my hostel on the outskirts of the city for the night to think it through. Then I called my dad on the pay phone and told him what happened. As I did, I got an urgent message from the front desk telling me Inspector Osorio wanted me to come by the station immediately.

"*Don't go,*" my father told me.

"*Are you serious?*"

"*You never got the message. Don't talk to anyone. Don't even pack. Get on the next plane to the USA. I don't care what city—*"

"*But, Dad—*"

"*You are a brown kid in a foreign country.*"

Henry is still chewing the book when I finish. Molly sits there, digesting it.

"Well, we know now she wasn't dead," Molly says.

"Yes."

"That has to be a relief."

I nod, not trusting my voice.

"Did you check for a pulse?"

"No."

"Because when you screamed, this Buzz guy burst right in?"

"Yes."

"Like he was waiting for you to wake up?"

"Yes," I say again.

"You must have wondered about that."

"Over the past twenty-plus years, I've considered every possibility. But I don't think my mind would let me go to what I now know is the truth."

"Which is?"

"I was scammed. I had a lot of money on me. A phone too. When I rushed out, I never even realized that it was gone. That was their play. Anna and Buzz were con artists. I was their mark. Anna's job was to get close to the mark. By drugging him and making him think he'd killed her, the mark would just run off. He wouldn't make a fuss. He wouldn't go to the police or press charges or any of that. Most of the time, the mark, I imagine, would just do what my father suggested. Run and never look back. And if the mark did report it, well, they cleared out of that room before anyone could find them."

"Seems like quite an effort," Molly says. "Couldn't they have just rolled you the first night?"

I shake my head. "I kept the money in a safe deposit box. That was my first night with it. I was going to move in with her."

Molly sat there. A tear rolled down her cheek. Watching her, I could feel two hands grab my heart and snap it in two. I don't think I've ever seen my wife look so sad.

"Molly?"

"You never told me."

"I never told anyone. Only my dad."

Molly swallows. "Nicole?"

I shake my head again. "Not even Nicole. Not even my mother."

"This huge part of you," Molly says, her voice sounding far away. "And you never told me."

"I'm sorry," I say. "I buried it."

She makes a face. "You didn't bury it."

"I didn't want it in our life."

She doesn't reply. She just sits there and breaks my heart.

"Molly?"

"Maybe you should stay with your dad tonight."

I feel what remains of my heart plummet in my chest. There is no anger in her tone. I wish there was.

"I don't want to worry my dad," I say.

"Then maybe a hotel or a friend. Just for tonight."

————

I end up at Craig's, for once not just to pick up my car. I was going to stay with Marty—Lord knows that would be a more upscale accommodation—but I hadn't spent much time with Craig recently, and I worry about him being lonely. Craig is excited for my visit. He ran to the supermarket and bought guac and salsa and Tostito chips ("the scoop shape one—I remember you like those") and Black Cherry Coke. Craig always has brandy on hand. He likes to mix it in his Black Cherry Coke. That may sound disgusting to you but that's only because it is.

Craig had taped a soccer match between Manchester City and Fulham from earlier today, and we watched it. I love watching soccer or football or whatever you want to call it, especially when I have no rooting interest. It's too stressful when you care, but when you don't, football has the most Zen quality to it, a gentle wave of back and forth, to and fro, with—and I can't stress this enough as an American—no time-outs or commercial breaks except at the half. I wish other sports could do that, but hey, I'm not naïve enough to think this isn't all about money. I'm old enough to remember when betting was against the law—what, ten years ago maybe?—but now there are more TV ads for betting apps than beers.

I would judge this if I cared more.

Craig has one son named Michael. He's grown and moved to San Francisco. There are a lot of family photos around. Craig's late wife, Cassie, is in every single one. I don't know how to say this without seeming unkind, but Cassie was the more ordinary-looking woman in every way, or maybe what I'm saying is kind in the sense that we should all have someone who looks at us and sees us the way Craig saw Cassie.

Craig falls asleep in his recliner. He's made up the spare bedroom—what used to be Michael's room—for me. I lay down and stare at the ceiling. I can hear Craig in the next room, still snoring in his recliner.

My phone buzzes at midnight. It's Molly. I pick up the phone and say, "You okay?"

"I can't sleep," she says.

"Me neither."

"We don't go to bed angry," Molly says.

"I'm not angry."

"Neither am I. Come home, Sami. I want you here with me."

"I'm sorry I didn't tell you about Spain."

"I don't care. I just want you back home with us."

"Craig is already asleep."

"Wake him and say you're coming home. Or just leave a note. Please?"

She doesn't have to ask me again. Craig understands and falls promptly back to sleep. My app says the train is delayed, so I splurge on an old-school yellow taxi. My father used to drive a cab. He then moved on to investing in taxi medallions. They used to have tremendous value—at their height, they were almost a million dollars a pop. He poured most of his savings into it and did well, and then the ride-share apps came along and now that million is maybe one hundred grand and my dad lost pretty much everything.

It's the late-night shift so it's Russian roulette about what kind of driver you're going to get. My driver is a chatty guy named Dmitri Scull, who is skinny and unshaven and wired. He tells me that he used to be in the advertising business.

"I came up with a great campaign for Verizon," Dmitri tells me.

I enjoy talking to taxi drivers. I regret that so few speak to you now. They all have their earphones in and are talking for hours on end to someone back home and I often wonder who loves them that much. Like with Cassie. Love is everywhere, if you look for it. "Have I seen the ad?" I ask.

"They didn't use it. But it was a brilliant idea. Want to hear it?"

"Sure."

"You know Bruce Springsteen?"

"Not personally."

"His song 'The Rising.'" Then Dmitri sings it for me. "'Come on up for the rising . . .'"

"I remember it," I say.

"So you just change one lyric," he explains. "'The Rising' becomes 'Verizon.'"

I smile and sing. "'Come on up for Verizon'?"

"Exactly."

We both sing it together for the rest of the ride: "'*Come on up for Verizon, come on up, lay your hands in mine . . .*'"

"Catchy, right?"

"Brilliant," I agree.

Molly opens the door before I knock. She is wearing the bright red nightgown that has always been my favorite. I wonder whether that's the reason she wore it, if she changed into it, or if it was just the red nightgown's turn in her rotation. Then I wonder why I'm asking myself such inane questions. She throws her arms around me. I hug her back with everything I've got. "I'm sorry," I say again. She shuts me up with a kiss. I kiss her back. She smells of honeysuckle and Neutrogena face soap, and no man can resist that combination.

In the morning, I reach for my phone and check my texts. The first is from a number I don't recognize.

> Molly looks good in red.

I jolt up. Molly sleeps next to me. I take a screenshot and send it to Marty.

> Find out whose number this is.

But I know the trace will go nowhere. It's so easy to send anonymous texts with any one of those readily available burner apps. Still, maybe Marty can get something from the number.

I also have a pretty good idea who sent it.

Tad Grayson.

At least that is what I think until I tiptoe out of bed and look at the street outside my bedroom window. As though I don't have enough going on in my brain, there, parked on the corner, is a dark blue Cadillac Escalade with a Connecticut license plate.

The Belmonds' car.

As I throw my clothes on, Molly starts to stir. "What's the matter?"

"It's okay, my love. Go back to sleep."

"You're going to lead with the patronizing again?"

She has a point. I say, "Victoria Belmond's car is parked outside."

"You think she's here?"

"She hasn't rung the bell, so no."

"Last time she came in an Uber without telling anyone."

"Right."

"So why is her car here?"

"That's what I'm going to ask."

"Should you call the cops?" Molly asks.

"And say what? An expensive car is parked on our street?"

"It is suspicious," Molly says with a smirk.

"I got this."

We agree that Molly will watch from the window, phone in hand, in case something goes wrong. I have a gun. I keep it locked and hidden and up high, and I know the stats on keeping a gun in your home so I will probably get rid of it as soon as Henry is old enough to move around. But I'm also a cop and have been heavily trained in how to use one. I get the pros and cons. I know what I'm doing.

Should I get it out now? Better safe than sorry?

I decide to leave the gun behind. I exit the building. The first thing I see is what we might call a suspicious-looking dude on the far street corner with a face tat, scraggly dirty-blond hair, faded denim vest, and mirrored sunglasses. He has the telltale brown bag clutched in one hand (for those who don't know what I mean, a bottle of booze is most likely in the bag). He raises the hand as I pass as though offering me a toast. I give a small nod back. I'm not sure what to make of him. Suspicious-looking dudes drinking in the early morning are not uncommon in this neighborhood, but something about this guy is tingling my spidey senses.

I turn right. As soon as the blue Cadillac Escalade comes into view, the driver door opens. Gun Guy steps out. He smiles at me and waves. My best pal. I quickly glance up at my window. Molly is there. I turn back toward Scraggly Dude. He's stumbling away now, almost out of sight. I approach Gun Guy. He keeps the smile on his face.

"Nice to see you again," he says when I get closer.

I am tempted to sucker-punch him. I have that right, but I don't know how it will play out here in the middle of the street. When I get closer to the car, he opens the back door for me to get in. I look inside to see who is there. No one.

"Did you send me a text this morning?" I ask.

"Not me," he says. "I'm more of an 'in-person' guy."

"Why are you here?"

"I was asked to bring you to the estate."

"The Belmonds' estate?"

He smiles again and gestures toward the opening. "Why don't you get in?"

"My mommy told me not to get into a car with a stranger."

"Oh, come on, Mr. Kierce. We are old friends by now, aren't we? Please. Make yourself comfortable."

"Pass," I say and start back toward my door. Is this a bluff? I am not even certain. I don't think I'm in any danger. He knows that I'm an ex-cop now. What is he going to do, drive me out someplace and dump my body? Seems clear that he wants to take me to the Belmonds. I don't know why or at whose request. But I'm curious. Still, I hope walking away will force him to divulge more information. Gun Guy is here to pick up and deliver a package. If he doesn't, I assume that his task will be viewed as a failure.

"It's her father," he says.

I stop. I don't ask whose father. There is a dance going on here in terms of names. I'm willing to sway with the music a bit.

"What does he want?"

"Above my pay grade."

"Why not call me?"

"Above my pay grade."

I press the first number on my speed dial. When Molly answers I tell her I'm going to take a ride with Gun Guy (I don't call him that) at the request of Victoria's father. She insists that we move over to FaceTime and keep it on me, just to be on the safe side. I agree, but again I'm not worried. Molly has seen the Escalade's license plate, and I've taken photos of Gun Guy and we know where he works.

When we arrive at the estate in Connecticut, the ornate gates slowly open. I say goodbye to my beloved as we head up the long driveway. It takes a full minute before the house comes into view. It's enormous, of course. Stately. There are some Victorian touches mixed with classic gray stone, and yet

197

something about it makes it difficult to know if it's a very old home in good shape or a newer home that aped some more opulent era's architecture.

As we circle to the front, a familiar young man opens the door and steps out.

It's Arthur from the White Shoe law firm.

I should be surprised to see him—and I guess I am—but it's almost as though all my worlds are colliding and being smushed down into one tiny space. When the car comes to a stop, I open the door before Gun Guy can do it. Arthur comes over with his hand extended. I shake it because why not.

"You work for Belmond?" I ask him.

"No," Arthur says. "I work for you."

"Then why are you here? Or better yet, why am I here?"

"I'm here at Mr. Belmond's request," Arthur says.

"But you represent me?"

"Yes. Mr. Belmond wants us to go over a few things before you meet. He felt that I could facilitate by making sure you have proper legal counsel to answer any questions you may have."

I stare at him. "Uh-huh. In English?"

"Mr. Belmond wants to meet with you."

"Yeah, I got that part."

"But before he does, he wants to make sure that you are both—" Arthur looks in the air as though searching for the word "—protected."

"Wait, how did Belmond even know that I know you?"

Arthur makes the skeptical face that reminds me that this

wouldn't be difficult for a man with Belmond's means to figure out and of course he is right.

"Mr. Belmond's chief counsel is Lenore Spikes."

"Am I supposed to know the name?"

"It doesn't matter, but yes. Anyway, Ms. Spikes has drawn up an NDA." Then he adds, "That stands for Non-Disclosure Agreement."

"I know what an NDA is, Arthur."

"This one is both pretty standard and pretty inflexible. You can't talk about anything that goes on with this meeting. You can't talk about the Belmonds. You can't reveal anything about the Belmond family or any interactions you have with them herewith."

I frown. "Did you just say 'herewith'?"

"I'm being the total pro."

"And why would I sign this NDA?"

"Three reasons. One, it is a precondition for the meeting about to occur."

"That's not a reason."

"Two, he has things he may wish to reveal to you. He wants to know you can be discreet."

I frown again. "Again not really a reason. And three?"

"Three, Mr. Belmond is willing to pay you one hundred thousand dollars to sign it."

That catches my attention. Arthur tries to keep a straight face.

"A hundred thousand dollars," I repeat.

"Yes."

"Just to sign an NDA?"

"Yes."

Wowza. Belmond clearly wants me to keep my mouth shut. I'm not sure what about. I assume Spain. But does he even know about that? Did his daughter tell him?

"And if I refuse to sign it?"

"You'll be driven back home immediately by Prince Charming over there. The family will have no further communication with you on any level whatsoever. If you go anywhere near them, their attorney will request a restraining order, and they are well enough connected to get it."

I try to think it through. "The hundred grand is for real?"

"Very much for real," Arthur says. "In fact, your attorney insisted that the money be wired to your Bank of America account the moment you sign it—before you meet Belmond."

"I could use that money," I say.

"I know."

"I feel like I'm being bought off."

"I assume so, yes. Do you want to tell me about it?"

I think about it. The only thing I know is Spain. What could I do with that? I can't even prove the young woman—my Anna—was Victoria Belmond. I suspect it. I think it's true. But I have zero proof. Even if I wanted to hurt the family, what could I do? Go to the press? And say what? I guess there's an outside chance that I could stir up some trouble and scandal. Maybe that tiny worry is enough for the rich. A hundred grand is a small price to pay to insure that doesn't happen.

One hundred thousand dollars, ladies and gentlemen.

Oh man oh man could I put that money to good use. I'm broke. I'm swimming in debt. And I'm also curious. Why does Belmond want to see me? If I refuse to sign and I'm driven back, my investigation into what really happened twenty-two years ago to me—and, more to the point, Victoria—hits a dead end. But if I sign, if I go in and talk to him . . .

One hundred thousand dollars, ladies and gentlemen.

"I'll sign," I say.

It's the only move. It's the only way I learn more. And if nothing comes from the meeting . . .

One hundred thousand dollars, ladies and gentlemen.

And there is one more thing here. If there is some attempt to cover up something worse, some kind of crime that I believe needs to be prosecuted, I'll find a way to break the NDA. Sue me, assholes. I don't have any money anyway except for . . .

I won't say it again.

Arthur opens the enormous front door and leads me inside.

"Wait," I say, "are you doing this pro bono?"

Arthur looks at me as though I'd asked him if the Easter Bunny was real. "I don't work for free, Kierce, but don't worry. That's part of what I negotiated for you in all this—attorney's fees."

"Savvy move," I say.

"Right? Also you wouldn't have the money to pay me if you didn't sign."

17

The house isn't what I expected. There is no marble or gold or tacky columns or original Picassos or any of that stuff. The house seems more inspired by the Smithsonian than anyone from the Gilded Age. The opening room isn't a ballroom or living room—it's a stunning two-floor library that reminds me of *Beauty and the Beast* except, well, more. There are signed first editions from Dickens, Fitzgerald, Hemingway, Harper Lee. I remember that when Victoria was found, the note was written by someone calling themselves the Librarian. Is there anything to that? Probably not. Rich people have libraries. It's one of their things.

There is a stegosaurus skeleton and a cosmonaut's spacesuit worn by Yuri Gagarin. There is the hatch to an Apollo capsule that landed on the moon. There are series of original letters between John Adams and Thomas Jefferson. I know all this—what these things are—because they have index cards next to them.

Two women are waiting for us at a wooden library table toward the back. There are tables in the middle of the library and the front of the library, but I suspect that we were sent this way so as to be impressed by the belongings. If that was the aim, mission accomplished, though I thought, *I don't know what impressing me with your overpriced artifacts is going to do for either of us.*

A Black woman in an impeccably tailored suit rises and stretches out her hand. I recognize her, though I don't know how. Like maybe she's a talking head on TV or been on the news or something like this. She has that look, whatever that means. She reeks of professionalism.

"Lenore Spikes," she says to me in a soothing FM-radio voice. "I'm chief counsel and senior vice president of Belmond Industries. This is Jill McClain. She is a notary public who will witness and notarize your signature. Your attorney has already provided us with your bank information so we should be able to wire the payment in a matter of seconds."

The four of us sit at the table. I sign. Lenore Spikes sends a message on her phone.

"The money is wired," Spikes says, rising. "Shall we?"

"One second."

I bring up my bank app. I don't use it very often and it takes me a minute or two to sign in. I look at the balance and whoa nelly, it's already updated. Because I know she worry-checks the account balance often, I send Molly a short text:

> Yes, there is an extra $100K in our account. I'll
> explain later.

I add a heart emoji. Molly counters almost immediately with that double-exclamation-point reply.

Arthur pulls me aside. "I'll wait here in case you need me."

"I'm not going to need you."

"I bill by the hour and Belmond is paying."

"Then again I might."

Arthur slaps my back. "Thatta boy."

Lenore Spikes leads me down a corridor. "Do you know anything about Archie?"

Archie Belmond. Victoria's father. "Not really."

"You're from Newark, right?"

"I was born there, yeah."

"Archie too. Beth Israel Hospital. He grew up next town over. In Irvington. No money. His father was a house painter, his mom filed for a storefront accountant. Archie was a high school math genius. When he was seventeen he came up with an idea for a home-monitoring device that allowed health care providers to track vital signs and symptoms. You know those stories about guys who start their businesses in their garage?"

I nod.

"Archie's family didn't have a garage. Or a car. There was a janitor who worked at the local Y. He knew about an unused room in the basement. No air-conditioning, barely any heat. That's where Archie started what is now Belmond Industries. And when Archie hit it big, he gave that janitor ten percent of the business. You don't know that part of the story. Archie didn't want the credit, and the janitor didn't want it out there. You see all this cool stuff in the library?"

I nod.

"Nothing stays more than two months at the house. That's why you see those index cards. The Belmonds loan them to museums. They're constantly in circulation. And the family only buys from private collections and makes sure the public now has the chance to see them—often for the first time. The Belmonds have created the largest charitable foundation in the country. You don't hear about it because Archie doesn't like the attention, especially for doing good. He makes the donations and insists there are no thank-yous, no banquets, no naming any buildings after him. It's not his way." Then: "You're wondering why I'm telling you all this."

I shrug.

"You think you're about to meet spoiled rich people. You're not. You have a picture in your mind of what they'll be like. You're wrong. Archie grew up with nothing. He met Talia, his wife, at Princeton. She was an American Legion scholarship kid from Columbus, Ohio. First generation to go to college. Her father worked for the post office. These are good people. And despite the trappings, they've been through a lot."

Lenore Spikes made a left and headed down the corridor toward a room with cathedral ceilings. "Want to hear the cheesy end of my story?"

"Sure."

"That janitor who owns ten percent of the company had a

daughter. She ended up going to law school and now works as the company's chief counsel."

"You're right," I say.

"How's that?"

"That is cheesy."

She smiles and opens the door. I enter a conservatory with a glass cathedral ceiling and an impressive amount of foliage. The four Belmonds—Dad (Archie), Mom (Talia), Son (Thomas the Tee), Daughter (Victoria)—stand in various locations as though a director placed them before the curtain rose. Victoria is in the right-hand corner, wringing her hands. I look over at her and she offers me a tentative smile. As for the others, I know more about them than I let on to Lenore Spikes. The Pink Panthers sent me biographical sketches. Thomas, who stands with a drink in his hand, is married with two daughters, lives down the block, works for Belmond Industries in the nebulous position of marketing vice president. By all accounts, he is a decent enough fellow, what they used to call a pillar of the community, but I also know that he had rough early years, with arrests that he'd have served prison time for had he been poor, but when you're rich it's breezily dismissed as youthful indiscretion and you get a pass. I don't begrudge the guy for that. I begrudge that we don't give others that same chance.

The mother, Talia Belmond, rose from a forest-green wing-back chair. She had the regal bearing, her hair completely gray and pulled back into a ponytail, highlighting her blue eyes and high cheekbones. She wore what looked like a men's white button-down shirt (I don't know why I say men's—doesn't a woman's white button-down blouse look the same?) with the sleeves rolled up on the knotty forearms.

And finally, the first to come over and greet me, is Archie, the family patriarch. He has a roly-poly quality, a little soft in the middle with a big smile and a bald head. He sticks out a pudgy hand and shakes mine with relish. He introduces himself. His wife follows suit. When his son approaches, I keep my hand at my side.

"Sorry about the other night," Thomas the Tee says to me.

"Yeah, that was messed up," I say. "Do you threaten to kill anyone who wanders onto your property?"

"We are security conscious," Thomas says. "But we would have never hurt you."

"Your man assaulted me, so that's a lie," I say.

"I meant—"

"You don't live here, do you, Thomas?"

"No, I don't."

"So what were you doing here that night?"

He stiffens. "Are you serious?"

"I am."

"My family lives here."

"And what, you decided to join your security detail?"

"As a matter of fact, yes. I was here visiting and then the sensor went off. It's been a while since someone trespassed."

"And your normal reaction is physical assault and threatening murder?"

"You trespassed." Thomas looks over at his father. Archie

Belmond clears his throat, throws on an awkward smile, and says, "I think it's time for everyone to leave so I can talk to Mr. Kierce alone. I just wanted everyone to meet you, so that you know that we stand as united in what we are about to discuss."

I'm not sure what that means, but I don't ask for clarification. The family files out. First Talia, who hasn't said a word, then Thomas. Before he leaves, he says, "I'm sorry about what happened. Truly."

He sounds sincere, but I choose not to respond. I try to meet Anna's—I know that sometimes I call her Victoria, but in my head, she's always going to be Anna, I think—eye but for a while she seems to be avoiding mine. She is last out and before she closes the door behind her, she finally looks at me and gives me the slightest nod of approval.

Archie Belmond and I are alone now. It was interesting what Lenore Spikes had said about the man. I always suspect the rich will look different or act different and most of the time they do. Not *special* or *better*. It isn't always something obvious like clothing or jewelry. Archie Belmond is wearing jeans and a blue pullover. Could have been Old Navy for all I knew. But still you can usually tell. Here I couldn't. There were no giveaways in Archie's looks or manner. He was comfortably nondescript.

"Thank you for coming to see me on such short notice," he begins. "I also apologize for all the legalese. You met Lenore?"

"Yes."

"So maybe you get it. She's a stickler for these things."

"I understand," I say.

"I will try not to waste more of your time. I know you've spoken to Victoria. I know you think maybe you saw her in Spain while she was . . . " He stops, closes his eyes.

I consider correcting him here, that there was no *think* or *maybe*, that I did indeed see his daughter, but what would be the point?

"It's been fourteen years since she came back. You know that, right?"

"I do, yes."

"So let me be honest here—you're not the first person to sign one of those agreements. We've hired dozens of investigators over the years—the first ones while Vic was missing, of course. The FBI stayed on it. I'm not saying they didn't. You have a child, right?"

"Yes," I say.

"No one cares about your child like you do. You know that, right?"

"I do."

"So we hired our own people. And then after, when we finally got Victoria back . . . she lost eleven years of her life. Just gone. Nothing. And I don't know if I want those years back for her—I imagine not—but the person or people who did this to her never got caught. Never paid a price. And Talia and I, we can't live with that."

He had a glass of what looked like iced tea. "Did someone offer you a drink?"

"I'm fine," I say.

"I understand you're a decorated police officer," Belmond continues.

"Used to be."

"And now a private investigator."

"I don't have a license."

"Arthur says you do jobs for him."

"I do."

"So I want you to do a job for me. For us, actually. The whole family."

"You said you hired other investigators."

"Yes."

"I imagine big ones with tremendous resources."

"Yes."

"Why would I learn more?"

Archie Belmond looked off, took a small sip, and said, "None of them knew about Spain."

I nod slowly. "So you believe me when I say I saw her?"

"Victoria sought you out after seeing your picture, not the other way around. So yes, I believe you."

So here we are.

He takes a deep gulp of iced tea now. "Was Victoria okay?" he asks. "I mean, when you were with her in Spain. Did she seem in pain or . . . ?"

"No," I say. "She wasn't in pain."

He nods, closes his eyes, takes another gulp. "Allow me to put my businessman cap on for a moment, if I may."

"Go ahead."

"Talia and I want to hire you to investigate what happened

to my daughter. You will work for us. You will tell me and only me what you know. The NDA also includes all the work you do for me as attorney product, so you can't be compelled to tell anyone what you learn. I want you to tell me everything you learn—and then, when we are done, when we know all we can about what happened to our daughter, I want you to have nothing to do with what we do with that information."

I think about this. "Let's say I get very lucky. Let's say I find the kidnapper."

"You tell only me."

"What about the police?"

"That's up to me. All work product belongs to me. I may share it with the police. Or I may choose not to."

"I'm not sure I like that."

"I'm sorry, Mr. Kierce, but this part is not negotiable. I'm not going to subject my still-traumatized daughter to new headlines or a lengthy trial. I won't let her be victimized again by whoever did this. Are we clear?"

I say nothing.

"If her kidnapper is found, you tell me. That's it. That's your role. What happens after doesn't concern you. You won't be involved."

He seems to be talking about vigilantism. Meting out justice and revenge via his own resources. I understand his viewpoint. The odds of me finding the people responsible are very low—but the odds I would find enough to arrest and convict after all these years are infinitesimal.

Belmond wants to handle it himself.

I understand that. But I don't like it.

Archie Belmond pushes through my hesitation. "Let's talk specifics and compensation," he says. "I want to hire you for the next three months to work exclusively on what happened to Victoria. Your pay will be half a million dollars plus all expenses."

I try not to look wide-eyed and slack-jawed, but I don't think I'm fooling anyone.

Half a million dollars, ladies and gentlemen.

Plus the one hundred thousand I already made just by coming here.

"Half of the money will be wired to you today," he continues. "Half when you finish in three months."

I'm a man of morals and scruples and all that, but seriously? Five hundred grand? That's not just money—that's *life-changing* money. That's a better (or at least easier) life for my family. I'm adding up the pros and cons of accepting this job, and the pros are winning big-time. My mind is swirling. I don't know if I'm being objective or seeing dollar signs, but if I say no, I probably get no more access to the family and learn nothing more. I don't want that. Yes, I realize that Archie Belmond is, in some sense, buying me off. If I agree to this, I can't ever tell my tale about Spain to . . . well, again, who would I tell it to anyway? Who'd believe me or care? What would I say happened? Still, that's clearly what Belmond is doing here, right? He is paying money to keep whatever happened in Spain a secret. Or is he? Does he already know? Does Victoria remember? Has she always remembered?

If I turn down this offer, I'll never know.

Odds are this investigation will go nowhere anyway. I'm good, damn good, but I'm not that good. If I refuse his offer, however, I'm out of the game. It's over. But if I accept, if I stay in the game, if I can keep swinging the bat, at least there's a chance.

Oh, and half a million dollars, ladies and gentlemen. Half a million!

I clear my throat. "I'll need access to everything—family members, old friends, police files, investigator reports."

"Of course," Belmond replies. "In turn, we will ask you to be discreet as possible."

"You don't want me to kick up attention. I get that."

"So are you in?"

I nod. "Yeah, I'm in."

"Fantastic. Let's start now, if you don't mind. What happened with you two in Spain?"

18

I'm hesitant to talk about Spain without Victoria present, but Archie Belmond explains: "Vic didn't ask you because she's not sure she wants to hear yet."

So I start to tell him. I do the meeting at the Discoteca Palmeras, the Lax Bros, all of that. I obviously don't go into lurid details about the nights spent in her apartment. I realize that may sound tame in comparison to the rest of what had happened, but this man is her father and so why go there? I keep emphasizing, perhaps to ease his way, that Victoria/Anna never seemed in distress. We had fun, I tell him. I fell hard for her and I thought she fell for me, but we were just kids on the European equivalent of spring break.

"So how did it end?" Archie Belmond asks.

And here is where I make a decision that surprises me. I had figured that I would come clean. The man is paying me good money. He has as much to lose here as I do. We are working together with the same aim—to find out what

214

really happened to his daughter and jointly what happened to me that morning in Spain. But something inside my brain—something old and instinctive and primitive—tells me that confessing to waking up with a bloody knife in my hand next to what I'd thought was the murdered corpse of his then-missing daughter would be unwise.

And what would be the point?

I had learned as a cop that you don't just toss out information willy-nilly. You hold as much back as you can. My father puts it better: You can always say something later, but you can't "unsay" something. I instead tell Archie Belmond what could generously be described as a partial truth. I tell him that I was conned—robbed—by his daughter and her partner, Buzz, that I woke up and my money was gone, and that we never saw one another again.

"Until she came to your class," Archie says to me as I finish.

"Yes."

"You're saying she robbed you."

"Or Buzz did. Or both."

Archie Belmond rubs his chin. "One thing I don't get."

I wait.

"When Vic came to your class, you knew who she was right away."

No reply from me.

"You haven't seen her in a quarter century. Her hair is changed. She's aged. She looks pretty different, I imagine. Yet you saw her across the room and immediately knew that this woman in her forties was the girl you knew in Spain. How?"

"It's a fair question," I say.

I had wondered this myself, except that I'm not telling him the full story, am I? I'm giving him a sanitized version. You might not remember a girl you dated or who rolled you. You *definitely* remember a girl who convinced you she'd been murdered, perhaps by you in some violent, drug-n-drunk haze. But I give him another answer that is probably true too.

"Maybe because she ran when I saw her," I say. "I don't think I knew right away. But when she ran, yeah, something clicked."

There are so many half-truths in the room already, even I'm not sure anymore how much bearing this had on anything.

"So what's your first step?" he asks me.

"I'd like to speak with your wife."

———

I find Talia Belmond in tennis whites heading to the court. I ask her whether we can talk before she starts playing. She looks at her watch a few beats longer than necessary. Still staring at the watch, she says, "May I ask you a question, Mr. Kierce?"

"Of course."

"Are we being stupid?"

"I'm not following," I say, though perhaps I am.

"This pursuit. Digging up the past."

"You want to know what happened to your daughter," I say. "That's natural."

"We are in a good place right now," Talia Belmond tells me. "As a family. All of us. Including Victoria. So shouldn't we just let sleeping dogs lie?"

"Is that a rhetorical question?" I ask.

"I'd like to hear your thoughts."

"It may sound self-serving with the money you're paying me," I say. "But no, you shouldn't let sleeping dogs lie. If you don't mind me mixing metaphors, I've seen a lot of people try to bury the past. It works for a little while. But whatever is buried, it eventually claws its way out of the ground."

She nods. "That's how I feel," she says. "Like whatever happened is still here, still with us, hiding in the closet or, yes, buried in the ground, and if we don't dig it up ourselves, it'll attack us by surprise."

"That makes sense."

"But I worry," she says. "Because there's trauma here. A lot of it."

"You know I used to be a cop."

"Yes, of course," she says.

"Cops do this a lot—dig up people's personal trauma for answers. It hurts. You have to be careful and do it slowly. Like one of those archeological digs where everything is fragile and so you use brushes instead of shovels or whatever. But do you know what I've learned from doing this a lot?"

"Tell me."

"Nothing heals trauma better than resolution and closure."

Talia Belmond studies my face. "Including your own?"

I don't say anything.

"Come now, Mr. Kierce. You don't think I know that you have some personal stakes in finding the answers?"

"No, I do," I admit. "Maybe you're right. Maybe I'm the one who needs closure and resolution."

"Sounds like we both do," she says. "So go ahead. Ask your questions."

I dive straight into the deep end of the pool. "You weren't home on that New Year's Eve."

"That's right."

"Can you tell me where you were?"

"I was in Chicago. My father had just gone into hospice, and I wanted to spend some time with him."

"Your husband didn't travel with you?"

"No, he stayed home."

"Did he go to any parties?"

"He stayed in."

"It was the end of the millennium. Nineteen ninety-nine and all that. I'm sure there were a lot of party invitations. Before your father went into hospice, had you been planning on attending one?"

"Why does that matter?" Before I can explain that I'm wondering whether anyone would think that the house might be empty, she holds a hand up to stop me. "Archie and I, we aren't New Year's Eve people. We never go out on New Year's Eve. We sort of take pride in that. Most years, we are asleep by midnight. But that year in particular? Archie was a little worried about Y2K. You remember all that?"

I nod. "That when the computers went from 1999 to 2000, no one was sure what would happen."

"Right. That computer systems wouldn't be able to distinguish between 1900 and 2000 and there would be chaos and power outages, stuff like that. We didn't stockpile like some people did, but Archie stayed home, just in case, so if something went wrong, he would be near the kids. Once we knew everything was okay with Y2K, Archie took our plane and flew up to meet me."

"Do you remember what time he arrived?"

"No, sorry. Very late. Probably three or four in the morning? I know I woke up next to him."

"Where were you staying?"

"At the Four Seasons, I think," she says, but I'm annoying her now. "Is this really important?"

It wasn't. "You stayed a few more days?"

"Yes. But my father stabilized, so we came back home."

I know already that her father died three weeks later. No reason to bring that up.

"Could I just quickly answer the rest of this part for you?" she asks. "No, I didn't think anything was wrong. I was focused on my father. Not hearing from Victoria wasn't that unusual. I also didn't hear from Thomas. This was twenty-five years ago. I didn't have a mobile phone. I was one of the final holdouts. I didn't like them then, and I like them less now. As Archie probably told you, he did get a few texts from Victoria's phone. One said 'Happy New Year.' He showed that one to me. Thomas got one from her too."

"When did you start to worry?"

"That's the thing."

"What is?"

"I called her mobile on January third. No answer, but again, it was a different era. None of us carried our phones all the time with us. So I didn't think that much about it. I was worried about my dad. My point is, you expect something like this to hit you all of a sudden. But my worrying about her, it wasn't like that. It was like a slow descent. I started to feel a nagging, then a worry, then finally, a bit of a panic. Even when we went to the police, I was hesitant. Victoria could be impetuous, rebellious even. I figured she had met a guy and run off for a few days. Or she was with a friend we didn't think about. You think a mother would know better, right? Like I should have had some kind of sixth sense. But I was oblivious. Or distracted. Or maybe there was some kind of self-defense mechanism thing going on and I subconsciously knew the truth and didn't want to face it."

The guilt was coming off her in waves. There is no reason to harp on this. It seems obvious now that Victoria's kidnapper had sent those texts or had coerced her into sending them. Then at some point, the kidnapper realized that the phone's location could be triangulated so they stopped and probably got rid of the phone. Still, those texts were clever. They kept the parental worry at bay and helped make the trail go cold.

"What?" she says.

"Would it sound weird if I just say, let's skip ahead eleven years to the day she came home?"

She smiles. "A little."

"Before I do, is there anything you can tell me about those eleven years that might help?"

"Nothing," she says quickly. "Most of the days, I was just numb. It was weird. You'd wake up every day and you couldn't believe this was your life. That you'd have to get out of bed and brush your teeth and then after, I don't know, a year, maybe two, you actually have your appetite back and there are days you almost feel okay, like you're living again, and then you remember that she's still gone and now on top of your everyday pain you feel the self-hatred because for a moment you forgot about her, and that for a moment, you maybe enjoyed something or smiled and that just feels like the worst outrage."

I say nothing.

"I imagined seeing Victoria. For real. Did Archie mention that to you?"

He had, briefly, but I didn't want to stop her, so I gave a small head shake.

"You know those scenes in TV shows where some guy is searching for a missing girl, maybe his girlfriend or something, and the guy thinks he sees her in a bar or a club and so he runs up to her and taps her on the shoulder and then she turns around and it's not her?"

"Sure."

"That was my life for a while. Once every, I don't know, three or four months I'd be in New York City and I would swear—swear—that Victoria was across the street and I could never get there in time. Or she was in a crowd at a concert at Madison Square Garden, but she would vanish before I could get to her. Once I was convinced that Victoria was a barista at a Starbucks. I ran home and dragged poor Archie back to the Starbucks with me. I made him check out every barista. He even paid the manager to show us photos of every barista who was off duty. Archie was so good to me. He tried to help me find an outlet. We started Vic's Place. Do you know what that is?"

I nod. "A charity for girls in trouble?"

"Yes. If we could help other girls, if something good could come out of what happened to our daughter, well, isn't there some kind of cosmic balance in that? We set up Vic's Place. I started volunteering there. A lot. And every once in a while—you could probably guess where I'm going with this—I would see a girl there and I'd be so sure that it was Victoria. I started seeing a therapist twice a week because of this." She stops, shakes her head. "I'm not making my point, am I?"

"I think you're doing fine."

"My point is, the therapist would want to dig into past trauma. That's what psychiatrists do, of course. What were my parents like? Was I ever sexually abused when I was a kid? How about that uncle who was a bit of a letch? That kind of thing. But it was none of that. I wasn't having mental issues—it's just that I wanted to know where my daughter was. Was she dead? Was she buried somewhere? Did she get dumped in the sea? Was she being held in someone's basement—or did she get hit on the head and lose her memory? Maybe she was just fine, just right around the corner, working at a Starbucks as a barista. The not-knowing was torture. So of course, *of course*, I imagined seeing her. And then one day, after eleven years"—tears fill her eyes now—"your baby finally comes home."

I try to handle this as gently as possible. "Can you tell me about that?"

"I didn't believe it. Ironic, I guess. I was always the one who imagined seeing her, but when they told me about finding a woman with her head shaven at that diner, I was too afraid to believe it. And when I first met her, I wasn't sure she was my baby. She didn't talk. The police asked her a ton of questions, but she wouldn't speak. For days. We took her home. Archie insisted. Got her around-the-clock care. We ran a DNA test right away. I gave blood for it. Archie's idea. It confirmed that she was Victoria. I sat with her twenty-four seven. I wouldn't leave. Not for a minute. I was afraid she'd vanish if I did. Or I'd wake up and it would have been a dream, like in the past. Then on the fourth day, she spoke to me for the first time."

"Do you remember what she said?"

"Of course. Victoria had a king-size bed in her room. She let me lie next to her. We were watching TV. *The Price Is Right* was on. I was holding her hand, and she said, 'Are you my mother?'"

I tilt my head. "That's the first thing she said?"

Talia Belmond nods. The tears come now. "It's not what you think. She wasn't asking me, like she didn't know. It wasn't a question."

"What then?"

Talia swallows. "It was her favorite book. When she was three. I used to read it to her every night. An old picture book called *Are You My Mother?* by P. D. Eastman. Do you remember it?"

"I do," I say.

"And when Victoria was little and I would tuck her in at night, she would never say, 'Read to me,' she would just say . . ."

". . . 'Are you my mother.'"

Talia blinks. "It's when I knew. More than any blood test. Anyway, that was the start. She slowly started talking. It took some time, but she came back to us. It was the most beautiful thing I will ever know in my lifetime. There is an old expression: A parent is only as happy as their saddest child."

I think about that. "Profound," I say, and I mean it.

"Yes. And so I want to know what happened to Victoria, Mr. Kierce. But the thing is, my daughter is indeed happy. Happiness is always fragile. For all of us. Like a bubble."

"And you're afraid I'll burst that bubble."

"I am, yes."

"I'll do my best not to."

My phone rang then. As I mentioned, I keep it on silent except for certain people. I look down and see the call is from

Molly. I excuse myself and move toward the corner as I put the phone up to my ear.

"Molly?"

"Where are you?"

"Still at the Belmonds. Everything okay?"

"No," she says. "Someone's stalking us."

19

According to the navigation app, the Belmond estate is forty-two minutes out from where Molly has dropped her pin on the Lower East Side.

Gun Guy keeps his foot on the gas, which I appreciate. I stay on the phone with Molly. She and Henry are now at Katz's Deli, the famed New York staple that claims to be the oldest deli in New York City. They have a big menu, but if you order anything other than a variant of the pastrami sandwich you deserve to be mocked and bullied. I tell her to stay there, not to leave, to make sure she has people around her and an eye on the door. I call Marty, but he's at a friend's bachelor party on the Jersey Shore. I'd try Craig, but really, what can he do? I consider calling the police, but again where would that go?

They're in an always-busy restaurant. They're safe.

I'm now, according to the navigation app, forty-three minutes out.

"When did you realize he was following you?" I ask.

"I saw him when I left the apartment," Molly says. "Then when I left Duane Reade."

"What does he look like?"

"Like central casting bad guy. Sunglasses even though it's cloudy. Long hair."

I sit up. "Face tat and denim jacket?"

"You saw him?"

"He was hanging outside when Belmond picked me up. Is he still out front? Can you still see him?"

"I'm not near a window."

I want to get a photo of the guy, but I don't want Molly taking any risks. I tell her to stay put. We keep driving. I tap my foot impatiently, ask her for updates. Fifteen minutes later, I get a text on my phone:

Don't like Molly in this blue outfit as much.

"Molly?"

"Yes?"

"What are you wearing?"

"This doesn't seem the time for flirtation, Sami."

"I'm not—"

"I know, I know. Sometimes I need a laugh, okay? It helps. I'm wearing the blue overalls."

Another text comes in:

Your wife's got a great bod. Tell her I like it when she shows it off just for me.

I take deep breaths, try to remain calm.

"What is it?" she asks.

"Another text came in," I say.

"Read it to me."

I don't want to, but I don't want to be accused of being patronizing again. So I do. When I finish, Molly says, "Am I being fashion-shamed by my stalker?"

"I love you in those overalls."

"But you're easy," she says. "Sami?"

"Yes?"

"How far away are you? I'm getting a little weirded out."

"Twelve minutes. Should I call the police?"

"No. There are two uniforms in here anyway."

"That's good. Just stay put."

"Who do you think he is?"

"I don't know."

I have been speaking in a low voice the whole time because I don't trust Gun Guy. For all I know, he's working directly with Scraggly Dude. I'm trying to surreptitiously watch him, see if he touches his phone or sends a message or anything. So far, he hasn't. He may be overhearing bits and pieces, but nothing I'm saying is going to help much.

Six minutes out.

I put the phone on mute and lean forward. "You still carrying your gun?" I ask him.

"I am," he says. "And yes, I got a carry permit. No, you can't borrow it."

"How about your other gun?"

"Other gun?" He chuckles. "Oh, you mean when we found you in the woods and we said we could kill you and plant it on you. That one?"

"Yeah," I say. "That one."

"That was all a bluff, Kierce."

Was it? "I'm employed by the Belmonds now too."

"I heard. Still can't borrow my gun."

"How long have you worked for the family?"

"Long time."

"When you were waiting outside my place, did you notice a guy with a face tattoo and long hair?"

"The one watching your place?"

"Yes."

"He was there when I arrived."

"What time was that?"

"Twenty minutes before you came out."

"He was standing there that whole time?"

"Yep. Not that I'm eavesdropping, but is he the guy following your wife?"

"Yes."

"He probably served time."

"What makes you say that?"

"Five dots tattoo on his eye," Gun Guy says. "Like the five on dice. Four dots on the outside representing walls, the one in the middle supposed to be you serving time. He's either a convict or wannabe. I didn't get wannabe vibes off him."

"You seem to know your stuff."

"I didn't get hired just because of my good looks."

"But come on," I say. "Those helped."

He smiles at that. "Sorry about the punch and the whole threatening-your-life thing."

"Are we having a moment?"

"God, I hope not."

"Do you know what the Belmonds hired me to do?"

"I think I can figure it out."

"Any insights you can offer?"

"Not a one."

"What's Victoria like?"

"I didn't get hired just because of my good looks," he repeats. "I'm also the soul of discretion."

"You're the total package, that's for sure."

"It's amazing I'm still single," he says. Then: "What are you going to do when you find this tattoo guy?"

"Ask him questions," I say.

"You're not a cop anymore."

"He's stalking my wife."

Gun Guy nods. "Fair point. You want me to stick around in case?"

I still don't trust him—or would it be more apt to say I see no reason to trust him? But I don't see much harm in having backup. We settle on a plan where he drops me off and circles around in his car nearby in case I need him.

When we are two blocks from Katz's, I get out of the back. The streets are packed, a mingling of locals and tourists seeking designer knockoffs and pastrami. I didn't bring earphones, so I tell Molly where I am and that I'm on my way and lower the phone. When I get closer, I slow my roll. No sign of Scraggly Dude. I stand on the corner of Avenue A where Boulton & Watt used to be. Katz's Deli is on the other side of Houston. I survey. Still no sign of Scraggly Dude. Molly had entered the deli forty-five minutes ago. He could have left. Or he could be hiding somewhere else.

I'm not sure how to play this.

I move off the corner and say to Molly, "I don't see him."

"Should we leave then?" she asks.

I wonder about that. I could have Molly walk out of Katz's and see whether anyone follows her, but I'm not prepared to use my wife and son as bait.

"No," I say.

I explain that I will come in and get them, but first, I want to circle the block a few more times. I switch the call over to Gun Guy. "You see him at all?"

"Negative," he says.

I take the next twenty minutes to search the streets. It is an awkward thing to do, what with him knowing what I look like. But I don't see him. I check my texts periodically, even though I've now set my phone to notify me if anything new comes in. Nothing else about my wife's wardrobe.

How long can I keep this up?

Molly says, "Henry is getting antsy. And by 'antsy' I mean thirty seconds until a full-fledged thermonuclear meltdown."

Enough. There is nothing to be done. I tell Gun Guy I'm calling it off. He says, "Roger that." I head into Katz's Deli and find Molly and Henry sitting in the back corner, Molly facing the door so she could see if Scraggly Dude entered. She stands as soon as I enter. I hurry over and scoop up Henry just as he's about to burst into tears. Seeing Daddy fends that off, at least for the moment. My son smiles at me, and I think about Talia Belmond and not knowing where her child was for eleven years, and the thought alone almost breaks me.

"What is it?" Molly says.

I shake it off. My wife stands. She has a take-out bag in her hand.

"What's that?" I ask.

"Pastrami sandwich on rye, mustard, slice of kosher dill," she says.

My favorite. "I love you, you know."

"I'd say I love you too, but I think this sandwich says it better."

"The way to a man's heart is through his stomach," I say.

"More like two inches lower than that."

I smile at her. The more nervous she gets, the more she jokes. "It's all going to be fine," I assure her.

"I know."

We start back home. Scraggly Dude (or should I call him Tattoo Face?) already knows where we live, so there is no point in trying to lose him or any of that. I attempt to spot him on the sly. Twice, I wait after turning a corner. Sometimes, without warning and in midsentence, I spin, seeing whether maybe I can catch him behind me or something. After I spin for the third time, Molly says, "Please stop that. You look like you're having a seizure."

When we get back home, I check the entire apartment thoroughly. No one here. Molly comes in and puts my sandwich on a plate. The sandwich is so stacked with meat I almost ask her whether it came with Lipitor. It's an old joke, but there's a reason they stick around.

"So," she says, "fill me in on what the Belmonds wanted."

I do. When I tell her about the money, she whips out her phone and checks the bank app.

"Oh my God," she says.

"Right?"

"It's . . . " She bites down on her lower lip and blinks away tears. I reach my hand across the table and put it on hers. She turns away for a second. It's hard for me to watch this. She never made me feel stupid or bad or guilty for being thrown off the force, even though getting fired was all my fault. I know that. I can chalk up my excesses to a need for justice and going the extra mile and all that. But it was dumb and careless.

My point?

Me losing my job has put us into a precarious financial position. We lost everything. We are in debt up to our eyeballs. Molly never wants me to feel bad about that, pretends it isn't a big deal, proudly and bravely battles through our bills, like so many of us are doing. But now, as I see her so overawed by our new bank balance she can't even look at me, I realize the toll my mistakes have taken upon the woman I love.

"It's for real," I tell her.

We sit there for a bit, holding hands, her looking away and then at our account balance, now in six figures from low fours, and back up again. Eventually she says, "If you keep holding my hand, you can't eat that sandwich."

"I can try with one hand."

"You'll make a mess."

She lets me go. I take a bite.

"It feels right, Sami," she says. "This job. This money. It feels good. Like kismet. You need to find out what happened to her too. It'll give you closure. It'll give her family closure. And maybe it'll give that poor woman closure, I don't know. It's the right thing. But this money, am I wrong to be excited about it?"

"You are not wrong."

I take another bite of the pastrami. It's too much food for now. I wrap it up and bring it to the refrigerator and as I do, my phone buzzes indicating an incoming call. A name doesn't pop up from my contacts, but I recognize the number. I debate stepping in the other room to take the call, but I don't think that's the right play here.

I hit the green answer button and say, "Hello?"

"I can't believe you have the same number."

"Hey, Ella," I say. Then: "So do you."

Ella is the older sister of my murdered fiancée, Nicole. It's been a long time, probably because we both remind the other of Nicole and neither of us needs that. The only connection between us was our love for Nicole. When she died, there was no reason for us to communicate anymore.

"So they freed him," she says.

"For now."

"And it's your fault."

I don't bother replying.

Ella says, "No one called to tell me."

"Someone should have."

"Would have been nice to get a heads-up," Ella says. "I found out when a reporter came to the salon for a quote."

Ella owns a hair salon in Queens called Bangs for the Memories.

"I'm sorry," I say.

"That's not why I called."

"Okay."

"He was creeping by the salon."

"Tad Grayson?"

"Yes."

I grip the phone tighter. "What do you mean, creeping?"

"What do you think I mean?" she snaps. "Like he was standing out front and watching. I'm inside, giving Delia a hair coloring and wax treatment, and I look out the store window and there he is."

"What did you do?"

"I went outside to confront him."

"And?"

"And he ran away. I called the cops. They told me I could try to get a restraining order, but I'd have to prove imminent danger or something."

"I'm sorry."

"Stop saying that," Ella says. Then: "I heard you're married now, got a kid."

"A son," I say. "His name is Henry."

"Nice. She would have smartened up. Nicole, I mean. Left your ugly ass before you tied the knot."

I again choose silence. Ella always thought I wasn't good enough for Nicole. I wasn't, but then again, I'm not good enough for Molly either.

"I saw his press conference on TV," Ella says.

I still don't reply.

"Tad was pretty convincing."

"Psychopaths can be."

"You think he's still dangerous?"

"Yes."

"To us?"

"Yes."

That's when I glance out the window, past our fire escape. And standing down on the street corner and leaning against a lamppost, staring straight up at me from two floors down with a smile on his face, is Scraggly Dude.

20

I don't hesitate.

"Call you back," I tell Ella and hang up. I throw open the window to the fire escape.

Molly stands. "Sami?"

"Stay here. I see him."

"Wait," Molly says.

I don't. I am already scuttling onto the fire escape. Funny. I've never been out here before. For one thing, we've never had a fire. For another, the escape outside our window appears rusty, unstable, and uninviting. When my feet land on it, I find it is indeed all three of those things. The thing shakes to the point where I fear it might just peel away from the brick and send me plummeting. It doesn't, of course.

"Sami?"

It's Molly again. I get it. She wants me to stop. Scraggly Dude could be armed and dangerous. I am being impulsive, possibly reckless, and my history with acting this way is not

237

good. I get all that, but I also can't help it. I once read that we humans are irrational because we are not well described by the rational-agent model. We believe that we make our own decisions with free will, but we don't. Never have.

So let's blame that.

Scraggly Dude has already spotted me coming after him and turned to run. He has a head start. It will be difficult to catch him—and if I do, he has size over me. There is little point to what I am doing. I should have stayed where I was. I should have snapped a photo of him and texted it to Marty or called the cops to help. That would seem the rational thing to do.

But would the cops do anything anyway? Would they get here in time, or would he slip away again?

I release the fire escape ladder so it will reach the ground, but it gets stuck on the rusted track. I hop on it, figuring my weight will get it moving. It doesn't budge. I don't have time to play around. I half climb, half slide to the bottom, hang off the last rung and drop to the ground. The drop is farther than I expected. I land hard, forcing me to roll rather than stand upright.

Scraggly Dude watches me for a few seconds, frozen perhaps in something like surprise, but he soon realizes what's going on and turns to run. He is round and chubby, and when he runs, his arms move like those inflatable noodles in front of car dealerships. Again I should pull up, but when I think of those texts about what Molly's wearing and about him scaring her—scaring my Molly—sorry, man, it would be irrational for me *not* to go after him with everything I have.

He made Molly feel unsafe. He made Molly call me for help.

You don't let that pass.

This may not surprise anyone, but I'm not a great athlete. I'm not saying I was last picked for kickball or anything like that. I was decidedly middling. I do not have terrific hand-eye coordination, and my footwork could best be described as lacking, but I do have speed and stamina. For now, that's all I need. I roll back to a stand and sprint after him.

Scraggly Dude has a block lead, but he is slow, lumbering, the noodle arms working like a drag rather than a propulsion. I swear I can feel grease coming off his long hair and spritzing my face as I get closer. He tries to veer right, but takes the turn too fast and nearly loses his footing. He looks at me over his shoulder. His face is red, his chest heaving.

I'm closing in.

The blood in me is rising.

There are people on Rivington Street. A few turn and stare. Most don't. I'm tempted to call out to stop him, that I'm police, but I'm not and I'm not sure how all that will play out.

Besides I'm gaining on him.

Scraggly turns down Clinton Street, heading toward Delancey. He passes Clinton's Exotic Plus and Deli, a place I've strolled by a hundred times, but I don't know if I want to have my sandwich made by the same guy selling vapes and hookah. That may be a "me" issue. Molly says I need to widen my horizons.

I continue to gain ground.

He suddenly swerves left toward a store called Lot-Less Closeouts. Picture a less-glamorous Dollar Tree, which I know is not easy. Molly sometimes buys cleaning supplies and gift bags at the Lot-Less. It may save money, but it isn't worth it. Scraggly Dude grabs the door handle. That slows him down enough. I dive at him, my body fully extended and horizontal. I wrap my arms around his knees and take him down like a cornerback making an open field tackle. I hear him grunt when he hits the pavement.

He shouts, "What the . . . ?"

I start to climb on top of him. He squirms away, kicks out at me. Nothing lands, but I can't quite get a grip on him. We both scramble to our feet.

Scraggly Dude holds up a hand and signals that he's trying to catch his breath. When he does, he pants, "Get the fuck away from me."

"Who are you? Why are you following my wife?"

"I don't have to tell you anything."

"Yeah, you do."

"Or what?"

I don't have a fast answer. That makes him smile.

"I'm going to walk away right now," Scraggly says. "You're not going to stop me."

He takes a step. I block his path. It's semicomical, I guess. People are beginning to stare. He is far larger than I am, but there is no way I'm letting him go.

"Why are you stalking my wife?"

Scraggly steps to the side, I step to the side. Then he steps at me. I try not to move back. It is one of those moments where one of us is waiting for the other to get physical. We stand now, my chin up against his chest.

"Get out of my way," he says.

"Who are you?"

"I don't have to tell you a goddamn thing."

He walks into me, his bulk pushing me back a bit. I don't know exactly what to do here. I've "caught" him, but what do I do now? He plans on just walking away. Do I, what, hold him captive? Beat the answer out of him in broad daylight? To prevent him from simply leaving, I will have to get more physical. He is big. He has the tats. He has probably spent time in prison. Of course, none of that bothers me. If it gets physical, I know I will win.

That probably sounds cocky. It's not.

I try to hold firm. He takes another step forward. I tilt off-balance and push him back. That's all he needs. He smiles and charges. I let him. We go to the ground.

And that is when I lose my shit.

I mentioned that I wasn't being cocky. Here's why. I have one strength as a fighter, but it is a very effective strength: I totally lose my shit. I am relentless, unstoppable. I just keep coming at you like some little Pakistani Terminator. Scraggly Dude punches me in the cheek hard. He dances back, think-ing the fight is over. I don't even blink. I just keep coming. He hits me with a body shot, lower ribs. Maybe he's cracked one, I don't know.

But I don't stop.

That's my superpower. I've been in scrapes before. I don't lose because there is no quit in me. I don't feel pain when the adrenaline starts pumping. Scraggly starts to turn away from me, realizing he may have bitten off more than he expected to chew. I jump on his back like something coming out of a tree. He stumbles under my weight, drops to his knees. I hang on until his face hits pavement.

Then I grab his hair and smash his face into the sidewalk. I pull him back up by the greasy hair, arching his back, my mouth near his ear.

"Who are you? What do you want with my wife?"

He smiles and I can see blood on his teeth. "Go fuck yourself."

I smash his face into the pavement again.

I pull back to do it again. And that's when someone hits me with a blindside tackle.

"Police! Stop resisting! Hands behind your back!"

Someone else leaps on me. Two uniformed cops are on me now.

"No," I say. "Listen to me—"

I'm face down now. One of the cops jumps up a little and lands with his knee against my spine. I know the move. I'd done the move. It hurts.

"Hands behind your back!"

I'm tempted to tell him I'm a cop, but when they find out I'm no longer one, that might be a mistake. They won't listen now anyway. I let them cuff me. I wonder whether Scraggly Dude is going to run. But he's not. He's just smiling.

"This guy is crazy, man," Scraggly says. "He just starts chasing me."

The officer looks at me. "Sir?"

"He sent my wife texts. He's been stalking her."

"Do you have any proof?" the cop asks me.

"He's cuckoo for Cocoa Puffs," Scraggly says. "I've never seen this guy before in my life. I'm standing on the corner of Avenue C and suddenly he's running after me like a psycho. Did you see what he did to me?"

Scraggly points to his bleeding mouth.

"Sir," the officer says to him, "would you like to press charges?"

"No, man. I just want to go home." He winks. "I got a hot wife and baby boy waiting for me."

Rage engulfs me. "He's lying."

The cop gives me a world-weary-cop sigh. "And again I ask, do you have any proof?"

"Bring us down to the precinct," I say. "My wife will tell you."

"Tell us what exactly?"

"That he's been stalking her."

"Stalking her how?"

"He was outside our apartment this morning. Then my wife went for a walk, and she saw him following her. Then I saw him just now staring up at her window."

"That's bullshit," Scraggly Dude says.

"He also sent two texts."

"Sir," the cop asks me, "do you know this man?"

"Not by name—"

HARLAN COBEN

"Does your wife know this man?"

"No."

"Because the fact that your wife saw the same man on the streets of New York City, even if intentional, is not a crime. You get that right? Do you have proof he was the one who sent you these texts?"

"Just bring us in."

"No, sir, we aren't going to waste time and resources bringing two douchenozzles into the station. It's your lucky day. We are going to let you both go with just a warning. You"—he points to Scraggly Dude—"get out of here. Now. You"—he points to me—"you wait with us for a few minutes and then head in the other direction. We clear?"

"Get his name," I say.

"We don't want his name. And if we got it, we are not giving it to you." Then he turns to Scraggly Dude. "Go."

Scraggly doesn't have to be told twice. He starts running with the noodle arms.

When they uncuff me, I quickly reach for my phone, so I can take a pic. I worry for a moment the two cops might startle, think I'm reaching for a gun, but they don't move in the slightest. Still, by the time I get my phone up, Scraggly Dude and his noodle arms are gone. A moment later, so are the cops. I get up off the curb.

A Pakistani man steps out of the door and says to me, "Turn on your AirDrop."

"Why?"

"Just do it please."

244

I do. The man clicks an icon on his phone—and a photograph of Scraggly Dude, clear as day, comes through. The man smiles at me.

"Thank you," I say to him.

He nods and disappears back into the store.

———

As I walk back to my apartment, I send a WhatsApp message to my special students to meet tonight. I also call my dad and ask him to come over tonight and hang with Molly and Henry, because I have class and I don't want to leave them alone. I stare at the picture of Scraggly Dude my Lot-Less friend had taken and zoom in on the face tattoos.

The five dots.

Gun Guy was right. He had served time.

I debate sending Marty the photograph of Scraggly Dude to get an ID, but while that works on television, it doesn't in real life. I've had cases—too many to name—where we had crystal-clear surveillance footage of suspects caught in the act, but we still can't figure out who they are. You have to post the pictures to the public or get them on television. That's how you get a name. You've undoubtedly seen on the local news or more recently, some social media account, the grainy surveillance photos in those "the police need your help in identifying the suspect" type stories.

Still I text Marty the photograph and ask him to help identify the guy.

Two seconds later, Marty calls. "What's this about?"

"The guy was following Molly." I fill him in. He agrees that the odds we will get something are slim, but he will see what he can do.

Then I add, "I got hired for a pretty big job."

"Nice," he says. "By?"

"The Belmond family."

Silence from Marty.

"No reaction?"

"You tell me out of the blue you might be able to solve the Victoria Belmond case, even ask me to get you info on the case, and boom, the family hires you."

"Yes."

"So either you were soliciting business in a cold-call fashion," Marty says, "or you aren't telling me your real connection to the case?"

Now I'm the silent one.

"I'm betting on the latter," Marty says.

I'm not sure how much to give here. "I may have seen her while she was missing."

"Victoria Belmond?"

"Yes."

"While she was kidnapped?"

"Yes."

"Where?"

"In Spain. I'd just graduated college. I met a girl in a bar. We hung out for a few days. I think it's her."

"I see," Marty says slowly. "We can get rid of the 'I think'

246

portion of that, can't we? You're pretty sure it was her, aren't you?"

"I am."

"Wow. So solving this case is a real possibility for you."

"I don't know how real."

"And if you need a law enforcement officer to get credit for an arrest, I'm standing right here."

I don't want to go into the whole NDA thing—in fact, have I breached it by telling Marty this?—or that part of my generous compensation involves leaving law enforcement out of it. "Look at you being all ambitious," I say. "I didn't know you had it in you, Marty."

"You have no idea," he says.

When we hang up, I place another call, this time to Lenore Spikes. I want to get an okay on travel expenses. I tell her the main thing I need and await pushback, but Lenore says, "No problem, I'm on it. Anything else?"

"Two things, actually," I say.

"Shoot."

"I need to interview Thomas Belmond."

"How's tonight?"

"I have a class, so I can't be there until maybe ten-ish."

"That's fine if it's fine with you. Thomas will be home."

"Okay," I say.

"What else?"

I switch hands. "I'll need to meet with Victoria again."

There is a hesitation.

"Ms. Spikes?"

"Lenore," she says quickly. "Call me Lenore. You under-stand that she doesn't remember anything?"

"She remembers some."

"The family doesn't want her—" she takes a moment to find the right word "—agitated."

"Neither do I."

"I'll get back to you on that. Best I can do."

She hangs up without another word.

Molly is waiting for me, and I fill her in on my encounter with Scraggly Dude. When I finish, I say to her, "I have some-thing of a plan."

"For?"

"For us."

"I'm all ears."

"I have a class tonight. Early. And then I need to drive up to see Thomas Belmond."

"Okay."

"I don't like the idea of leaving you and Henry alone, so I invited my father over."

Molly arches an eyebrow. "Seriously? Your father?"

"Just until I get back."

"You invited your father because you're worried about us."

"Yes."

"And what, pray tell, do you think your father is going to be able to do? Like, if that guy comes back, is your father going to fight him off? Your father, Sami. He can't fight his way out of a wet paper bag."

"Fair point," I say.

"Luckily your son and I love having your dad over anyway."

"But I should probably get someone to watch the place. Maybe I'll ask Marty to park in front or something."

"We'll be fine. We will stay in."

I think about that.

"You said you have something of a plan," Molly says.

"Yes."

"Was the plan having your father defend us?"

"No," I say with a smile. "The plan is brilliant."

She arches an eyebrow. I love when she does that. "Do tell."

"We pack suitcases," I say.

"Oooh, go on."

"For you, me, and Henry."

"We're going on a trip?"

"We are," I say. "We leave tomorrow night."

"And where are we going?"

My smile widens. "The Costa del Sol of Spain."

21

When I start passing out the papers to the class, Golfer Gary asks, "Oh man, is this a pop quiz?" "I hate those."

"This isn't fair, Kierce," Lenny whines. "No one told us we had to study."

"It's not a pop quiz," I say. "It's a Non-Disclosure Agreement. I have a case. I thought it might be fun for you to participate."

"Like being junior detectives?"

"Something like that."

"Do we get badges?" Raymond asks.

I hadn't noticed him before, but he wasn't on the student list. "What are you doing here, Raymond?"

"Right," he says with a chuckle. "Like you don't need my help."

I look at Debbie. She shrugs. "He followed me," she says.

"No badges," I say. "Read it over. If you're okay with it, Polly here is a notary. She'll witness your signatures."

"And if we aren't okay with it?"

"I'll have to ask you to leave," I say. "My client has insisted on complete discretion. If you can't abide by that, buh-bye."

Unsurprisingly, no one leaves. They barely read the document—except for Raymond, who has broken out a monocle like the Planters Peanuts guy. The rest quickly line up to sign. Polly carefully notarizes them. Raymond asks, "Can I get a definition for the word 'the' in the last paragraph?"

"It means you're free to leave whenever you want, Raymond."

"Funny one, Kierce."

Raymond signs, Polly notarizes. That's everyone.

Debbie says, "Okay, so what's the case?"

"We have two, actually," I say.

They wait.

"First case you already know about."

"Victoria Belmond?" Polly asks.

"Yes."

"Who is hiring us?"

Us. Already with the *us.* "It's confidential. Always. Everything about this case is confidential. Ethically. Morally. And legally. Are we all clear?"

"Do we get paid?" Raymond asks.

"No. It's part of your studies. I have assignments for all of you. Well, not you, Raymond."

"Better," Raymond says. "Let me fly solo."

"Like a witch on an airplane wing," I say.

Raymond likes that. He makes a finger gun and drops the hammer. "Exactamundo."

"What kind of assignments?" Gary asks.

"Mostly background and research. There might be some surveillance too."

"What's the second case?" Polly asks.

I swallow because this is hard to say. "The murder of Nicole Brett."

Silence.

They all know.

I figure one of them will ask a question. But none of them do. They just sit in silence and wait.

I clear my throat. "A man named Tad Grayson was convicted of the murder, but he was recently released from prison on a technicality. If we can get enough new evidence, perhaps we can get the Manhattan DA to retry him. Nicole Brett was a decorated rookie police officer with the NYPD when Tad Grayson gunned her down. She was—"

My voice catches. I stop for a second.

Polly stands. "We know who she was, Kierce."

I look around at the solemn, pitying faces and say, "I'll brief everyone on their assignments."

———

Thomas Belmond's converted farmhouse is stone and tasteful and rich and clean and decorated like it's ready for its *Architectural Digest* closeup. Thomas and his wife, Madeline, also fit the bill. Thomas looks like he's getting off a yacht in Hyannis Port. He is youthful and healthy and tan. He sports an untucked blue Oxford shirt, jeans, sockless loafers. His face is beneath-the-skin clean-shaven and glowing. Madeline is a central casting match for him. She is lovely and blond and trim and has perfect skin and perfect teeth. Neither has a sweater tied around the neck, but I feel as though they should.

One of their two daughters bounds down the stairs as I arrive.

"Carly is picking me up in two," she says to her parents, not yet seeing me. "Stacy's upstairs studying. She's got the Calculus midterms tomorrow."

Vicki notices me and before her parents need to prompt her, she comes over to me and sticks out her hand. "Hi, I'm Vicki."

"I'm Sami Kierce."

"Nice to meet you, Mr. Kierce."

Vicki smiles at me with Mom's perfect smile. I smile back. She is a breath of fresh air, the sort of person who walks in a room and you can't help but feel the room is made better. Her parents understandably beam. I know from the bios the Pink Panthers prepared that Vicki is eighteen, a senior in high school, and it strikes me how youthful and vibrant she is, even during this short meet and greet, and how she is at the exact same stage of life as her aunt Victoria was when she vanished.

"What time will you be back?" her father asks.

"Not long. We're just going to watch *The Bachelor* at Jamie's."

Vicki hugs her parents. Not a duteous touch. A bona fide

embrace. Both Thomas and Madeline close their eyes and soak it in. It almost feels unreal to me, like I'm watching a performance, except there is the definitive whiff of authenticity to it. This isn't a show for me. This is what they're like.

"Nice to meet you, Mr. Kierce," Vicki says, heading to the front door.

"You too," I say.

A moment later, Vicki is gone. We all just stand there as though a tornado has passed through and left everything intact.

"Please," Madeline says. "Let's sit in the living room."

They take the plush sofa with floral patterns. I take a matching armchair across from them.

"Would you like something to drink, Mr. Kierce?" Madeline asks me.

I tell her to call me Sami and say that I'll have what they're having. Turns out it's iced tea. It's too late at night for iced tea, but I find some people get comforted when you accept their hospitality.

Thomas crosses his legs, then uncrosses them. He tries to smile but it falters. Then he says to me, "I don't know how I feel about this."

"This being?" I ask.

"Opening this all up again. Kicking the beehive. We all want to know the truth, but . . . "

He stops. Madeline takes his hand. I see the concern on her face.

"Never mind," Thomas says, forcing back up the

still-faltering smile. "Ask me anything. What do you want to know?"

"Can you tell me about that New Year's Eve?"

The faltering smile drops off his face like I just told him his dog died. Madeline looks concerned.

"Thomas?" she says.

"It's my fault, Mr. Kierce," he says to me. "You probably know that."

"I'm not here looking to place blame."

"Victoria called me that night. I didn't answer."

He's so agitated, I worry Madeline will ask me to leave.

"Let's start at the beginning," I say. "Victoria and her friends planned to celebrate the new millennium at McCabe's Pub in New York City. They needed someone twenty-five years old to sign a release. Is that correct?"

Thomas nods. "That was irresponsible of me."

"But understandable," I say, trying to seem a sympathetic ally. "My older brother used to buy me beers when I was in high school. I appreciated that."

This isn't true, but you see what I'm doing.

"I was a mess back then," Thomas says. "I imagine you've done some background work."

"I have."

"So you know I drank too much. I had four DUIs. There was a minor drug charge when I was in college."

"Thomas, I'm not here to relitigate any of that. But you said what happened was your fault. Could you tell me what you mean by that?"

He takes a deep breath.

Madeline whispers, "It's okay, honey." She gives me a semibaleful look. "It's hard for him," she says. "Bringing this all up."

"I'm sorry for that," I say, and I mean it. Thomas seems genuinely distraught, and I don't want to add to that. According to the locals, Thomas is a good guy. He contributes to lots of causes. He has stayed out of trouble. I'm still pissed off about his behavior when I trespassed, but I get what it's like to be overprotective of a loved one. Here is something I'm just going to say with the huge caveat that yes, it's a snap judgement and snap judgements are often wrong: I think what I see in front of me is basically a good man. Maybe it was the hug from the daughter. Maybe it's the way his lovely wife cares about him. His sister's disappearance was obviously a huge trauma for him. I get that, and I sympathize. It won't make me back off. A good detective recognizes and worries about sensibilities, but he doesn't let them deter him.

I turn my attention back to Thomas and wait.

"I drove Vic to that party," he says. "She and one of her friends—Caroline, I think—wanted to get there early to set up."

"Set up?"

"Decorate the room, hang up New Year's posters, stuff like that." Thomas smiles at his wife while still speaking to me. "Vic was that kind of kid. Always responsible. Always looking out for others." Now he turns back to me. "Do you want to hear something awful?"

I don't know how to reply, so I just try to look interested.

"I was already half wasted when I drove her."

"Do you think she knew?"

"That I was under the influence? Probably. I was just oblivious. Vic was my goofy little sister. I was too wrapped up in my own stuff to see her, you know what I mean?"

I nod that I do.

"I was in a very dark place back then. My girlfriend, Lacy, had just dumped me. I was spiraling." He smiles now. It's no longer faltering, but it may be the saddest smile I've ever seen. "And Victoria saw that."

"What do you mean?"

"Vic saw how low I was. During that ride. She tried to talk me into staying."

"At McCabe's Pub?"

"Yes. She said she was worried about me, that she didn't want me to be alone. So she kept saying I should go to her party." The sad smile is still there. "And you know something? I almost did. I remember pulling up to the bar and her trying one more time to convince me and I almost said yes, but I mean, if there is anything more pathetic than being alone on New Year's Eve, it's going to your little sister's high school party when you're twenty-five years old."

Fair point. "You said you broke up with your girlfriend."

"She broke up with me, yes. The day before."

"This would be Lacy Monroe?"

"That's right."

"But you told the FBI you ended up at her place that night."

"I did. That's just it. After I dropped off my sister, I came back home and hung out by myself in our home theater. I had quite the pity party. I watched an old movie. I drank a lot. I did a fair number of drugs. I mean, I was blitzed. At some point, Lacy called me."

I nod. "According to the FBI file, that would have been at 1:21 a.m."

"That sounds about right."

"What did Lacy say?"

"It was a classic drunk dial. She missed me, she loved me, she was sorry and wanted me back. You know the deal."

"All too well," I say.

Thomas sits up a little. "I hope it's not insensitive for me to say I know. When Mom wanted to hire you, our security guys at Belmond did a quick background check. They said you drank."

"I did," I say.

"But you've been sober for several years now."

"Yes."

"Good," Thomas says. "I'm glad. It's not an easy journey."

I don't know whether he's working me with this bonding moment or if it's legit. Don't care either. "So after Lacy called," I continue, "you went to her place?"

"Yes. She dumped me a few days later. Our whole relationship was what they now correctly label 'toxic.'"

"Okay," I say. "You mentioned before that your sister also called you that night."

He swallows. "That's right."

"According again to the phone records, this was at 11:04 p.m., a few minutes before she's spotted leaving McCabe's Pub."

He says nothing. Madeline says nothing.

"And," I add, "the call only lasted one minute."

"That's because I didn't answer," Thomas says. He closes his eyes. Again I've seen some good acting in my time, and I'm not saying I buy everything he's saying, but there is little doubt in my mind that his regret is authentic.

Madeline looks at her husband, his head lowered now, and again I see the concern on her face.

"Maybe we should take a little break?" Madeline suggests.

"No," Thomas says. "I'm fine, really. We need to get through this, okay?"

She nods. "Of course."

"I didn't answer my sister's call," he says.

"Okay," I say.

"I don't know if I was too wasted to pick up or if, I don't know, I was so caught up in my own drama that I just ignored my little sister or, who knows, maybe I wanted to keep the line open in case Lacy called." He stops to take a breath. "I don't know. I don't remember. I just know that her call ended up going to voice mail."

"What did it say?" I ask.

The question seems to surprise him. "Her voice mail?"

"Yes."

He shakes his head. "Nothing."

I wait for him to elaborate. You wait, you sometimes get gold.

"I just heard a lot of party noise in the background."

"On the voice mail?"

"Yes."

"But no words?"

"Nothing I could make out. Maybe Vic meant to hang up. Maybe she didn't realize her phone was still on."

I mull that over and try to lay out the tracks in my mind. Victoria is at a big millennium party in New York City she helps arrange. Something happens. She reacts by calling her brother. He doesn't answer. Then she rushes out into the street where she's seen by the CCTV camera.

"When did you listen to the voice mail?" I ask.

"You mean play it back?"

"Yes. When did you hear this message of party noise?"

"I don't know. Thing is, I almost never check my voice mail. It could have been days later."

"But you can't remember when?"

Madeline seems annoyed by this line of questioning. "What does that have to do with anything?"

"I'm wondering how it all went down," I say. "Like, did you hear her message and think *That's odd*. Did you check your voice mail before or after the family started to get worried about Victoria. That kind of thing."

"What difference does any of that make?" Madeline asks.

"Probably none," I admit. "But this is how you investigate.

You try to put together a timeline and see where something goes awry." I turn back to Thomas. "Do you remember when you first listened to the voice mail?"

"I don't." He thinks about it a bit and adds, "But I don't remember thinking it was a big deal, so it must have been before we were worried about her."

"I assume you no longer have the voice mail?"

"From twenty-five years ago? No, sorry."

"Do you have a theory on why Victoria called?"

"Seems obvious." A tear escapes his eye and rolls down his cheek. "Something happened at the party, and she wanted a ride home."

He stops again. Madeline whispers some words of comfort, but I don't think he can hear them right now. I don't have a follow-up question, so I stay silent.

After some time passes, Thomas continues: "Victoria was a teenage girl, and instead of watching her, instead of taking care of her, we were all distracted by our own stuff. I was all caught up in my Lacy drama. My mom was consumed with what was happening with my grandfather. I can make all the excuses I want—Victoria texted us, we thought she was with friends, whatever—but why weren't we more worried when she didn't come home?"

I shift in the chair. "What about your dad?"

"What about him?"

"You said 'we were all distracted.' We've covered your issues with Lacy. Your mom was distracted with her father's illness. What about your dad?"

Thomas frowns at that. "Dad was busy with work, I guess. He was also helping Mom with my grandfather. If you're trying to imply—"

"I'm not trying to imply anything," I say. "He was home on New Year's Eve, correct?"

"Yes."

"Did you see him at all?"

"No. I pretty much stayed in the home theater."

"How about when you left to go to Lacy's?"

"I didn't see him, no. He may have already been on his way to Chicago by then. Why are you asking—?"

Time to switch gears. "Can I ask you something else?"

Thomas clears his throat. "Of course."

"You're sober now."

"I am. Twenty-five years."

"That would mean you quit right around the time your sister disappeared."

"You have to hit rock bottom before you get help. We both know that, don't we? Maybe it was melodramatic for me to declare 'It's my fault,' but the hard truth is, if I had been sober, everything would have turned out differently. So I got help. I went to rehab. I joined the church. I met Madeline. We have two children. You just met our oldest. We named her Victoria—Vicki—after my sister. But odd as it sounds, it's a little like Covid."

"Covid?" I repeat. "How so?"

"I realize this will sound like a strange comparison, but remember how we all felt when the world first shut down for

Covid? Like everything had changed forever. Like the world would never be the same—and now, just a few years later, poof, you can barely remember it. That's kind of how it felt after Victoria came home. I don't know if it's blocking or just a new gratitude about life, but my parents are great, Madeline and I are great—even Victoria seems happy. I daresay—and I know how this will sound—we are all better off now. You go through something this horrible, you appreciate what matters more. That's the thing with tragedy. It's awful and cruel, but it's a great teacher. You can't put a silver lining on something so horrific, but the truth is, I don't know where I'd be if this hadn't happened. I'd never have met Madeline. There'd be no Vicki, no Stacy. Blessing, curse, I don't know."

I sit back and cross my legs. I give his words time to settle.

"Do you have a theory on what happened to your sister?" I ask.

"I did. I mean, before we met you and learned about Spain. I thought someone had kidnapped her and locked her away."

"And now?"

"Now," Thomas says, gripping his wife's hand, "I worry it was something worse."

22

The Belmonds' travel agent knew her stuff. She arranged early check-in at the five-star Higueron Hotel in Fuengirola. Molly gasps when we enter the suite.

"Oh. My. God."

I smile. "Right?"

I have Henry in one arm. I put my other around Molly as we gaze out the open window. The Mediterranean is laid out in front of us like a shimmering blanket, a gentle breeze blowing through the windows. Molly closes her eyes and soaks it in. We smell the salt air. For my part, I am experiencing no déjà vu to my previous visit to Spain because the difference between crowding into a youth hostel with the Lax Bros clogging the shared toilet and this opulent luxury suite overlooking the sea with my wife and child is, to put it mildly, transformative.

"Maybe we should move here," Molly says.

"To Spain?"

"To this hotel suite."

"We'd get bored."

Molly tilts her head. "Would we?"

I follow her gaze back out the window. "Yeah," I say. "But not for a while."

"When do you have to leave for your appointment?"

I check my watch. I was able to set up a meeting with Carlos Osorio, the young police inspector I reported to twenty-two years ago, under the guise (honest guise, if you will) of being a private investigator working for the Belmond family. Osorio is still with the same police department, having risen to the rank of comisario, which you don't have to be a major linguist or top-notch crime fighter to deduce means "commissioner."

"I have an hour," I say.

She comes closer to me. "Do you know what I hear is good for jet lag?"

"Uh, your son is awake."

"A walk in the sun, silly."

"Oh."

"Don't look so crestfallen. It'll be fun."

And it was. An hour later, I leave my wife and son by a gorgeous infinity pool laying on something called a Balinese bed. Forget the suite—I think Molly could live on that bed and never be bored.

When the taxi drops me off at the El Puerto Hotel, the déjà vu doesn't just come back—it rises in a rush and slaps me across the face. Some things have changed, sure, but not a lot. I glance toward the more crowded beach, and I swear I can see a couple of kids who look just like Anna and me on a blanket right where we used to lie. The memories are charging at me so fast I almost duck. It's a harsh blast, a strobing kaleidoscope of a slideshow, and I can't tell whether the memories are good or bad. I am trying to maintain my composure, focus on the job, remember that perhaps Anna too was a victim. But when I think of what came after, how it derailed me, I can't help feeling rage at her too.

Twenty-two years ago, when I reported the "murder" to Carlos Osorio, I was a cleanly shaven scrawny lad. Now I'm weathered and bearded and look completely different. Osorio does not, though even in his youth, he had looked like an old soul. The years have been kind to Comisario Osorio. Other than some graying at the temples, there is zero change.

We shake hands and move into his office. He offers me an espresso, promising me that it will help with the jet lag. I don't know if that's true, but I can say that whatever he serves me hits like jet fuel. It's also spectacular. He gets to the point fast.

"So what is the Belmonds' interest in Fuengirola?" he asks. "I would think Marbella would be more their speed."

The No Shit Elites had discovered that before joining the academy Osorio had spent three years studying in Cambridge. That explained the perfect British accent.

"Do you recognize me?" I ask.

He studies my face. "Should I?"

"We met," I say. "Over twenty years ago. My name is Sami Kierce."

He sits back, folds his hands, rests them on his stomach. "I thought you were here on behalf of the Belmonds."

"I am. Twenty-two years ago, I was another young tourist staying at a hostel. I came to you because I thought a girl I was kinda seeing had been murdered. You dismissed it as my being high or drunk, but you did go back with me to her apartment."

"And there was no body," he finished for me.

"You remember?"

"Not really, no. But I would remember if there had been one, wouldn't I?"

"I guess that's true."

Osorio possesses the kind of world-weary face only we cops seem to cultivate. His skin has a leathered tan that can only be derived from years of sun exposure. "What do you want from me, Mr. Kierce?"

"None of this surprises you, does it?"

Osorio rubs his chin. "You came to Spain as an American college student, correct?"

"I'd just graduated."

"Backpacking with friends through Europe?"

"Something like that."

"And when you reported this to me, did you tell me the whole story? Or did you leave out some key details?"

"I left out some key details," I say.

Osorio strokes his chin. "Do you still think you saw a murdered woman that day?"

"No." Then I add, "So you do remember me?"

Osorio chooses not to answer. "You probably figured out by now that you were scammed."

"And you knew right away," I say.

"Yes. It wasn't an uncommon crime, but your case was somewhat unusual."

"In what way?"

"Various forms of that con were common in those days. A girl would seduce a young tourist. The mark, if you will. She would wait until the mark was comfortable and then she'd rob him. The problem was, the mark would often report it to the police. He would be able to identify her. She would have to move on or at least change locations. So some con artists became, shall we say, more creative. They'd fake an illness or something worse and convince the mark it was his fault. The mark would run in a panic and never report it. Because if he did, he feared he'd end up in jail. Sound familiar?"

"It does."

Osorio grins. "That's why you didn't tell me everything. You'd have implicated yourself, wouldn't you have?"

"I would, yes," I admit.

"Most scams were simpler. The woman would fake a drug overdose. The accomplice would say something like, 'You bought the drugs' or 'When we take her to the hospital, they'll arrest you for possession, just go.' So the mark would take the out. They never really cared about the girl. She was just fun or sex to them. Your con—a dead woman with a knife in her chest or whatever—those were rare. Or who knows, maybe a lot of people got conned that way, but to your credit, you were one of the few, maybe the only one, who still felt morally obligated to report it."

"Yeah, I'm great," I say, flashing back to the last time I was in the station. "You could have told me. You could have let me off the hook."

"I planned to," he replies. "I left a message at your hostel. But you ran home, remember?"

"You still could have called."

"I didn't have your phone number. You also didn't come fully clean with me. I had no obligation to follow up."

"Or maybe someone in the police department was getting a kickback."

"Oh, I don't know about that. But beach towns like this, we survive on tourism. Amplifying news about crimes does little to enhance our business model."

"So you look the other way."

"You're being melodramatic, Mr. Kierce. But let's also be realistic. If you had stayed, perhaps we would have tracked down the two people who committed this petty crime. That's all it was. She wasn't *really* dead, remember? Maybe they'd have been charged if you testified against them—but then you'd have to admit possessing illegal drugs in a foreign country. Do you see my point?"

"Clear as the Mediterranean Sea," I say.

"Can I ask you a question?"

"Go ahead."

"What does this have to do with the Belmonds?" Osorio

asks. "Or was using their name just a ruse to get a meeting with me?"

"It was no ruse," I say.

Osorio spreads his hands. "Then?"

"The girl who ran that con on me—the one I thought had been murdered."

"What about her?"

"She was Victoria Belmond."

Osorio blinks, absorbs the words. "The kidnapped daughter?"

"The very," I say. "The FBI has had no clue where she was for the eleven years she was missing. Now we know that she was in Fuengirola three years after she vanished, running scams on at least one naïve, young tourist."

Osorio sits back. "I don't even know what to say. Are you sure it's the same girl?"

"Yes."

"Have you met her?"

"Just recently for the first time."

"I assume you asked her about robbing you?"

"She claims no memory of those eleven years."

Osorio rubs his chin again. "I remember reading that," he says. "But come on. Amnesia? That has to be a lie, don't you think?"

"I don't know," I say. "But I need your help."

"How?"

"She didn't run that con on her own. She had an accomplice. He went by the name Buzz."

Osorio arches a skeptical eyebrow. "Buzz?"

"Yes. He was also her drug dealer."

"More likely, her handler," Osorio says.

"Meaning?"

"Look, twenty-two years ago—that was before we fully understood about trafficking and all that. But this is how it worked: You know, I'm sure, that a lot of young women—and men too—were forced into sex slavery."

"Yes."

"These were often run by organized crime families. They were into a lot of illicit things, of course. Not just sex. They exploited other avenues for revenue."

"For example?"

"For example, a destitute, desperate young woman look-ing for work could be told there's a job waiting for her at a tourist destination, something like waitressing or being a club hostess. Once she arrives, her handler takes her pass-port away and forces her into other lines of work—sex work being the most obvious. But some of the girls would be put out on the streets to beg. Some would be taught to pickpocket or shoplift or roll men. And some would run more elaborate cons."

"Like the one on me."

"Precisely."

I try to put it together. Did Victoria get kidnapped and was then forced into a life of petty crime? It seems a stretch. She certainly wasn't destitute or desperate. And what do I make of her memory loss? Is that for real? Is it a cover? I try to rewind to the beginning, to that New Year's Eve party above McCabe's Pub.

Something made Victoria call her brother that night.

Something made her leave the party.

What?

What could have led a seemingly well-adjusted girl from a well-to-do family from celebrating the new millennium with rich high school friends to running low-rent cons on naïve tourists in the Costa del Sol?

"I remember when the Belmond girl was found," Osorio says to me. "It was in a restaurant or something?"

"Yes, a diner."

"So how can I help?"

"We need to find Buzz."

"Twenty-two years later?"

"A guy like that," I say. "I probably wasn't his first mark or his last."

Osorio sees it now. "You think he's in the system."

"I think there's a good chance. We start back at that summer. I can give you a general description. White guy. I'd say one meter eighty, maybe ninety-five kilograms. I'm guessing around forty years old then. He had a Dutch accent, and I remember Anna telling me he was from Amsterdam. Don't know if that's true or not. When I met him, he had purple-spiked hair and a nose ring. He said he worked as a DJ."

Osorio writes this all down. "Did this Buzz say where he worked?"

"No."

"Twenty-two years ago," Osorio says. "That won't be in the computer. We didn't start digital storage until 2008, so they'll be in physical form."

"Like mug shot books?"

"Yes."

"Can we access them?"

"They're in a warehouse in Málaga."

"How long will that take?"

"Can you come back in two hours?"

"Sure."

I rise to leave.

"It was cruel," Osorio says. "That con. You were just a kid, and you thought you'd done something terrible. It's haunted you."

I say nothing.

"That's what I should have seen, but I wasn't much more than a kid either. Like I said, I didn't have your phone number. But I could have found it. I should have. I should have called you and told you the truth. I'm sorry about that."

I don't trust my voice, so I nod what I hope is a thanks and head outside.

23

I head to the beach and take off my shoes and socks. The sand is hard, gritty, crushed-shell-like. The Jersey Shore is much better. Sorry, it is. Better waves too. I don't stay long. I get my shoes back on and walk over to the Discoteca Palmeras. I stare up at the façade. I don't feel anything because I don't think I ever saw the place's exterior in the daytime. I can't tell whether it's changed in the past two decades. Have you ever stayed in a nightclub until closing when they turn the houselights on and it's like a totally different experience? It's a sobering sight when a nightclub is scrubbed of its makeup and mood lighting, when it is exposed to the harsh morning glare.

I am focused on the case—on finding out the truth about what happened to Victoria Belmond and to a lesser degree me—but I can't help thinking about the financial windfall that has risen me up like that church song about angels' wings. I don't want it to matter. I don't want to let money change me or any of that. But I feel a lightness in my chest, and I know Molly does too. I'm not sure we consciously understood the burden that debt had placed upon our shoulders—what the heavy weight was doing to us physically, mentally, emotionally. I wanted to be that old Loggins and Messina song about even though we ain't got money, I'm so in love with you honey, but the truth is far more complex.

In sum, I had to be careful that the money didn't cloud my vision.

A young man sees me staring at the club entrance. He walks past me without so much as a nod and starts to unlock the door.

"Buenos días," I say.

I speak fluent Spanish. Not as well as Osorio speaks English, but pretty close. I took it in high school like a lot of American youth and learned very little. But after my experience here, after Anna, I developed a sudden desire to master Spanish. You'd probably attribute this to some kind of perverse reaction to trauma, offer up some sort of pat psychological explanation for my need to learn the language of the country that had caused me such angst. You'd be right. It's pretty much that simple, I guess. Or maybe a part of me knew that I would one day return to find the answer.

I'm getting very deep today.

The young man—I would say he's somewhere between twenty and twenty-five—nods.

"I used to come here," I say in Spanish. "When I visited here twenty-two years ago."

He does not look impressed.

"Do you know if anyone is still around from those days?" I ask.

"My grandfather maybe."

"Do you know where I can find him?"

"The Santa Maria cemetery in Mijas," the young man says. He shakes his head. "Twenty-two years ago." He chuckles. "Didn't Franco rule this country then?"

Great. I spent years mastering Spanish so I could understand all the nuance of a sarcastic kid.

I try to find the old apartment building where it all went down. It's gone now, along with all the others, replaced with newer high-rises. Good riddance, I guess, though part of me hoped that it was still there and I could convince Osorio to get his lab guys in there and swab every bit of it in search of . . . well, now I know it wasn't blood, so what's the point?

I head back to the beach and look for some place that doesn't look too touristy. I order two dishes—the lightly breaded boquerones with tomatoes and the house paella, which is unlike anything we peasant Americans think of as paella. I probably shouldn't, but it would be almost criminal to enjoy these delicacies without a glass of Rioja Blanco from the Viura grape. So I order one of those too.

I call Molly. She answers in a singsong voice. Again it's not just that we are staying in a five-star hotel in Spain. It's the money.

"Where are you?" I ask.

"On the Balinese bed."

"The same one?"

"We haven't moved much."

"How's Henry?"

"He's napping. Or should I say, he's having a siesta."

"It's like you're half Spanish already."

"I know, right? I'm also drinking something called a Tinto de Verano."

"What's that?"

"Heaven."

A call breaks in. I explain to Molly that it's Osorio and switch over.

"Come back," Osorio says.

I pay the check and hurry toward the station. Osorio brings me to a room that they probably use for interrogations. Thick binders are piled on the table. Lots of them. On the cover are the words FOTOS DE DETENIDOS. I don't need my Spanish mastery to figure out what that means.

"How are they categorized?" I ask.

"By date."

"How about by crime or physical descriptions?"

"No, sorry."

"Are foreigners in a separate binder?"

"No. I was wrong about that."

"So," I say. "Just by date."

"Afraid so."

I let loose a long breath. "Okay."

"You want something to drink?"

I'm tempted to ask for a Rioja Blanco. "I'm good."

"Let me know if you need anything."

I expect this to take hours. It doesn't. I find him in fifteen minutes.

I started with July 11, 2003, the day I ran from Spain, figuring Buzz and "Anna" remained active after me. The mug shots are much like the ones in the USA—two photos of the face, one a frontal view, the second a profile.

I was just settling in, getting a little rhythm going, when I hit pay dirt.

Buzz still had the purple spiked hair and nose ring. The date on the photo is four months after he'd scammed me. There is no name listed under the mug shot. There is no crime. There is just a number—9039384.

I lift the large binder, keeping it open to the correct page, and bring it to Osorio's office.

"Found him," I say.

Osorio looks at me over his reading glasses. "Let me see."

I hand him the book. He studies the mug shot for a moment.

"Do you recognize him?"

"He is not completely unfamiliar," Osorio says. "But there were a lot of guys who looked like this turd back in the day."

"Do we know what he was arrested for?"

"We can't put the name or crimes on here for privacy reasons. Article 18.4 of the Spanish Constitution protects personal data, including mug shots and police records."

"Meaning?"

"Meaning this can't be accessed by the general public."

"But you're not the general public."

"True, but you are. So step back and don't look over my shoulder."

Osorio types the number into his computer and starts to read. I wait.

"Well?"

"His name is Harm Bergkamp."

"Harm?"

"Apropos name, no? He is a citizen of the Netherlands. He was thirty-six years old at the time of his arrest. This was a year after you left. He has a fairly extensive record, all minor things. Petty robberies. It's what I told you before. Even if we caught him back then, what crime had he really committed— stealing under a thousand dollars from you and, what, pretending someone was dead?"

"And this arrest?"

"Assault." Osorio squints and reads. "Seems our friend Harm got into a fight in a room at the El Puerto Hotel."

"Did he stand trial?"

He shakes his head. "All charges dropped." He keeps reading. "Oh, this is interesting."

"What?"

"According to the record, the man he attacked was an American named Frank Ache. Bergkamp claimed self-defense, saying that Ache first attacked his girlfriend, a woman named—" he looks up at me "—Anna Marigold."

Boom.

He continues to read. I am not patient.

"What?" I ask.

"Give me a second."

I take out my phone and google Anna Marigold. Nothing significant. I hit the image search. A bunch of textile patterns of marigold flowers designed by a woman named Anna Spiro pop up. I try putting the name in quotes—"Anna Marigold"— but still get nothing. Then again had I really expected to get anything worthwhile? No. I try "Harm Bergkamp," but the results are all in Dutch. I click through a few, but they all seem to be about someone with the name who died in 1876.

Finally, Osorio lets loose a deep breath, sits back, and rubs his face. "Okay, so here's the deal."

I put my phone down and lean toward him.

"It's like what happened to you. Anna met Ache at the Discoteca Palmeras. She faked a drug overdose. Not death. But like, really out of it. The problem was, from what I can gather here, Bergkamp got held up and didn't get there in time. So Ache kept shaking her and shaking her. Anna tried to keep her eyes closed and pretended to be out of it. But how long can you pull that off? So he figures out she's faking it and she'd already stolen his money and hidden it. So Ache loses it and starts beating her."

The broken nose, I think. The shattered cheekbone. Could this be how she got them?

"Harm Bergkamp arrives, sees her in trouble. He jumps on Frank Ache to stop him. That's the assault. It turns super ugly. Hotel security intercedes. Bergkamp and Ache both get arrested. Anna Marigold has to go to the hospital."

He stops and reads some more.

"And?" I say.

"And that's it. Charges dropped. My guess is, neither side wanted to pursue it."

"How badly was Anna hurt?"

"Doesn't say. It just says that she was hospitalized in Málaga."

"Can we get records?"

"From that long ago? Doubt it. And what are you going to learn? There won't be pictures."

"So," I say, "how do we get Harm Bergkamp's current whereabouts?"

24

With the help of Polly and the Pink Panthers, I find Harm three days later in, of all places, Nashville, Tennessee.

Or should I say Buzz? Or Buzzy?

Harm Bergkamp now goes by the name—get this—Buzzy Berg. He works on low-budget horror films, using local breweries and abandoned buildings as locations. His movies are universally terrible and three steps below what we used to call "straight-to-video." I tried to watch one called *Bed, Bloodbath and Beyond*, but I'm not good with gore and that's pretty much all the films offer.

I use the Belmond name again, this time saying that the family is interested in financing a film. That kind of offer clears a schedule, though I don't think Buzzy is all that busy. Buzzy isn't Bizzy, if you will. I'll let that alliteration stay a moment.

Buzzy tells me to meet him at the Gaylord Opryland Resort.

What he doesn't tell me is that the Gaylord is the largest non-casino hotel in the world. Yes, the world. I looked it up before I got here. It has nearly three thousand rooms and over three million square feet of space, all located—I kid you not—under a giant glass sphere overloaded with foliage, so you feel as though you're trapped in the world's largest terrarium. I wish Molly and Henry were with me, but they decided to stay a few extra days in Spain and who could blame them?

I meet Buzz by an indoor riverboat—I don't know or care where it goes. Even though his purple hair and nose ring have been replaced by a shaved head and one hoop earring, I recognize the man right away.

"Buzzy Berg," he says with a floppy-fish handshake.

"Samuel Pierce," I say. It's a favorite alias for obvious reasons. I didn't use Sami Kierce with him because way back when he knew my name and might possibly remember it. For a moment, he hesitates, and I imagine that there is a flicker of recognition in his eyes. He still gives me a big smile and leads me on a path under an indoor waterfall.

I notice Buzz has a very prominent limp. He didn't have that when I knew him.

"We are just prepping for a scene," he tells me.

We is Buzzy and a guy with a ZZ Top beard holding a camera who Buzzy introduces as Dale. Dale doesn't pay me much attention, and I return the favor. My attention, my full attention for a moment, is on the "dead" woman on the bed drenched in blood, the knife sticking out of her chest. I turn my head away fast. Buzzy notices and chuckles.

283

"I do all my own props and special effects," he says. "Good work, right?"

"Yes," I manage. Then I say, "Where did you hone that skill?"

"Everywhere. It's my first love." Then: "Take five, Dale."

Dale doesn't have to be told twice.

"Tell me more about that," I say.

"About what?"

"How you started in the business. How you honed your craft."

"I'm from Holland. You can probably hear my accent."

"Not much of it," I say. And that's true. He sounds almost American now. "How long have you lived in the States?"

"Oh, gosh. More than twenty years now."

"And before that?"

"Europe. I started as a production assistant, if you can believe it. Worked my way up."

"Where in Europe?" I ask.

"Oh, all over. But that was a long time ago. Your timing is great because I have some close Hollywood friends who want to star in my new horror rom-com *Romeo and Ghouliet*. Especially since my last film won the Gore award. You probably know it. Anyway, I don't like to name drop or anything, but I've been talking to Lenny DiCaprio."

"Lenny?"

"That's what his friends call him. I mean, come on, you don't think his friends call him Leonardo, do you?"

Buzzy chuckles.

"I thought they call him Leo," I say.

That stops the chuckles, but he recovers. "No, no, Leo is what his *public* friends call him. See, when you get to know him—"

I need to move this along. "Your real name is Harm Berg-kamp, isn't it?"

The smile flickers. "Sure, of course. Who in the business uses their real name? Did you know Vin Diesel is really Mark Sinclair? Michael Caine was Maurice Micklewhite? Judy Garland was Frances Gumm? Gumm. Can you imagine the *Wizard of Oz* with Frances Gumm as Dorothy? Doesn't Buzzy Berg sound better?"

"It does," I agree, though it sounds like the name of a Hollywood agent.

"Right, exactly. It's a good name. You want something in this life, you have to envision it. Buzzy Berg is the name of a big movie producer. So I envisioned it, I repeated it, and"— he spread his hands—"here we are, Mr. Pierce."

"Kierce," I say.

"Pardon?"

"My last name is Kierce. Like Pierce but with a *K*. And my first name is Sami." I spell it for him. I see something cross his face, like maybe five percent recognition. I push on. "We knew each other twenty-two years ago. In the Costa del Sol of Spain."

"Ah." He looks at me now. Everything about him changes, but I can't say from what. Is it fear, anger, resentment, regret— I don't know. "Are you taping this?" he asks me.

"No."

"I remember you now. It was, what, a few hundred dollars in another country a quarter century ago. The statute of limitations has long run out."

"I know."

"Are you here for revenge then?"

"No, not that either."

"What then?"

"I want some answers. That's all. And then I'll let you be."

"And if I refuse?"

"I would rather not start with the threats."

"And I would rather not relive my sordid past. And so I'll ask again: If I refuse?"

"I'll do all I can to make you miserable. The people who set up this meeting. The Belmonds. You know who they are?"

"Of course."

"I am asking these questions on their behalf, not mine."

"On their behalf?"

"Yes. You do not want them on your bad side."

He frowns. "How can my past have anything to do with the Belmonds?"

"If you refuse," I continue, ignoring his question for the time being, "they'll use their vast resources, influence, and connections to make your life miserable."

"I don't really understand any of this," Buzz says.

"Tell me about Anna."

A small smile comes to his face. "Are you sure this is for the Belmonds?"

"I am sure," I say as firmly as I can muster. "Tell me about Anna."

"You liked her, didn't you?" There is a bit of cruelty to the smile now. "What makes you think I know where she is now?"

"I didn't ask where she is now," I say. "I want you to tell me about her. Her full name. Where she grew up. How you two met."

"Why?" he asks.

"How about starting with how you two met?"

He leaned back. "It would make a hell of a movie, actually. But I think I'll pass."

"You're right," I say. "No one will care about an old robbery. But a kidnapping—a prominent, unsolved one—well, that's a different story."

"What the hell are you talking about?"

He seems genuinely befuddled. He'd been locked onto my interest being personal, a search for Anna, but even with the Belmond name, he wasn't going down the excuse/evasion route one would expect a kidnapper to take. In fact, this was the main reason why I had the Belmonds call. The plan had been thus: If he'd been involved in the kidnapping—if he'd known who Anna really was—he most likely would have panicked when the Belmonds called. Lenore Spikes had investigators watching him to see whether he bolted so he could be followed. But he didn't. He clearly welcomed the meeting. That meant either he wasn't directly involved in the kidnapping—or that he had brass balls and was playing the ultimate game of bluff.

"Just tell me about Anna."

"We were both part of the program."

"What program?"

"I don't know Anna's exact story. But they were all variations of the same thing. There was a feeder agency. They find vulnerable girls. And boys. When they arrive, a group of men—hard men, awful men—train them. And yes, I don't really mean train. They brutalize them. Do you really need to hear all this?"

"I don't," I say.

"People think these girls only come from Eastern Europe or somewhere like that. That's not true. You just want lost children, ones with no one who gives a shit about them. Ones where no one will care that they vanish. There's more than you think. Everywhere."

"And Anna was one of them?"

He nods. "They paired her with me. Our job was to rob tourists. Like you."

I know it isn't relevant to this case, but I have to ask. "Why didn't you do that?"

"Do what?"

"Just rob me?"

"We did."

"You know what I mean."

He nods. He gets what I'm asking. "We had flair. Anna and me. We liked to make it more. I know that sounds cruel. I was working on my craft." He gestures to the "dead" woman on the bed. "That's the truth. Special effects. It was also effective.

If you convince someone they committed murder . . . Can I add, sorry, it was fun?"

I keep my tone steady. "And risky."

"Not really. I always came into the room fast, so they wouldn't check her vitals. You were also drugged. I think we gave you too much. It took forever for you to wake up. I had to practically carry you out of the room. And even if someone did get suspicious, what could they do? Report us? I was caught once. Working with another girl. The police laughed. What's the charge for faking like you're dead?"

Osorio had pointed out something similar. "So what happened to Anna?" I ask.

"I don't know. Eventually the girls get used up. So they let them go. Or they run. Or they end up in prison or dead."

"She never told you her real name?"

"She said her name was Anna Marigold. She said she grew up near Penn State. That her mother died young and left her with a sister. The sister married a man who abused her every which way. She saw a chance to run away." He shrugs. "That might have been the truth, that might have been a lie. I don't know."

"But that's what Anna told you?"

"That's what Anna told me, yes. I was working with four girls at the time."

"You mean you were their handler?"

"Use whatever term you like. It's not accurate. But we would be running four scams at any one time. We kept it up for another six months after you left, then Anna took off for a while."

"Took off?"

"Yes."

"Why?"

"Not important. Some kind of illness."

There is something on his face when he says this. Something I don't like.

"Anyway, maybe a year after you—I don't remember—Anna came to me and we started up again. She hooked up with the wrong man. Or kid, I should say. He was seventeen, flashing a lot of money. The kind of guy we loved to take down. Except we didn't know his family was connected. It all went sideways. She got beaten up. I got arrested. But this guy, his family was relentless. They went after us. She, I don't know. To be honest, I thought maybe Anna was dead, so your visit, I mean, I guess she got away. That's when I got out of the business too."

We sit there a moment.

"You said she came through an agency?"

"All the girls did. It wasn't a real agency, of course. Our economy relies on scams, you know that, don't you? You ever watch daytime TV? Buy gold, buy insurance you don't need. We all scam in our way. This agency used to have kiosks in malls. They'd stop people and say, hey, you could be a model. All you need is a portfolio, which could be arranged for a fee. A con job. And sometimes, they'd spot something else, someone more vulnerable."

"Do you remember the name of the agency?"

"Radiant Allure. Funny how I remember that."

"Is there anything else you can tell me about Anna?"

"I know what you must think of me. But there is more to it. I had my own sadistic handler. I came from an orphanage too. I thought they were sending me to film school in Spain. That's what they told me. I was going to work as a production assistant on a real Spanish film. And when it all went wrong with that mobster's kid, my handler told them where to find us. They held me down. Three men. Flipped me on my stomach. Two sat on my legs. The third straddled my back and held me by the hair. The fourth man . . . " He stops and licks his dry lips. "He had a hacksaw. He sawed through my Achilles tendon. I spent four months in a hospital. Then I moved here."

I say nothing.

"I don't tell you that for sympathy. You come here and tell me that you're looking for Anna and it involves a high-profile kidnapping. So I assume you're talking about the Belmonds' daughter. You think that Anna had something to do with it. I don't believe that. I'm not saying she was a saint. She wasn't. She was a survivor and clever. But she took care of the other girls. She wouldn't kidnap one. For all I know, you want to hurt Anna. You want to put her in prison or get some kind of revenge. And it isn't like the Belmonds hired a random private detective. It's you. Someone she conned years ago. And if Anna got away, I'm happy for her. She made it. And I'll tell you something else, Sami Kierce, though you won't believe it. She cared about you. Those cons? We ran them for a day or two at the most. She kept making excuses to keep you around. Because she was falling in love with you. I had to put my foot down. I told her we were taking too long. The bosses wouldn't be happy. I think she was planning to run away with you. So if you're looking for a bad guy or someone to blame, it's me. Let her be."

I believe him. I know that sounds crazy. But I do.

"I only want what's best for her too," I say.

"Then maybe don't try to sell her out to a rich family."

"That's not what I'm doing," I say. "We already found her."

"What are you talking about?"

"She's Victoria Belmond."

"What?" He shakes his head and smiles. "My god, talk about the ultimate con."

"What?"

"Pretending to be a long-lost heiress."

"The family ran DNA tests."

"Are you serious?"

"I am."

"Wow." He shakes his head, trying to comprehend. "So the Anna I knew . . . was like a rich heiress?"

"Something like that."

"So why are you asking me what happened? Why don't you ask her?"

"She says she doesn't remember."

"How can she not remember?"

I shrug. "Some kind of amnesia."

"Do you believe that?"

"I don't know."

"So you're, what, still trying to find her kidnappers?"

"Yes."

Buzzy shakes his head. "I don't know what to say."

"If you reveal anything, the weight of this family will come down on you. If you don't, they will indeed finance your next film."

"That's nice," he says. "I'll take the financing. I can use it. But between us, I don't need the threats or the payoffs. Anna and I, we went through hell together. We survived. If she ever remembers, we will always have a bond."

"You exploited her."

"She won't think that. Either way, tell her if she ever needs me, I'll be there. But Sami?"

"What?"

"Let this be. Whatever she and I did, it was a long time ago." And then, using the exact same words I heard from Talia Belmond, he says: "Let sleeping dogs lie."

25

I check in at the desk at the offices of a charity called the
Abeona Shelter and ask for Jennifer Schultz. The building
is located on the corner of Hudson and Harrison Streets
in Tribeca. It was the New York Mercantile Exchange until
1977, but it's always looked more like a cool fire station to me.

How did I end up here?

It started with a call from Polly after I downloaded my
meeting with Harm Bergkamp to the Pink Panthers.

"I found something strange on the Radiant Allure modeling
agency," Polly said.

"Okay."

"So the agency closed in 2004 when the two founders,
Eunice and Vernon Schultz, retired."

"Do we know where the Schultzes are now?"

"Both dead. Eunice died of cancer about a year after retir-
ing. That might have been why they retired, I don't know. The
husband, Vernon, died in 2018. He was eighty-two."

"So what's the weird part?"

"We found their daughter. Jennifer Schultz. She said she would talk to you. In truth, she seemed anxious to."

And here I am.

I'm led into a conference room where a woman I recognize as Jennifer Schultz from my Google searches awaits me. Without so much as a hello or handshake, she asks, "Why are you asking about my parents' old agency?"

No reason to pull punches. "You know why."

"Pardon?"

"Your working here," I say, spreading my arms. "It's almost too on the nose, don't you think?"

The Abeona Shelter is an international organization that rescues children from danger. Abeona was the child-protecting Roman Goddess of safe returns, ergo the name of this place. The charity does a lot of good work, from what I'm told.

"What do you mean," Jennifer asks, squinting, "by 'too on the nose'?"

"I mean that your parents were involved in child trafficking. You felt guilty about it, which is understandable. You wanted to make amends. And now you work here."

She looks stunned. But I can also see I struck gold.

"You're not much for beating around the bush," Jennifer says.

"Sometimes. But not right now."

"I loved my parents," she says.

"I'm sure you did."

"They were good to me and my three siblings. We were

a happy family. And the vast majority of their clients—the young people who engaged the modeling agency's services—received exactly what they ordered: a modeling portfolio with professional headshots. Several of those young people became models. Many more were placed in good jobs in the entertainment and food industry."

I impatiently gesture with my hand for her to get through this and when she does, I say, "When did you find out the truth?"

But she's not ready yet. "I can show you testimonials from clients who said the Radiant Allure agency changed their lives."

"I'm sure you can. Doesn't make up for it though, does it?"

Silence.

"How did you find out?" I ask again.

"My mom," Jennifer says. "On her deathbed." Her eyes are on my face, but they are looking way past me. "She wanted me to understand. It was a tiny percentage of the teens, she told me. She and Dad only did it to the most hopeless cases—the kids who had nothing and no chance. And the profit from these interactions helped the Radiant Allure agency help other young people, ones who could be reached. 'You can only tend the garden you can reach,' Mom liked to say—it's an old Buddhist expression, I think—and these girls could not be reached." She looks up at me. "I loved my mother with all my heart, and the last thing I said to her on her deathbed was that I would never forgive her."

We both stop now. The silence is pushing against the walls

and windows. I let it. So does she. Part of me wants to reach out a comforting hand. I try to do that with a gaze instead. She seems to get it and gives me the smallest nod. Then she gestures for me to sit. I do. She takes the chair across from me.

"So yes," Jennifer Schultz says, "I work here to make amends. It's obvious and clumsy and inadequate."

"But it's something," I finish for her.

"Yes. Who are you looking for?"

"She went by the name Anna Marigold. She was sent to Spain."

"When?"

"Early 2000s."

"A long time ago," Jennifer Schultz says. A pendant of a butterfly hangs from a gold chain around her neck. She reaches for it now. "Funny. I kept waiting for someone to come to me like this, someone who lost a loved one they cared deeply about—or at least, someone that was missed. But you're the first. Are you a relative?"

"No."

"So maybe my mom was right."

We both know she wasn't, so neither one of us has to say it.

"What else do you know about the girl?"

I tell her most of what I learned from Harm Bergkamp. She takes notes. I tell her about Anna Marigold coming from somewhere near Penn State and the dead mother and then living with the aunt. I tell her how she worked cons with another man in Spain. Jennifer nods along as she scribbles. The story is not an unfamiliar one to her, I guess.

I don't tell her that I was one of Anna Marigold's "victims." I don't want her to think my motives are anything but pure.

"Do you know if this Anna Marigold is still alive?" Jennifer Schultz asks me.

"She is."

Jennifer Schultz fiddles with the butterfly pendant like prayer beads. "Is she okay?"

"Yes."

"But she has questions about her past."

"Something like that," I say.

"I have a private database, but it's huge. Do you know how the Radiant Allure agency operated?"

"Tell me."

"Our agency mostly worked out of kiosks in malls. Young girls would walk by—boys too—and we'd approach them and say that they were attractive and had a great look and maybe they should consider modeling. Really lay it on thick with the false flattery. Then we would try to sell them a modeling port-folio. Basically a photo shoot. Some people called it a scam, but our prices were competitive and hey, we weren't the first business to sell a dream."

"Did you work in the agency?"

"Yep. All four of us kids did. It was our after-school job. Good training for life. The agency had kiosks in dozens of malls throughout Pennsylvania and Ohio."

"You said you have a private database."

"Yes. I can't make it public for privacy reasons. It would

lead to many false claims and lawsuits. Do you have a photo of what Anna looked like back then?"

I realize that I don't. There are still a few grainy photos of Victoria Belmond from that time period, so I google them. Not many. I see Anna in Victoria's face, especially the eyes, but that might be mind games. I find the few photos taken right after Victoria was found, the paparazzi ones with no hair and shot from a distance because the FBI and her parents protected her privacy—these are slightly more accurate. Jennifer Schultz tells me to AirDrop them to her. I hesitate.

"Can I trust you keep her identity a secret?" I ask.

"Of course."

I AirDrop the best photo. She studies it on her phone. I don't say Victoria Belmond's name, and I can't tell whether she's figured it out.

"I have a team working with me," I say to her. "They can do AI on this photograph and put hair on her head and de-age her, maybe clean up the image a little."

"That might help," Jennifer says. Then she looks up at me. "What's going on, Mr. Kierce?"

"I have a tougher question for you," I say.

She waits.

"Could your parents have been involved in a kidnapping?"

She blinks. Then she says, "In what way?"

"I don't know. The obvious, for one—would they ever just kidnap a girl?"

"It would be easy for me to say, 'Of course not,' but . . . "

She doesn't finish the thought. She doesn't have to. "I don't think so. They needed the self-justification, I think."

"Did your parents ever help move someone?"

"Move someone?"

"Like maybe someone brought your parents a girl to hide overseas?"

She frowns. "You think someone brought my parents this girl so they could hide her in Spain?"

"Maybe. I don't know."

"Okay then." Jennifer places both hands on the table and pushes herself to a standing position. "I'll start going through the database. Oh, and a more innocent possibility, Mr. Kierce."

I turn.

"The girl you're looking into—you think she was kidnapped."

"Probably."

"But there are many who don't believe that, right? I mean, a lot of people think Victoria Belmond just ran away."

Ah. So she does recognize the image in the photo.

"That's right, isn't it?" she presses.

"Yes."

"So maybe that's how my parents got involved," she says.

"How do you mean?"

"If Victoria Belmond wanted to run away and never be found," Jennifer Schultz says, "my parents would be the best at making that happen."

———

300

Still mulling over Jennifer Schultz's last words, my phone vibrates. The caller ID reads BELMOND, so I pick it up.

"Hello?"

"Lenore said you wanted to talk to me." It's Victoria.

"Could we meet?" I ask.

"Is everything okay?"

"I was in Spain."

Silence.

"Victoria?"

"I'm here," she says. "You found something?"

"I can come out to you."

"No. My parents will ask a lot of questions. I'll come to you."

26

The children's playground is built on top of a cemetery. James J. Walker Park is in Greenwich Village on Hudson Street between St. Luke's Place and Clarkson Street on top of what used to be aptly and not subtly called St. John's Burying Ground. Even now, something like ten thousand corpses lie beneath the baseball diamond, the pickleball courts, the bocce courts, the children's playground—and even the bench where I now sit with Victoria Belmond.

The only visible remnant of the park's macabre past is the Firemen's Memorial, a nearly seven-foot-high marble sarcophagus dedicated in 1834 to two very young firemen who died their very first day on the job. According to the memorial's epithet, "Here are interred the bodies of Eugene Underhill, aged 20 years 7 months and 9 days, and Frederick A. Ward, aged 22 years 1 month and 16 days"—meaning that their remains are still in this sarcophagus sitting on a fence against a kids' baseball field. For those who need an additional reminder, the bronze plaque, which I always read no matter how often I come here, reads:

> THIS GROUND WAS USED AS A CEMETERY BY
> TRINITY PARISH DURING THE YEARS 1834–1898.
> IT WAS MADE A PUBLIC PARK BY THE CITY OF
> NEW YORK IN THE YEAR 1897–8. THIS MONUMENT
> STOOD IN THE CEMETERY AND WAS REMOVED TO
> THIS SPOT IN THE YEAR 1898.

Welcome to New York.

Lots of benches in New York City are sponsored—that is, someone donates money and gets a little plaque on the backrest—and this one is dedicated to someone with the last name Madoff. I don't want to know more. Victoria and I sit no more than ten yards from the monument. Behind us, children are squealing on slides and climbing bars. In front of us, through the chain-link fence, little kids are shagging grounders and fielding pop-ups with enthusiasm and chatter. I like watching baseball. I think it's the nostalgic echo. I see a field and I still remember the first time my father took me to a game at Shea Stadium when I was six. I still remember the smell of the grass and the echo when a small white ball connected with the wood of a bat. My dad bought me two pennants that day, one for the Mets, one for the visiting Houston Astros. "Because you should respect your opponent," he explained. When I got home, I hung those pennants on my wall over my bed. As I aged, the colors faded, but I kept them on that bedroom wall until I came back from Spain and rid my room of all childish things.

I didn't throw the pennants away, by the way. They are stored in a box in the basement. Make of that what you will.

Victoria and I haven't started talking yet. A coach hits ground balls to three boys at shortstop. They take turns fielding the ball and throwing it to first base. There is a joyous and Zen routine to this, and for a few moments we just bask in this swaying back-and-forth.

"I didn't know you were going to Spain," Victoria says. "I guess I should have guessed."

I wait. The coach hits a grounder. The tallest of the shortstops scoops it up as though there's a giant magnet in his glove and throws the ball to the first baseman.

"What did you find?" she asks.

"Enough."

We keep our eyes on the baseball diamond.

"I found out how I was scammed. I found out you did it to others. I found out you eventually crossed the wrong people. And I found Buzz."

That gets her attention. "You found him?"

"Yes."

"Where is he?"

"Nashville."

"Tennessee?"

I nod.

She turns away, so I can't see her face.

I say, "You didn't know where he was, did you?"

It takes her a second. "No, of course not."

"No, I mean . . ." I stop, try again. "Your father had me sign an NDA. You know that, right?"

"Yes."

"I wouldn't betray your trust anyway," I say. "But even if I wanted to, I couldn't. Legally, I mean."

"I don't know what you're talking about."

"Yeah, you do," I say. "Buzz told me when you two ran your scams on naïve tourists, it usually lasted a day or two. Get in, get out, move on to the next mark. But you took longer with me. You kept stalling. I don't know whether Buzz was full of shit or not, but he thought that you had genuine feelings for me."

She still won't face me.

"You remember me," I say.

I lean forward now, so I can see her profile. Her eyes are squeezed shut.

"Victoria?"

Her eyes stay closed.

"Please," I say. "For my sake, if not yours." I turn my body toward hers. My hands are shaking. "You remember me, don't you?"

And then she finally says it. "Yes."

I almost ask her to say it again, but I don't want to slow the momentum. "You remember Buzz too."

"How is he?"

"He's okay."

"What's he doing?"

"He works in film."

She smiles now. "He loved films. We watched so many together and he would talk about how it was lit and the special effects. He was always testing that stuff. That's why he wanted to go big when we faked a death—show his skills. But I shouldn't have let him do that to you."

"You did that to others?"

"Yes. But they were nasty, little boys. I didn't feel sorry for them at all. They ran and never looked back. But you . . . I knew what we did would haunt you. I'm so sorry."

I don't know what to say to that. I wait. I want to see what she will say next.

"And Harm wasn't lying, Sami. I did fall for you. He saw it before I did, I think. You were like this beacon of goodness in all this dark. I wasn't worthy of it, but at least I could bask in it a little while. You know? You'd smile at me, and it felt like all the bad would go away. Like we could be happy. It was almost cruel. Being with you. You were everything I wanted, so yes, I kept making excuses, even though I knew it wouldn't last. But I never forgot you. Or how I felt. Or what I did to you. And when I saw your photo on the news, when I looked you up and realized you hadn't become a doctor like you said and so much had gone wrong, that's why I came to see you. To let you know you hadn't killed anyone. To let you know it was all okay and that I was sorry for what I'd done to that wonderful, sweet boy."

Her words pummel me. They are supposed to be kind, but

I don't deserve them. She was right there, right in front of me, suffering, in trouble, and was I able to see or help?

"So why did you run?"

"When you saw me, I panicked. I knew that you recognized me. So you'd know I was alive and nothing bad happened that night. And I just . . ." She shakes her head. "It's not just about you and me, is it, Sami?"

"What do you mean?"

She shakes her head again.

"Did you ever have amnesia?" I ask.

"I want you to promise me something first."

"What?"

"Because it's not so black-and-white. What happened. Some of it is real and some of it is not. But the important things? The things that really matter? Those are real."

I have no idea what she's talking about, so I nod to keep her talking.

"They are such good, decent people, my family. What happened, all those years of torment, it haunts them. They were so hurt, and now I need to protect them. Do you understand?"

"No, not really."

"You sense it, don't you?"

"Sense what?"

"That they are kind. That they've been hurt and damaged, but when you strip away all the money and trappings, you can see their goodness."

I think about it because it seems to mean so much to her. "I guess I do."

HARLAN COBEN

"And I love them with all my heart, Kierce. Mom, Dad, Thomas, Maddy, my nieces—especially my nieces. I love them. And I love my life. You need to understand that."

"Okay," I say, just to say something because I don't know what she's getting at. "So what happened on New Year's Eve? How did you end up in Spain?"

"Promise me first."

"Promise you what?"

"That you won't hurt them. That you'll protect them."

"Protect them from what?" Then seeing that isn't going to get me anywhere, I go for the surrender: "I promise. I'll protect them."

"How did Harm end up in Nashville?"

"I don't really know. He said something about you guys scamming the wrong guy. Do you remember that?"

"Yeah," she says. "He's the one who beat me."

"The broken nose and shattered cheekbone," I say.

She nods.

"Buzz said you both ran after he got released. But they caught him. He walks with a limp now."

She closes her eyes again. "We were both damaged goods, Harm and me. I know we were con artists, but when you're in it, it doesn't seem so bad. You see some brat flashing money at a ritzy resort. So you take some. What's the big deal? And Harm—I'm so glad he's okay."

"He said the same thing about you."

"Wait. So he knows . . . ?"

308

"He does now, yeah. He said to tell you that if you ever need him, he'd be there."

It is then, right then, before she or I say another word, I see her eyes look past me and widen in shock. And then everything goes wrong. I don't know if I heard the gunshot first or if I felt the hot bullet on my shoulder, a searing, blistering pain as it tore the skin. And I wonder now, as I wondered then, at the very moment, if the bullet had been a centimeter lower, if that first bullet had hit my shoulder bone in full instead of skimming the top, if that would have stopped the bullet or slowed it down enough so that it wouldn't have continued and hit Victoria on the side of her neck.

Blood spurts from her artery.

She slumps down like someone has ripped all the bones from her body. I jump toward her. A cacophony of screams thrums in my ears. I reach out and grasp her neck, clasping my hand over her wound. At a distance it probably looks like I'm choking her. Her blood pours through my fingers, coating my hand. I grip tighter.

That's when the second bullet hits me.

This one isn't a skim. I try to fight through it, try to hold on to her neck, but it feels as though a giant hand has smacked me on the back. My entire body jerks forward, my head landing on the corner of the bench. I blink and try to fight it off. But I can't anymore. I am lost.

And then there is blackness.

They bury Victoria Belmond five days later.

I stand by a tree, in the distance, my arm in a sling, still somewhat high on the opioids.

Turns out one of those baseball coaches hitting grounders in the park was an ER doctor named Ken Liss. Once he was sure that his kids were down and safe, once everyone seemed certain that the shooter had run off, Liss hurried over to Victoria Belmond, but there was nothing to be done. For my part, I was flat on my back, my eyes blinking into the sun, nearly floating in a thick pool of blood, very little of which, it turns out, was my own.

She bled out lying next to me.

Some would find poignancy or karma in that, my blinking into the sunlight once again, lying next to her dead body twenty-two years after she pretended something similar. But I am not one of them. I have been through my share of tragedies and the truth is each one gets a little easier. The first cut is indeed the deepest. You mourn so deeply, and when that wound is finally healed the scar tissue is so thick and protective that you can never quite get there again. You won't let yourself. And so right now, as I watch the private family burial, I don't cry.

But this death is crushing me.

Victoria/Anna was only forty-two years old. And now she is dead.

That's pretty much the sum of it.

The second bullet hit me in the back near my upper shoulder. It was never life-threatening, but the throbbing pain seems to never quiet. It will take a while to heal, maybe months or even a year before I'm all the way back. The doctors did not want me to come today, but I have to be here. There is a certain momentum to everything in life. I am near the end, close to having all the answers, and I've lost a few steps now.

I can't waste more time.

I had visitors at the hospital. Molly, of course. My dad. Arthur spent more time with me, in part making sure that even if the Belmonds may want to terminate my employment, I get all monies due. In fact, Arthur wants to insist that I get extra cash, some kind of workman's comp for suffering an injury on the job. I tell him to let that go. The Belmonds have lost a daughter. Twice, in a sense. Their loss is unfathomable. I can see it now in their thousand-yard stares. They spent eleven years in the dark thinking she was gone forever. They got a reprieve, a miracle, and now, fourteen years later, when everything seemed pretty damn good, grief has thrown them back into that bottomless, dark pit.

From this distance, I can see and even feel the devastation. Archie, Talia, Tom, Madeline, Vicki, Stacy—they all have the grief-stricken faces of someone surprise-punched in the gut. Talia and Archie are leaning on one another—literally, that is—and I keep looking for the poignant or meaningful when there is nothing.

The casket is lowered. Talia Belmond's knees buckle. Archie, fighting off his own collapse, holds her up. Thomas steps forward first. He throws ceremonial dirt on top of the casket. Archie half carries Talia toward the recently dug hole. They both do the same. Archie keeps his eyes on the casket. The sadness emanating off him almost makes me take a step back. He raises his eyes and meets my gaze. I try to hold it, try to offer up something like sorrow or regret.

Archie signals for Thomas to help his mother. Thomas takes her arm, and Archie trudges toward where I'm standing alone. I brace myself, not sure what he is going to say or do. As he walks toward me, I remember Victoria's last words—her last request.

That I protect them.

When Archie reaches me, I say the obvious: "I'm so sorry."

"Thank you," he says. He gestures toward my sling. "How are you?"

"I'll be fine."

Archie looks up and blinks into the sky. "We don't blame you," he says. "I want you to know that. And yet . . ."

I stay silent.

"I don't understand any of this," he says. "What sort of danger did you bring to our lives?"

The pain in his voice almost makes me recoil, but I fight it off. He doesn't mean to hurt me here. He genuinely doesn't get it, but then again neither do I.

"I shouldn't have hired you. I should have just let it be. But I tried to control it instead. And you can't. Not back then. Not now." His eyes meet mine. "I blame myself. I killed her by stirring this all up."

It's not true, but it won't do any good to tell him that.

"Mr. Belmond," I say, clearing my throat. "We still need to find her kidnapper."

He looks lost. "What?"

"It could be connected—"

"Don't the police think the man you got released from prison did it?"

That is the most common theory right now—that I was the intended target, not her. According to Marty, the police are investigating the possibility that Tad Grayson wanted revenge on me and that Victoria was just an innocent bystander.

Made sense.

"The police dragged Tad Grayson in for questioning, but his lawyer, Kelly something—"

"Neumeier," I say.

"Right, whatever. She came with him. She asked the police what hard evidence they had tying her client to the shooting. When no one had a decent answer other than this revenge motive, she smiled and said, 'Come on, Tad. Let's get you back to your mother.'"

"Yes," I say. "And that's a strong possibility. But before she died, Victoria told me some things you should know."

"Like what?"

"I don't know if now is the right time—"

"Don't start with that," Archie snaps. "What did she say?"

I let loose a deep breath. "That she remembered Spain. That she remembered me—"

"Hold up. Are you saying her memory returned?"

I don't know how to word this to a grieving father, so I just spit it out. "I think she always remembered."

I expect this to shock him, but I don't see that here. Then again, he's grieving and numb and maybe nothing can shock him anymore.

"What else did she say?" he asks.

"That she loved her family more than anything," I reply. "That you were all kind and decent. She made me promise to protect you."

His eyes close. A moan escapes his lips. I should let it go, but I can't.

"What did she mean by that?"

He doesn't reply. I press a bit more.

"Protect you from what, Mr. Belmond?" I ask. "What do you need protection from?"

Archie Belmond takes a step back. "I don't know," he says, his voice strained now but no longer just from grief. There is something else there, but I can't put my finger on what it is. "But it's over now. Do you hear me? Please let us be."

He doesn't wait for a reply. He turns then and walks away. I stay where I am. Soon the silence is shattered by leaf blowers and lawn mowers and the whir of the yellow backhoe tractor as it covers her casket with the remaining pile of dirt. My shoulder is throbbing. I don't care. I'm in mourning too, I guess, though it's a very different version from anything I've experienced before. I am not a religious man, but I do my versions of a prayer. It is mostly asking the dead what my next step should be. There is no answer, of course. I didn't expect one.

I reach into my pocket, shake out a pain pill, and swallow it. I don't have to worry about operating a vehicle. Craig dropped me off with my own car. He ran to some Price Club to stock up on items and he's on his way back now. I turn to head toward the parking lot where he'll be waiting for me. That's when I realize that Talia Belmond is standing behind me.

"They think she was hit by a bullet intended for you," she says to me.

I say nothing.

"Do you think that's true?"

"It's the most likely theory," I say.

"But not definitive?"

"No. Not definitive."

Talia Belmond looks toward where I'd been standing with Archie Belmond minutes earlier. "What did my husband tell you?"

"To let it go."

"That's understandable. He means well." Then she turns and starts toward the black car. "But don't listen to him."

27

I go back to the hospital under one condition—that the doctors allow my students to visit. The hospital rules are only four visitors at a time, so Polly, Gary, Lenny, and Debbie are allowed in the room. The rest, I'm told, are waiting in the lobby, though the staff strongly requested (demanded?) that Raymond wait outside.

"They want us to rotate," Gary says. "So everyone can see you."

"I'm not sure I'm up for that," I say.

Polly steps forward. "We all chipped in and got you this."

She hands me a huge Stanley-brand mug with a straw sticking out of the top. On the side it reads:

WORLD'S BEST TEACHER

"That's really nice," I say. "Thank you."

Debbie says, "Read the other side."

"What?"

She turns the cup around. I see one word there:

NORBURY

I can't help but smile. Norbury is mentioned in one of my favorite Sherlock Holmes tales, "The Adventure of the Yellow Face." What made this story so memorable—what I taught my class—is that Sherlock Holmes messed up in his deductions here. The point: Even Sherlock is not infallible. None of us is. And at the end of this sentimental and surprisingly modern story about mixed marriages, after a shaken Holmes and Watson return to Baker Street, Sherlock tells his dearest friend:

"Watson, if it should ever strike you that I am getting a little overconfident in my powers, or giving less pains to a case than it deserves, kindly whisper 'Norbury' in my ear, and I shall be infinitely obliged to you."

"Norbury," Gary says.

"Norbury," Polly adds.

I hold up my hand before Lenny says it. "Yeah, okay, I get it."

"So now what?" Lenny asks. "Are we done with this case?"

I notice that Polly already has her laptop out. She sets it on that food table tray with the PowerPoint up.

"I guess not." I look up at their expectant faces. "What have you got?"

"We are working on various prongs involving both cases

you asked us about. For the sake of simplicity, we will call one case the Victoria Belmond Case and the other the Tad Grayson Case."

"I wanted us to call it the Nicole Brett Case," Lenny says. "Because that way we are naming the cases for the victims, not the perps."

"Except," Polly says, "there may be two victims now. Nicole Brett and—"

"Calling it the Tad Grayson case is fine," I say. "Let's not get mired in semantics. What do you want to show me?"

"We are still tracking down the man who was following your wife, the one you refer to as Scraggly Dude. We have a theory now, based on what you told us, and have engaged Detective Marty McGreggor in helping us with this."

"My old partner?"

"Former," Polly says in her teacher voice. "Not old."

I bit back the sigh. "How did you meet Marty?"

"Downstairs that day you were shot. He was visiting too. We were in the lobby."

"Good-looking guy," Lenny says.

"You guys came the day I was shot?"

"Of course."

I look at them. "I should be touched," I say, "but oddly, I'm not."

Gary spreads his hands. "None of us has much of a life, so . . ."

"Speak for yourself," Polly snaps but she's smiling as she does. She clears her throat and puts on the business voice.

"We are coordinating with Jennifer Schultz and her Radiant Allure agency database. But nothing so far. Our theory right now is that the woman Victoria Belmond used the agency as a cover story, but you never know."

That theory is wrong, but I let it go for now. "Okay," I say.

"Get to it," Gary says with a sigh. "This is what she does. She draws everything out like she's the final chapter of an Agatha Christie novel."

"I do not," Polly says. "Everything is in context."

"Just tell him already."

"Fine." Polly sighs. "We tried to create a list of Victoria Belmond's high school friends who might have been at the party. We got six names from the FBI files via Detective Marty McGreggor. None of them would talk to us. But we were able to get school records and yearbooks. We cross-checked through them to see possible attendees. For example, Victoria Belmond was in the French club and on the field hockey team. So anybody who was on both of those were likely to have been at the New Year's Eve party. Using a pretty simple software program, we could figure out who would have been Victoria's close friends and likely to have gone to that party."

They all look at me.

"Okay."

"We also—I don't know how to put this or even why we did this. It was Debbie's idea. But we also put into the equation your cases from your time on the police force."

I frown. "My cases?"

"Yes."

"Why?"

Debbie says, "Because you're linked into this, Kierce."

I look over at her.

"Victoria Belmond vanishes," Debbie says. "You're the only one who sees her in eleven years."

"We all figured it would go nowhere," Gary adds.

"Even me, to be honest," Debbie says.

The hospital room is far too warm and clammy, but I still feel the chill. "So?"

"So the last case before you left the force was the murder at Farnwood, an estate owned by the Burkett family."

"Right."

And even before Polly says it, I flash back to my conversation with Thomas Belmond, to what he told me about driving his sister to that New Year's Eve party.

"I drove Vic to that party. She and one of her friends— Caroline, I think . . . "

Caroline . . .

Polly is nodding as though she can read my mind. "Victoria Belmond's best friend in high school," she says, "was Caroline Burkett."

———

I will skip the part where my doctors remind me that I had promised not to leave the hospital again if they gave me permission to go to Victoria Belmond's funeral.

Marty rushes me to Farnwood, the uber-opulent Burkett

estate made notorious by the murder that the entire world witnessed. There is an old man at the gate. He scowls at us, but he hits the button. The gates creak open so slowly it's hard to see it move with the naked eye. We head up the drive, past a tennis court, past a soccer pitch. The house itself is a nineteenth-century English country home with Gothic elements like gargoyles and mullioned windows. It is built with Elizabethan red brick, perfectly symmetrical with turreted Tudor-style wings.

Standing there, dead center as though working the symmetrical lines, is the formidable figure of Judith Burkett. She is nearly eighty, but she still commands your attention. Her posture is ramrod pure, her head high. You can sense her elegance and charisma because she has both in droves, but I know that it's all in the pursuit of evil. When we stop, she moves toward the car as though she is on a runway. She smiles at me. The glamour is still there. Her eyes are still steely.

"Mr. Kierce," she says, stressing the word *Mister* because last time we met, she knew me as *Detective*, and she undeniably wants to rub my downfall in my face. "Delighted to see you again."

She holds out her hand, and I hesitantly shake it. She senses my discomfort, so she tightens her grip and makes me be the one to pull away. I want to say something or do something, including punching an old woman in the face, but I need information from her.

Marty gets out of the car too. He was the one who set up this meeting. He seemed surprised that Judith Burkett agreed to see me. I was not. Some people avoid confrontation. Some relish it. I'd figured that she wouldn't be able to resist.

Judith Burkett smiles at Marty and says, "Detective McGreggor, is it?"

"Yes, ma'am."

Ma'am. I want to slap him.

"I'd like you to wait down by the gate please."

She dismisses Marty with a nod and gestures for me to follow her. We head inside the foyer. You expect the décor to be antique-y, and while it is lavish enough to reflect the family's wealth and former status, there are a lot of modern touches in the carpeting and upholstery. We stop in front of the enormous family portrait—Judith, her husband Joseph, and their four children—Andrew, Joe, Caroline, and Neil. Everyone is looking forward except for Andrew because when the painting was created, he was already dead. Now Joseph Senior is dead. Joe Junior too is dead. Shot in Central Park. Judith stops and stares up at the portrait and waits for me to speak.

"I would like to talk to Caroline," I say.

"Caroline," she replies, "isn't here."

"When will she be home?"

Still staring at the portrait, Judith smiles. "I can't say for sure, I'm afraid. But not soon." She finally turns away from the portrait. "I'm told you want information on Victoria Belmond. Isn't that why you're here?"

"Yes."

"Such a tragedy. The poor girl survives such a long, cruel

ordeal only to get caught in street fire meant for someone else." She tsk-tsks. "Our families used to be very close. Did you know that?"

"I knew Caroline and Victoria were friends."

"Best friends," Judith adds.

She smiles again. It kills me that so many died or were made sick to pay for this grand house and this tacky portrait—that this odious woman is allowed to enjoy these lavish grounds and breathe this fine air and smile like she is doing right now.

But I hold my tongue. "That's why I'd like to talk to Caroline," I say instead.

"I don't really understand," Judith says with an exaggerated tilt of her head. "What could Caroline tell you about Victoria's death? Wasn't the shooter aiming for you?"

"We don't know for sure."

"But surely you can't think someone wanted to kill Victoria."

"Someone kidnapped her. Someone held her for eleven years. We are digging into that too."

"And you think that led to her death?"

"I don't know," I say. "It's possible. Either way, she should have justice for what was done to her."

"After her death?" Judith playfully arches an eyebrow. "Do you think the kidnapper matters to the dead?"

"I'm not deep enough for such meanderings," I say, "but at worst, it could stop someone from doing it again."

"That's true, I suppose."

"The night Victoria disappeared," I say, trying to get us back on track, "there was a New Millennium party at McCabe's Pub."

"I'm well aware."

"And Caroline was there."

"Of course. In fact, Caroline cohosted with Victoria."

"Where is Caroline?" I ask again.

She spins back toward the portrait. Now her eyes land on her only daughter. "Are you familiar with the Solemani Recovery Center?"

I am. It's a very high-end, exclusive rehab center. "That's where she is?"

Judith nods. "I'll inform them of your visit, so they can—" she pauses as though thinking of the right word "—prepare Caroline. Will tomorrow morning work for you?"

"Any chance I could see her today?"

A tight smile now. "I'm afraid not, no."

"Is Caroline okay?"

Judith bites down on her lower lip. "I'm not sure she is ready for visitors, but if it will help the Belmonds, we are both more than willing to cooperate."

"I appreciate that," I say, spitting nails.

We stand there. She is taller and so moves closer, but I'm used to that. She can't intimidate me that way.

"I'll be on my way," I say.

"Did you know that I used to see Talia Belmond?" Judith says to me, and there is something teasing in her voice. "Professionally speaking, I mean."

I didn't expect that. "You were Talia's therapist?"

324

"Her doctor, yes. After her daughter vanished, well, you can imagine. I can't say very much about our sessions, of course."

"But she started seeing you after Victoria disappeared? Talia Belmond, I mean."

"Yes. She had severe trouble dealing with the trauma"— Judith flashes her razor-sharp smile at me—"and of course, the guilt."

She waits for me to prompt her. I play my part.

"The guilt," I say.

"Yes."

"Because she didn't report her daughter was missing right away," I say. "Because she was away that night."

"Not just away," Judith says. The teasing is back. She's enjoying this. Part of me wants to strangle her, but most of me is just weary of the injustice of it all.

I give the expected line as though I've overrehearsed it. "What do you mean, not just away?"

Judith is suddenly coy. "I really shouldn't say more. Patient-client confidentiality."

"Talia Belmond was in Chicago that night."

"That's true, yes."

"Her father was dying."

"Also true."

"Then?"

"The Belmonds are new money. You probably know that. When they first became wealthy, my husband and I welcomed them into our circle. Many did not. We got Talia on the board of the philharmonic. Made sure that she and Archie were allowed into the right clubs. I hosted them in this very house. Our children became close. Thomas used to play soccer on that pitch with Andrew and Joe. Victoria and Caroline were inseparable. When Victoria vanished, Caroline too suffered severe trauma. You can imagine. Her best friend walks out of a party they're cohosting—and never returns. And when Talia Belmond was at her lowest, when she needed professional help to deal with her daughter's kidnapping, I was there for her—first as her friend, and then as her doctor."

She turns again and stares at that damn painting.

"And yet when we Burketts had our troubles, when the accusations around my family started to swirl, Talia Belmond never reached out to me. Never called. Never sent a note to see how we were doing. So do I owe Talia Belmond loyalty? I don't think so."

I wait. She is making the argument for me. It's a stupid, nonsensical argument, but so be it. There is no reason to push when she was already doing all the pushing.

"Before I say anything else, I have a question for you, Mr. Kierce."

"Okay."

"Have you seen my granddaughter?"

She is talking about Lilly. Lilly is four years old now.

"No," I say.

This is a lie.

I see Lilly a lot. I'm still in her life—and always will be if it's up to me. I have made a vow to protect Lilly from monsters.

Monsters like her grandmother.

326

I see Judith Burkett's eyes well up. "Is that the truth?" she asks. "You haven't seen Lilly?"

I have no qualms about lying to her. "I haven't seen her, no."

She turns and studies my face. I don't know whether she sees the lie or not. I don't really care one way or the other.

"She was meeting a man," Judith Burkett says. "In Chicago."

I feel a rushing in my head. I know what she means. I understand the implication. But I still mutter, almost against my will: "What?"

"Talia Belmond," Judith says, turning back to the portrait. "She wasn't just going to Chicago to see her sick father. Talia was meeting a man. That's why she wasn't focused on their daughter. And that's why she still blames herself for what happened that night to Victoria."

28

"Give me the keys," I tell Marty.

"What?"

"Just give them to me please."

"But you're a terrible driver. And you're recovering from a bullet wound."

My hand is out, palm up. He reluctantly drops the keys into it. I get in the driver's side. He takes the passenger seat.

"What happened?" Marty asks. "What did she say?"

I shake him off. Not now. It's not time to talk it out yet.

I can't drive away from Farnwood fast enough. It is almost as though the ghosts are chasing me away. I am trying to process what I learned. Judith could be lying, of course. She is manipulative and vindictive, but the thing is, she is also highly self-interested. There is a method to her madness usually, and making up this story just to . . . I don't know . . . make it harder for me to figure out the case or to toy with me doesn't seem enough. She is cruel enough, of course, but for her, cruelty serves a purpose.

Her accusation also has the ring of truth.

I don't bother calling ahead. I just find myself reaching another stupid rich-people's gate in front of the driveway. I give my name to the guard. It's someone who wasn't here last time I was, so he's looking at me and my crappy car like I just dropped dog feces on their lawn. That infuriates me. Bad enough when the rich look down upon you, but why are the people they hire—people no wealthier than you—even worse? Like they're snobby by proxy. That infuriates me too. Everything infuriates me. The stupid gate, as I wait for the guard to call up to the house, infuriates me. I want to hit the accelerator and crash through it.

"Marty?"

"What?"

"Do you mind staying down here?"

"Seriously?"

I look at him. He sighs and gets out as the guard finally opens the stupid gate. I drive up to the house, but as I do, as I get closer, I slow my roll.

Their daughter is dead.

It might even be my fault.

Probably was. No matter how you sliced it. If the bullet was meant for me, well, that's the obvious way. But if it wasn't, if my investigation had somehow awakened the past, then it is still on me.

Perhaps that explains my fury. I'm redirecting it. I'm not furious with the gate. I am furious with myself. As I see the house rise before me, I flash back to when I first trudged through those woods in search of Anna Marigold, the old ghost from my past, and since that first day, I've had so many theories swirling in my head, so many attempts at trying to figure out the truth, that I've come to realize that the only thing I know is that I can't trust anyone or anything. I am not a paranoid sort, and that's not what I'm feeling now, but this is akin to paranoia, I guess, a feeling that reality is perhaps conspiring against clarity.

Archie and Talia are both at the door when I arrive, standing side by side. When I park, Archie steps in front of his wife as though offering protection and says, "I told you this was over."

"I know," I say, as I move toward them, pointing my chin toward Talia, "but she told me to stay on it."

Archie turns to his wife with surprise. "Talia?"

"Someone took her from us," she says.

"The police are investigating—"

"I'm not talking about now. I'm talking about then. It changed the course of her life. Don't you see? If she wasn't kidnapped, her life would have been completely different. She would have never met Kierce. She wouldn't have been in the park with him. She'd be alive."

"Talia—"

"I don't want to let this go," she pleads. "I want to know what happened to our daughter that night when she left the

party. Don't you? Archie? Please, don't we need to know?
Both of us?"

He opens his mouth, but for a few moments no words
come out. "I thought we put it behind us," he says, "the day
she came home."

She shakes her head. "You put it behind you."

"And you?"

"I tried to ignore it. Like I jammed it into a box in the back
of my closet. But our daughter is dead now. And I need those
answers." Talia Belmond doesn't wait for him to say more.
"Have you learned something new?"

"I need to talk to you," I say to her. "Alone."

"No," she says.

"Mrs. Belmond—"

"Talia," she says, correcting me. "And you can say whatever
you need to with Archie here."

"I was just with Judith Burkett," I say. "I think it is better
if we talk alone."

But even as I say it, I can tell that won't be necessary. Their
faces say it all. They both know. They both know what Judith
Burkett told me. Without conscious thought, or so it seems,
they take each other's hand. I can't say who initiated it or if
they both just moved at the same time. But there they are,
standing together, ready to face me as one.

"It's not better alone," Talia says.

They stand there, steadying themselves as though they
are standing on the beach awaiting a wave that they know
will sweep them away. I flash back to Anna's last request

that I protect them, and I want to tell her that I don't know how.

"Judith told you why I went to Chicago," Talia says.

Again I've learned to use silence. I simply nod.

Archie says, "I don't see the relevance. How long have you been married?"

"Not quite a year."

"You'll have ups and you'll have downs. Our youngest child was about to leave home for college. Empty nest syndrome. We didn't tell Thomas or Victoria, but we had decided on a trial separation. It wasn't for us—we realized that pretty fast. In the end I think it made our marriage stronger."

Did it? I wonder. I don't say this out loud.

"I didn't go through with it," Talia says. "I might have. I was still in the lobby, almost five in the morning, trying to work up the courage to go to his room. I kept crying. And suddenly Archie was there. He wasn't supposed to come. He was supposed to stay home. But, I don't know, maybe he sensed something. Either way he stopped me from making a huge mistake. His arrival felt like a blessing, like we'd been saved."

I see Archie shut his eyes as she speaks as though warding off blows.

"We talked that whole next day. And the day after. We saw that we were both still in love with one another. We saved our marriage and came home in the best place we'd been in in years."

And, I think to myself, you took your eye off the ball. Again, no need to say it. They know. It explains a lot about their guilt. It explains why they didn't see the warning signs when their daughter didn't contact them. *Protect them*, Victoria had asked, and so I won't point out that their neglect had probably contributed to what had happened. I suspect they had already pointed it out to themselves every morning for eleven long, hard torturous years. What pain. What horror. I wonder what it must have been like to live with that kind of guilt for those eleven years, and again I think I'm starting to understand why Anna—I notice I'm going back and forth on what to call her—wanted me to protect them.

"I'm sorry to bring this up," I say.

"It has nothing to do with what happened to Victoria," Talia says a little too firmly. "It helped make us what we are today."

Which is what? I ask myself. I believe what Victoria told me. That they were happy. That they are good, decent people. But I think about it from another perspective too. Their marriage suffers a rupture. They claim that they fixed it in Chicago and maybe they did, but then the aftermath—their daughter's disappearance—had to change everything. Was the renewed marital bond based on the idea that they still loved one another—or was the bond forged in tragedy?

And does it matter?

I try to put it together. New Year's Eve 1999. Talia goes to Chicago to meet a man. Victoria leaves her party in New York City. Are they connected? Add in that Thomas drives Victoria to McCabe's Pub and then heads home to sulk. And then there's Archie, who stays behind because he was worried about Y2K—but ends up in Chicago blocking his wife's possible cheating rendezvous.

Something isn't adding up.

"Who was the man?"

"It doesn't matter," Archie says.

"It doesn't," Talia adds. "He was a college boyfriend named Steven Ricci. He moved to Miami. He died four years ago."

I look at Archie. "You were supposed to stay home that night," I say. "Because of Y2K worries."

"Yes."

"Yet you ended up taking a private flight there at, what, three, four in the morning."

"Earlier," he says quickly. Too quickly. And something starts niggling at the base of my skull.

"Why?"

"I told you. I stayed around in case there was any danger from Y2K. Once that danger had passed, I decided to join Talia."

I stand there and let the moment weigh on us. We all feel it. Something isn't adding up.

"Did you know Talia was meeting Ricci?"

He swallows hard. "No," he says. "I had no idea."

"It must have been devastating."

He lowers his head. Talia steps forward.

"Forget what I said before," she tells me. "Leave us alone."

"Do you want to fill me in?" Marty asks.

"Not yet."

Marty shifts the car into drive. "Back home then?"

"Can we make a stop first?"

"Where?"

"The cemetery."

"The one you were just at?"

"Yep."

Marty seems puzzled by the request, but he honors it.

The cemetery is a mile away from the Belmonds' estate. Marty parks and I tell him to wait, that I won't be long. I get out. The car door echoes when I close it. I weave my way through the tombstones until I find the freshly repacked earth. I didn't have a chance to do this at the funeral. It wasn't my place, what with the family asking for and getting privacy. There have been no obituaries in the paper. The funeral arrangements were kept confidential. Her murder was a news story, of course, but not as big a one as you might imagine. The world is so easily distracted by shiny new stories. We are in a constant whirlwind of scroll. Everything is a blur. Nothing is worthy of our attention for more than a day, two at the most anymore, and if the Belmond family doesn't feed the story—if nothing new happens—it will vanish from that scroll.

But I don't want that for her.

I don't mean in terms of the public. I don't care about that, and I suspect Victoria would relish the privacy. I mean in terms of me. Her death means something to me. She meant something to me. It might not have been true love, like with Molly, but that doesn't mean it wasn't something special and unique. We connected. You might think what she did to me in Spain was unforgivable or you might think she was a victim of horrible circumstances or you might land in the middle. I don't care about any of that. Right now, I am thinking about that first dance in Spain and twenty-two years later, being with her when she gasped her final breath in New York City. So I want to acknowledge all that. That she mattered to me too. I want to pay my respects. I want to do right by her.

By us.

So I sit on the grass next to the freshly packed dirt. I reach out and put my hand on top of where her remains lie. I am sorting through it all, for her sake, and I realize that everyone connected to this is lying to me. I don't know why yet. But I'm not fully buying the story about why Archie Belmond ended up in Chicago. I think about the Belmonds, all of them, and I think about how the trajectory of their lives changed that New Year's Eve, and somehow, I don't think it's only because of the obvious.

A theory is starting to form. It's an ugly one. But my mind can't help but go there. I remember Sherlock's axiom, the one I put on that blackboard the very first day of class:

It is a capital mistake to theorize before one has data. Insensibly one begins to twist facts to suit theories, instead of theories to suit facts.

But there is a caveat to this. As long as you keep an open mind, it doesn't hurt to test whatever theory you've come up with. I'm not new to this case. In a sense, I've been working on it for twenty-two years. So now, in memory of the woman buried beneath me, the one who suffered and scraped and fought and made a good life for herself only for some worthless piece of shit to snuff it out, I am going to find the truth.

Or that is what I am telling myself.

Because she didn't ask me to find the truth, did she? She made it clear what she wanted from me.

"Promise me first."

"Promise you what?"

"That you won't hurt them. That you'll protect them."

So will the truth protect them? And if it won't—if it ends up the truth will hurt them—will I have to break my final promise to her?

"Kierce?" It's Marty. "You okay?"

I nod.

"Your doctor called. So did Molly. We made a deal I'd have you back by now."

Standing is hard, what with your arm in a sling. Marty comes over to help me, but I shake him off. I get up with a grimace. I brush off the dirt with one hand.

By the time we drive back to the hospital, I'm hurting pretty good, but I don't want to take another pill. Molly is there. She hugs me gently, sniffs, and says, "You need a shower."

"It's a hospital," I say. "Can't you give me a sponge bath?"

"I'm glad you're feeling better. But no. Get showered and in bed."

She helps with that. Night falls. I make her leave. She and Henry are staying with her sister because I don't want them home without me until I know it's safe. I fall asleep. Not deeply. I call it hospital sleep. It's a shallow snooze, skimming the surface of consciousness. I don't know if it's the machine's beeping or the lowered voices or just the fact that you're in this place that houses so much fear and pain. The doctor tells me I can be released the day after tomorrow, and like any rational human being I am ecstatic.

I get a text message right before I fall asleep. It's from Judith Burkett:

> Caroline will see you tomorrow at noon. Don't
> be tardy.

Tardy. Who uses the word *tardy* except when you're talking about school?

Then:

> Please don't upset her.

I hit the thumb emoji on both messages because I don't want to say anything to her. Then I pound my pillow and try to make myself comfortable. It doesn't work, but eventually the drugs do.

It is early the next morning when a whisper awakens me.

"Kierce?"

I don't move, don't even open my eyes. I recognize the voice. It's Polly.

"Gary's watching for the nurse," Polly says in the same soft whisper. "Visiting hours don't start for another three hours. But we found something we need you to see."

I blink my eyes open. I'm still groggy from the drugs. "Polly?"

"You were right about Scraggly Dude," she says.

"What?" I try to sit up. "What did you find?"

"We did what you suggested—went through all the inmates who spent any time in the past eighteen years at Sing Sing Correctional Facility. We sorted them in reverse chronological order, which is why it took so long. Naturally it was a huge job. The guy you call Scraggly Dude? He was clean-shaven back then. His hair was short too."

"But you found him?"

"Yeah. We did. His name is Brian Powell. And guess who his cellmate was for a full six months."

I knew it and yet I still can't believe it. "Tad Grayson?"

She nods.

I stand quickly. "Do you know where Powell lives?"

"In Newark. We have an address."

I roll my legs off the bed. "Help me get dressed."

29

Gary drives my old Ford Taurus. Polly sits in the front seat next to him. I'm spread out in the back. Every pothole hits me like a dagger. I close my eyes and ride it out. Polly fills me in as we drive. I text Marty and Molly that I am fine and will be back soon. I don't tell them my destination. Neither are very happy with me. They are made no happier when I inform them that I'm with my students.

"His name is Brian Powell," Polly says in that voice she must have learned watching old *Law and Order* episodes. "He's fifty-four. Been in and out of the joint since he was eighteen."

Gary frowns. "Joint?"

"What?"

"Did you really just say 'joint,' Polly?"

"I'm using common vernacular."

"Common for who? Bugsy Siegel?"

"Whom," she says.

"What?"

"Common for whom, not who—"

"Guys," I say. Then: "When was Powell in Sing Sing with Tad Grayson?"

"Nine years ago," Polly says.

"And how long has Powell been free?"

"Same answer."

"Nine years?"

"Yes."

"Long time." I think about that. "Any arrests since then?"

"Not even a parking ticket," she says, aping another line from old TV shows. "Powell got off parole in 2021. He's worked in a Price Club warehouse in Bloomfield for the past six years."

We take the Lincoln Tunnel out to Route 21 and cross over Mulberry. As we pull onto Goble Street, I see Debbie and Raymond. Raymond is wearing cotton briefs—what we used to call tighty-whities—over his jeans and a shower cap on his head.

From the backseat, I say, "Uh, what are they doing here?"

"Keeping an eye on the place," Gary says.

"Raymond?"

"He fits in," Polly says.

"So out of place he's in place, if you catch my drift," Gary adds.

I guess they have a point.

"They've been watching the block since six," Polly says.

"Six this morning?"

"Yep." Gary steers toward the curb. "If Powell left, they would have followed him. Raymond's an earlier riser. Big morning guy. Did you know that?"

We pull into the spot in front of the address. We are in the southern part of Newark's Ironbound district, about a mile from the Prudential Center where the New Jersey Devils play.

"Apartment C," Polly says. "First floor on the right."

The building is a converted two-family rectangular structure with beige aluminum siding that isn't pretending to be anything but beige aluminum siding. The architecture and design are pure no-nonsense functionality. You couldn't make the façade more conformist without traveling back in time to a 1980 East Bloc country.

Debbie and Raymond come over to me.

"See anything?" I ask.

"A total smoke show of a hottie lives across the street," Raymond informs me. "Has an ass that makes me want to open a proctology practice for one."

"Gross," Debbie says. "And she wasn't a smoke show."

"Was so," Raymond insists. He takes out his phone. "Like the great Sir Mix-A-Lot would sing, 'I wanna get with ya, and take your picture.' So I took a few. And video. Look, Kierce."

Debbie shakes her head. "She was a six."

Raymond is offended. "A six?!"

"A seven tops."

"Hey, don't go disrespecting my future ex-wife." Then to Kierce: "Smoke Show walked by an hour ago, but my heart is still beating." Raymond opens the top two buttons of his shirt. "Here, feel for yourself."

He juts out his chest toward me, which I guess is preferable to a lower alternative.

"I'm good, Raymond."

"Kierce?" he says, buttoning back up.

"What?"

Raymond leans conspiratorially closer. "Can you loan me money, you know, for a ring?"

"A ring?"

"When Smoke Show comes back, I want to propose. The ass was that ripe."

I sigh and tell everyone to stay on the other side of the street, but when I cross toward Powell's residence, Gary follows me. He is wearing his customary golf shirt, this one way too fitted so it looks like he's smuggling a bowling ball. The shirt's logo is a foot with wings on it in a color so orange Gary could double as a parking cone.

"You should have backup," Gary says in a way of explanation.

I shake my head. "All of you watch too much TV."

We get to the door. I knock. No answer. I knock again. Still no answer.

From behind us, Polly reads a message from her phone: "Powell hasn't shown up to work this week."

"How do you know?" I ask.

"We sent two of the Three Dead Hots down to the warehouse."

"Which ones?"

343

"I can't tell them apart," Polly says. "Anyway, they flirted with some workers during a smoking break."

Gary looks at me. "Should we bust the door down?"

"No, we shouldn't bust the door down."

A familiar car makes the turn and hurries down the street. It's Marty. I should be surprised, but I'm not. He pulls in front of Powell's residence, gets out, and slams the door hard to make some kind of point.

Raymond shout-whispers from across the street. "Kierce," he says, pointing at Marty. "Smoke Show is back."

Debbie rolls her eyes. "That's a man, dumbass."

Marty storms toward where I'm standing on the stoop. "What the hell, Kierce?"

"How did you find me?"

"Molly has your location on her Find My Phone."

"Oh," I say, "right."

Marty is not hiding his annoyance. "What's going on? You're supposed to be in the hospital."

"The guy who was following Molly, the one with the scraggly long hair you said we couldn't find."

Marty sighs. "I never said we couldn't—"

"He lives here. They"—I sweep my arm to indicate Gary, Polly, Debbie, and yep, Raymond—"found him."

Raymond shouts, "You're welcome, Smoke Show."

I shake my head at Raymond. He holds his hands up in apologetic surrender.

"His name is Brian Powell," I tell Marty. "And he was cellmates with Tad Grayson at Sing Sing."

Marty's eyes widen. "Wait, what?"

Gary steps forward. "There's no answer at the door, and Powell didn't show up for work."

Marty looks toward me. I turn and knock on the door again as if to confirm Gary's words. I try the knob. The door is locked. Marty steps forward and knocks on the door too. Like his knock is official and that's going to work better.

"Mr. Powell," Marty shouts. "This is the police. Please open this door."

We wait. I press my ear against the wood. Nothing.

Marty says, "This isn't my jurisdiction. Let me call the local Newark precinct and see if we can get someone over here to assist us."

"We don't have time for that," Golfer Gary says. Then he snaps his finger as though he's come up with an idea: "Besides, I hear someone inside screaming for help."

Marty looks confused. "What?"

"There it is again," he says. Gary is obviously making this up. There are no screams. There are no sounds at all. "It's an emergency. He's in trouble. Break down the door. Can't you do that when you hear someone screaming like that?"

Marty puts his hands up. "Just wait—"

"I can't," Gary says. "Not when someone is in danger."

And then without warning, Gary rears back more athletically than I would have imagined and kicks the door with his heel. The wood splinters, and the door gives way, banging open. Raymond whoops and applauds. Debbie claps too. Gary bows.

Marty and I stand there for a moment, too stunned to move, then Marty says, "Everyone wait out here." He looks hard at me. "Including you."

"Yeah no," I say to him.

Marty knows better than to push it. "Okay, but the rest of you stay out here."

"Wait," Raymond says, nudging Debbie. "That's not Smoke Show. That's a man."

Marty steps in. I follow. The lights are off. The shades are all pulled down. We move in slowly. Marty has a gun on his hip. He doesn't take it out, but he keeps his hand on it, just in case. It is hot in the apartment. The air is stale, still, heavy. It feels like we're walking through a beaded curtain.

We veer into the kitchen, but by now we both sense what we will find. You can just feel it. It isn't woo-woo and I'm sure there is an actual scientific explanation. But we both just know. It isn't so much a smell, though that's there now, as a texture, a forced stillness. You always know before you find it and actually confirm it with your eyes, as though some kind of spectral figure is tapping you on the shoulder and beckoning you to follow.

We find Brian Powell in a kitchen chair, his head flat on the table, his long hair congealed in the massive amount of blood.

———

Marty calls it in and tells me to wait outside. I listen. My students are hushed. When I'm out on the stoop, I call Arthur and fill him in. He tells me not to say a word to the police or anyone else until he arrives. I don't. I move across the street and encourage my students to leave before the police arrive. There is nothing against the law with doing that. I have their names and contact information and can provide them if necessary. They disperse, though Raymond vows to come back to woo Smoke Show.

Golfer Gary agrees to stay with me because I will need a ride up to the Solemani Recovery Center soon to see Caroline Burkett, the cohost of that now-notorious New Millennium party.

Marty looks a little piqued when he comes out. He is a good cop and a better man. He doesn't handle scenes of violence well. His empathy is not well served here. I still remember the way he looked at me after PJ fell off the roof because of my negligence. I think his disappointed face hurt me more than that police inquisition.

When Arthur arrives, he says to Marty, "Don't talk to my client. He's not answering any questions."

"It's okay," I say to Arthur. "Marty?"

"Bullet to the back of the head," Marty says.

Just like with Nicole. I take deep breaths.

"A gun was left behind. I assume it's the murder weapon. Ballistics will tell us if it's a match with the bullet we pulled out of you. We will also be coordinating this murder investigation with the Newark police. We're already looking into the obvious."

"That being?" I say, just because I want to hear him say it.

"That Tad Grayson is behind this all. That he shot you and killed Victoria Belmond and his former cellmate Brian Powell."

I check my watch. "I have to go."

"Back to the hospital?"

I shake my head. "Not quite yet."

"Kierce."

"I'm visiting Caroline Burkett. She was at the party the night Victoria Belmond was kidnapped."

"Then I'm sure the FBI spoke to her back then."

"She's a Burkett, Marty. You think Judith would have let her say anything incriminating?" I put my hand on his shoulder. "Let me do this. Then we can worry about my little flesh wound, okay?"

Marty looks at Arthur. They are both tall men, and my standing between them makes us look like a bar graph with a dip in the economy. "I know you want to play hardball," Marty says over my head, "but Kierce is going to have to give a statement."

"I know," Arthur says. "He'll give one later. With counsel present. Right now, he has someplace he has to be."

Marty lets loose a deep breath. Still looking at Arthur and over me, he says, "It's all a little too neat, don't you think?"

"What is?" Arthur asks.

"That Tad Grayson would hire his cellmate."

"I'm not following," Arthur says.

Marty shrugs. "It's just that it's pretty stupid, don't you think? If Tad Grayson is behind this all, why would he be dumb enough to hire someone we could so easily trace back to him?"

Arthur nods in agreement. "Not just someone in the same prison as him," he adds. "But his actual cellmate."

"Exactly," Marty says. "It's all just a little too convenient."

Now they both look down at me. I say nothing.

"One of my most respected colleagues represents Tad Grayson. She worked hard to get his conviction overturned. She wouldn't do that unless she truly believes someone is innocent."

They both look at me again and wait.

"I have to go," I say, and then I get in the passenger seat of Gary's car.

30

We are ten minutes into the drive when Gary says, "There is something else you need to know. It came in while we were waiting on the police."

"What?"

"Open up my iPad."

I lift it out of the slot in the console between us and turn it on. When it comes to life, I recognize the old black-and-white still frame from the CCTV video of Victoria Belmond leaving McCabe's Pub at 11:17 p.m. on December 31, 1999, the night she vanished.

"What's up?" I ask.

"So we did a deeper dive into that old video footage."

"Okay."

"I know the FBI and other investigators did too back in the day, but the world is different now. Anyway, you see Victoria on the sidewalk, right?"

"Right."

"When you hit play, you'll see the next eight seconds after Victoria Belmond walks by. That's all we have, but that's all we need. There are other people on the street, of course. I think we counted fourteen. Not a surprise. Typical New York City street on New Year's Eve. But eight seconds after Victoria walks by, you'll see another woman hurrying in the same direction. Like she's trying to catch her. Coming from the left, she's the third woman to appear after Victoria Belmond. The screen will stop on her. Go ahead. Hit play."

I do as he says and tap the play arrow with my index finger. Again the black-and-white images are blurry and shot from above and you mostly get Victoria's back. I've seen this video before, of course, but something about it is bothering me this time. I can't put my finger on it. But I don't focus on that right now—no time—and now another girl walks by, moving quickly as though, as Gary pointed out, maybe she's trying to catch up to Victoria.

The video freezes.

I squint. I use my fingers to zoom in, but that just makes the image blurrier. I can see the girl has blond hair and a ponytail, but like with Victoria Belmond, you really can't see her face.

"So," Gary continues, "like I said, there are fourteen people in this video. The Pink Panthers tried a new way to identify them."

"How?" I ask.

"They took the high school yearbook and scanned every photo of girls in the same graduating class as Victoria into some kind of new AI image search program. It's pretty beta and not precise yet, but it could tell, for example, what girls would match the general description and hairstyle."

"I assume they found a match?"

"Only one," Gary says, his eyes on the road. "Just this girl."

"So who is she?"

"According to the AI program, there's ninety-eight point seven percent likelihood that it's Caroline Burkett."

I fall back in my seat.

"Do you want to talk this out?" Gary asks.

"Not right now."

I close my eyes and try to find the connections. Victoria Belmond leaves the party she's throwing. Caroline Burkett, her cohostess, follows her.

Why?

I guess I'll have to ask her.

We get off the highway, make too many quick turns, and then we drive down a long, narrow, tree-lined street until we reach an unmarked dead end. There are no visible structures on this road. No signs either. Nothing. If you don't know where the Solemani Recovery Center is, you're not supposed to find it. It's that kind of place. We start up the small dirt drive until—yep, you guessed it—we reached a guard booth and a gate. The guard approaches Gary's car as we slow down.

"May I help you?"

I roll down my window and do the talking. "I'm here to see Caroline Burkett."

"Name?"

"Sami Kierce."

The guard saunters back to his little hut. He picks up the phone, his baleful eyes on me as if worried I might steal the silverware. A moment later, he hangs up and comes back out. "Drive up to the guest lot. It'll be on the right. Someone will meet you there."

I salute him.

The guard leans into the car. "Sir?" He is talking now to Gary.

"Yes?"

"Please do not leave the vehicle for any reason."

"Got it."

The gate is one of those arms. The guard presses a button, and the arm lifts. We start up the drive.

"Suppose I have to pee," Gary says.

"What did you do when you'd have to pee in the middle of a golf course?"

"Duck behind a tree."

"Seriously?"

"Literally, every man does it. It's almost a rite of passage."

I shake my head. "Golfers are weird."

Buildings of rain-gray stone emerge. Old buildings. Classy buildings. But you feel the solace, the refuge, the nature. If you're rich and an addict, the Solemani seems like a pretty sweet getaway.

A young woman in a golf cart is waiting for us in the guest lot. She wears a peach aviation scarf like a flight attendant.

353

"May I see your ID please?"

I hand her my driver's license. She takes out her mobile phone, snaps a pic of my ID, and hands it back to me. Then she invites me to sit with her in the cart.

"Caroline is waiting for you in Brocklehurst Hall. I'll take you there."

As we drive up the hill, we pass a fountain with a statue of what looks like the Virgin Mother. I look at her. She smiles.

"Until 1978, this place was a Catholic convent. My understanding is it was full of nuns."

Well, yes, I think. If it'd been a convent, there would indeed be nuns.

"All the nuns who lived here took a vow of poverty."

"If you're going to take a vow of poverty," I say, "this seems a nice place to do it."

She laughs at that and pulls up to yet another gray edifice.

"Here we are. Just go through the doors."

I get buzzed in by yet another security guard. They make me walk through a metal detector, which seems more for show than anything else. Why now? Why didn't you do that back at the gate? A woman meets me on the other side of the detector with a smile and a handshake.

"Hello, my name is Kate Boyd. I'm a facilitator at the Solemani. Caroline is waiting for you in the solarium. I'll show you the way."

Kate Boyd's heels clack and echo in the empty corridor. Interesting. The place feels very much like a convent, all silent and stone, and yet Ms. Boyd chooses to wear heels that she has to know will echo in this corridor like a gunshot. Why? Why not wear something with a soft sole?

Caroline Burkett is already standing when I enter the room. She's talking to a man I recognize as Christopher Swain. We never met before, Mr. Swain and I, but I know that he is yet another victim of the Burketts' evil. I'm sad to see that a year later, Swain is still here. When he sees me, Swain takes both of Caroline's hands in his. He looks at her and nods. She nods back. Then he turns, stares at me for a few long moments, and leaves without another word.

I expect Caroline to look as I've seen her before—mousy, reedy, frail, blinking a lot as though she's about to be slapped. But she's not any of that today. It's a different Caroline Burkett. Her posture is straight. Her eyes are steady. I wonder whether this place has been good for her or if it is just that this is the first time I've seen her out of the presence of her mother.

"I'll leave you two," Kate Boyd says, "if that's okay with you, Caroline."

"It is," she says.

"I'll be nearby just in case. Just call if you want me to come back in."

"Thank you, Kate," Caroline says.

We both stand there as the heel clack fades away. Caroline wears a black turtleneck and matching pants. No jewelry. Very little makeup. Again this is a different woman than the one I saw when I would visit Farnwood.

Caroline says, "You're here about Victoria."

"Yes."

"I didn't know she'd been murdered until today. They don't allow us to watch the news in here. No phones, no internet, no social media."

"Sounds nice," I say, and I try a smile.

Caroline returns it. "It is, yes."

The solarium looked like a recent addition that's trying to fit in but not quite working. The roof is domed. The plants look too green—I wonder whether they are fake. There are two leather chairs in the center of the room. Caroline invites me to sit. I do. She takes the other chair.

"What do you want to know, Mr. Kierce?"

I always carry one of those detective pads with me. Sometimes I use it, not because I won't remember—I always remember the important stuff—but for effect. For some people, it relaxes them. For others, it makes them wary. Right now, I leave the pad and pen in my pocket and dive right in.

"When was the last time you saw Victoria?" I ask.

There is no hesitation in Caroline's reply: "December thirty-first, 1999."

"The day she went missing?"

"Missing," Caroline repeats, and then tilts her head. "I thought Victoria was kidnapped."

"She probably was," I say.

"Probably?"

"There were a lot of blanks in her memory," I say, but I don't like the fact that suddenly I'm the one answering the questions. "You two were close friends, correct?"

"Yes. In high school."

"In fact," I continue, "I'm told that you two were the ones who arranged the New Year's party at McCabe's Pub."

"That's true."

"Whose idea was the party?"

Caroline puts a hand to her chin. "You know something? I'm not sure. I think we were just talking about what we should do that night. It was a big deal, of course. New millennium and all that. We both figured there'd be a party—maybe at her house or, more likely, Farnwood. The Burketts threw a lot of parties there, as you might imagine. But my parents were having their own shindig, and Victoria and I wanted to do our thing. We wanted to feel like grown-ups, you know?"

"You said you hadn't seen Victoria since the night of that party."

"That's right."

"So eleven years later, when Victoria came back . . . ?"

"No, I didn't see her."

"Why not? I mean, you two had been close friends. You must have been happy or at least relieved when you heard she'd been found?"

"I was. Very much so. And I did reach out to her. I think some of the other girls did too. At first, we were told she needed time to recover. She was in extensive therapy. At some point, the family made it clear that it could be harmful for Victoria to look backwards. After a while, I think we all just moved on."

"You never bumped into her?"

"Never. For a while we heard rumors that she was living in Costa Rica. The Belmonds have an estate there. But I don't know if that was true. I never saw her in town or at any restaurants, if that's what you mean."

I nod. "Can you tell me about the night Victoria vanished?"

Her face darkens. "It was really hard on me."

"I'm sure it was," I say, laying on the empathy with my best hangdog face. "You were close friends. You cohosted a party together. And then, poof, she just vanishes. That had to be traumatic for you."

"It was."

"Do you remember the last time you saw her that night?" When I see her stiffen, I backpedal a bit. "Or maybe start at the beginning. How did you and Victoria arrive at McCabe's Pub?"

"Thomas. Her brother."

"Thomas drove you?"

"Yes." She makes a face. "He was drunk. We kept trying to get him to pull over so one of us could drive."

"But he wouldn't listen?"

"He wouldn't listen," she echoes. "I think back in those days, there used to be some rule about being nineteen in order to drive in Manhattan. Thomas may have mentioned that—that we were too young so even if we wanted to take the wheel, it wouldn't have been legal." She smiles. "I think Victoria countered by saying something like, 'Well, drunk driving isn't legal either.'"

"Touché," I say, sharing in the joke. "Anything else you remember about that ride?"

Caroline thinks about it. "Not really. Victoria and Thomas were pretty tight. He was upset about something—I can't remember what anymore . . ."

"Maybe a girl?"

"Yeah, maybe. Vic told him he should come to our party. I remember that. I was kind of mortified."

"About her brother coming?"

"Yes."

"Why?"

"Because he was too old and obnoxious and drunk."

"Right," I say. "So he drops you off at McCabe's Pub. You and Victoria are the first there. So I guess you, what, set up?"

"Yes. It wasn't a big deal. Some balloons. We ordered those glasses with the year 2000 on it. Hats, streamers, noisemakers. Like that."

"And then your guests arrive."

"Yes."

"And the party gets going."

"Yes."

"Anything strange you remember?"

She starts squirming. "Nothing really."

"What 'not really'?"

"What? Oh. No. Nothing."

"So what's the next thing you remember?"

"I don't know. It was just a party."

Time to get to it. "When did you realize that Victoria was missing?"

"I'm not sure I ever really realized it."

Her hands are in her lap now. She's staring down at them.

"What do you mean?" I ask.

"I mean, I remember we turned on the TV and watched the countdown to midnight. Then we watched the ball drop in Times Square. Prince's '1999' was on. And I think maybe I looked for Victoria. To celebrate the moment with her. But I didn't see her."

"Did that surprise you?"

She shrugs. "I guess. I was a little tipsy by then. It didn't seem like a huge deal."

"How about at the end of the night? Did you notice her missing then?"

"I don't really remember. I left with a big group of friends. There were a few other groups like that. I guess I thought she joined up with one of them."

I nod. I meet her eye. She looks away.

"I'm debating my next move here, Caroline."

"What do you mean?"

"I mean, I know you're lying to me."

"What?"

"So," I continue, "I'm wondering why. Did you do something to Victoria that night? What are you trying to cover up?"

"I'm not lying—"

"We have a CCTV of you following Victoria on the street outside the bar at 11:17 p.m."

Her face goes white.

"I also know the police tried to interview you, but back then, your family blocked it. I don't know why. I don't even care why. But it's been twenty-five years, Caroline. Victoria was your friend. She's dead now." Then I lay it on thick because why not. I lean in closer and almost take her hand. "This is about you too," I say to her in a low voice. "Before that night, you were on a great life path. Success. Happiness. You were smart. People liked you. You liked them." This is all bullshit, but I know she will buy into this narrative. We always buy into narratives we like. My mother was a private college guidance counselor. She used to give students a "personality" test. She always told them the same "result" when it was over: "You're the kind of person who, if your mother tells you to do something like clean your room, you might not do it right away, but if you *really* want something, if you put your mind to it, you are the first to get something done." My mother said this every time to every student, and every time the student and the student's parents would nod in agreement because we all like this narrative for ourselves.

I was counting on Caroline wanting the same with this.

"I'm not here to hurt you," I say. "Whatever happened, it stays between us. That's a promise. But I need to know. And more than that, Caroline, you need to tell me. I don't want to say the truth shall set you free, but—"

"You're right." The tears start flowing down her face. "It's my fault."

I sit back and wait.

"That night. It changed everything. I wanted to face it, tell the truth right away, but my mother . . . she told me never to speak of it. Insisted, really. So I jammed it inside of me. My mother even sent me away. Like now. Like whenever I have a problem—or should I say, when I *am* a problem. We Burketts don't face up to our problems. We hide them here instead."

I don't say anything. Life and cop lesson: Don't derail someone when they are on the right track.

"What happened to Victoria that night," Caroline continues, "was my fault."

I fight to stay still. I give Caroline Burkett my most open, trusting face. "I am with you," this face says. "I get it. I will listen and respect you and not judge." These are the things I am trying to manifest on my face. It has worked for me in the past. I'm hoping it will work again.

"This was 1999," Caroline says. "Today, no big deal. But 1999 . . ."

I still say nothing.

"Victoria and I were more than friends."

She looks up to meet my eye. I hold it and try to encourage her to continue.

"That wouldn't have played well in our high school. I was dating the varsity quarterback, like some stupid cliché. Buff Danelo. He was there that night. He didn't know about me and Victoria, of course. No one did. Buff just thought I wanted to save myself. But he was my, I don't know, I guess you'd call it a beard?" She looks off, over my shoulder, her head tilting to the left. "Victoria was my first love and when I think about it, when I think back on my entire life, maybe the only one I've ever had. Because I never got over losing her. We didn't break up. We didn't grow tired of one another or outgrow one another or fade away. None of that. One moment we were inseparable, hopelessly in love, hiding it behind the façade of being best friends. And the next moment, just when our relationship seemed to be at its best, Victoria was just—" Caroline stops, shrugs "—gone."

I still say nothing.

"I had too much to drink that night. That's the excuse I use. But really, it was about that time in our lives. New year, new millennium, new me. And I just loved Victoria so much. It had been exciting keeping it a secret, but now it felt suffocating. Like I'd lose her if we didn't take the next step. Do you know what I mean?"

"I do," I say.

"I wanted to tell the whole world about us. I didn't care. And Buff, ugh, he was all over me. Started grabbing my ass and slobbering in my ear about how we would start the new year off with a bang, ha ha, gross, and I look across the room and there's Victoria, leaning against the bar. She's talking on her phone, and she has that look on her face, this one she gets when she's really *really* focused, and she's so adorable wearing this white dress and she just looks so damn beautiful I thought my heart would burst out of my chest." Caroline rubs her hands in her lap. "I don't know why I did it. I should have known better. But I couldn't stop myself. I just pushed Buff off me and I stormed over to Victoria and I grabbed her face and I told her that I loved her and then I kissed her. Just like that. I kissed her so hard and with such hunger, and do you want to know something?"

I keep my voice gentle. "Tell me."

"She kissed me back." Caroline's smile is wistful. "It was the best kiss of my life."

An old-school grandfather clock strikes the hour. It echoes off the solarium glass. In the distance I hear Kate Boyd's heel-clacks again. I worry that she might interrupt our flow.

"That must have been a nice moment," I say, just to keep things moving.

"It was."

I still try to go with my most gentle voice. I feel as though my voice is trying to carry a bubble without making it pop. "So what happened after the kiss?"

"Buff. Buff happened."

"Your boyfriend?"

"He runs over and he pushes me. Pushes me really hard. Right in the middle of the kiss. With my eyes closed. I stumble into her, and we both fell to the floor. Hard. And it was like reality hit when we hit the floor. You know? Our eyes opened. I looked up. Most people were wrapped up in their own stuff, but others were staring down at us now, and it was like we both knew nothing would ever be the same. One of Buff's meathead friends started laughing at us. Another called us dykes and then I heard 'lesbo' and 'lez be friends' and what I really remember is the Goo Goo Dolls are on the boombox, that song 'Slide,' and they're singing, 'I wanna wake up where you are, I won't say anything at all,' and suddenly Victoria is up and she's running toward the stairs. It's like the jeers are chasing her, you know. She runs down the stairs to the first floor, where another party is happening, of course. Everyone is partying everywhere. There's so much noise and everyone is drunk. She's stumbling. I'm stumbling. I called her name. But she couldn't hear it over all the noise. The Goo Goo Dolls were on downstairs too. I guess it was all one big music system, and now the singer, John something, I can never remember his last name, he's panicked in the song and he's asking this girl if she loves the life she killed and the priest is on the phone, your father hit the wall, your mother disowned you, and it's like he's singing to me, to us, and I'm swimming through people to try to find Victoria, to tell her it's okay, that I'll just tell our friends I was so drunk I thought she was Buff. That I'd protect her. But I couldn't find her. And then, finally, I saw her by the door. So I tried to get there. Some guy grabbed me on the way, 'Hey, what's the rush, sweetcheeks.' You'd get that all the time back in those days, and when I pushed him, he said, "Come on, be friendly, how about an end-of-the-year kiss' and I pushed him harder and shouted, 'Get off me,' but by the time I broke free, Victoria was gone."

Her eyes are closed as she tells me all this. Her hands mime pushing away the man who grabbed her. I've seen this before. Caroline is not just remembering—she is "there," if you will, more reliving it than recalling it. It's almost self-hypnosis.

Caroline's face reddens from something akin to exertion.

She takes a few deep breaths. They don't seem to calm her. Her eyes stay closed.

"Caroline?"

Damn. It's Kate Boyd.

Caroline's eyes flutter open.

"Caroline, are you okay?"

It takes her a few moments to orient herself. I'm wondering about my play here.

"She's fine," I say. "This is just an emotional moment for both of us."

"Caroline?" she says again.

"We're fine, Kate," Caroline finally spits out. "I don't really appreciate you disturbing us."

"I just wanted—"

"I told you I'd call you if I needed anything. This facility is supposed to be a two-way street when it comes to respect and privacy."

Boyd bristles at that. "It is."

"You're not respecting my privacy right now, are you?"

"I wasn't listening in, if that's what you—"

"Please leave us. And don't come back until we call you."

Boyd almost bows as she exits. Caroline looks at me. I worry the moment is gone now. Her eyes are open. She's back in this solarium instead of McCabe's Pub.

I try to take her back. "You said Victoria ran outside?"

She says nothing for a moment. She just stares at me, as though I've just magically materialized in front of her, and she has no idea why.

"Victoria hurried past a CCTV camera," I continue. "A few seconds later, you did too."

Caroline keeps staring.

"And then," I say, "Victoria vanished. Poof. Like that. You never saw her again, right?"

"Never," she repeats.

I lean in closer. "What happened, Caroline?"

Silence.

"Did you catch up to her?" I ask.

Her voice is far away. "Yes."

"And then?"

She blinks now, like the Caroline I knew at Farnwood. She starts gesturing and shrugging, as though she can't quite get the words out. "Victoria hugged me," Caroline says. "She said it would all be fine."

I try to look the question at her rather than speaking one. She stays quiet, so I finally ask, "And then what happened?"

"She held up her phone."

"Her phone?"

"She told me that Thomas was in a bad way."

I feel the small chill start at the back of my neck. "What do you mean?"

"She loved him. You know that, right?"

"I do."

"He was the older brother, but she was always the one looking out for him. I guess he called her. Drunk out of his mind. That's who she'd been talking to when I went over and kissed her."

I swallow. "Thomas was at home, right?"

"Home?"

"Yes. After he dropped you two at McCabe's Pub, didn't he go home?"

"Oh no," Caroline says. "He was far too drunk. In fact, Victoria took his keys to make sure."

I swallow again. "So where was he?"

"He was at another bar down the street. She figured he'd be safe there, but I guess he kept drinking and then he called her sobbing. Anyway, she said she was going to check up on him."

"Did she?"

"Yes. I mean, I watched her go into the bar."

"And then?"

Caroline shrugs. "That's the last time I ever saw her."

31

Golfer Gary is waiting for me in his Range Rover. "Debrief please."

I don't say anything. He reads the room—or to be more precise, the car—and shifts into drive without another word.

Thomas lied to me. Did his parents know?

I check my phone for messages. Molly and Marty both called. I call Molly first.

"You're being an idiot," Molly says.

"I'm heading back to the hospital right now."

"Don't bother."

"Huh?"

"I got you discharged. Come home. I have a bed ready for you."

"And a sponge bath?"

"Don't push it," she says. "But yes."

I switch hands. "I love you," I say.

"You should." Then she adds, "You have that voice."

"What voice?"

"The this-case-is-a-total-mess voice."

"You know me well."

"Do you want to tell me about it?" she asks.

"Not right now. I need to sort through it."

"But later," she says.

"Later."

"Maybe after the sponge bath."

"Certainly not before," I say.

I call Marty next. He answers on the first ring and asks, "What did you learn?"

"You first," I say.

"A preliminary ballistic test on the gun found at Brian Powell's murder scene indicates it was the same weapon used on you and Victoria Belmond."

I'm not surprised.

"It's also the same type of gun used on Nicole Brett years ago. You probably realized that already."

"I did."

"Not the same gun, of course. But the same type. A Walther PPK. Hell of a coincidence."

I don't want to get into that now. "Powell's time of death?"

"Hard to know. The ME still has him on the table, but the estimate is between thirty-six and forty-eight hours ago."

I ask the obvious question. "Did you bring Tad Grayson in for questioning?"

"We tried. His lawyer said he will not cooperate. He has

an alibi of sorts. Witnesses place him at the hospice with his mother pretty much nonstop—he has a cot in her room—but I guess he could have sneaked out a window or something. The place isn't exactly Fort Knox with the security. I mean, who'd want to break into a hospice?"

My phone buzzes. I check and see the incoming call is from Jennifer Schultz at the Abeona Shelter. I tell Marty I'll talk to him later and switch over.

Jennifer Schultz says, "I almost stopped."

"Stopped?"

"Looking. I saw on the news Victoria Belmond had been killed in a street shootout. Were you with her?"

"Yes."

"Were you the other person shot?"

"Yes."

"Are you hurt?"

"I'm fine."

"You told me Victoria Belmond wanted answers. But she's dead now. So what would be the point in digging it all up? This isn't easy for me. These were my parents."

Gary keeps glancing at me out of the side of his eyes.

"But you kept looking anyway," I say.

"Yes."

"And?"

"When can you come to my office?" Jennifer Schultz asks me. "This isn't the kind of thing you discuss over the phone."

———

An hour later, I am back at the offices of the Abeona Shelter with Jennifer Schultz. When we are both seated, she spins her computer monitor around and when she does, when I see the image on the screen, it's like someone walloped me with a two-by-four.

I am not hiding what I'm feeling.

"I assume that's her," she says.

It's more than her. It's the Anna I knew. Maybe a year or two younger than when we first met. I am suddenly transported to the Discoteca Palmeras and she's catching my eye on the dance floor. Just like that. It's like I said before—if I ask you to picture a face from twenty-five years ago, you'll struggle. You remember and you don't remember. The image is more manu-factured, more stitched together through the prism of nostal-gia, emotion, reality. But this—this is the Anna that I knew.

The image is of a modeling headshot. I'm no expert, but the lighting, framing, composition, all that looks pretty pro-fessional. Anna stares into the camera in a mildly inviting way—beautiful, yes, but not intimidatingly so. She is smil-ing, but it looks forced and I'm having trouble finding any-thing resembling joy in it.

She also looks scared to me.

Nothing obvious. Could be projection. But there is fear there, a backing away as though even the camera means to harm her, and it makes my heart ache.

"Her real name is Anna Marston," Jennifer Schultz tells me. "My father was the original point of contact on this. He was working the King of Prussia mall when she walked by him. Alone. No friends. That was sometimes a sign, I guess. What teenage girl wanders a mall alone? Like she's prey. I assume my father gave her his usual sales pitch. You're beautiful. You have a certain something." Jennifer says this all quickly, like she just wants to get through it, which would make sense. "Anna made it clear that she couldn't afford a modeling portfolio, another sign of weak prey. Dad would have then said something like he saw so much potential in her he would give her a"—again quote fingers—"'scholarship,' and he'd pay for the portfolio himself. Depending on the situation, he might have taken Anna to the food court to get something to eat. Or the Gap or Limited and buy her an outfit for the shoot. She'd be deeply moved by his kindness, even if a bit wary. A girl like Anna is not used to kindness, especially from men. My guess is, my mother would come in at this point and take over. A matronly woman would be less threatening to a young girl."

I stare at the photo and shake my head.

"It's grooming," Jennifer says. "And yes, it's awful."

"What do you know about her?" I ask.

"Anna Marston is sixteen years old in the photo. The picture was taken February tenth, 2001. She was born in State College, Pennsylvania, to a single mother. Don't know who her father was—not sure she did. Her mother worked in a cafeteria in the East Halls at Penn State. She died when Anna was nine. Don't know from what. Anna then moved in with her aunt in Spruce Creek because that was the only family left. The aunt was an abusive junkie. Lots of guys in and out.

Some nice, most not. Anna was pretty. You know the deal. I don't have to spell it out. I guess Spruce Creek is known for its fly-fishing. One of the fly-fishing instructors took a special interest in Anna. So she ran away. She'd been on the run three weeks when she met my father at the mall."

I look at this photograph. I think about the girl I met not long after all this. I'm overwhelmed and trying to stay on course.

"Is that aunt still alive?" I ask.

"I don't know. I couldn't find her, but I didn't really look all that hard."

"So what happened to Anna then?"

"I don't know for sure, but I think we can speculate. The agency probably told her they had a job for her overseas. Modeling, waitressing, babysitting, whatever. They sent her there. They got their pay. And she was gone. My parents wouldn't ask for a follow-up because they didn't want to know. But she'd either be forced into the sex trade or into some kind of money-making scheme. You mentioned she worked scams with some Dutch guy. Maybe that wasn't as bad as some other tracks, but my guess is it was pretty damn awful."

We sit there. Jennifer Schultz shows me some other modeling shots of Anna. Full-body ones. They were all casual, appropriate, nothing risqué in the slightest. They looked like ads we would see in old Sunday newspaper circulars for stores like Sears and JC Penney. Do they still have those? Do people still page through ads in a thick Sunday newspaper? I don't know and I don't know why I'm thinking about such nonsense or maybe I do know. Maybe it's a stall, a preventative, because I am finally putting the pieces together and I don't want to face this truth.

That doesn't stop Jennifer Schultz from asking the obvious: "Is this the woman who was passing herself off as Victoria Belmond?"

I knew, didn't I? The clues were all there from day one. Why did she insist on being such a recluse? Why wouldn't she see old friends like Caroline Burkett? Why did they hire me in the first place? Why did she lie about not remembering Spain?

"Kierce?"

I don't know the details. Not yet. But I'm there now.

"Was the murdered woman Victoria Belmond or not?"

I don't say the answer, not out loud, but I think it.

She was Victoria Belmond. And she was not.

32

Underneath it all, I'm a cop. Now. Before. Prenatally, I sometimes think.

That's the funny thing about my life trajectory. I was supposed to be a physician. That had been my plan from as young as I can remember. If I hadn't gone to Spain and met Anna, I would have gone to Columbia University medical school that fall. I'd have done the four years. I'd have picked a specialty—I was interested in cardiology—and gone on to my internship and residency and would have never crossed paths with Nicole or met Molly and there would be no Henry.

I would have never become a cop.

All pretty obvious.

But now I wonder—because another part of me feels, *knows*, I was always meant to be a cop. It's in my blood, even now, even after getting thrown off the force and knowing that I will never be able to return. I'm not saying it was God's will or any of that. I don't think I'm that important. I don't think any of us are. We human beings are startlingly, amazingly, narcissistic. I remember my father, the amateur scientist, pointing this out to me once:

"Earth is 4.6 billion years old, Sami. If you scale that down to forty-six years, do you know how long human beings have been here?"

"No."

"Guess. It's important. How long out of those forty-six years have humans roamed the earth?"

"Twenty years?"

"Less."

"Ten years."

He smiles and shakes his head. "Four hours. Out of forty-six years, we humans have been on this planet for a mere four hours. The industrial revolution started a minute ago. Yet we humans believe God created all this just for us."

I think about that a lot. It keeps me humble, I guess. Our insignificance in the scheme of things. That doesn't make life less valuable to me. It makes it more.

Okay, enough with the philosophical meandering. My point is, I don't want to sound too self-serious, but maybe I was destined to be a cop. I can't let that part of me go, which is why I am teaching a course on criminology. Now that the clues are starting to pour in, now that I feel the answer is tantalizingly close, I need to step up.

I can't have my students figure it out before me.

Not out of ego. My students have been amazing and more than proved themselves. They should be proud of what they've done. But it has to be on me at the end. There's no other way. So I've divided them up. One hand won't see what the other is doing. They will report their findings only to me. We have all worked this case hard and like real cops. Maybe harder. We have no agenda other than solving the case. We may not have a badge but in today's world, perhaps that's an advantage not a hindrance, especially since I also have Marty, whom I've nicely bullied into running certain tests for me.

This takes a week.

I remained patient. I gathered all the findings. I analyzed the data in private.

I've come up with the answer.

When I do, I call Archie Belmond and tell him I need to see the family. He knows it is something big. I can hear it in his voice or maybe he hears it in mine. We set up a time to meet at the Belmonds' estate.

Marty insists on driving me. I would argue, but I know he won't listen. This is the deal I made with him and Molly. I would argue, but my body is still sore, and I need someone to drive me anyway, so what's the point?

Besides, to be fair, I really can't predict how the Belmonds will react. I'm about to pull the pin out of a grenade and toss it at them. You know what they say: You never know who is going to make the sacrifice and jump on the grenade, who is going to panic and run—and who is going to pick it up and toss it back at you.

Or something like that.

When Marty pulls through the gate and up to the front of

the house, I'm barely surprised to see Arthur standing there. I get out of the car and tell Marty to stay here. He nods. He has done all I've asked and then some.

"Marty?"

"What?"

"Thank you."

He nods again. "I'm going to leave the car windows open. Scream like a lunatic if you need me."

Arthur waits at the same spot he'd stood when last we were here together.

"What are you doing here?" I ask him.

"As your attorney, I'm supposed to remind you of your legal commitments and responsibilities."

"You drove all the way up here to tell me that?"

"What part of 'billable hours paid by the Belmonds' is confusing to you?"

I put a hand on his shoulder. "It's all good."

"It's not though. These people have lawyers who can crush you."

"My lawyer is way better."

Arthur smiles. "Truth."

I tap his shoulder again and move past him. As I do, I look up and see Talia Belmond standing by a window. She looks down at me. Our eyes meet. I don't know what to do. I raise my hand and give a small, stupid wave. She just stares back. I don't know what to make of that.

I go inside where Gun Guy awaits me. He has one of those metal detector wands, though it looks slightly more high tech.

HARLAN COBEN

"Empty your pockets," he tells me, pure Airport-TSA in his tone. I do. He waves the wand over me. He pats me down, checking for a wire. I don't have one. He is thorough. He knows what he's doing.

"They're waiting in the conservatory," Gun Guy says.

"Does anybody *not* rich refer to a room as a conservatory?"

"I'll keep your phone and belongings safe for you."

"Afraid I'll get robbed?"

Gun Guy shakes his head.

"What?"

"I'm disappointed. I expect wittier rejoinders from you."

"If it helps," I say, "I've let myself down too."

As I head toward the conservatory, I walk past Lenore Spikes. She doesn't say anything either, just gives me a solemn look. I guess that I'm supposed to get some deeper meaning from this look too, but I don't, so I give her a semisarcastic salute and enter.

Archie and Thomas, father and son, stand shoulder to shoulder, primed for my entrance. I get why. I have been joking around because that's what I do, but I know that when we leave this room (er, conservatory)—and not to sound overly melodramatic—but our lives will never be the same.

"Where's Talia?" I ask.

"She won't be joining us," Archie says. "Please have a seat."

"You two sit," I reply. "I need to stand and pace."

Here we are, in this decked-out "conservatory," and I can't help feeling like I'm Hercule Poirot gathering all the suspects, except that there are only two in the room, and with the way

380

I dress and act, the more probable detective hero I'm emanating here is Columbo. Like in that show, we all know the guilty parties. Sort of. With Columbo, he knows it right away. That's the fun. We just wonder how he will catch them. I'm not that quick, but I catch on eventually.

The two men do sit. Thomas is wearing a white Oxford cotton shirt, khakis, loafers. Archie has a gray sweater vest over a blue shirt. Both cross their legs the same way, left ankle over right knee. I see the father-son echo in their faces, in their mannerisms, in the way they cross their legs.

I see no reason to ease my way into this. Not yet. So I start with Thomas.

"You lied about the night your sister disappeared," I say without preamble. "You didn't drop her off at McCabe's Pub and head home. Victoria took your keys, so you couldn't drive back, even if you wanted to. So instead, you sat in a bar down the street. Is that about right?"

Thomas looks over at his father. Archie says, "We know you've talked to Caroline Burkett."

I'm not surprised. I figured at some point he would put people on me too. "I don't care," I say. I look back at Thomas. "Is that what happened? You stayed at a bar down the street? Victoria had your keys?"

Thomas simply nods. I start pacing.

"You told me before that you'd broken up with your girlfriend. A Lacy Monroe. You said she dumped you and you weren't taking it well. That part was true. You also claimed that your sister called you, per the phone records at 11:04, and that her call went to voice mail. But it didn't go to voice mail, did it?"

He looks at his father. His father nods at him.

"No," Thomas says, "I sat on a barstool at that bar and I was getting drunker and drunker. The bartender told me I should leave. So I called her to tell her I had to go, but she didn't answer. So I hung up. That's why there's no record of that. But a few minutes later, she saw my missed call on her phone."

"And she called you back."

"Yes."

"What did she say?"

He swallows. "She asked me if I was okay."

"And what did you say?"

"Nothing coherent. I just blubbered."

"So your sister left her party to check on you?"

"Yes."

"Because she was worried about you."

Thomas squeezes his eyes shut and doesn't answer. Archie fights to keep his expression blank.

"You were in bad shape."

"Yes."

"So I assume Victoria drove you home."

Thomas manages a nod. "We wanted to get back in time to watch the ball drop. There was no traffic on the road, so we thought we could make it. I remember the car radio was on. An AM news station—1010 WINS." He deepens his voice and mimics a radio announcer. "'You give us twenty-two minutes, we'll give you the world.'" Thomas looks up at me. "They still around? That station?"

"I think so," I say.

"Victoria drove. I was slumped next to her. I was pretty out of it, but I remember that radio station. She was staring at the road. You know. Concentrating. And I say to her, 'I'm sorry I'm such a fuckup,' and she says that we're about to enter a whole new millennium, and we both need to make resolutions. I said okay, like what? She said I had to stop drinking and doing drugs. Pleaded with me, really. I said I would. But I didn't mean it. She probably knew that. Wasn't the first time we had this conversation. She said she was going to be stronger too. More honest. And even in my state I could tell something had happened at the party. I asked her what was wrong, and she just said, 'Caroline, everyone knows about that now.'"

I stop midpace. "So you already knew about your sister and Caroline Burkett?"

"Yeah," Thomas says. "I was the only one she told. That's what we were like, Vic and me." He gets lost in that thought for a moment or two, but then he shakes it off. "Anyway, we were on Route 95 listening to that radio station when it got to midnight. I remember watching her face as she counted down out loud with the radio. I tried to count out loud too, but I was so wasted. I just sat there and smiled instead. Here I am, on the biggest party night of the year, and I'm watching my sister's face going light and dark in passing headlights."

I nod and start pacing again. "So then you two arrived home."

"Yes."

"What time?"

"Don't know. A little after midnight, I guess."

"And then what happened?"

Silence.

I can feel the entire room shut down. I turn to Archie. "You told me you were home that night."

"I was."

"How did you welcome in the new year?"

"Watching Dick Clark on TV with our dog Winslow."

"Just you two?"

"Just us two. I told you. I was worried about Y2K."

"Did you hear them come home?"

"I heard the car pull up, yes."

"Did you see them?"

"I saw Victoria. She came in, said, 'Happy New Year, Dad.' Then she kissed me on the cheek."

I am not sure I have ever heard a sadder voice than Archie Belmond's right now.

"What happened after that?" I ask.

Silence.

I switch gears. "I know the woman I met in Spain wasn't your daughter, Victoria."

No reaction.

"Her name was Anna Marston. She grew up in Spruce Creek, Pennsylvania. She looked like your daughter. Not exact or anything. But the two of them probably could have gone to bars and switched IDs and nobody would have noticed."

Silence.

"So the woman found in the diner in Maine wasn't your daughter. It was Anna pretending to be Victoria. It was a setup. Another scam, I guess. But of course, she couldn't pull that off on her own. Even after eleven years, you'd know she wasn't your daughter. You'd run a DNA test. There is only one way this fraud could work—"

I pause. I hope they will say something. They don't.

"—and that's if you set it up yourself. Not her. You."

Still nothing. So I push on.

"And that's what you did. I don't know all the details, but you were smart about it. You shaved her head. That's what people noticed first. It made a casual observer think that's why she looked different. You pretended to be super protective of her—so no one would get too close. You threw in that nonsense about 'the Librarian' to distract. You had Anna play mute, so no one would notice the different voice. You insisted on getting her to your doctors right away, so she'd be under your supervision, not the FBI's. You used your money and influence to isolate her from scrutiny, and if anyone noticed that she looked a little different, well, eleven years had passed. People change in eleven years, especially if they've been held hostage. Anna was a little thinner than Victoria, but that also made sense if she'd been held against her will. You had your people work the search engines—if someone searches for 'Victoria Belmond' the photos that pop up are blurry Photoshops your people made up and paid to get higher engagement. Those look more like Anna than Victoria. And then the kicker. You ran a DNA test. Or least you claimed to. Did you fix the results or just lie about taking it?"

"Lied about taking it," Archie says right away. "The FBI wanted to do their own, of course. I said I wouldn't trust the results unless my own lab ran it. We just made it up. Who would question a father about something like that?"

I stop my pacing again. I give him a few seconds.

"Just so we are clear," Archie continues, "lying about a DNA test is not against the law. None of what you are describing is. There is no law against pretending someone else is your daughter. That's not an arrestable offense."

I am not sure how to respond to that. It's true, I guess. What would be the charge? But it's also beside the point. And I don't want him or Thomas defensive. They know I have them. That's clear. They've calculated the pros and cons and realized with my NDAs and their power and money and influence and all that, it is probably better to give me at least *some* truth to control the situation.

But I need it all. I just have to tread gently to get it.

"How did you find Anna?"

Archie smiles. "Kismet."

"What do you mean?"

"When Victoria . . . vanished, we founded a charity in her name."

"Vic's Place," I say.

He nods. "My wife runs it. She goes often. Do you remember

how I told you Talia started imagining she was seeing Victoria? Like at Starbucks?"

"Yes."

"That's what happened again. Talia rushed home from the charity one day saying the same thing about Anna. She swore she'd finally found Victoria, that I had to see for myself. By now, it had been eleven years. And Talia . . . " He closed his eyes, took a deep breath, started again. "I drove down to Vic's Place. I met Anna. And even I—I mean, she really reminded me of Vic. I sat with her in Vic's Place for hours. We really connected. It was like . . ."

He stops, shakes his head, starts again. "She opened up to me. Told me how she ended up here—her single mom getting beaten to death by some drunks when she was a kid, her neglectful aunt, all the abuse she suffered. She'd ended up in Spain—you know that, of course—but she'd crossed the wrong people and had to get out. She stole enough money to buy a ticket to JFK, but once she landed, she had nowhere to go. Someone on the street told her about Vic's Place, so here she was. She was grateful to be here. I asked about her plans. She had none. I know how this will sound, but I really liked her. She was a survivor. She had such strength. You met her. You know."

I remind myself that I need to tread gently here. "So you, what, decided to make it appear that she was your daughter?"

"Yes," Archie says.

Just like that. I knew it, of course. Had figured it out a while back. But to hear him just say it like that still hit me anew.

"As you pointed out, she wasn't an exact match but they resembled each other, like sisters maybe. We also had eleven years of aging to explain that. Plus the shaved head, yes. Plus, right, we paid search engines so that the photos you'd get if you searched for Victoria would be ones we recently Photoshopped. It was enough."

"Seems like a big risk," I say.

"What do you mean?"

"That someone would see through her."

"No, not really. For all the reasons you mentioned. We had the resources to keep the media and law enforcement at arm's length. We used her supposed fragile mental health to get her home right away. The FBI and press might have wanted us to cooperate more, but when the family tells you she doesn't remember, what can you do? You move on to other cases."

Archie sits a little straighter, warming up to the story now. "But even if someone did figure it out, so what? Suppose we were somehow caught. What laws were we breaking? It might be weird or even unethical, but if you found out we wanted someone to pretend to be our daughter—that's not against the law."

I had no answer to that.

"Even if you left here now and defied the NDA and told the world about it—well, for one thing you could never prove any of this. But even if you could, what could you charge us with?"

"But I could prove it," I say.

"What?"

388

"I got DNA from Anna's body during the recent autopsy after she was killed."

"You what?"

"I also swiped Thomas's glass of iced tea when I was at his house. I tested his DNA against the DNA from the police morgue. There's no sibling match."

For the first time I see the pain leave Archie's face and the cold businessman emerge. He points a finger at me. "Now that—stealing DNA from a corpse—that's against the law."

"I know," I say.

"And she's now been cremated."

"I know that too. You cremated her in case someone wanted to exhume the body for the DNA. You were smart. You were careful."

"We broke no laws," he says again.

"True," I agree. "You just paid a woman to pretend to be your missing daughter."

Archie's eyes widen, and I worry I've gone too far.

Thomas speaks up. "It wasn't like that."

I turn to him. "So what was it like?"

"You won't understand."

I spread my hands. "Try me."

"I thought the whole idea was crazy too, but—and this is going to sound even crazier—it worked. Once she came into our lives, we all grew to love Anna. She became my sister. Not just playing a part. She *was* my sister. I loved her like that. I confided in her. Like I used to with Victoria. You met my daughter at my house. Vicki. We named her for my real sister—but for both my daughters, she was their favorite aunt. Hell, their favorite relative. They traveled together. She took them out on their birthdays. My daughters—her nieces—haven't stopped crying since she was murdered."

"Do they know the truth—"

"No, of course not."

"—that she wasn't really their aunt Victoria."

"But she was," Thomas insists. "To them. To me. To all of us. That's the point. I loved her. And she loved us. I know that with every fiber of my being. You may not believe that—"

But of course, I do believe it.

Anna's last words still ring in my ear:

"I love them with all my heart, Kierce. Mom, Dad, Thomas, Maddy, my nieces—especially my nieces. I love them. And I love my life."

"—but we became a family," Thomas says. "A good family. A loving family. She brought us together. Healed us."

"I didn't force her into this," Archie says. "I told her she could change her mind at any time. We'd let her go. But she didn't want to leave."

I see Anna's pleading face in the park again:

"I love them. And I love my life."

"She was happy," Archie says. "We were happy. That's the crazy part. We all became better people for it. And as for my wife—" He stops here, bites down on his knuckle, closes his eyes. When he starts up again, his voice has a choke in it. "It saved Talia's life. I can't put it any plainer than that. My wife lived through eleven years of hell. Every day waking up and wondering what had happened to her daughter. She imagined fresh hells every single morning. You spoke to Judith Burkett. I'm sure she told you about my wife's suffering. The pain and guilt of not knowing—and now suddenly she had her daughter back. Don't you see?"

But suddenly I didn't see it.

How had I missed this?

"Hold up," I say.

I thought I had it. It's why I wanted to see the whole family. Including Talia.

But I was wrong. I had put so much of it together but not this part.

But it makes sense, doesn't it?

It is all starting to fit.

"Your wife didn't know," I say.

"Of course not."

"She wasn't in on this."

"Don't you see?" Archie says. "Talia was the whole motivation for doing this."

I shake my head in disbelief. "She was the mark."

"No, not like that," he says. "Don't you get it? My wife was drowning every day. For eleven years. Every day she woke up crying, wondering where Victoria was. I tried everything to comfort her. But nothing worked. Until this. Until I made 'Victoria' come home to her."

My brain is swirling. "So the reason you hired Anna to play Victoria—"

"*Hired* isn't the right word."

"Whatever the hell you want to call it," I snap. "The reason was . . . to fool your wife?"

"Not fool her. Give her back what she'd lost."

It's starting slowly to sink in.

"And your wife was skeptical at first," I say. "I remember she told me that. Then, what, you told Anna to ask her to read that kids book?"

"*Are You My Mother?*"

"Right. Jesus. That's so damn manipulative."

"I was trying to save her life," he says. "Talia was in such pain. I was trying to end it for her."

"By lying?"

"We all live a lie, Kierce."

"Oh please don't hand me that bullshit."

"It worked," Archie says again. "Don't you see? You can call it whatever you want, but it eased her pain. Talia was happy again. We all were. Even Anna. You told me so yourself." He gestures toward his son. "Tell him, Kierce. Tell Thomas what she made you promise before she died."

I look at him. "She wanted me to protect you."

"Our feelings were not a lie," Archie says. "They were reality."

"So where did it go wrong?" I ask. "You are all living in this fantasy world for thirteen years. What happened?"

Thomas takes that one. "You, Kierce."

"Me?"

"She recognized you in the news," Archie says. "All those articles about your fall from grace. It unnerved her. You'd been fired. Disgraced. She felt responsible. She said it was the same way Talia had been tortured by not knowing—you were suffering the same thing. She wanted to make it right."

This fit in with what Anna told me in the park. "So she came to my class," I say.

"Yes. She thought that would have been the end of it, I think. None of us counted on you being resourceful enough to track her down. And once you showed up, I knew you'd never let it go. You'd keep digging."

"So you decided to, what, control the situation?"

"As much as I could, yes," Archie says. "That's what I do. For the best of reasons. Let's face it. I was right, wasn't I? You'd have never let it go."

Probably true, I think.

"At least by hiring you, I had some leverage and protection. The NDA. The money. You'd have to tell me all your findings. Like right now. Whatever else you might think this is, this is you doing your job. I hired you to investigate. Now you are simply reporting your findings per your employment contract."

"Wow, that's some spin."

No reply.

"That only leaves us with one question," I say.

I wait. They wait.

We are at it now.

I've been intentionally circling because I didn't want them to shut down too early. Like I said, there are a lot of avenues to the truth. I just had to be careful not to force my way through barriers. But now, to keep within this piss-poor metaphor, we are on the final road and there is still a big roadblock ahead and sadly, I have no choice.

I have to ram through it, consequences be damned.

I know it. And they know it. Thomas closes his eyes and tightens his fists, as though bracing for the blow. So I lower the boom.

"What happened to Victoria?"

Their heads drop. Like father, like son. Their eyes stay on the floor. I will have to do the talking here.

"She's dead, isn't she?"

Silence.

"She died that night. On January 1, 2000."

Silence.

"How did it happen?"

Silence.

"I have a theory if you're ready to hear it."

They are not. I don't care.

"It starts with your alibis. Thomas, you said your girlfriend, Lacy Monroe, called you to reconcile. According to the phone records, that would have been at 1:21 a.m. That sound right?"

He still looks down, but he nods.

"I found Lacy," I tell him. "She lives in Portland now. She confirmed for me that she did call you then, just like you said, but that you didn't get to her place until five a.m., some four hours later. But she only lived two miles from you. The FBI noticed this discrepancy too, by the way. Part of why people had doubts about you. But they figured maybe you were so drunk you passed out again, so they dismissed it." I turn to his father. "Archie, you originally had no plans to go to Chicago. But suddenly you wanted an alibi, and what better one than surprising your wife on your private plane?"

"I don't see your point," Archie says. "This proves nothing."

"True," I say. "Not on its own. But it makes one wonder. All that commotion—all of those time gaps and the need to fill them with alibis—leads me to believe that Victoria died that night, sometime after she drove Thomas home on New Year's Day. It begins to create a timeline. Shall I go on?"

Silence.

"New York started E-ZPass in 1993. Believe it or not, they still have electronic records going back that far. That night, Thomas, you and your sister drove your BMW E36 with a license plate KTR-478 into the city. Just as you said. E-ZPass has a record of it. In fact, during the months before, you used the car a lot—it shows up on a ton of E-ZPass records. But guess what?" I move closer to Thomas. "After that night, it was never used again. Not one toll crossing. My theory? You got rid of the car because it was evidence. Do you see how our timeline is starting to take shape?"

They still won't look up, but I know that I'm close.

"So now I ask myself, what happened? You and Victoria arrive home. I believe that. It fits. So how did she die? Well, we know it's related to your BMW E36 because you got rid of it. Could Victoria have crashed the car herself? No. If she did, well, to parrot your father, there's no law against that. You would just have called the police." I turn now back to his father. "And it doesn't make sense that you, Archie, would have been behind the wheel. Again same thing: If you were driving and she ended up dead, it would just be a terrible accident."

I pace again. I pace back and forth and then I stop so that I'm looming over Thomas, so close to him that he is staring down at my shoes.

"So it had to be you, Thomas. That's the only thing that makes sense. You told me you had four DUIs. I checked the records—it was actually six. You had seriously injured two people in a drunk driving incident just two months earlier, on November eighth. Your father's money got you off. But it wouldn't this time, not again. Not if you killed your own sister."

Silence.

"You've kept this secret for too long," I say. "Tell me what happened."

From behind me, I hear Archie say, "It can't leave this room."

I spin toward him.

"What we are about to tell you is just a hypothetical," Archie continues. "That's all. We admit nothing."

"Archie," I say, "I don't have any listening devices. I can't prove any of this. You've made that abundantly clear. You want to control me, but you're smart enough to know right now that the only way to do that is to tell me the truth. Because if you don't, I'll just keep coming at you."

He knows I mean it. He looks over at his son. Thomas's shoulders go slack. Now he too finally looks up at me. Thomas wants to tell me. I can see that now. He needs to do this, to unburden himself in some way.

I move away from him now. I give him space.

"We got home," Thomas says in pure monotone. "Just like I told you. We pulled up to the front door. It was freezing out. Victoria turned off the car. She kissed my cheek and told me she was going inside to see Dad. I sat there. I was drunk. There were also drugs in the car. A lot of them. I opened the glove compartment. Some spilled out onto the floor. Coke. I took a few snorts. That woke me up. But I didn't leave the car. I called Lacy on my phone again. She still didn't answer. I'm sitting in the cold and I'm drunk and I'm jealous. I know Lacy is out with Jim DeLapp and I can't stand the thought of them together. I'm losing my mind. So I take another snort. And another. I call Lacy again. And again. It's so cold I can see my breath. In my head, it was like I became a giant fire-breathing dragon. I remember thinking that. And then finally my phone rings. And it's Lacy."

Thomas looks across the room. I sneak a glance at Archie Belmond. His face is covered in tears.

"So I answer it. And Lacy is hysterical. She's telling me she loves me, that she was just using Jim DeLapp to make me jealous, that she needs to see me, that I've always been the one. I tell her I'll be right there, don't move, don't worry, I'm coming. So I hang up and slide over to the driver's side. I start up the car. Lacy needs me. I'm getting her back. I gotta get there fast. I hit the gas pedal and the car accelerates. I can't slow down. I won't slow down. I have to get to Lacy. So

I press down on the gas again, pedal to the metal, and I'm flying down the driveway and it's cold and maybe it's slippery, I don't know, but I'm going so fast now, out of control, but I don't care and I take the turn too hard and the car goes off the pavement, onto the grass, and I can't stop and suddenly, in the headlights, I see Victoria staring back at me."

I close my eyes.

"She's just standing there. Frozen. You know. Like they say about a deer in the headlights. And she's right by that tree, the old one we used to have in the yard. See, after she kissed Dad, she decided to take Winslow for a walk. That's the kind of person she was. She took Winslow for a walk and now it's like she's trapped in the car headlight beam and everything slows down and ramps up and so I slam on the brake except it's not the brake, it's the gas pedal again and I speed up and crash and wrap the car around that big oak tree. The airbag explodes in my face and I can hear the car hissing. I open the door and fall out and look at the hood of the car and the top half of Victoria is lying flat on it. Winslow is licking her face. Her eyes are open, staring, unblinking, just like when I saw her in the headlights. And I start to scream and scream . . ."

He stops. We all stop. I'm holding my breath. It feels like the entire room is. I can see it now. I can see it all in my mind's eye. And part of me swears it can still hear his screams. Like they're still echoing and if we stay still enough, they'll get louder and louder.

But we aren't done yet.

I turn to Archie. "Did you hear the screams?"

"I heard the crash," he says, the tears cascading down his face. "I ran outside. I ran down the hill. I see my daughter. My beautiful, perfect daughter, the one who just a few minutes earlier had kissed my cheek and wished me a happy new year . . ."

He starts to lose it.

"Don't," I warn. "Not now. We have to get through this."

"That's it," Archie manages to say.

"No, it's not."

"You know the rest."

"I need to hear it," I say.

He finally nods, wipes his face with his sleeves, tries to gain some composure. "I rush over to her. I'm trying to fix her, you know, like maybe there is some way to make this not have happened. I'm a fixer. It's what I do. I control things. I can . . . But she's . . . she's dead. There's no doubt about it. And Thomas is screaming we need to get help, we need to call someone. He takes out his phone . . ."

"I was going to call nine-one-one," Thomas adds.

"And suddenly I hear myself say, 'Wait.'" Archie sits up, looks at me. "I don't remember my brain telling me to say it. There I am, standing over my dead daughter, lost, devastated—but it was like I could suddenly see everything so clearly. Like seeing the worst thing imaginable had honed my mind, gave me clarity. And do you know what I asked myself?"

"No," I say. "What?"

"I'd lost one child. Do I want to lose two?"

It's as though the room temperature drops twenty degrees.

"I could see three or four moves ahead," Archie Belmond continues. "We would call the police. They would arrive en masse. Victoria would be dead. Thomas would be arrested. He had a record. Like you said. Including drunk driving for the seventh time. There would be a maximum vehicular manslaughter charge at a minimum. Drugs were in the car. Cocaine. Add that charge on too. Can't sweep this one away. Even with money and influence, Thomas would be in prison for years. No way around that. They'd make an example out of him, I bet. And what good would that do for Victoria? She loved Thomas. She wouldn't want that for him. And no matter what—and this is the key—Victoria would still be dead. We couldn't bring her back. Death is final. What good would it do to destroy her brother too?"

He says it again: "I'd lost one child. Do I want to lose two?"

I nod. "So you didn't call the police."

"No."

"What did you do with her body?"

"We buried her. In our woods. We burned it later. There's no trace anymore, if that's what you're thinking."

"That's not what I'm thinking."

"It was the worst thing I ever did. Thomas and I, we found shovels in the garage. We buried her. I buried my own daughter. I still don't know how. The ground was hard. But I was in a fugue state. We both were, I guess. I can't describe it to you. I had become like a machine. Maybe because it hurt too much to feel. I just kept saying to myself, I'd lost one child, I can't lose another. We cleaned up the scene. We put the car in the garage. You're right. We never used it again. A few months later, we took it to a salvage yard in Vermont. Had it crushed and shredded and recycled. I was so analytical about it all. I told Thomas to go to Lacy's. That was important. Act normal. Give us alibis. I woke up my pilots. Got my plane ready. I used the excuse that Y2K hadn't caused any problems, so I needed to see my wife. You know all this."

I nod again.

"I'm still seeing three or four moves ahead. Victoria was supposed to be away with her friends after the party. We could use that. Everyone knows about trails going cold, that when time passes, it makes it harder on the police. So I tried to maximize that. I sent those texts from her phone to explain why we didn't report her missing for so long. Then I realized the police might be able to triangulate the phone. I destroyed it with a hammer."

He stops. "Kierce," he finally says. "You have a son."

"Yes."

"What wouldn't you do to save him?"

I don't reply.

"And it worked. You know what I mean? Thomas didn't go to jail. He got the help he needed. He turned his life around. His sister—I know, I know—but Vic would be so proud of the man he's become."

Sure, it worked, I think to myself. All you have to do is kill your own sister to hit rock bottom. They should contact rehab centers and tell them they've found the cure.

I think this. I don't say it. I need him to keep talking.

"So you fly to Chicago," I say.

"Yes. I was going to tell Talia what happened. I mean, how could I not? I thought she would understand because it was the same for her—do we lose one child or both? But when I landed, something changed."

"She was with the other man."

"Well, yes, that was part of it, though in truth, I barely cared. It was nothing in the grand scheme of things. But even before that, I'm sitting on the plane and I'm rehearsing in my mind what I'm going to tell Talia, and it sounded reasonable in my ears—we have a chance to save one of our children—but once I was there, once I saw Talia's face, I mean, how could I tell her? How could I know how she'd react? She isn't much of an actress, my wife. It's what I love about her. She didn't have that kind of guile. How could I be sure she wouldn't turn Thomas in? Could she really pretend well enough to fool the police or her friends or her family for the rest of our lives? And when I thought about the pain I was in—the pain of losing my daughter—could I maybe spare her that too?" He glances away briefly. "I love my wife. I didn't want that for her."

"So you didn't tell her."

"I didn't tell her."

"You just made her live with the lie."

"Don't you see? She would have to live with a lie no matter what. If I tell her what I'd done, she'd be forced to live with the same lie Thomas and I had to live with—pretending her daughter had been kidnapped or run off. If I don't tell her,

402

she lives with the lie of not knowing the truth. You tell me, Kierce. Which is better?"

I don't reply.

"Those were my options that night. Do I lose one child that night—or do I lose two? Do I make my wife part of my lie—or do I let her live with what I thought was a more comforting lie? I did what I thought was best. And if I could go back in time and do it again, I don't know if I would change much. Thomas is strong and healthy now. My wonderful granddaughters, the apples of our eyes, would not be here. You've heard the expression that you have to break a few eggs to make an omelet? I don't know about that, but the eggs were broken anyway—I could leave a mess or I could try to make an omelet."

I can't help but frown at that. "Jesus, is that what you tell yourself?"

"Tragedy is a hell of a teacher. It's just too damn cruel."

I remember Thomas telling me the same thing.

"But I was wrong on one thing," Archie continues. "Dead wrong. Or so I thought for a long time."

"That being?"

"Maybe I should have told Talia the truth," he says. "By not telling her what really happened, I gave her hope. People think hope is a good thing, but it's not. Every day my wife woke up and hoped—hoped—that today would be the day we would find Victoria. The not-knowing was debilitating."

I understood this. I had said something similar to Talia.

"Nothing heals trauma better than resolution and closure."

403

"I am a problem solver," Archie continues. "I never give up. I keep searching for solutions. But I didn't know what to do. I couldn't solve this one. Not for a long time."

"And then you met Anna."

"Yes."

"Problem solved," I say.

"I know you don't believe that, but—"

I hold up my hand to silence him. I don't want to hear it again. "And how about now?"

"What do you mean?"

"Will you tell Talia the truth now?"

Archie Belmond frowns. "What sense would that make? Can you imagine the additional pain it would cause?"

"The truth will set you free," I say.

"You're not that naïve, Kierce." Archie clears his throat, and I can almost feel a shift in the room. He stands now, sturdy on his own two feet. "I can help you and your family more," he says, his voice returning to normal. "You've done remarkable work. I think a bonus—"

"I want the money I'm owed," I say. "Not a penny more from you."

He nods and wisely chooses silence.

I don't know what to do here anyway. I can't prove any of this. Archie knew that coming into this meeting. He's still in control. There is no real evidence. It was all so long ago. Even if I could prove it, the statute of limitations on vehicular manslaughter has passed. Thomas wouldn't serve any time.

What would be the point?

To be fair, I understand the terrible choices Archie as a father faced that night. I'm furious about what he did, but I also get it. Lose two kids or lose one. That was how he saw it. A cold calculation—but was it also an accurate one? Suppose Henry had a sister, and something like this happens? What would I do? Not what Belmond did, I hope, but I get it. What happened broke them all—maybe Archie most especially.

I turn to leave now.

"What are you going to do?" Archie asks.

I don't respond. I just hear Anna's words ring in my ear.

"Promise me first."

"Promise you what?"

"That you won't hurt them. That you'll protect them."

I think about that. And then I walk away.

Epilogue

THREE WEEKS LATER

"Class dismissed," I say.

They all came to this week's No Shit, Sherlock class.

The Pink Panthers still huddled together, but tonight they sat closer to the Three Dead Hots podcast girls. Lenny and Gary hung together. Debbie had sat in the back with Raymond, wearing a yellow sleeveless mesh shirt, as he clipped his toenails again.

Now, everyone files by me as they leave. I've seen videos online where first-grade teachers greet their students with some kind of complicated handshake before each class. We do something similar at the end with fist bumps.

"Don't worry," Gary says to me. "We'll get him."

He is talking about Tad Grayson. We seem no closer to

putting him back behind bars. There is nothing tying him to Nicole anymore, and the Newark police have so far drawn a blank on the murder of Brian Powell.

I thank him and move on.

The Three Dead Hots linger and are last to leave. I know why. "We're going to hit a few clubs on the way home," their leader, Carrie, says to me.

"How many is a few?" I ask.

"Like, three. We're going to talk about the upcoming podcast. Wanna join?"

"Hard pass," I say, but I smile as I do.

"You're a warrior, Kierce."

I don't know what that means in this context, but I thank her for it.

After they exit, Marty calls me. "Where are you?"

I don't like the tone of his voice.

"Just finished class."

"I thought that was last night."

"I'm running an extra track now," I say. "For new students. Like one is regular No Shit and one is Advanced Placement No Shit."

"Come by my place."

"When?"

"Now."

"Can I go home and check in with Molly first?"

"Call her on the way."

He hangs up.

I don't like that either.

I get to the subway station and call Molly before I descend. She answers with a happy, "Hello, handsome."

I will tell you an unpleasant truth. Molly and I are enjoying our life with financial freedom. We are relaxed. We breathe easier. We sleep better. And that sucks. Has the Belmond money influenced what I'm doing in terms of Victoria? Hard to say. Money can warp perceptions though, so this analysis may be too kind to myself.

"I'll be late."

"The Dead Hots talk you into clubbing?"

"They tried again, but no, it's Marty."

"He wants to see you?"

"Yes."

"And it can't wait until the morning?"

"He says no."

"I don't like that," Molly says.

I tell her me neither and hang up. I hurry to the subway and get off at Eighty-First Street and take the elevator up to the penthouse of the Beresford. Marty is waiting for me.

"So what is it?"

"It's a video from the Victoria Belmond murder scene," he says.

"Now? It's been almost a month."

"I know. I just got it myself." Marty moves over to the couch. I follow. He tees up the video on his laptop. "So you remember there were kids playing baseball there?"

"Yes."

"A father was filming his son at batting practice—right before you and Victoria got shot. He didn't think to hand it over it until now because his camera was facing the other way." He types something on his laptop. "Look at the guy leaning against the backstop on Hudson."

He spins the monitor, so it faces me.

I expect to see Brian Powell or Tad Grayson.

But I see neither.

Instead, I see Raymond.

———

Many hours later, I stand in front of the Tranquil Pines hospice center.

I enter. A man behind Plexiglas is playing with his phone. He is surprised to see a visitor at this hour. He puts down the phone and sits up.

"We're closed," the man says.

I lean in closer. "Which room is Mrs. Grayson's? I'm here to see her son Tad."

There is a voice from down the corridor. "What do you want?"

I turn and I see Tad Grayson standing fifteen feet away. His eyes are red. His face is gaunt.

"She just died," he says to me. "My mom. At least, she got to see me set free. She can rest in peace."

I say nothing.

"Why are you here, Kierce?"

"I wanted to talk to you."

Tad Grayson shakes his head. "Now?"

I say nothing.

"I don't want to talk to you," he says. "My mother just died."

"Okay," I say.

"I'm done, Kierce."

I wait.

"I don't care if you believe me anymore. I'm done."

I say nothing.

"I tried to show you the truth. I was framed. And then Powell, I mean, why would I ever be stupid enough to hire him of all people? I just got out of prison, what, a few days before—and I'm crazy enough to call on my own cellmate? So that's it. I'm done. I don't care if you don't believe me anymore. Who are you to me anyway? You can't see what's so plainly obvious."

"What's so plainly obvious, Tad?"

"It's the real killer who's behind this."

"I know that," I say.

That surprises him. "You do?"

"That's why I'm here. I know who did it. And we have the proof."

I hold out the video still for him to see. He hesitates, but eventually he snatches the photograph from my hand. I let him examine it.

Then I say, "That's you, right?"

It took Debbie and me an hour to find Raymond. He was staying in a shelter at the Armory in Washington Heights. As he'd promised, Raymond had indeed decided to "fly solo" like an airplane-carrying witch. That meant following Tad

Grayson everywhere and videotaping him as often as possible. Raymond had captured Grayson climbing out of his mother's hospice room window. He had been there when Grayson ducked down an alley to put on the ski mask and black sweatshirt. He had even followed Grayson to a Staten Island landfill where he dumped the ski mask and clothes after he shot Victoria and me.

When I asked Raymond why he hadn't shown all this to me, he simply shrugged and said, "You didn't ask."

"It was a nice move," I say now to Tad Grayson. "Hiring Powell—making it so obvious it was you that anyone reasonable would think it *can't* be you."

Grayson smiles as he looks through the photographs. "My lawyers bought it, didn't they? So did the cops."

"That they did."

"Powell did me some good though. He followed you to the park."

"It's why you had to kill him."

"Would have killed him anyway."

"You killed Nicole. You killed Victoria. You killed Powell."

"Not sure it will do me any good to deny it."

"No," I say. "It won't. I'm curious though. Were you trying to kill me in the park—or were you aiming for her?"

"Truth?"

I shrug. "Why not?"

"I wasn't sure who to kill. That was the problem. I've always wanted to kill you, of course. But then your pain would be over. So I figured that I would kill this other woman who clearly mattered to you first. Then maybe I would kill your wife. Then I would kill your little boy. That would be the best of all. And then, after that, you. But I wasn't sure if that makes sense. I think that distracted me. Threw off my aim a little." He grins. "Still, I'm happy to have killed her. She meant something to you, didn't she?"

"She did."

"And it's your fault she died," he says. "That'll make the trip back inside much easier. I assume you're taping this."

"It's a live mic," I say, tapping my chest. And then I add, "Okay, guys."

The cops swarm in, but I don't wait to see the arrest. I don't need to. I head out into the cool night. I pull up the collar on my coat. Marty is there. I nod at him, but I have one more place to go. He lets me be. I take the subway to Craig's and take my car. I drive back up to the recently dug grave. The sun is starting to rise. There is no marker here. I'm sure they ordered a tombstone that would read Victoria Belmond. I don't know how I feel about that. This is Anna. Anna Marston. But maybe she was Victoria Belmond too. Like I said before. She was Victoria. And she was not.

It's not my place to decide.

But I need to tell her what I'm doing.

I can calculate it like Archie. I can look at the various angles and odds and try to figure out what would produce the best result. I think about them all—Archie, Talia, Thomas, Madeline, Vicki, Stacy. I think about young Victoria Belmond and how her drunk brother crushed her against a tree and how her father buried her in the woods, and I know that while there has been plenty of anguish, there is no chance for real justice. No one is going to prison. No one is going to get convicted of anything. I don't know whether they should.

But mostly, I think about you, Anna.

You took on the role of Victoria Belmond. I bet you thought it was the best thing that ever happened to you. After so much heartache, you had a family. After a life of abuse, you found your people. They loved you, and you loved them. I don't doubt that. I believed you when you told me that you loved them. I believed them when they told me the same about you.

So in a sense, as Archie Belmond told me, it was the best move for all.

Except, Anna, you're dead.

Maybe that's on me. Maybe I'm just trying to deflect blame from myself, but I'm wondering right now—if Archie Belmond had called the police that night, if Thomas Belmond had faced the music for what he did—you, my brief love, would probably still be alive. Maybe you would have found your way to a better life without Archie Belmond's offer. Or not. Maybe if Archie and Thomas had told the truth, everyone would have been worse off. Probably. And that's the point. There are no guarantees.

Which is why you shouldn't calculate the odds.

Which is why you should seek the truth.

The truth may not set you free, but it is still the way to go.

That's what I concluded. Or let's keep it vague—*someone* concluded. That someone leaked the information to the

413

Three Dead Hots. They are about to embark on a podcast on the Victoria Belmond kidnapping with a new theory involving her death and replacement. That's why they asked me to go clubbing. So they can ask me about it.

I'll continue to give them a hard pass.

I too was left with a terrible choice, Anna. That's what I've been thinking these past few weeks. Not as terrible as the one that Archie Belmond faced. But something similar. But I opted in the end to keep seeking the truth over what the odds might call "better."

And what about the promise I made to you?

That I wouldn't hurt them. That I would protect them.

I admit that will haunt me.

But then again, who is to say that the truth won't be the very thing that finally protects them?

I stand back up and look down at the mound of earth.

One more thing, Anna, before I go.

Your autopsy revealed parturition scars on the pelvic bones. No need to go into details, but that means at some point you gave birth.

So I wonder about that too.

About when you gave birth.

About how Harm Bergkamp told me about that time you took off six months after I left Spain.

Am I reading too much into this, Anna?

Or like too many before us, did you just want to protect me?

Either way, you've left me with little choice.

I need to keep seeking the truth now, don't I?

Acknowledgments

The author (love using the third person here) wishes to thank the following:

Daniel Stashower (who knows Sherlock Holmes better than Sir Arthur Conan Doyle), Fred Friedman, Ben Sevier, David Shelley, Lyssa Keusch, Danielle Thomas, Beth deGuzman, Karen Kosztolnyik, Jonathan Valuckas, Matthew Ballast, Staci Burt, Andrew Duncan, Taylor Parker-Means, Alexis Gilbert, Quinne Rogers, Tiffany Porcelli, Joseph Benincase, Albert Tang, Liz Connor, Rena Kornbluh, Rebecca Holland, Mari Okuda, Jennifer Tordy, Ana Maria Allessi, Nita Basu, Michele McGonigle, Rick Ball, Selina Walker, Charlotte Bush, Claire Bush, Lucy Hall, Venetia Butterfield, Alice Gomer, Kirsten Greenwood, Jade Unwin, Phoenix Curland, Anna Curvis, Barbora Sabolova, Meredith Benson.

As always, I thank Diane Discepolo and Lisa Erbach Vance.

Letícia Rodrigues and Flávia Silva remain instrumental in their support and research capabilities. Thank you for all you do.

All mistakes are on these people. They're the experts, not me.

I'd also like to give a quick shout-out to Richard Belthoff, Kate Boyd, Jim DeLapp, Ken Liss, Kelly Neumeier, Trevor Rennie, and Dmitri Scull. These people (or their loved ones) made generous contributions to charities of my choosing in return for having their name appear in this novel. If you would like to participate in the future, email giving@harlancoben.com.

About the Author

Harlan Coben is a No. 1 *New York Times* bestselling author and one of the world's leading storytellers. His suspense novels are published in forty-six languages and have been No. 1 bestsellers in more than a dozen countries, with eighty million books in print worldwide. His Myron Bolitar series has earned the Edgar, Shamus and Anthony Awards, and several of his books have been developed into Netflix original series, including the No. 1 global hit *Fool Me Once*, *The Stranger*, *The Innocent*, *Gone for Good*, *The Woods*, *Stay Close* and *Hold Tight*, as well as the Amazon Prime series adaptation of *Shelter*. He lives in New Jersey.

For more information you can visit:

HarlanCoben.com
X: @HarlanCoben
Facebook.com/HarlanCobenBooks
Instagram: @HarlanCoben
Netflix.com/HarlanCoben

Bringing a book from manuscript to what you are reading is a team effort, and Penguin Random House would like to thank everyone at Century who helped to publish *Nobody's Fool*.

PUBLISHER
Selina Walker

EDITORIAL
Rose Waddilove
Charlotte Osment

DESIGN
Glenn O'Neill

PRODUCTION
Helen Wynn-Smith

INVENTORY
Lizzy Moyes

UK SALES
Alice Gomer
Kirsten Greenwood
Rhian Steer
Phoenix Curland
Emily Harvey

INTERNATIONAL SALES
Anna Curvis
Barbora Sabolova

PUBLICITY
Charlotte Bush
Rhiannon Carroll

MARKETING
Lucy Hall

AUDIO
James Keyte
Meredith Benson

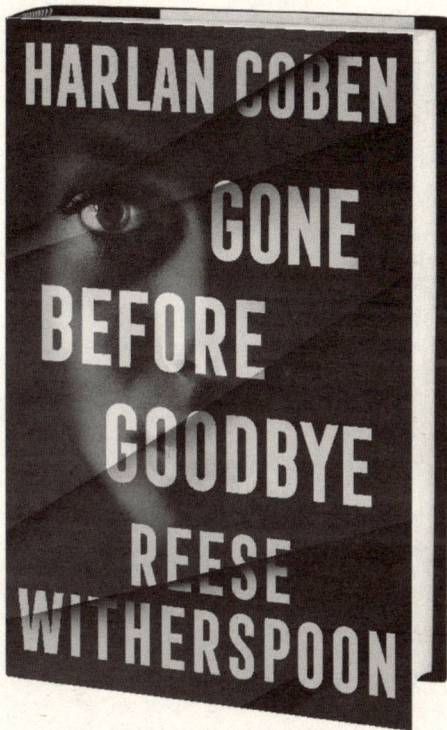